"ANACH[...] [...]eur scientist o[...] [...]ay to untold r[...] [...]

"BLACK CHARLIE" by Gordon R. Dickson—Art, is it what separates us from other species . . . or unites us with them?

"FONDLY FAHRENHEIT" by Alfred Bester—Who must bear the responsibility for crime, an android or his master?

"THE COLD EQUATIONS" by Tom Godwin—When it comes to survival, the rules of space can never be changed, especially not when death is the major factor in the equation.

"THE DEEP RANGE" by Arthur C. Clarke—When the sea has become humanity's last and best source of food, a man will vie against the killers of the deep to keep his sea herd safe.

These are just five of the future forecasts you'll find in—

ISAAC ASIMOV PRESENTS THE GREAT SF STORIES 16

ISAAC ASIMOV

PRESENTS

THE GREAT SF STORIES #16

(1954)

EDITED BY ISAAC ASIMOV AND MARTIN H. GREENBERG

DAW BOOKS, INC.
DONALD A. WOLLHEIM, PUBLISHER

1633 Broadway, New York, NY 10019

Cover art by Angus McKie

DAW Book Collectors No. 709.

First DAW Printing, May 1987.

1 2 3 4 5 6 7 8 9

PRINTED IN THE U.S.A.

ACKNOWLEDGMENTS

CONTENTS

1954 INTRODUCTION

In the world outside reality it was another year filled with violence. On May 7, the French fortress at Dien Bien Phu fell to Vietnamese Communist forces after a long siege. On July 20 France agreed to leave the Northern part of Vietnam, in an arrangement which also provided for the removal of Communist forces from Southern Vietnam as well as Laos and Cambodia. Hanoi was taken over by Communist troops on October 8. Pierre Mendes-France had become Premier of France on June 18.

On a happier note, the St. Lawrence Seaway got under way with the signing by President Eisenhower of a bill on May 13. On September 8, the South East Asia Defence Treaty (SEATO) was signed as a Pacific equivalent of NATO. And on September 27 Senator Joseph McCarthy of Wisconsin was found to have acted improperly by a United States Senate Committee, and on December 2, he was condemned by his colleagues in that august body, bringing an end to one of the most shameful chapters in American political history.

One of the most important events of the year was the ruling by the U.S. Supreme Court, in the case of Brown vs. the School Board of Topeka, Kansas, that segregation by race in education was a violation of the Fourteenth Amendment to the Constitution, a decision that became a watershed in the history of race relations in the United States.

Canada and the U.S. began construction of the "DEW line" (Distant Early Warning) of radar stations across northern Canada, stations that would pick up numerous aliens and UFO's in the science fiction movies of the late 1950's.

During 1954 Ernest Hemingway won the Nobel Prize for Literature, television sets could be found in 22,000,000 American homes, and J. Robert Oppenheimer lost his job and his security clearance in what might have involved only rumors of "Questionable loyalty." The top plays of the year included *The Pajama Game* by Adler and Ross, *Cat On a Hot Tin Roof* by Tennessee Williams, which won the Pulitzer Prize for Drama, Mac Hyman's *No Time for Sergeants, Separate Tables* by Terence Rattigan, and *The Teahouse of the August Moon* by John Patrick. Roger Bannister of Great Britain ran the mile in 3:59:4, breaking the four minute barrier, a feat that many had said could never be done.

1954 saw Billy Graham hold a series of massive evangelical meetings in several countries, the year that Theodore Roethke won the Pulitzer Prize for Poetry for "The Waking." The New York Giants won the World Series by defeating the Cleveland Indians four games to none. Linus Pauling (who would achieve fame in other areas later on) won the Nobel Prize for Chemistry for his research into the nature of molecular forces. The best films of the year included REAR WINDOW directed by Alfred Hitchcock, DIABOLIQUE, the Academy-Award winning ON THE WATERFRONT directed by Elia Kazan and based on the book by Budd Schulberg, and Fredrico Fellini's great LA STRADA. Chagall painted "The Red Roofs."

The first solar battery able to produce electricity from the sun's rays was unveiled by the Bell Telephone Company in 1954. The USS Nautilus became the first nuclear powered ship. In the first of what was to become an annual event, a Jazz Festival was held in Newport, Rhode Island. Francoise Sagan published BONJOUR TRISTESSE, while Isaac Deutscher wrote the first part of his famous biography of Trotsky,

THE PROPHET ARMED. Saul Bellow's THE ADVENTURES OF AUGIE MARCH received rave reviews.

In 1954 the United States contained fifty-eight percent of all the telephones and sixty percent of all the cars in the world—we contained six percent of the world's population. Three Americans—Enders, Weiler, and Robbins—received the Nobel Prize in Medicine for their efforts to isolate the polio virus. The top songs of the year included "Hey There," "Hernando's Hideaway," "Young at Heart," "Mister Sandman," and "Three Coins in the Fountain," but Rock and Roll was just around the corner. Vic Seixas and Doris Hart were the top tennis players in the world.

People began to worry about the disposal of radioactive waste in 1954, but Picasso painted "Sylvette," and William Golding published THE LORD OF THE FLIES, which might qualify as science fiction. Other major books of the year included LUCKY JIM by Kingsley Amis and Bruce Catton's A STILLNESS AT APPOMATTOX, which won the Pulitzer Prize for History. Michigan State defeated UCLA in the Rose Bowl, and the top amateur golfer was a guy named Arnold Palmer.

Death took Enrico Fermi, Reginald Marsh, Oskar Straus, Henri Matisse, Colette, and Lionel Barrymore.

Melvin Kaminsky was Mel Brooks.

In the real world it was another outstanding year as a number of fine science fiction and fantasy novels were published, including several in hardcover, marking the beginning of the end of an era which had seen serialized novels waiting a decade or more for book publication. Noteworthy books included I AM LEGEND by Richard Matheson, A MIRROR FOR OBSERVERS by Edgar Pangborn, THE LONG WAY BACK by Margo Bennett, an excellent novel by a genre outsider, MISSION OF GRAVITY by Hal Clement (Harry Stubbs), THE BIG BALL OF WAX by Shepherd Mead, SHADOW IN THE SUN by Chad Oliver, MESSIAH, by Gore Vidal, and the first two volumes of Tolkien's seminal LORD OF THE RINGS trilogy.

The rapidly changing science fiction magazine market,

under stress by television and paperback books, saw the death of DYNAMIC SCIENCE FICTION, TWO COMPLETE SCIENCE ADVENTURE BOOKS, COSMOS SCIENCE FICTION AND FANTASY MAGAZINE, and ORBIT SCIENCE FICTION. But the great loss of the year was the passing of WEIRD TALES, which had been in publication since 1923 and which had published much fine science fiction in addition to its more famous horror stories. One magazine, IMAGINATIVE TALES, started publication during 1954.

In the real world, more important people made their maiden voyages into reality: in February—Thomas N. Scortia with "The Prodigy," Robert Silverberg with "Gorgon Planet"; in March—Robert F. Young with "Stop Over"; in April—Kenneth Bulmer with "First Down"; in May—Barrington J. Bayley with "Combat's End"; in July—Brian W. Aldiss with "Criminal Record" and Avram Davidson with "My Boyfriend's Name is Jello"; in August—William F. Nolan with "The Joy of Living" and Bob Shaw with "Aspect"; and in September—"Edmund Cooper with "The Jar of Latakia."

Fantastic films (in terms of category, not always quality) included THE ATOMIC KID, the ever popular THE BOWERY BOYS MEET THE MONSTERS, the wonderful THE CREATURE FROM THE BLACK LAGOON, the campy GOG, KILLERS FROM SPACE, the better off having been left there MONSTER FROM THE OCEAN FLOOR, the failed RIDERS TO THE STARS, THE ROCKET MAN, the slushy THE SNOW CREATURE, TARGET EARTH!, the effective and memorable THEM! (it was a big year for exclamation points), the not so great TOBOR THE GREAT, and one of the highlights of the year, 20,000 LEAGUES UNDER THE SEA.

The family gathered in San Francisco for the Twelfth Science Fiction Convention, which we called SFCon.

Let us travel back to that honored year of 1954 and enjoy the best stories that the real world bequeathed to us.

THE TEST

BY RICHARD MATHESON (1926–   )

THE MAGAZINE OF FANTASY AND SCIENCE FICTION,
JANUARY

*Richard Matheson was the Stephen King of his time—a
writer who made the everyday dangerous and danger an
everyday worry. His influence on the field of modern horror is
enormous, and is finally being recognized. 1987 should see
the publication of his complete short stories in two volumes, a
body of work that can stand with the best in speculatve
fiction. A long association with Hollywood found him producing screenplays and teleplays, but may have cost his readers
many notable prose works. The man who produced I AM
LEGEND (1954) and THE SHRINKING MAN (1956) is assured of greatness, but I'll take his short fiction any day. He
had some eight existing stories adapted for THE TWILIGHT
ZONE, and did many teleplays directly for that beloved show,
a relationship that helped to make it the landmark that it
became.*

*"The Test" is a good example of his ability to write solid
science fiction and is a story that clearly and movingly antici-
pates sf's concern with social issues like overpopulation. Its
concern for the problems of the elderly in society makes it
read like it was written this year. (MHG)*

*And yet I wonder. Matheson was twenty-eight when this
story was published. A mere kid! He is sixty now.*

When he wrote this story he was entitled (I suppose) to think of an eighty-year-old man as incredibly old, and as being in his second childhood. Some octagenarians are, I know. But I also know some who seem to be totally alert. My dear wife, Janet, has an aunt who is ninety-two years old and entirely alive.

I certainly hope this will be my case. I am six years further into the vale of years than Matheson is. So far my mind seems to be clicking on all cylinders but—if I make eighty—

I suppose it's a sign of the strength of the story that it interested me when it was first written, and it makes me terribly uneasy now. (IA)

The night before the test, Les helped his father study in the dining room. Jim and Tommy were asleep upstairs and, in the living room, Terry was sewing, her face expressionless as the needle moved with a swiftly rhythmic piercing and drawing.

Tom Parker sat very straight, his lean, vein-ribbed hands clasped together on the table top, his pale blue eyes looking intently at his son's lips as though it might help him to understand better.

He was eighty and this was his fourth test.

"All right," Les said, reading from the sample test Doctor Trask had gotten them. "Repeat the following sequences of numbers."

"Sequence of numbers," Tom murmured, trying to assimilate the words as they came. But words were not quickly assimilated any more; they seemed to lie upon the tissues of his brain like insects on a sluggish carnivore. He said the words in his mind again—*sequence of . . . sequence of numbers*—there he had it. He looked at his son and waited.

"Well?" he said, impatiently, after a moment's silence.

"Dad, I've already given you the first one," Les told him.

"Well . . ." His father grasped for the proper words. "Kindly give me the—the . . . do me the kindness of . . ."

Les exhaled wearily. "Eight-five-eleven-six," he said.

The old lips stirred, the old machinery of Tom's mind began turning slowly.

"Eight . . . f—ive . . ." The pale eyes blinked slowly. "Elevensix," Tom finished in a breath, then straightened himself proudly.

Yes, good, he thought—very good. They wouldn't fool him tomorrow; he'd beat their murderous law. His lips pressed together and his hands clasped tightly on the white tablecloth.

"What?" he said then, refocusing his eyes as Les said something. 'Speak up," he said, irritably. "Speak *up*."

"I gave you another sequence," Les said quietly. "Here I'll read it again."

Tom leaned forward a little, ears straining.

"Nine-two-sixteen-seven-three," Les said.

Tom cleared his throat with effort. "Speak slower," he told his son. He hadn't quite gotten that. How did they expect anyone to retain such a ridiculously long string of numbers?

"What, *what*?" he asked angrily as Les read the numbers again.

"Dad, the examiner will be reading the questions faster than *I'm* reading them. You—"

"I'm quite aware of that," Tom interrupted stiffly, "quite aware. Let me remind you . . . however, this is . . . not a test. It's study, it's for *study*. Foolish to go rushing through everything. *Foolish*. I have to learn this—this . . . this *test*," he finished, angry at his son and angry at the way desired words hid themselves from his mind.

Les shrugged and looked down at the test again. "Nine-two-sixteen-seven-three," he read slowly.

"Nine-two-six-seven——"

"Six*teen*-seven, Dad."

"I said that."

"You said six, Dad."

"Don't you suppose I know what I said!"

Les closed his eyes a moment. "All right, Dad," he said.

"Well, are you going to read it again or not?" Tom asked him sharply.

Les read the numbers off again and, as he listened to his father stumble through the sequence, he glanced into the living room at Terry.

She was sitting there, features motionless, sewing. She'd turned off the radio and he knew she could hear the old man faltering with the numbers.

All right, Les heard himself saying in his mind as if he spoke to her. All right, I know he's old and useless. Do you want me to tell him that to his face and drive a knife into his back? You know and I know that he won't pass the test. Allow me, at least, this brief hypocrisy. Tomorrow the sentence will be passed. Don't make me pass it tonight and break the old man's heart.

"That's correct, I believe," Les heard the dignified voice of his father say and he refocused his eyes on the gaunt, seamed face.

"Yes, that's right," he said hastily.

He felt like a traitor when a slight smile trembled at the corners of his father's mouth. I'm cheating him, he thought.

"Let's go on to something else," he heard his father say and he looked down quickly at the sheet. What would be easy for him? he thought, despising himself for thinking it.

"Well, come on, Leslie," his father said in a restrained voice. "We have no time to waste."

Tom looked at his son thumbing through the pages and his hands closed into fists. Tomorrow, his life was in the balance and his son just browsed through the test paper as if nothing important were going to happen tomorrow.

"Come on, come on," he said peevishly.

Les picked up a pencil that had string attached to it and drew a half-inch circle on a piece of blank paper. He held out the pencil to his father.

"Suspend the pencil point over the circle for three minutes," he said, suddenly afraid he'd picked the wrong question. He'd seen his father's hands trembling at meal times or fumbling with the buttons and zippers of his clothes.

Swallowing nervously, Les picked up the stop watch, started it, and nodded to his father.

Tom took a quivering breath as he leaned over the paper and tried to hold the slightly swaying pencil above the circle.

Les saw him lean on his elbow, something he wouldn't be allowed to do on the test; but he said nothing.

He sat there looking at his father. Whatever color there had been was leaving the old man's face and Les could see clearly the tiny red lines of broken vessels under the skin of his cheeks. He looked at the dry skin, creased and brownish, dappled with liver spots. Eighty years old, he thought—what does a man feel when he's eighty years old?

He looked in at Terry again. For a moment, her gaze shifted and they were looking at each other, neither of them smiling or making any sign. Then Terry looked back to her sewing.

"I believe that's three minutes," Tom said in a taut voice.

Les looked down at the stop watch. "A minute and a half, Dad," he said, wondering if he should have lied again.

"Well, keep your eyes on the watch then," his father said, perturbedly, the pencil penduluming completely out of the circle. "This is supposed to be a test, not a—a—a *party*."

Les kept his eyes on the wavering pencil point, feeling a sense of utter futility at the realization that this was only pretense, that nothing they did could save his father's life.

At least, he thought, the examinations weren't given by the sons and daughters who had voted the law into being. At least he wouldn't have to stamp the black INADEQUATE on his father's test and thus pronounce the sentence.

The pencil wavered over the circle edge again and was returned as Tom moved his arm slightly on the table, a motion that would automatically disqualify him on that question.

"That watch is slow!" Tom said in a sudden fury.

Les caught his breath and looked down at the watch. Two and a half minutes. "Three minutes," he said, pushing in the plunger.

Tom slapped down the pencil irritably. "*There*," he said. "Fool test anyway." His voice grew morose. "Don't prove a thing. Not a thing."

"You want to do some money questions, Dad?"

"Are they the next questions in the test?" Tom asked, looking over suspiciously to check for himself.

"Yes," Les lied, knowing that his father's eyes were too weak to see even though Tom always refused to admit he needed glasses. "Oh, wait a second, there's one before that," he added, thinking it would be easier for his father. "They ask you to tell time."

"That's a foolish question," Tom muttered. "What do they——"

He reached across the table irritably and picked up the watch and glanced down at its face. "Ten-fifteen," he said, scornfully.

Before Les could think to stop himself, he said, "But it's eleven-fifteen, Dad."

His father looked, for a moment, as though his face had been slapped. Then he picked up the watch again and stared down at it, lips twitching, and Les had the horrible premonition that Tom was going to insist it really was ten-fifteen.

"Well, that's what I meant," Tom said abruptly. "Slipped out wrong. Course it's eleven-fifteen, any fool can see that. Eleven-fifteen. Watch is no good. Numbers too close. Ought to throw it away. Now——"

Tom reached into his vest pocket and pulled out his own gold watch. "Here's a *watch*," he said, proudly. "Been telling perfect time for . . . sixty years! That's a watch. Not like *this*."

He tossed Les' watch down contemptuously and it flipped over on its face and the crystal broke.

"Look at that," Tom said quickly, to cover the jolting of embarrassment. "Watch can't take anything."

He avoided Les' eyes by looking down at his own watch. His mouth tightened as he opened the back and looked at Mary's picture; Mary when she was in her thirties, golden-haired and lovely.

Thank God, she didn't have to take these tests, he thought—at least she was spared that. Tom had never thought he could believe that Mary's accidental death at fifty-seven was fortunate but that was before the tests.

He closed the watch and put it away.

"You just leave that watch with me, tonight," he said

grumpily. "I'll see you get a decent . . . uh, *crystal* tomorrow."

"That's all right, Dad. It's just an old watch."

"That's *all* right," Tom said. "That's all right. You just leave it with me I'll get you a decent . . . crystal. Get you one that won't break, one that won't break. You just leave it with me."

Tom did the money questions then, questions like *How many quarters in a five-dollar bill?* and *If I took thirty-six cents from your dollar, how much change would you have left?*

They were written questions and Les sat there timing his father. It was quiet in the house, warm. Everything seemed very normal and ordinary with the two of them sitting there and Terry sewing in the living room.

That was the horror.

Life went on as usual. No one spoke of dying. The government sent out letters and the tests were given and those who failed were requested to appear at the government center for their injections. The law operated, the death rate was steady, the population problem was contained—all officially, impersonally, without a cry or a sensation.

But it was still loved people who were being killed.

"Never mind hanging over the watch," his father said, "I can do these questions without you . . . hanging over that watch."

"Dad, the examiners will be looking at their watches."

"The examiners are the examiners," Tom snapped. "You're not an examiner."

"Dad, I'm trying to help y——"

"Well, help me then, *help* me. Don't sit there hanging over that watch."

"This is your test, Dad, not mine," Les started, a flush of anger creeping up his cheeks. "If——"

"My test, yes, my test!" his father suddenly raged. "You all saw to that, didn't you? All saw to it that—that——"

Words failed again, angry thoughts piling up in his brain.

"You don't have to yell, Dad."

"I'm not yelling!"

"Dad, the boys are sleeping!" Terry suddenly broke in.

"I don't care if—!" Tom broke off suddenly and leaned back in the chair, the pencil falling unnoticed from his fingers and rolling across the tablecloth. He sat shivering, his thin chest rising and falling in jerks, his hands twitching uncontrollably on his lap.

"Do you want to go on, Dad?" Les asked, restraining his nervous anger.

"I don't ask much," Tom mumbled to himself. "Don't ask much in life."

"Dad, shall we go *on?*"

His father stiffened. *"If you can spare the time,"* he said with slow, indignant pride. *"If you can spare the time."*

Les looked at the test paper, his fingers gripping the stapled sheets rigidly. Psychological questions? No, he couldn't ask them. How did you ask your eighty-year-old father his views on sex?—your flint-surfaced father to whom the most innocuous remark was "obscene."

"Well?" his father asked in a rising voice.

"There doesn't seem to be any more," Les said. "We've been at it almost four hours now."

"What about all those pages you just skipped?"

"Most of those are for the . . . the physical, Dad."

He saw his father's lips press together and was afraid Tom was going to say something about that again. But all his father said was, "A fine friend. Fine friend."

"Dad, you——"

Les' voice broke off. There was no point in talking about it any more. Tom knew perfectly well that Doctor Trask couldn't make out a bill of health for this test the way he'd done for the three tests previous.

Les knew how frightened and insulted the old man was because he'd have to take off his clothes and be exposed to doctors who would probe and tap and ask offensive questions. He knew how afraid Tom was of the fact that when he redressed, he'd be watched from a peephole and someone would mark on a chart how well he dressed himself. He knew how it frightened his father to know that, when he ate in the government cafeteria at the midpoint of the day-long examination, eyes would be watching him again to see if he dropped a fork or a spoon or knocked over a glass of water or dribbled gravy on his shirt.

"They'll ask you to sign your name and address," Les said, wanting his father to forget about the physical and knowing how proud Tom was of his handwriting.

Pretending that he grudged it, the old man picked up the pencil and wrote. I'll fool them, he thought as the pencil moved across the page with strong, sure motions.

Mr. Thomas Parker, he wrote, *2719 Brighton Street, Blairtown, New York.*

"And the date," Les said.

The old man wrote, *January* 17, 2003, and something cold moved in the old man's vitals.

Tomorrow was the test.

They lay beside each other, neither of them sleeping. They had barely spoken while undressing and when Les had leaned over to kiss her good night she'd murmured something he didn't hear.

Now he turned over on his side with a heavy sigh and faced her. In the darkness, she opened her eyes and looked over at him.

"Asleep?" she asked softly.

"No."

He said no more. He waited for her to start.

But she didn't start and, after a few moments, he said, "Well, I guess this is . . . it." He finished weakly because he didn't like the words; they sounded ridiculously melo-dramatic.

Terry didn't say anything right away. Then, as if thinking aloud, she said, "Do you think there's any chance that——"

Les tightened at the words because he knew what she was going to say.

"No," he said. "He'll never pass."

He heard Terry swallowing. Don't say it, he thought,

pleadingly. Don't tell me I've been saying the same thing for fifteen years. I know it. I said it because I thought it was true.

Suddenly, he wished he'd signed the *Request for Removal* years before. They needed desperately to be free of Tom, for the good of their children and themselves. But how did you put that need into words without feeling like a murderer? You couldn't say: I hope the old man fails, I hope they kill him. Yet anything else you said was only a hypocritical substitute for those words because that was exactly how you felt.

Medical terms, he thought—charts about declining crops and lowered standard of living and hunger ratio and degrading health level—they'd used all those as arguments to support passage of the law. Well, they were lies—obvious, groundless lies. The law had been passed because people wanted to be left alone, because they wanted to live their own lives.

"Les, what if he passes?" Terry said.

He felt his hands tightening on the mattress.

"Les?"

"I don't know, honey," he said.

Her voice was firm in the darkness. It was a voice at the end of patience. "You have to know," it said.

He moved his head restlessly on the pillow. "Honey, don't push it," he begged. "Please."

"Les, if he passes that test it means five more years. *Five more years*, Les. Have you thought what that means?"

"Honey, he can't pass that test."

"But, what if he does?"

"Terry, he missed three quarters of the questions I asked him tonight. His hearing is almost gone, his eyes are bad, his heart is weak, he has arthritis." His fist beat down hopelessly on the bed. "He won't even pass the *physical*," he said, feeling himself tighten in self-hatred for assuring her that Tom was doomed.

If only he could forget the past and take his father for what he was now—a helpless, interfering old man who was ruining their lives. But it was hard to forget how he'd loved and respected his father, hard to forget the hikes in the country, the fishing trips, the long talks at night and all the many things his father and he had shared together.

That was why he'd never had the strength to sign the request. It was a simple form to fill out, much simpler than waiting for the five-year tests. But it had meant signing away the life of his father, requesting the government to dispose of him like some unwanted garbage. He could never do that.

And yet, now his father was eighty and, in spite of moral upbringing, in spite of life-taught Christian principles, he and Terry were horribly afraid that old Tom might pass the test and live another five years with them—another five years of fumbling around the house, undoing instructions they gave to the boys, breaking things, wanting to help but only getting in the way and making life an agony of held-in nerves.

"You'd better sleep," Terry said to him.

He tried to but he couldn't. He lay staring at the dark ceiling and trying to find an answer but finding no answer.

The alarm went off at six. Les didn't have to get up until eight but he wanted to see his father off. He got out of bed and dressed quietly so he wouldn't wake up Terry.

She woke up anyway and looked up at him from her pillow. After a moment, she pushed up on one elbow and looked sleepily at him.

"I'll get up and make you some breakfast," she said.

"That's all right," Les said. "You stay in bed."

"Don't you want me to get up?"

"Don't bother, honey," he said. "I want you to rest."

She lay down again and turned away so Les wouldn't see her face. She didn't know why she began to cry soundlessly; whether it was because he didn't want her to see his father or because of the test. But she couldn't stop. All she could do was hold herself rigid until the bedroom door had closed.

Then her shoulders trembled and a sob broke the barrier she had built in herself.

The door to his father's room was open as Les passed. He looked in and saw Tom sitting on the bed, leaning down and fastening his dark shoes. He saw the gnarled fingers shaking as they moved over the straps.

"Everything all right, Dad?" Les asked.

His father looked up in surprise. "What are you doing up this hour?" he asked.

"Thought I'd have breakfast with you," Les told him.

For a moment they looked at each other in silence. Then his father leaned over the shoes again. "That's not neces-sary," he heard the old man's voice telling him.

"Well, I think I'll have some breakfast anyway," he said and turned away so his father couldn't argue.

"Oh . . . *Leslie*."

Les turned.

"I trust you didn't forget to leave that watch out," his father said. "I intend to take it to the jewelers today and have a decent . . . decent crystal put on it, one that won't break."

"Dad, it's just an old watch," Les said. "It's not worth a nickel."

His father nodded slowly, one palm wavering before him as if to ward off argument. "Never-the-less," he stated slowly, "I intend to——"

"All right, Dad, all right. I'll put it on the kitchen table."

His father broke off and looked at him blankly a moment. Then, as if it were impulse and not delayed will, he bent over his shoes again.

Les stood for a moment looking down at his father's gray hair, his gaunt, trembling fingers. Then he turned away.

The watch was still on the dining-room table. Les picked it up and took it in to the kitchen table. The old man must have been reminding himself about the watch all night, he thought. Otherwise he wouldn't have managed to remember it.

He put fresh water in the coffee globe and pushed the buttons for two servings of bacon and eggs. Then he poured two glasses of orange juice and sat down at the table.

About fifteen minutes later, his father came down wearing his dark blue suit, his shoes carefully polished, his nails manicured, his hair slicked down and combed and brushed. He looked very neat and very old as he walked over to the coffee globe and looked in.

"Sit down, Dad," Les said. "I'll get it for you."

"I'm not helpless," his father said. "Stay where you are."

Les managed a smile. "I put some bacon and eggs on for us," he said.

"Not hungry," his father replied.

"You'll need a good breakfast in you, Dad."

"Never did eat a big breakfast," his father said, stiffly, still facing the stove. "Don't believe in it. Not good for the stomach."

Les closed his eyes a moment and across his face moved an expression of hopeless despair. Why did I bother getting up? he asked himself defeatedly. All we'd do is argue.

No. He felt himself stiffening. No, he'd be cheerful if it killed him.

"Sleep all right, Dad?" he asked.

"Course I slept all right," his father answered. "Always sleep fine. Fine. Did you think I wouldn't because of a——"

He broke off suddenly and turned accusingly at Les. "Where's that watch?" he demanded.

Les exhaled wearily and held up the watch. His father moved jerkily across the linoleum, took it from him and looked at it a moment, his old lips pursed.

"Shoddy workmanship," he said. "Shoddy." He put it carefully in his side coat pocket. "Get you a decent crystal," he muttered. "One that won't break."

Les nodded. "That'll be swell, Dad."

The coffee was ready then and Tom poured them each a cup. Les got up and turned off the automatic griller. He didn't feel like having bacon and eggs either now.

He sat across the table from his stern-faced father and felt hot coffee trickling down his throat. It tasted terrible but he knew that nothing in the world would have tasted good to him that morning.

"What time do you have to be there, Dad?" he asked to break the silence.

"Nine o'clock," Tom said.

"You're sure you don't want me to drive you there?"

"Not at all, not at all," his father said as though he were

talking patiently to an irritably insistent child. "The tube is good enough. Get me there in plenty of time."

"All right, Dad," Les said and sat there staring into his coffee. There must be something he could say, he thought, but he couldn't think of anything. Silence hung over them for long minutes while Tom drank his black coffee in slow, methodical sips.

Les licked his lips nervously, then hid the trembling of them behind his cup. Talking, he thought, talking and talking—of cars and tube conveyers and examination schedules—when all the time both of them knew that Tom might be sentenced to death that day.

He was sorry he'd gotten up. It would have been better to wake up and just find his father gone. He wished it could happen that way—*permanently*. He wished he could wake up some morning and find his father's room empty—the two suits gone, the dark shoes gone, the work clothes gone, the handkerchiefs, the socks, the garters, the braces, the shaving equipment—all those mute evidences of a life gone.

But it wouldn't be like that. After Tom failed the test, it would be several weeks before the letter of final appointment came and then another week or so before the appointment itself. It would be a hideously slow process of packing and disposing of and giving away of possessions, a process of meals and meals and meals together, of talking to each other, of a last dinner, of a long drive to the government center, of a ride up in a silent, humming elevator, of——

Dear God!

He found himself shivering helplessly and was afraid for a moment that he was going to cry.

Then he looked up with a shocked expression as his father stood.

"I'll be going now," Tom said.

Les's eyes fled to the wall clock. "But it's only a quarter to seven," he said, tensely. "It doesn't take that long to——"

"Like to be in plenty of time," his father said firmly. "Never like to be late."

"But my God, Dad, it only takes an hour at the most to get to the city," he said, feeling a terrible sinking in his stomach.

His father shook his head and Les knew he hadn't heard. "It's early, Dad," he said, loudly, his voice shaking a little.

"Never-the-less," his father said.

"But you haven't *eaten* anything."

"Never did eat a big breakfast," Tom started. "Not good for the——"

Les didn't hear the rest of it—the words about lifetime habit and not good for the digestion and everything else his father said. He felt waves of merciless horror breaking over him and he wanted to jump and throw his arms around the old man and tell him not to worry about the test because it didn't matter, because they loved him and would take care of him.

But he couldn't. He sat rigid with sick fright, looking up at his father. He couldn't even speak when his father turned at the kitchen door and said in a voice that was calmly dispassionate because it took every bit of strength the old man had to make it so, "I'll see you tonight, Leslie."

The door swung shut and the breeze that ruffled across Les' cheeks chilled him to the heart.

Suddenly, he jumped up with a startled grunt and rushed across the linoleum. As he pushed through the doorway he saw his father almost to the front door.

"Dad!"

Tom stopped and looked back in surprise as Les walked across the dining room, hearing the steps counted in his mind—*one, two, three, four, five.*

He stopped before his father and forced a faltering smile to his lips.

"Good luck, Dad," he said. "I'll . . . see you tonight." He had been about to say, "I'll be rooting for you"; but he couldn't.

His father nodded once, just once, a curt nod as of one gentleman acknowledging another.

"Thank you," his father said and turned away.

When the door shut, it seemed as if, suddenly, it had

become an impenetrable wall through which his father could never pass again.

Les moved to the window and watched the old man walk slowly down the path and turn left onto the sidewalk. He watched his father start up the street, then straighten himself, throw back his lean shoulders and walk erect and briskly into the gray of morning.

At first Les thought it was raining. But then he saw that the shimmering moistness wasn't on the window at all.

He couldn't go to work. He phoned in sick and stayed home. Terry got the boys off to school and, after they'd eaten breakfast, Les helped her clear away the morning dishes and put them in the washer. Terry didn't say anything about his staying home. She acted as if it were normal for him to be home on a weekday.

He spent the morning and afternoon puttering in the garage shop, starting seven different projects and losing interest in them.

Around five, he went into the kitchen and had a can of beer while Terry made supper. He didn't say anything to her. He kept pacing around the living room, staring out the window at the overcast sky, then pacing again. It had been threatening to rain all day.

"I wonder where he is," he finally said, back in the kitchen again.

"He'll be back," she said and he stiffened a moment, thinking he heard disgust in her voice. Then he relaxed, knowing it was only his imagination.

When he dressed after taking a shower, it was five-forty. The boys were home from playing and they all sat down to supper. Les noticed a place set for his father and wondered if Terry had set it there for his benefit.

He couldn't eat anything. He kept cutting the meat into smaller and smaller pieces and mashing butter into his baked potato without tasting any of it.

"What is it?" he asked as Jim spoke to him.

"Dad, if grandpa don't pass the test, he gets a month, don't he?"

Les felt his stomach muscles tightening as he stared at his older son. . . . *gets a month, don't he?*—the last of Jim's question muttered on in his brain.

"What are you talking about?" he asked.

"My Civics book says old people get a month to live after they don't pass their test. That right, isn't it?"

"No, it *isn't*," Tommy broke in. "Harry Senker's grandma got her letter after only two weeks."

"How do *you* know?" Jim asked his nine-year-old brother. "Did you *see* it?"

"That's enough," Les said.

"Don't *have* t'see it!" Tommy argued. "Harry told me that——"

"That's *enough*!"

The two boys looked suddenly at their white-faced father.

"We won't talk about it," he said.

"But what——"

"*Jimmy*," Terry said, warningly.

Jimmy looked at his mother, then, after a moment, went back to his food and they all ate in silence.

The death of their grandfather means nothing to them, Les thought bitterly—nothing at all. He swallowed and tried to relax the tightness in his body. Well, why *should* it mean anything to them? he told himself; it's not their time to worry yet. Why force it on them now? They'll have it soon enough.

When the front door opened and shut at six-ten, Les stood up so quickly, he knocked over an empty glass.

"Les, *don't*," Terry said suddenly and he knew, immediately, that she was right. His father wouldn't like him to come rushing from the kitchen with questions.

He slumped down on the chair again and stared at his barely touched food, his heart throbbing. As he picked up his fork with tight fingers, he heard the old man cross the dining-room rug and start up the stairs. He glanced at Terry and her throat moved.

He couldn't eat. He sat there breathing heavily, and picking at the food. Upstairs, he heard the door to his father's room close.

It was when Terry was putting the pie on the table that Les excused himself quickly and got up.

He was at the foot of the stairs when the kitchen door was pushed open. "Les," he heard her say, urgently.

He stood there silently as she came up to him.

"Isn't it better we leave him alone?" she asked.

"But, honey, I——"

"Les, if he'd passed the test, he would have come into the kitchen and told us."

"Honey, he wouldn't know if——"

"He'd know if he passed, you know that. He told us about it the last two times. If he'd passed, he'd have——"

Her voice broke off and she shuddered at the way he was looking at her. In the heavy silence, she heard a sudden splattering of rain on the windows.

They looked at each other a long moment. Then Les said, "I'm going up."

"Les," she murmured.

"I won't say anything to upset him," he said, "I'll . . ."

A moment longer they stared at each other. Then he turned away and trudged up the steps. Terry watched him go with a bleak, hopeless look on her face.

Les stood before the closed door a minute, bracing himself. I won't upset him, he told himself; I *won't*.

He knocked softly, wondering, in that second, if he were making a mistake. Maybe he should have left the old man alone, he thought unhappily. But he found himself knocking again.

In the bedroom, he heard a rustling movement on the bed, then the sound of his father's feet touching the floor.

"Who is it?" he heard Tom ask.

Les caught his breath. "It's me, Dad," he said.

"What do you want?"

"May I see you?"

Silence inside. "Well . . ." he heard his father say then and his voice stopped. Les heard him get up and heard the sound of his footsteps on the floor. Then there was the sound of paper rattling and a bureau drawer being carefully shut.

Finally the door opened.

Tom was wearing his old red bathrobe over his clothes and he'd taken off his shoes and put his slippers on.

"May I come in, Dad?" Les asked quietly.

His father hesitated a moment. Then he said, "Come in," but it wasn't an invitation. It was more as if he'd said, This is your house; I can't keep you from this room.

Les was going to tell his father that he didn't want to disturb him but he couldn't. He went in and stood in the middle of the throw rug, waiting.

"Sit down," his father said and Les sat down on the upright chair that Tom hung his clothes on at night. His father waited until Les was seated and then sank down on the bed with a grunt.

For a long time they looked at each other without speaking, like total strangers, each waiting for the other one to speak. How did the test go? Les heard the words repeated in his mind. How did the test go, how did the test go? He couldn't speak the words. How did the——

"I suppose you want to know what . . . happened," his father said then, controlling himself visibly.

"Yes," Les said, "I . . ." He caught himself. "Yes," he repeated and waited.

Old Tom looked down at the floor for a moment. Then, suddenly, he raised his head and looked defiantly at his son.

"I didn't go," he said.

Les felt as if all his strength had suddenly been sucked into the floor. He sat there, motionless, staring at his father.

"Had no intention of going," his father hurried on. "No intention of going through all that foolishness. Physical tests, m-mental tests, putting b-b-*blocks* in a board and . . . Lord knows what all! Had no intention of going."

He stopped and stared at his son with angry eyes as if he were daring Les to say he had done wrong.

But Les couldn't say anything.

A long time passed. Les swallowed and managed to summon the words. "What are you . . . going to do?"

"Never mind that, never mind," his father said, almost as

if he were grateful for the question. "Don't you worry about your Dad. Your Dad knows how to take care of himself."

And suddenly Les heard the bureau drawer shutting again, the rustling of a paper bag. He almost looked around at the bureau to see if the bag were still there. His head twitched as he fought down the impulse.

"W-ell," he faltered, not realizing how stricken and lost his expression was.

"Just never mind now," his father said again, quietly, almost gently. "It's not your problem to worry about. Not your problem at all."

But it is! Les heard the words cried out in his mind. But he didn't speak them. Something in the old man stopped him; a sort of fierce strength, a taut dignity he knew he mustn't touch.

"I'd like to rest now," he heard Tom say then and he felt as if he'd been struck violently in the stomach. I'd like to rest now, to rest now—the words echoed down long tunnels of the mind as he stood. Rest now, rest now . . .

He found himself being ushered to the door where he turned and looked at his father. *Goodbye.* The word stuck in him.

Then his father smiled and said, "Good night, Leslie."
"Dad."

He felt the old man's hand in his own, stronger than his, more steady; calming him, reassuring him. He felt his father's left hand grip his shoulder.

"Good night, son," his father said and, in the moment they stood close together, Les saw, over the old man's shoulder, the crumpled drugstore bag lying in the corner of the room as though it had been thrown there so as not to be seen.

Then he was standing in wordless terror in the hall, listening to the latch clicking shut and knowing that, although his father wasn't locking the door, he couldn't go into his father's room.

For a long time he stood staring at the closed door, shivering without control. Then he turned away.

Terry was waiting for him at the foot of the stairs, her face

drained of color. She asked the question with her eyes as he
came down to her.

"He . . . didn't go," was all he said.

She made a tiny, startled sound in her throat. "But——"

"He's been to the drugstore," Les said. "I . . . saw the
bag in the corner of the room. He threw it away so I wouldn't
see it but I . . . saw it."

For a moment, it seemed as if she were starting for the
stairs but it was only a momentary straining of her body.

"He must have shown the druggist the letter about the
test," Les said. "The . . . druggist must have given him . . .
pills. Like they all do."

They stood silently in the dining room while rain drummed
against the windows.

"What shall we do?" she asked, almost inaudibly.

"Nothing," he murmured. His throat moved convulsively
and breath shuddered through him. *"Nothing."*

Then he was walking numbly back to the kitchen and he
could feel her arm tight around him as if she were trying to
press her love to him because she could not speak of love.

All evening, they sat there in the kitchen. After she put the
boys to bed, she came back and they sat in the kitchen
drinking coffee and talking in quiet, lonely voices.

Near midnight, they left the kitchen and, just before they
went upstairs, Les stopped by the dining-room table and
found the watch with a shiny new crystal on it. He couldn't
even touch it.

They went upstairs and walked past the door of Tom's
bedroom. There was no sound inside. They got undressed and
got in bed together and Terry set the clock the way she set it
every night. In a few hours they both managed to fall asleep.

And all night there was silence in the old man's room. And
the next day, silence.

ANACHRON

BY DAMON KNIGHT (1922–   )

WORLDS OF IF, JANUARY

Damon Knight is back (see "To Serve Man" Vol. 12, and "Four In One," Vol. 15 of this series) and causing us problems. 1954 saw the publication of at least three outstanding stories by him, in addition to the present selection: "Natural State," GALAXY, January; "Special Delivery," GALAXY, April; and the wonderful "Rule Golden," SCIENCE FICTION ADVENTURES, June. They all deserve (at least in my view) inclusion in this book, but in addition to the numbers problem, all of them are long, the first and last mentioned being novellas.

This is not to say that "Anachron" is here by way of compensation—it is one of Damon's best stories, and for some reason, one of his least reprinted, an added bonus as far as I'm concerned. It also appeared in IF, my favorite magazine of my 1950's. (MHG)

I. suppose that every science fiction writer of any note whatever has tried his hand on stories involving time-travel paradoxes at one time or another. (One of mine was "The Red Queen's Race" in Vol. 11 of this series.)

To my way of thinking it is precisely because time-travel involves such fascinating paradoxes that we can conclude, even in the absence of other evidence, that time-travel is

*impossible. I have the feeling that the Universe (or Reality, if
you prefer) allows no paradoxes. To be sure, there is such a
thing as "quantum weirdness" in which quantum theory
seems to contain irrefutable paradoxes, but because of that I
am beginning, very reluctantly, to veer toward Einstein's
view that quantum theory is incomplete and that there is
something deeper that has yet to be reached. (IA)*

The body was never found. And for that reason alone, there
was no body to find.

It sounds like inverted logic—which, in a sense, it is—but
there's no paradox involved. It was a perfectly orderly and
explicable event, even though it could only have happened to
a Castellare.

Odd fish, the Castellare brothers. Sons of a Scots-English-
woman and an expatriate Italian, born in England, educated
on the Continent, they were at ease anywhere in the world
and at home nowhere.

Nevertheless, in their middle years, they had become settled men. Expatriates like their father, they lived on the island
of Ischia, off the Neapolitan coast, in a palace—*quattrocento,*
very fine, with peeling cupids on the walls, a multitude of
rats, no central heating and no neighbors.

They went nowhere; no one except their agents and their
lawyers came to them. Neither had ever married. Each, at
about the age of thirty, had given up the world of people for
an inner world of more precise and more enduring pleasures.
Each was an amateur—a fanatical, compulsive amateur.

They had been born out of their time.

Peter's passion was virtu. He collected relentlessly, it would
not be too much to say savagely; he collected as some men
hunt big game. His taste was catholic, and his acquisitions
filled the huge rooms of the palace and half the vaults under
them—paintings, statuary, enamels, porcelain, glass, crystal,
metalwork. At fifty, he was a round little man with small,
sardonic eye and a careless patch of pinkish goatee.

Harold Castellare, Peter's talented brother, was a scientist.
An amateur scientist. He belonged in the nineteenth century,

as Peter was a throwback to a still earlier epoch. Modern
science is largely a matter of teamwork and drudgery, both
impossible concepts to a Castellare. But Harold's intelligence
was in its own way as penetrating and original as a Newton's
or a Franklin's. He had done respectable work in physics and
electronics, and had even, at his lawyer's insistence, taken
out a few patents. The income from these, when his own
purchases of instruments and equipment did not consume it,
he gave to his brother, who accepted it without gratitude or
rancor.

Harold, at fifty-three, was spare and shrunken, sallow and
spotted, with a bloodless, melancholy countenance; on his
upper lip grew a neat hedge of pink-and-salt mustache, the
companion piece and antithesis of his brother's goatee.

On a certain May morning, Harold had an accident.

Goodyear dropped rubber on a hot stove; Archimedes took
a bath; Becquerel left a piece of uranium ore in a drawer with
a photographic plate. Harold Castellare, working patiently
with an apparatus which had so far consumed a great deal of
current without producing anything more spectacular than
some rather unusual corona effects, sneezed convulsively and
dropped an ordinary bar magnet across two charged terminals.

Above the apparatus a huge, cloudy bubble sprang into
being.

Harold, getting up from his instinctive crouch, blinked at it
in profound astonishment. As he watched, the cloudiness
abruptly disappeared and he was looking *through* the bubble
at a section of tesselated flooring that seemed to be about
three feet above the real floor. He could also see the corner of
a carved wooden bench, and on the bench a small, oddly
shaped stringed instrument.

Harold swore fervently to himself, made agitated notes,
and then began to experiment. He tested the sphere cautiously
with an electroscope, with a magnet, with a Geiger counter.
Negative. He tore a tiny bit of paper from his notepad and
dropped it toward the sphere. The paper disappeared; he
couldn't see where it went.

Speechless, Harold picked up a meter stick and thrust it

delicately forward. There was no feeling of contact; the rule went into and through the bubble as if the latter did not exist. Then it touched the stringed instrument, with a solid click. Harold pushed. The instrument slid over the the edge of the bench and struck the floor with a hollow thump and jangle.

Staring at it, Harold suddenly recognized its tantalizingly familiar shape.

Recklessly he let go the meter stick, reached in and picked the fragile thing out of the bubble. It was solid and cool in his fingers. The varnish was clear, the color of the wood glowing through it. It looked as if it might have been made yesterday.

Peter owned one almost exactly like it, except for preservation—a viola d'amore of the seventeenth century.

Harold stooped to look through the bubble horizontally. Gold and rust tapestries hid the wall, fifty feet away, except for an ornate door in the center. The door began to open; Harold saw a flicker of umber.

Then the sphere went cloudy again. His hands were empty; the viola d'amore was gone. And the meter stick, which he had dropped inside the sphere, lay on the floor at his feet.

"Look at that," said Harold simply.

Peter's eyebrows went up slightly. "What is it, a new kind of television?"

"No, no. Look here." The viola d'amore lay on the bench, precisely where it had been before. Harold reached into the sphere and drew it out.

Peter started. "Give me that." He took it in his hands, rubbed the smoothly finished wood. He stared at his brother. "By God and all the saints," he said. "Time travel."

Harold snorted impatiently. "My dear Peter, 'time' is a meaningless word taken by itself, just as 'space' is."

"But, barring that, time travel."

"If you like, yes."

"You'll be quite famous."

"I expect so."

Peter looked down at the instrument in his hands. "I'd like to keep this, if I may."

"I'd be very happy to let you, but you can't."

As he spoke, the bubble went cloudy; the viola d'amore was gone like smoke.

"There, you see?"

"What sort of devil's trick is that?"

"It goes back. . . . Later you'll see. I had that thing out once before, and this happened. When the sphere became transparent again, the viol was where I had found it."

"And your explanation for this?"

Harold hesitated. "None. Until I can work out the appropriate mathematics—"

"Which may take you some time. Meanwhile, in layman's language—"

Harold's face creased with the effort and interest of translation. "Very roughly, then—I should say it means that events are conserved. Two or three centuries ago—"

"Three. Notice the sound holes."

"Three centuries ago, then, at this particular time of day, someone was in that room. If the viola were gone, he or she would have noticed the fact. That would constitute an alteration of events already fixed; therefore it doesn't happen. For the same reason, I conjecture, we can't see into the sphere, or—" he probed at it with a fountain pen—"I thought not—or reach into it to touch anything; that would also constitute an alteration. And anything we put into the sphere while it is transparent comes out again when it becomes opaque. To put it very crudely, we cannot alter the past."

"But it seems to me that we did alter it. Just now, when you took the viol out, even if no one of that time saw it happen."

"This," said Harold, "is the difficulty of using language as a means of exact communication. If you had not forgotten all your calculus . . . However. It may be postulated (remembering of course that everything I say is a lie, because I say it in English) that an event which doesn't influence other events is not an event. In other words—"

"That, since no one saw you take it, it doesn't matter whether you took it or not. A rather dangerous precept,

Harold; you would have been burned at the stake for that at one time."

"Very likely. But it can be stated in another way or, indeed, in an infinity of ways which only seem to be different. If someone, let us say God, were to remove the moon as I am talking to you, using zero duration, and substitute an exact replica made of concrete and plaster of Paris, with the same mass, albedo and so on as the genuine moon, it would make no measurable difference in the universe as we perceive it—and therefore we cannot certainly say that it hasn't happened. Nor, I may add, does it make any difference whether it has or not."

" 'When there's no one about on the quad,' " said Peter.

"Yes. A basic and, as a natural consequence, a meaningless problem of philosophy. Except," he added, "in this one particular manifestation."

He stared at the cloudy sphere. "You'll excuse me, won't you, Peter? I've got to work on this."

"When will you publish, do you suppose?"

"Immediately. That's to say, in a week or two."

"Don't do it till you've talked it over with me, will you? I have a notion about it."

Harold looked at him sharply. "Commercial?"

"In a way."

"No," said Harold. "This is not the sort of thing one patents or keeps secret, Peter."

"Of course. I'll see you at dinner, I hope?"

"I think so. If I forget, knock on the door, will you?"

"Yes. Until then."

"Until then."

At dinner, Peter asked only two questions.

"Have you found any possibility of changing the time your thing reaches—from the seventeenth century to the eighteenth, for example, or from Monday to Tuesday?"

"Yes, as a matter of fact. Amazing. It's lucky that I had a rheostat already in the circuit; I wouldn't dare turn the current off. Varying the amperage varies the time set. I've had it up to what I think was Wednesday of last week—at any rate, my smock was lying over the workbench where I left it, I remember, Wednesday afternoon. I pulled it out. A curious sensation, Peter—I was wearing the same smock at the time. And then the sphere went opaque and of course the smock vanished. That must have been myself, coming into the room.''

''And the future?''

''Yes. Another funny thing, I've had it forward to various times in the near future, and the machine itself is still there, but nothing's been done to it—none of the things I'm thinking I might do. That might be because of the conservation of events, again, but I rather think not. Still farther forward there are cloudy areas, blanks; I can't see anything that isn't in existence now, apparently, but here, in the next few days, there's nothing of that.

''It's as if I were going away. Where do you suppose I'm going?''

Harold's abrupt departure took place between midnight and morning. He packed his own grip, it would seem, left unattended, and was seen no more. It was extraordinary, of course, that he should have left at all, but the details were in no way odd. Harold had always detested what he called ''the tyranny of the valet.'' He was, as everyone knew, a most independent man.

On the following day Peter made some trifling experiments with the time-sphere. From the sixteenth century he picked up a scent bottle of Venetian glass; from the eighteenth, a crucifix of carved rosewood; from the nineteenth, when the palace had been the residence of an Austrian count and his Italian mistress, a hand-illuminated copy of De Sade's *La Nouvelle Justine*, very curiously bound in human skin.

They all vanished, naturally, within minutes or hours—all but the scent bottle. This gave Peter matter for reflection. There had been half a dozen flickers of cloudiness in the sphere just futureward of the bottle; it ought to have vanished, but it hadn't. But then, he had found it on the floor near a wall with quite a large rat hole in it.

When objects disappeared unaccountably, he asked himself, was it because they had rolled into rat holes, or because
some time fisher had picked them up when they were in a
position to do so?

He did not make any attempt to explore the future. That
afternoon he telephoned his lawyers in Naples and gave them
instructions for a new will. His estate, including his half of
the jointly owned Ischia property, was to go to the Italian
government on two conditions: (1) that Harold Castellare
should make a similar bequest of the remaining half of the
property and (2) that the Italian government should turn the
palace into a national museum to house Peter's collection,
using the income from his estate for its administration and for
further acquisitions. His surviving relatives—two cousins in
Scotland—he cut off with a shilling each.

He did nothing more until after the document had been
brought out to him, signed and witnessed. Only then did he
venture to look into his own future.

Events were conserved, Harold had said—meaning, Peter
very well understood, events of the present and future as well
as of the past. But was there only one pattern in which the
future could be fixed? Could a result exist before its cause
had occurred?

The Castellare motto was *Audentes fortuna juvat*—into
which Peter, at the age of fourteen, had interpolated the word
"*prudentesque*": "Fortune favors the bold—and the prudent."

Tomorrow: no change; the room he was looking at was so
exactly like this one that the time sphere seemed to vanish.
The next day: a cloudy blur. And the next, and the next . . .

Opacity, straight through to what Peter judged, by the
distance he had moved the rheostat handle, to be ten years
ahead. Then, suddenly, the room was a long marble hall
filled with display cases.

Peter smiled wryly. If you were Harold, obviously you
could not look ahead and see Peter working in your laboratory. And if you were Peter, equally obviously, you could not
look ahead and know whether the room you saw was an
improvement you yourself were going to make, or part of a

museum established after your death, eight or nine years from now, or . . .

No. Eight years was little enough, but he could not even be sure of that. It would, after all, be seven years before Harold could be declared legally dead. . . .

Peter turned the vernier knob slowly forward. A flicker, another, a long series. Forward faster. Now the flickering melted into a grayness; objects winked out of existence and were replaced by others in the showcases; the marble darkened and lightened again, darkened and lightened, darkened and remained dark. He was, Peter judged, looking at the hall as it would be some five hundred years in the future. There was a thick film of dust on every exposed surface; rubbish and the carcass of some small animal had been swept carelessly into a corner.

The sphere clouded.

When it cleared, there was an intricate trail of footprints in the dust, and two of the showcases were empty.

The footprints were splayed, trifurcate, and thirty inches long.

After a moment's deliberation Peter walked around the workbench and leaned down to look through the sphere from the opposite direction. Framed in the nearest of the four tall windows was a scene of picture-postcard banality: the sunsilvered bay and the foreshortened arc of the city, with Vesuvio faintly fuming in the background. But there was something wrong about the colors, even grayed as they were by distance.

Peter went and got his binoculars.

The trouble was, of course, that Naples was green. Where the city ought to have been, a rankness had sprouted. Between the clumps of foliage he could catch occasional glimpses of gray-white that might equally well have been boulders or the wreckage of buildings. There was no movement. There was no shipping in the harbor.

But something rather odd was crawling up the side of the volcano. A rust-orange pipe, it appeared to be, supported on hairline struts like the legs of a centipede, and ending without rhyme or reason just short of the top.

While Peter watched, it turned slowly blue.

One day further forward: now all the display cases had been looted; the museum, it would seem, was empty.

Given, that in five centuries the world, or at any rate the department of Campania, has been overrun by a race of Somethings, the human population being killed or driven out in the process; and that the conquerors take an interest in the museum's contents, which they have accordingly removed.

Removed where, and why?

This question, Peter conceded, might have a thousand answers, nine hundred and ninety-nine of which would mean that he had lost his gamble. The remaining answer was: to the vaults, for safety.

With his own hands Peter built a hood to cover the apparatus on the workbench and the sphere above it. It was unaccustomed labor, it took him the better part of two days. Then he called in workmen to break a hole in the stone flooring next to the interior wall, rig a hoist, and cut the power cable that supplied the time-sphere loose from its supports all the way back to the fuse box, leaving him a single flexible length of cable more than a hundred feet long. They unbolted the workbench from the floor, attached casters to its legs, lowered it into the empty vault below, and went away.

Peter unfastened and removed the hood. He looked into the sphere.

Treasure.

Crates, large and small, racked in rows into dimness.

With pudgy fingers that did not tremble, he advanced the rheostat. A cloudy flicker, another, a leaping blur of them as he moved the vernier faster—then there were no more, to the limit of the time-sphere's range.

Two hundred years, Peter guessed—A.D. 2700 to 2900 or thereabout—in which no one would enter the vault. Two hundred years of "unliquidated time."

He put the rheostat back to the beginning of that uninterrupted period. He drew out a small crate and prized it open.

Chessmen, ivory with gold inlay, Florentine, fourteenth century. Superb.

Another, from the opposite rack.

T'ang figurines, horses and men, ten to fourteen inches high. Priceless.

The crates would not burn, Tomaso told him. He went down to the kitchen to see, and it was true. The pieces lay in the roaring stove untouched. He fished one out with a poker; even the feathery splinters of the unplaned wood had not ignited.

It made a certain extraordinary kind of sense. When the moment came for the crates to go back, any physical scrambling that had occurred in the meantime would have no effect; they would simply put themselves together as they had been before, like Thor's goats. But burning was another matter; burning would have released energy which could not be replaced.

That settled one paradox, at any rate. There was another that nagged at Peter's orderly mind. If the things he took out of that vault, seven hundred-odd years in the future, were to become part of the collection bequeathed by him to the museum, preserved by it, and eventually stored in the vault for him to find—then precisely where had they come from in the first place?

It worried him. Peter had learned in life, as his brother had in physics, that one never gets anything for nothing.

Moreover, this riddle was only one of his perplexities, and that not among the greatest. For another example, there was the obstinate opacity of the time-sphere whenever he attempted to examine the immediate future. However often he tried it, the result was always the same: a cloudy blank, all the way forward to the sudden unveiling of the marble gallery.

It was reasonable to expect the sphere to show nothing at times when he himself was going to be in the vault, but this accounted for only five or six hours out of every twenty-four. Again, presumably, it would show him no changes to be made by himself, since foreknowledge would make it possi-

ble for him to alter his actions. But he laboriously cleared one
end of the vault, put up a screen to hide the rest and made a
vow—which he kept—not to alter the clear space or move the
screen for a week. Then he tried again—with the same result.

The only remaining explanation was that sometime during
the next ten years something was going to happen which he
would prevent if he could; and the clue to it was there, buried
in that frustrating, unbroken blankness.

As a corollary, it was going to be something which he
could prevent if only he knew what it was . . . or even when
it was supposed to happen.

The event in question, in all probability, was his own
death. Peter therefore hired nine men to guard him, three to a
shift—because one man alone could not be trusted, two might
conspire against him, whereas three, with the very minimum
of effort, could be kept in a state of mutual suspicion. He also
underwent a thorough medical examination, had new locks
installed on every door and window, and took every other
precaution ingenuity could suggest. When he had done all
these things, the next ten years were as blank as before.

Peter had more than half expected it. He checked through
his list of safeguards once more, found it good, and thereafter
let the matter rest. He had done all he could; either he would
survive the crisis or he would not. In either case, events were
conserved; the time-sphere could give him no forewarning.

Another man might have found his pleasure blunted by
guilt and fear; Peter's was whetted to a keener edge. If he had
been a recluse before, now he was an eremite; he grudged
every hour that was not given to his work. Mornings he spent
in the vault, unpacking his acquisitions; afternoons and evenings, sorting, cataloguing, examining and—the word is not
too strong—gloating. When three weeks had passed in this
way, the shelves were bare as far as the power cable would
allow him to reach in every direction, except for crates whose
contents were undoubtedly too large to pass through the
sphere. These, with heroic self-control, Peter had left
untouched.

And still he had looted only a hundredth part of that

                  Damon Knight

incredible treasure house. With grappling hooks he could have extended his reach by perhaps three or four yards, but at the risk of damaging his prizes; and in any case this would have been no solution but only a postponement of the problem. There was nothing for it but to go through the sphere himself and unpack the crates while on the other ''side'' of it.

Peter thought about it in a fury of concentration for the rest of the day. So far he was concerned, there was no question that the gain would be worth any calculated risk; the problem was how to measure the risk and if possible reduce it.

Item: He felt a definite uneasiness at the thought of venturing through that insubstantial bubble. Intuition was supported, if not by logic, at least by a sense of the dramatically appropriate. Now, if ever, would be the time for his crisis.

Item: Common sense did not concur. The uneasiness had two symbols. One was the white face of his brother Harold just before the water closed over it; the other was a phantasm born of those gigantic, splayed footprints in the dust of the gallery. In spite of himself, Peter had often found himself trying to imagine what the creatures that made them must look like, until his visualization was so clear that he could almost swear he had seen them.

Towering monsters they were, with crested ophidian heads and great unwinking eyes; and they moved in a strutting glide, nodding their heads, like fantastic barnyard fowl.

But, taking these premonitory images in turn: first, it was impossible that he should ever be seriously inconvenienced by Harold's death. There were no witnesses, he was sure; he had struck the blow with a stone; stones also were the weights that had dragged the body down, and the rope was an odd length Peter had picked up on the shore. Second, the three-toed Somethings might be as fearful as all the world's bogies put together; it made no difference, he could never meet them.

Nevertheless, the uneasiness persisted. Peter was not satisfied; he wanted a lifeline. When he found it, he wondered that he had not thought of it before.

He would set the time-sphere for a period just before one of the intervals of blankness. That would take care of accidents, sudden illnesses, and other unforeseeable contingencies. It would also insure him against one very real and not at all irrational dread: the fear that the mechanism which generated the time-sphere might fail while he was on the other side. For the conservation of events was not a condition created by the sphere but one which limited its operation. No matter what happened, it was impossible for him to occupy the same place-time as any future or past observer; therefore, when the monster entered that vault, Peter would not be there any more.

There was, of course, the scent bottle to remember. Every rule has its exception; but in this case, Peter thought, the example did not apply. A scent bottle could roll into a rat hole; a man could not.

He turned the rheostat carefully back to the last flicker of grayness; past that to the next, still more carefully. The interval between the two, he judged, was something under an hour: excellent.

His pulse seemed a trifle rapid, but his brain was clear and cool. He thrust his head into the sphere and sniffed cautiously. The air was stale and had a faint, unpleasant odor, but it was breathable.

Using a crate as a stepping stool, he climbed to the top of the workbench. He arranged another crate close to the sphere to make a platform level with its equator. And seven and a half centuries in the future, a third crate stood on the floor directly under the sphere.

Peter stepped into the sphere, dropped, and landed easily, legs bending to take the shock. When he straightened, he was standing in what to all appearances was a large circular hole in the workbench; his chin was just above the top of the sphere.

He lowered himself, half squatting, until he had drawn his head through and stepped down from the crate.

He was in the future vault. The sphere was a brightly luminous thing that hung unsupported in the air behind him, its midpoint just higher than his head. The shadows it cast spread black and wedge-shaped in every direction, melting into obscurity.

Peter's heart was pounding miserably. He had an illusory stifling sensation, coupled with the idiotic notion that he ought to be wearing a diver's helmet. The silence was like the pause before a shout.

But down the aisles marched the crated treasures in their hundreds.

Peter set to work. It was difficult, exacting labor, opening the crates where they lay, removing the contents and nailing the crates up again, all without disturbing the positions of the crates themselves, but it was the price he had to pay for his lifeline. Each crate was in a sense a microcosm, like the vault itself—a capsule of unliquidated time. But the vault's term would end some fifty minutes from now, when crested heads nodded down these aisles; those of the crates' interiors, for all that Peter knew to the contrary, went on forever.

The first crate contained lacework porcelain; the second, shakudō sword hilts; the third, an exquisite fourth-century Greek ornament in *repoussé* bronze, the equal in every way of the Siris bronzes.

Peter found it almost physically difficult to set the thing down, but he did so; standing on his platform crate in the future with its head projecting above the sphere in the present— like (again the absurd thought!) a diver rising from the ocean—he laid it carefully beside the others on the workbench.

Then down again, into the fragile silence and the gloom. The next crates were too large, and those just beyond were doubtful. Peter followed his shadow down the aisle. He had almost twenty minutes left: enough for one more crate, chosen with care, and an ample margin.

Glancing to his right at the end of the row, he saw a door. It was a heavy door, rivet-studded, with a single iron step below it. There had been no door there in Peter's time; the whole plan of the building must have been altered. *Of course!* he realized suddenly. If it had not, if so much as a single tile or lintel had remained of the palace as he knew it, then the sphere could never have let him see or enter this particular

here-and-now this—what would Harold have called it?—this
nexus in space-time.

For if you saw any now-existing thing as it was going to
appear in the future, you could alter it in the present—carve
your initials in it, break it apart, chop it down—which was
manifestly impossible, and therefore . . .

And therefore the first ten years were necessarily blank
when he looked into the sphere, not because anything unpleasant was going to happen to him, but because in that time
the last traces of the old palace had not yet been eradicated.

There was no crisis.

Wait a moment, though! Harold had been able to look into
the near future. . . . But—of course—Harold had been about
to die.

In the dimness between himself and the door he saw a rack
of crates that looked promising. The way was uneven; one of
the untidy accumulations of refuse that seemed to be characteristic of the Somethings lay in windrows across the floor.
Peter stepped forward carefully—but not carefully enough.

Harold Castellare had had another accident—and again, if
you choose to look at it in that way, a lucky one. The blow
stunned him; the old rope slipped from the stones; flaccid, he
floated where a struggling man might have drowned. A fishing boat nearly ran him down, and picked him up instead. He
was suffering from a concussion, shock, exposure, asphyxia-
tion and was more than three quarters dead. But he was still
alive when he was delivered, an hour later, to a hospital in
Naples.

There were, of course, no identifying papers, labels or
monograms in his clothing—Peter had seen to that—and for
the first week after his rescue Harold was quite genuinely
unable to give any account of himself. During the second
week he was mending but uncommunicative, and at the end
of the third, finding that there was some difficulty about
gaining his release in spite of his physical recovery, he
affected to regain his memory, gave a circumstantial but
entirely fictitious identification and was discharged.

To understand this as well as all his subsequent actions, it is only necessary to remember that Harold was a Castellare. In Naples, not wishing to give Peter any unnecessary anxiety, he did not approach his bank for funds but cashed a check with an incurious acquaintance, and predated it by four weeks. With part of the money so acquired he paid his hospital bill and rewarded his rescuers. Another part went for new clothing and for four days' residence in an inconspicuous hotel, while he grew used to walking and dressing himself again. The rest, on his last day, he spent in the purchase of a discreetly small revolver and box of cartridges.

He took the last boat to Ischia and arrived at his own front door a few minutes before eleven. It was a cool evening, and a most cheerful fire was burning in the central hall.

"Signor Peter is well, I suppose," said Harold, removing his coat.

"Yes, Signor Harold. He is very well, very busy with his collection."

"Where is he? I should like to speak to him."

"He is in the vaults, Signor Harold. But . . ."

"Yes?"

"Signor Peter sees no one when he is in the vaults. He has given strict orders that no one is to bother him, Signor Harold, when he is in the vaults."

"Oh, well," said Harold. "I daresay he'll see me."

It was a thing something like a bear trap, apparently, except that instead of two semicircular jaws it had four segments that snapped together in the middle, each with a shallow, sharp tooth. The pain was quite unendurable.

Each segment moved at the end of a thin arm, cunningly hinged so that the ghastly thing would close over whichever of the four triggers you stepped on. Each arm had a spring too powerful for Peter's muscles. The whole affair was connected by a chain to a staple solidly embedded in the concrete floor; it left Peter free to move some ten inches in any direction. Short of gnawing off his own leg, he thought sickly, there was very little he could do about it.

The riddle was, what could the thing possibly be doing here? There were rats in the vaults, no doubt, now as in his own time, but surely nothing larger. Was it conceivable that even the three-toed Somethings would set an engine like this to catch a rat?

Lost inventions, Peter thought irrelevantly, had a way of being rediscovered. Even if he suppressed the time-sphere during his lifetime and it did not happen to survive him, still there might be other time-fishers in the remote future—not here, perhaps, but in other treasure houses of the world. And that might account for the existence of this metal-jawed horror. Indeed, it might account for the vault itself—a better man-trap—except that it was all nonsense; the trap could only be full until the trapper came to look at it. Events, and the lives of prudent time-travelers, were conserved.

And he had been in the vault for almost forty minutes. Twenty minutes to go, twenty-five, thirty at the most, then the Somethings would enter and their entrance would free him. He had his lifeline; the knowledge was the only thing that made it possible to live with the pain that was the center of his universe just now. It was like going to the dentist, in the bad old days before procaine; it was very bad, sometimes, but you knew that it would end.

He cocked his head toward the door, holding his breath. A distant thud, another, then a curiously unpleasant squeaking, then silence.

But he had heard them. He knew they were there. It couldn't be much longer now.

Three men, two stocky, one lean, were playing cards in the passageway in front of the closed door that led to the vault staircase. They got up slowly.

"Who is he?" demanded the shortest one.

Tomaso clattered at him in furious Sicilian; the man's face darkened, but he looked at Harold with respect.

"I am now," stated Harold, "going down to see my brother."

"No, Signor," said the shortest one positively.

"You are impertinent," Harold told him.

"Yes, Signor."

Harold frowned. "You will not let me pass?"

"No, Signor."

"Then go and tell my brother I am here."

The shortest one said apologetically but firmly that there were strict orders against this also; it would have astonished Harold very much if he had said anything else.

"Well, at least I suppose you can tell me how long it will be before he comes out?"

"Not long, Signor. One hour, no more."

"Oh, very well, then," said Harold pettishly, turning half away. He paused. "One thing more," he said, taking the gun out of his pocket as he turned, "put your hands up and stand against the wall there, will you?"

The first two complied slowly. The third, the lean one, fired through his coat pocket, just like the gangsters in the American movies.

It was not a sharp sensation at all, Harold was surprised to find; it was more as if someone had hit him in the side with a cricket bat. The racket seemed to bounce interminably from the walls. He felt the gun jolt in his hand as he fired back, but couldn't tell if he had hit anybody. Everything seemed to be happening very slowly, and yet it was astonishingly hard to keep his balance. As he swung around he saw the two stocky ones with their hands half inside their jackets, and the lean one with his mouth open, and Tomaso with bulging eyes. Then the wall came at him and he began to swim along it, paying particular attention to the problem of not dropping one's gun.

As he weathered the first turn in the passageway the roar broke out afresh. A fountain of plaster stung his eyes; then he was running clumsily, and there was a bedlam of shouting behind him.

Without thinking about it he seemed to have selected the laboratory as his destination; it was an instinctive choice, without much to recommend it logically. In any case, he realized halfway across the central hall, he was not going to get there.

He turned and squinted at the passageway entrance; saw a blur move and fired at it. It disappeared. He turned again awkwardly, and had taken two steps nearer an armchair which offered the nearest shelter, when something clubbed him between the shoulderblades. One step more, knees buckling, and the wall struck him a second, softer blow. He toppled, clutching at the tapestry that hung near the fireplace.

When the three guards, whose names were Enrico, Alberto and Luca, emerged cautiously from the passage and approached Harold's body, it was already flaming like a Viking's in its impromptu shroud; the dim horses and men and falcons of the tapestry were writhing and crisping into brilliance. A moment later an uncertain ring of fire wavered toward them across the carpet.

Although the servants came with fire extinguishers and with buckets of water from the kitchen, and although the fire department was called, it was all quite useless. In five minutes the whole room was ablaze; in ten, as windows burst and walls buckled, the fire engulfed the second story. In twenty a mass of flaming timbers dropped into the vault through the hole Peter had made in the floor of the laboratory, utterly destroying the time-sphere apparatus and reaching shortly thereafter, as the authorities concerned were later to agree, an intensity of heat entirely sufficient to consume a human body without leaving any identifiable trace. For that reason alone, there was no trace of Peter's body to be found.

The sounds had just begun again when Peter saw the light from the time-sphere turn ruddy and then wink out like a snuffled candle.

In the darkness, he heard the door open.

BLACK CHARLIE

BY GORDON R. DICKSON (1923–   )

GALAXY SCIENCE FICTION, APRIL

A Canadian who came to the United States as a teenager, Gordon R. Dickson has been quietly building a most impressive body of work in science fiction for almost thirty-five years. Although best known for his "Dorsai" novels that form part of what he calls his "Childe Cycle," his more than fifty published sf works include such notable novels as THE ALIEN WAY (1965), ALIEN ART (1973), TIME STORM (1977), and THE FAR CALL (1978), as well as the excellent fantasy THE DRAGON AND THE GEORGE (1976). His remarkable story on the theme of leadership, "Call Him Lord," won a Nebula Award in 1966.

"Black Charlie," is his finest early story, one that reflects his long-standing theme of what it means to be human, and the sometimes thoughtless ways that beings treat each other. Gordon Dickson enjoys a major reputation as a writer of adventure science fiction, which sometimes obscures the deep sense of compassion that runs through his work. (MHG)

I believe this is Gordie's first appearance in this series. (Correct me if I'm wrong. Marty) (You're right, Isaac.)

If so, this is the time for me to explain that some writers show peculiar differences between their personalities and their writing. In real life, for instance, I'm such a lady's man, and I have written a number of books of raunchy limericks—and yet my fiction is entirely pure and wholesome.

Well, to begin with Gordie is a lovable character and one of his most lovable characteristics is his apparently hopeless disorganization. I remember once listening to him give a talk at a science fiction convention with several pages of notes before him. In no time, he had them hopelessly tangled up and was staring at them with an almost comic dismay.

So keen an impression did that make on my mind that the next story of his that I read I approached very cautiously, expecting it to be disorganized. Not so. His writing is straight-forward and clear. Don't ask me to explain this. (IA)

You ask me, what is art? You expect me to have a logical answer at my fingertips because I have been a buyer for museums and galleries long enough to acquire a plentiful crop of gray hairs. It's not that simple.

Well, what is art? For forty years I've examined, felt, admired, and loved many things fashioned as hopeful vessels for that bright spirit we call art—and I'm unable to answer the question directly. The layman answers easily—beauty. But art is not necessarily beautiful. Sometimes it is ugly. Sometimes it is crude. Sometimes it is incomplete.

I have fallen back, as many men have in the business of making like decisions, on *feel* for the judgment of art. You know this business of *feel*. Let us say that you pick up something—a piece of statuary or, better, a fragment of stone, etched and colored by some ancient man of prehistoric times. You look at it. At first it is nothing, a half-developed reproduction of some wild animal, not even as good as a grade-school child could accomplish today.

But then, holding it, your imagination suddenly reaches through rock and time, back to the man himself, half squatted before the stone wall of his cave—and you see there not the dusty thing you hold in your hand—but what the man himself saw in the hour of its creation. You look beyond the physical reproduction to the magnificent accomplishment of his imagination.

This, then, may be called art—no matter what strange guise it appears in—this magic which bridges all gaps between the artist and yourself. To it, no distance, nor any difference, is too great. Let me give you an example from my own experience.

Some years back, when I was touring the newer worlds as a buyer for one of our well-known art institutions, I received a communication from a man named Cary Longan, asking me, if possible, to visit a planet named Elman's World and examine some statuary he had for sale.

Messages rarely came directly to me. They were usually referred to me by the institution I was representing at the time. Since, however, the world in question was close, being of the same solar system as the planet I was then visiting, I spacegraphed my answer that I would come. After cleaning up what remained of my business where I was, I took an interworld ship and, within a couple of days, landed on Elman's World.

It appeared to be a very raw, very new planet indeed. The port we landed at was, I learned, one of the only two suitable for deepspace vessels. And the city surrounding it was scarcely more than a village. Mr. Longan did not meet me at the port, so I took a cab directly to the hotel where I had made a reservation.

That evening, in my rooms, the annunciator rang, then spoke, giving me a name. I opened the door to admit a tall, brown-faced man with uncut, dark hair and troubled, green-brown eyes.

"Mr. Longan?" I asked.

"Mr. Jones?" he countered. He shifted the unvarnished wooden box he was carrying to his left hand and put out his right to shake mine. I closed the door behind him and led him to a chair.

He put the box down, without opening it, on a small coffee table between us. It was then that I noticed his rough, bushcountry clothes, breeches, and tunic of drab plastic. Also an embarrassed air about him, like that of a man unused to city dealings. An odd sort of person to be offering art for sale.

"Your spacegram," I told him, "was not very explicit. The institution I represent—"

"I've got it here," he said, putting his hand on the box.

I looked at it in astonishment. It was no more than half a meter square by twenty centimeters deep.

"There?" I said. I looked back at him, with the beginnings of a suspicion forming in my mind. I suppose I should have been more wary when the message had come direct, instead of through Earth. But you know how it is—something of a feather in your cap when you bring in an unexpected item. "Tell me, Mr. Longan," I said, "where does this statuary come from?"

He looked at me a little defiantly. "A friend of mine made them," he said.

"A friend?" I repeated—and I must admit I was growing somewhat annoyed. It makes a man feel like a fool to be taken in that way. "May I ask whether this friend of yours has ever sold any of his work before?"

"Well, no . . ." Longan hedged. He was obviously suffering—but so was I, when I thought of my own wasted time.

"I see," I said, getting to my feet. "You've brought me on a very expensive side trip merely to show me the work of some amateur. Good-by, Mr. Longan. And please take your box with you when you leave!"

"You've never seen anything like this before!" He was looking up at me with desperation.

"No doubt," I said.

"Look. I'll show you . . ." He fumbled, his fingers nervous on the hasp. "Since you've come all this way you can at least look."

Because there seemed no way of getting him out of there, short of having the hotel manager eject him forcibly, I sat down with bad grace. "What's your friend's name?" I demanded.

Longan's fingers hesitated on the hasp. "Black Charlie," he replied, not looking up at me.

I stared. "I beg your pardon. Black—Charles Black?"

He looked up quite defiantly, met my eye, and shook his head. "Just Black Charlie," he said with sudden calmness. "Just the way it sounds. Black Charlie." He continued unfastening the box.

I watched rather dubiously as he finally managed to loosen the clumsy, handmade wooden bolt that secured the hasp. He was about to raise the lid, then apparently changed his mind. He turned the box around and pushed it across the coffee table.

The wood was hard and uneven under my fingers. I lifted the lid. There were five small partitions, each containing a rock of fine-grained gray sandstone of different but thoroughly incomprehensible shape.

I stared at them—then looked back at Logan to see if this weren't some sort of elaborate joke. But the tall man's eyes were severely serious. Slowly, I began to take out the stones and line them up on the table.

I studied them one by one, trying to make some sense out of their forms. But there was nothing there, absolutely nothing. One vaguely resembled a regular-sided pyramid. Another gave a foggy impression of a crouching figure. The best that could be said of the rest was that they bore a somewhat disconcerting resemblance to the kind of stones people pick up for paperweights. Yet they all had obviously been worked on. There were noticeable chisel marks on each one. And, in addition, they had been polished as well as such soft, grainy rock could be.

I looked up at Longan. His eyes were tense with waiting. I was completely puzzled about his discovery—or what he felt was a discovery. I tried to be fair about his acceptance of this as art. It was obviously nothing more than loyalty to a friend, a friend no doubt as unaware of what constituted art as himself. I made my tone as kind as I could.

"What did your friend expect me to do with these, Mr. Longan?" I asked gently.

"Aren't you buying things for that museum place on Earth?" he said.

I nodded. I picked up the piece that resembled a crouching animal figure and turned it over in my fingers. It was an awkward situation. "Mr. Longan," I said. "I have been in this business many years——"

"I know," he interrupted. "I read about you in the newsfax when you landed on the next world. That's why I wrote you."

"I see," I said. "Well, I've been in it a long time, as I say, and I think I can safely boast that I know something about art. If there is art in these carvings your friend has made, I should be able to recognize it. And I do not."

He stared at me, shock in his greenish-brown eyes.

"You're . . ." he said, finally. "You don't mean that. You're sore because I brought you out here this way."

"I'm sorry," I said. "I'm *not* sore and I *do* mean it. These things are not merely not good—there is nothing of value in them. Nothing! Someone had deluded your friend into thinking that he has talent. You'll be doing him a favor if you tell him the truth."

He stared at me for a long moment, as if waiting for me to say something to soften the verdict. Then, suddenly, he rose from the chair and crossed the room in three long strides, staring tensely out the window. His callused hands clenched and unclenched spasmodically.

I gave him a little time to wrestle it out with himself. Then I started putting the pieces of stone back into their sections of the box.

"I'm sorry," I told him.

He wheeled about and came back to me, leaning down from his lanky height to look in my face. "Are you?" he said. "*Are* you?"

"Believe me," I said sincerely, "I am." And I was.

"Then will you do something for me?" The words came in

a rush. "Will you come and tell Charlie what you've told me? Will *you* break the news to him?"

"I . . ." I meant to protest, to beg off, but with his tortured eyes six inches from mine, the words would not come. "All right," I said.

The breath he had been holding came out in one long sigh. "Thanks," he said. "We'll go out tomorrow. You don't know what this means. Thanks."

I had ample time to regret my decision, both that night and the following morning, when Longan roused me at an early hour, furnished me with a set of bush clothes like his own, including high, impervious boots, and whisked me off in an old air-ground combination flyer that was loaded down with all kinds of bush-dweller's equipment. But a promise is a promise—and I reconciled myself to keeping mine.

We flew south along a high chain of mountains until we came to a coastal area and what appeared to be the swamp delta of some monster river. Here, we began to descend— much to my distaste. I have little affection for hot, muggy climates and could not conceive of anyone wanting to live under such conditions.

We set down lightly in a little open stretch of water—and Longan taxied the flyer across to the nearest bank, a tussocky mass of high brown weeds and soft mud. By myself, I would not have trusted the soggy ground to refrain from drawing me down like quicksand—but Longan stepped out onto the bank confidently enough, and I followed. The mud yielded, little pools of water springing up around my boot soles. A hot rank smell of decaying vegetation came to my nose. Under a thin but uniform blanket of cloud, the sky looked white and sick.

"This way," said Longan, and led off to the right.

I followed him along a little trail and into a small, swampy clearing with dome-shaped huts of woven branches, plastered with mud, scattered about it. And, for the first time, it struck me that Black Charlie might be something other than an expatriate Earthman—might, indeed, be a native of this planet, though I had heard of no other humanlike race on other

worlds before. My head spinning, I followed Longan to the
entrance of one of the huts and halted as he whistled.

I don't remember now what I expected to see. Something
vaguely humanoid, no doubt. But what came through the
entrance in response to Longan's whistle was more like a
large otter with flat, muscular grasping pads on the ends of its
four limbs, instead of feet. It was black with glossy, dampish
hair all over it. About four feet in length, I judged, with no
visible tail and a long, snaky neck. The creature must have
weighed one hundred to, perhaps, one hundred and fifty
pounds. The head on its long neck was also long and narrow,
like the head of a well-bred collie—covered with the same
black hair, with bright, intelligent eyes and a long mouth.

"This is Black Charlie," said Longan.

The creature stared at me, and I returned his gaze. Abruptly,
I was conscious of the absurdity of the situation. It would
have been difficult for any ordinary person to think of this
being as a sculptor. To add to this necessity, an obligation, to
convince it that it was *not* a sculptor—mind you, I could not
be expected to know a word of its language—was to pile
Pelion upon Ossa in a madman's farce. I swung on Longan.

"Look here," I began with quite natural heat, "how do
you expect me to tell——"

"He understands you," interrupted Longan.

"Speech?" I said incredulously. "Real human speech?"

"No," Longan shook his head. "But he understands actions." He turned from me abruptly and plunged into the
weeds surrounding the clearing. He returned immediately
with two objects that looked like gigantic puffballs and handed
one to me.

"Sit on this," he said, doing so himself. I obeyed.

Black Charlie—I could think of nothing else to call him—
came closer, and we sat down together. Charlie was half
squatting on ebony haunches. All this time, I had been carrying the wooden box that contained his sculptures, and now
that we were seated, his bright eyes swung inquisitively
toward it.

"All right," said Longan, "give it to me."

I passed him the box, and it drew Black Charlie's eyes like a magnet. Longan took it under one arm and pointed toward the lake with the other—to where we had landed the flyer. Then his arm rose in the air in a slow, impressive circle and pointed northward, from the direction we had come.

Black Charlie whistled suddenly. It was an odd note, like the cry of a loon—a far, sad sound.

Longan struck himself on the chest, holding the box with one hand. Then he struck the box and pointed to me. He looked at Black Charlie, looked back at me—then put the box into my numb hands.

"Look them over and hand them back," he said, his voice tight. Against my will, I looked at Charlie.

His eyes met mine. Strange, liquid, black, inhuman eyes, like two tiny pools of pitch. I had to tear my own gaze away.

Torn between my feeling of foolishness and a real sympathy for the waiting creature, I awkwardly opened the box and lifted the stones from their compartments. One by one, I turned them in my hand and put them back. I closed the box and returned it to Longan, shaking my head, not knowing if Charlie would understand that.

For a long moment, Longan merely sat facing me, holding the box. Then, slowly, he turned and set it, still open, in front of Charlie.

Charlie did not react at first. His head, on its long neck, dropped over the open compartments as if he was sniffing them. Then, surprisingly, his lips wrinkled back, revealing long, chisel-shaped teeth. Daintily, he reached into the box with these and lifted out the stones, one by one. He held them in his forepads, turning them this way and that, as if searching for the defects of each. Finally, he lifted one—it was the stone that faintly resembled a crouching beast. He lifted it to his mouth—and, with his gleaming teeth, made slight alterations in its surface. Then he brought it to me.

Helplessly I took it in my hand and examined it. The changes he had made in no way altered it toward something

recognizable. I was forced to hand it back, with another
headshake, and a poignant pause fell between us.

I had been desperately turning over in my mind some way
to explain, through the medium of pantomime, the reasons
for my refusal. Now something occurred to me. I turned to
Longan.

"Can he get me a piece of unworked stone?" I asked.

Longan turned to Charlie and made motions as if he were
breaking something off and handing it to me. For a moment,
Charlie sat still, as if considering this. Then he went into his
hut, returning a moment later with a chunk of rock the size of
my hand.

I had a small pocket knife, and the rock was soft. I held the
rock out toward Longan and looked from him to it. Using my
pocket knife, I whittled a rough, lumpy caricature of Longan
seated on the puffball. When I was finished, I put the two
side by side, the hacked piece of stone insignificant on the
ground beside the living man.

Black Charlie looked at it. Then he came up to me—and,
peering up into my face, cried softly, once. Moving so
abruptly that it startled me, he turned smoothly, picked up in
his teeth the piece of stone I had carved. Soon he disappeared
back into his hut.

Longan stood up stiffly, like a man who has held one
position too long. "That's it," he said. "Let's go.'

We made our way to the combination and took off once
more, headed back toward the city and the spaceship that
would carry me away from this irrational world. As the
mountains commenced to rise, far beneath us, I stole a glance
at Longan, sitting beside me at the controls of the combination. His face was set in an expression of stolid unhappiness.

The question came from my lips before I had time to
debate internally whether it was wise or not to ask it.

"Tell me, Mr. Longan," I said, "has—er—Black Charlie
some special claim on your friendship?"

The tall man looked at me with something close to
amazement.

"Claim!" he said. Then, after a short pause, during which he seemed to search my features to see if I was joking, "He saved my life."

"Oh," I said. "I see."

"You do, do you?" he countered. "Suppose I told you it was just after I'd finished killing his mate. They mate for life, you know."

"No, I didn't know," I answered feebly.

"I forget people don't know," he said in a subdued voice. I said nothing, hoping that, if I did not disturb him, he would say more. After a while he spoke. "This planet's not much good."

"I noticed," I answered. "I didn't see much in the way of plants and factories. And your sister world—the one I came from—is much more populated and built up."

"There's not much here," he said. "No minerals to speak of. Climate's bad, except on the plateaus. Soil's not much good." He paused. It seemed to take effort to say what came next. "Used to have a novelty trade in furs, though."

"Furs?" I echoed.

"Off Charlie's people," he went on, fiddling with the combination's controls. "Trappers and hunters used to be after them, at first, before they knew. I was one of them."

"You!" I said.

"Me!" His voice was flat. "I was doing fine, too, until I trapped Charlie's mate. Up till then, I'd been getting them out by themselves. They did a lot of traveling in those swamps. But, this time, I was close to the village. I'd just clubbed her on the head when the whole tribe jumped me." His voice trailed off, then strengthened. "They kept me under guard for a couple of months.

"I learned a lot in that time. I learned they were intelligent. I learned it was Black Charlie who kept them from killing me right off. Seems he took the point of view that I was a reasonable being and, if he could just talk things over with me, we could get together and end the war." Longan laughed, a little bitterly. "They called it a war, Charlie's people did." He stopped talking.

I waited. And when he remained quiet, I prompted him. "What happened?" I asked.

"They let me go, finally," he said. "And I went to bat for them. Clear up to the Commissioner sent from Earth. I got them recognized as people instead of animals. I put an end to the hunting and trapping."

He stopped again. We were still flying through the upper air of Elman's World, the sun breaking through the clouds at last, revealing the ground below like a huge green relief map.

"I see," I said, finally.

Longan looked at me stonily.

We flew back to the city.

I left Elman's World the next day, fully believing that I had heard and seen the last of both Longan had Black Charlie. Several years later, at home in New York, I was visited by a member of the government's Foreign Service. He was a slight, dark man, and he didn't beat about the bush.

"You don't know me," he said. I looked at his card— *Antonio Walters*. "I was Deputy Colonial Representative on Elman's World at the time you were there."

I looked up at him, surprised. I had forgotten Elman's World by that time.

"Were you?" I asked, feeling a little foolish, unable to think of anything better to say. I turned his card over several times, staring at it, as a person will do when at a loss. "What can I do for you, Mr. Walters?"

"We've been requested by the local government on Elman's World to locate you, Mr. Jones," he answered. "Cary Longan is dying——"

"Dying!" I said.

"Lung fungus, unfortunately," said Walters. "You catch it in the swamps. He wants to see you before the end—and, since we're very grateful to him out there for the work he's been doing all these years for the natives, a place has been kept for you on a government courier ship leaving for Elman's World right away—if you're willing to go."

"Why, I . . ." I hesitated. In common decency, I could not refuse. "I'll have to notify my employers."

"Of course," he said.

Luckily, the arrangements I had to make consisted of a few business calls and packing my bags. I was, as a matter of fact, between trips at the time. As an experienced traveler, I could always get under way with a minimum of fuss. Walters and I drove out to Government Port in northern New Jersey and, from there on, the authorities took over.

Less than a week later, I stood by Longan's bedside in the hospital of the same city I had visited years before. The man was now nothing more than a barely living skeleton, the hard vitality all but gone from him, hardly able to speak a few words at a time. I bent over to catch the whispered syllables from his wasted lips.

"Black Charlie . . ." he whispered.

"Black Charlie," I repeated. "Yes, what about him?"

"He's done something new," whispered Longan. "That carving of yours started him off, copying things. His tribe don't like it."

"They don't?" I said.

"They," whispered Longan, "don't understand. It's not normal, the way they see it. They're afraid——"

"You mean they're superstitious about what he carves?" I asked.

"Something like that. Listen—he's an artist . . ."

I winced internally at the last word, but held my tongue for the sake of the dying man.

". . . an artist. But they'll kill him for it, now that I'm gone. You can save him, though."

"Me?" I said.

"You!" The man's voice was like a wind rustling through dry leaves. "If you go out—take this last thing from him— act pleased . . . then they'll be scared to touch him. But hurry. Every day is that much closer. . . ."

His strength failed him. He closed his eyes, and his straining throat muscles relaxed to a little hiss of air that puffed between his lips. The nurse hurried me from his room.

The local government helped me. I was surprised, and not a little touched, to see how many people knew Longan. How many of them admired his attempts to pay back the natives by helping them in any way he could. They located Charlie's tribe on a map for me and sent me out with a pilot who knew the country.

We landed on the same patch of slime. I went alone toward the clearing. With the brown weeds still walling it about, the locale showed no natural change, but Black Charlie's hut appeared broken and deserted. I whistled and waited. I called. And, finally, I got down on my hands and knees and crawled inside. But there was nothing there save a pile of loose rock and a mass of dried weeds. Feeling cramped and uncomfortable, for I am not used to such gymnastics, I backed out to find myself surrounded by a crowd.

It looked as if all the other inhabitants of the village had come out of their huts and congregated before Charlie's. They seemed agitated, milling about, occasionally whistling at each other on that one low, plaintive note which was the only sound I had ever heard Charlie make. Eventually, the excitement seemed to fade, the group fell back, and one individual came forward alone. He looked up into my face for a brief moment, then turned and glided swiftly on his pads toward the edge of the clearing.

I followed. There seemed nothing else to do. And, at that time, it did not occur to me to be afraid.

My guide led me deep into the weed patch, then abruptly disappeared. I looked around surprised and undecided, half inclined to turn about and retrace my steps by the trail of crushed weeds I had left in my floundering advance. Then a low whistle sounded close by. I went forward and found Charlie.

He lay on his side in a little circular open area of crushed weeds. He was too weak to do more than raise his head and look at me, for the whole surface of his body was criss-crossed and marked with the slashings of shallow wounds, from which dark blood seeped slowly and stained the reeds in which he lay. In Charlie's mouth I had seen the long chisel-teeth of his kind, and I knew what had made those wounds. A gust of rage went through me, and I stooped to pick him up in my arms.

He came up easily, for the bones of his kind are cartilaginous, and their flesh is far lighter than our human flesh. Holding him, I turned and made my way back to the clearing.

The others were waiting for me as we came out into the open. I glared at them—and then the rage inside me went out like a blown candle. For there was nothing there to hate. *They* had not hated Charlie. They had merely feared him—and their only crime was ignorance.

They moved back from me, and I carried Charlie to the door of his own hut. There I laid him down. The chest and arms of my jacket were soaked from his dark body fluid, and I saw that his blood was not clotting as our own does.

Clumsily, I took off my shirt and, tearing it into strips, made a poor attempt to bind up the torn flesh. But the blood came through in spite of my first aid. Charlie, lifting his head, with a great effort, from the ground, picked feebly at the bandages with his teeth, so that I gave up and removed them.

I sat down beside him then, feeling sick and helpless. In spite of Longan's care and dying effort, in spite of all the scientific developments of my own human race, I had come too late. Numbly, I sat and looked down at him and wondered why I could not have come one day earlier.

From this half stupor of self-accusation I was roused by Charlie's attempts to crawl back into his hut. My first reaction was to restrain him. But, from somewhere, he seemed to have dredged up a remnant of his waning strength—and he persisted. Seeing this, I changed my mind and, instead of hindering, helped. He dragged himself through the entrance, his strength visibly waning.

I did not expect to see him emerge. I believed some ancient instinct had called him, that he would die then and there. But, a few moments later, I heard a sound as of stones rattling from within—and, in a few seconds, he began to back out. Halfway through the entrance, his strength finally failed him. He lay still for a minute, then whistled weakly.

I went to him and pulled him out the rest of the way. He turned his head toward me, holding in his mouth what I first took to be a ball of dried mud.

I took it from him and began to scrape the mud off with my fingernails. Almost immediately, the grain and surface of the sandstone he used for his carvings began to emerge—and my hands started to shake so hard that, for a moment, I had to put the stone down while I got myself under control. For the first time, the true importance to Charlie of these things he had chewed and bitten into shape got home to me.

In that moment, I swore that whatever bizarre form this last and greatest work of his might possess, I would make certain that it was accorded a place in some respectable museum as a true work of art. After all, it had been conceived in honesty and executed in the love that took no count of labor, provided the end was achieved.

And then, the rest of the mud came free in my hands. I saw what it was, and I could have cried and laughed at the same time. For, of all the shapes he could have chosen to work in stone, he had picked the one that no critic would have selected as the choice of an artist of his race. For he had chosen no plant or animal, no structure or natural shape out of his environment, to express the hungry longing of his spirit. None of these had he chosen—instead, with painful clumsiness, he had fashioned an image from the soft and grainy rock—a statue of a standing man.

And I knew what man it was.

Charlie lifted his head from the stained ground and looked toward the lake where my flyer waited. I am not an intuitive man—but, for once, I was able to understand the meaning of a look. He wanted me to leave while he was still alive. He

wanted to see me go, carrying the thing he had fashioned. I
got to my feet, holding it, and stumbled off. At the edge of
the clearing, I looked back. He still watched. And the rest of
his people still hung back from him. I did not think they
would bother him now.

And so I came home.

But there is one thing more to tell. For a long time, after I
returned from Elman's World, I did not look at the crude
statuette. I did not want to, for I knew that seeing it would
only confirm what I had known from the start, that all the
longing and desires in the world cannot create art where there
is no talent, no true visualization. But at the end of one year I
was cleaning up all the little details of my office. And,
because I believe in system and order—and also because I was
ashamed of myself for having put it off so long—I took the
statuette from a bottom drawer of my desk, unwrapped it, and
set it on the desk's polished surface.

I was alone in my office at the time, at the end of a day,
when the afternoon sun, striking red through the tall window
beside my desk, touched everything between the walls with a
clear, amber light. I ran my fingers over the grainy sandstone
and held it up to look at it.

And then—for the first time—I saw it, saw through the
stone to the image beyond, saw what Black Charlie had seen,
with Black Charlie's eyes, when he looked at Longan. I saw
men as Black Charlie's kind saw men—and I saw what the
worlds of men meant to Black Charlie. And, above all,
overriding all, I saw art as Black Charlie saw it, through his
bright alien eyes—saw the beauty he had sought at the price
of his life, and had half found.

But, most of all, I saw that this crude statuette was *art*.

One more word. Amid the mud and weeds of the swamp, I
had held the carving in my hands and promised myself that
this work would one day stand on display. Following that
moment of true insight in my office, I did my best to place it
with the institution I represented, then with others who knew
me as a reputable buyer.

But I could find no takers. No one, although they trusted me individually, was willing to exhibit such a poor-looking piece of work on the strength of a history that I, alone, could vouch for. There are people, close to any institution, who are only too ready to cry, "Hoax!" For several years, I tried without success.

Eventually, I gave up on the true story and sold the statuette, along with a number of other odd pieces, to a dealer of minor reputation, representing it as an object whose history I did not know.

Curiously, the statuette has justified my belief in what is art, by finding a niche for itself. I traced it from the dealer, after a time, and ran it to Earth quite recently. There is a highly respectable art gallery on this planet which has an extensive display of primitive figures of early American Indian origin.

And Black Charlie's statuette is among them. I will not tell which or where it is.

DOWN AMONG THE DEAD MEN

BY WILLIAM TENN (PHILIP KLASS 1920–   )

GALAXY SCIENCE FICTION, JUNE

Professor Klass returns to this series with what is perhaps his most somber and powerful story, one much more serious than the biting satire and broad humor that features in most of his work. "Down Among the Dead Men" is remarkable in several respects, and is at least a decade ahead of its time in subject matter and treatment. It reads like a commentary on the Vietnam War, on the ecology movement, and on the Nixon Presidency, and remains one of the most powerful anti-war statements in science fiction. 1954 saw the publication of at least three other excellent stories by him. "The Tennents" (F & SF, April), "Project Hush" (GALAXY, February), and the superb "Party of the Two Parts" (GALAXY, August), which we just could not squeeze into this book. (MHG)

It seemed to me in my younger and more carefree days that everyone was essentially anti-war; that if war was forced upon a people it had to be fought with grim distaste, at the very best.

And yet to my astonishment, I find that nowadays there are people (even among the brotherhood of science fiction writers) who are earnestly talking about war not being so terrible; that it's a natural and ineradicable human activity.

*Maybe it's because since Vietnam, we have struck at care-
fully chosen enemies—at the mighty armies and navies of
nations like Cambodia, Grenada, Nicaragua, and Libya.
Or perhaps they dream of a fairy-tale Star Wars barrier from behind which they can attack without fear of
reprisal.*

*But to me it's stories like "Down Among the Dead Men"
that gives one the feel of what war is like, when you strip
away the Rambo-crap. (IA)*

I stood in front of the Junkyard's outer gate and felt my
stomach turn over slowly, grindingly, the way it had when I
saw a whole terrestrial subfleet—close to 20,000 men—blown
to bits in the Second Battle of Saturn more than eleven years
ago. But then there had been shattered fragments of ships in
my visiplate and imagined screams of men in my mind; there
had been the expanding images of the Eoti's box-like craft
surging through the awful, drifting wreckage they had created, to account for the icy sweat that wound itself like a flat
serpent around my forehead and my neck.

Now there was nothing but a large, plain building, very
much like the hundreds of other factories in the busy
suburbs of Old Chicago, a manufacturing establishment
surrounded by a locked gate and spacious proving grounds—
the Junkyard. Yet the sweat on my skin was colder and
the heave of my bowels more spastic than it had ever
been in any of those countless, ruinous battles that had
created this place.

All of which was very understandable, I told myself. What
I was feeling was the great-grandmother hag of all fears, the
most basic rejection and reluctance of which my flesh was
capable. It was understandable, but that didn't help any. I
still couldn't walk up to the sentry at the gate.

I'd been almost all right until I'd seen the huge square can
against the fence, the can with the slight stink coming out of
it and the big colorful sign on top:

DON'T *WASTE* WASTE
PLACE *ALL* WASTE HERE

remember—

WHATEVER IS WORN CAN BE SHORN
WHATEVER IS MAIMED CAN BE RECLAIMED
WHATEVER IS USED CAN BE RE-USED
PLACE *ALL* WASTE HERE

—*Conservation Police*

I'd seen those square, compartmented cans and those signs in every barracks, every hospital, every recreation center, between here and the asteroids. But seeing them, now, in this place, gave them a different meaning. I wondered if they had those other posters inside, the shorter ones. You know: "We need all our resources to defeat the enemy—and GARBAGE IS OUR BIGGEST NATURAL RESOURCE." Decorating the walls of this particular building with those posters would be downright ingenious.

Whatever is maimed can be reclaimed . . . I flexed my right arm inside my blue jumper sleeve. It felt like a part of me, always would feel like a part of me. And in a couple of years, assuming that I lived that long, the thin white scar that circled the elbow joint would be completely invisible. Sure. Whatever is maimed can be reclaimed. All except one thing. The most important thing.

And I felt less like going in than ever.

And then I saw this kid. The one from Arizona Base.

He was standing right in front of the sentry box, paralyzed just like me. In the center of his uniform cap was a brand-new, gold-shiny Y with a dot in the center: the insignia of a sling-shot commander. He hadn't been wearing it the day before at the briefing; that could only mean the commission had just come through. He looked real young and real scared.

I remembered him from the briefing session. He was the one whose hand had gone up timidly during the question period, the one who, when he was recognized, had half risen, worked his mouth a couple of times and finally blurted out: "Excuse me, sir, but they don't—they don't smell at all bad, do they?"

There had been a cyclone of laughter, the yelping laughter of men who've felt themselves close to the torn edge of hysteria all afternoon and who are damn glad that someone has at last said something that they can make believe is funny.

And the white-haired briefing officer, who hadn't so much as smiled, waited for the hysteria to work itself out, before saying gravely: "No, they don't smell bad at all. Unless, that is, they don't bathe. The same as you gentlemen."

That shut us up. Even the kid, blushing his way back into his seat, set his jaw stiffly at the reminder. And it wasn't until twenty minutes later, when we'd been dismissed, that I began to feel the ache in my own face from the unrelaxed muscles there.

The same as you gentlemen. . . .

I shook myself hard and walked over to the kid. "Hello, Commander," I said. "Been here long?"

He managed a grin. "Over an hour, Commander. I caught the eight-fifteen out of Arizona Base. Most of the other fellows were still sleeping off last night's party. I'd gone to bed early: I wanted to give myself as much time to get the feel of this thing as I could. Only it doesn't seem to do much good."

"I know. Some things you can't get used to. Some things you're not *supposed* to get used to."

He looked at my chest. "I guess this isn't your first sling-shot command?"

My first? More like my twenty-first, son! But then I remembered that everyone tells me I look young for my medals, and what the hell, the kid looked so pale under the chin— "No, not exactly my first. But I've never had a blob crew before. This is exactly as new to me as it is to you. Hey, listen, Commander: I'm having a hard time, too. What say we bust through that gate together? Then the worst'll be over."

The kid nodded violently. We linked arms and marched up to the sentry. We showed him our orders. He opened the gate and said: "Straight ahead. Any elevator on your left to the fifteenth floor."

So, still arm in arm, we walked into the main entrance of the large building, up a long flight of steps and under the sign that said in red and black:

HUMAN PROTOPLASM RECLAMATION CENTER
THIRD DISTRICT FINISHING PLANT

There were some old-looking but very erect men walking along the main lobby and a lot of uniformed, fairly pretty girls. I was pleased to note that most of the girls were pregnant. The first pleasing sight I had seen in almost a week.

We turned into an elevator and told the girl, "Fifteen." She punched a button and waited for it to fill up. She didn't seem to be pregnant. I wondered what was the matter with her.

I'd managed to get a good grip on my heaving imagination, when I got a look at the shoulder patches the other passengers were wearing. That almost did for me right there. It was a circular red patch with the black letters TAF superimposed on a white *G*-4. TAF for Terrestrial Armed Forces, of course: the letters were the basic insignia of all rear-echelon outfits. But why didn't they use *G*-1, which represented Personnel? *G*-4 stood for the Supply Division. *Supply!*

You can always trust the TAF. Thousands of morale specialists in all kinds of ranks, working their educated heads off to keep up the spirits of the men in the fighting perimeters— but every damn time, when it comes down to scratch, the good old dependable TAF will pick the ugliest name, the one in the worst possible taste.

Oh, sure, I told myself, you can't fight a shattering, no-quarter interstellar war for twenty-five years and keep every pretty thought dewy-damp and intact. But not *Supply*, gentlemen. Not this place—not the Junkyard. Let's at least try to keep up appearances.

Then we began going up and the elevator girl began announcing floors and I had lots of other things to think about.

"Third floor—Corpse Reception and Classification," the operator sang out.

"Fifth floor—Preliminary Organ Processing."

"Seventh floor—Brain Reconstitution and Neural Alignment."

"Ninth floor—Cosmetics, Elementary Reflexes, and Muscular Control."

At this point, I forced myself to stop listening, the way you do when you're on a heavy cruiser, say, and the rear engine room gets flicked by a bolt from an Eoti scrambler. After you've been around a couple of times when it's happened, you learn to sort of close your ears and say to yourself, "I don't know anybody in that damned engine room, not anybody, and in a few minutes everything will be nice and quiet again." And in a few minutes it is. Only trouble is that then, like as not, you'll be part of the detail that's ordered into the steaming place to scrape the guck off the walls and get the jets firing again.

Same way now. Just as soon as I had that girl's voice blocked out, there we were on the fifteenth floor ("Final Interviews and Shipping") and the kid and I had to get out.

He was real green. A definite sag around the knees, shoulders sloping forward like his clavicle had curled. Again I was grateful to him. Nothing like having somebody to take care of.

"Come on, Commander," I whispered. "Up and at 'em. Look at it this way: for characters like us, this is practically a family reunion."

It was the wrong thing to say. He looked at me as if I'd punched his face. "No thanks to you for the reminder, Mister," he said, "Even if we are in the same boat." Then he walked stiffly up to the receptionist.

I could have bitten my tongue off. I hurried after him. "I'm sorry kid," I told him earnestly. "The words just slid out of my big mouth. But don't get sore at me; hell, I had to listen to myself say it, too.''

He stopped, thought about it, and nodded. Then he gave me a smile. ''O.K. No hard feelings. It's a rough war, isn't it?''

I smiled back. ''Rough? Why, if you're not careful, they tell me, you can get killed in it.''

The receptionist was a soft little blonde with two wedding rings on one hand, and one wedding ring on the other. From what I knew of current planet-side customs, that meant she'd been widowed twice.

She took our orders and read jauntily into her desk mike: ''Attention Final Conditioning. Attention Final Conditioning. Alert for immediate shipment the following serial numbers: 70623152, 70623109, 70623166, and 70623123. Also 70538966, 70538923, 70538980, and 70538937. Please route through the correct numbered sections and check all data on TAF AGO forms 362 as per TAF Regulation 7896, of 15 June, 2145. Advise when available for Final Interviews.''

I was impressed. Almost exactly the same procedure as when you go to Ordnance for a replacement set of stern exhaust tubes.

She looked up and favored us with a lovely smile. ''Your crews will be ready in a moment. Would you have a seat, gentlemen?''

We had a seat gentlemen.

After a while, she got up to take something out of a file cabinet set in the wall. As she came back to her desk, I noticed she was pregnant—only about the third or fourth month—and, naturally, I gave a little, satisfied nod. Out of the corner of my eye, I saw the kid make the same kind of nod. We looked at each other and chuckled. ''It's a rough, rough war,'' he said.

''Where are you from anyway?'' I asked. ''That doesn't sound like a Third District accent to me.''

''It isn't. I was born in Scandinavia—Eleventh Military District. My home town is Goteborg, Sweden. But after I got my—my promotion, naturally I didn't care to see the folks

any more. So I requested a transfer to the Third, and from
now on, until I hit a scrambler, this is where I'll be spending
my furloughs and Earth-side hospitalizations.''

I'd heard that a lot of the younger sling-shotters felt that
way. Personally, I never had a chance to find out how I'd feel
about visiting the old folks at home. My father was knocked
off in the suicidal attempt to retake Neptune 'way back when
I was still in high school learning elementary combat, and my
mother was Admiral Raguzzi's staff secretary when the flagship
Thermophylae took a direct hit two years later in the famous
defense of Ganymede. That was before the Breeding Regulations, of course, and women were still serving in administra-
tive positions on the fighting perimeters.

On the other hand, I realized, at least two of my brothers
might still be alive. But I'd made no attempt to contact them
since getting my dotted Y. So I guessed I felt the same way
as the kid—which was hardly surprising.

"Are you from Sweden?" the blonde girl was asking.
"My second husband was born in Sweden. Maybe you knew
him—Svén Nossen? I understand he had a lot of relatives in
Oslo.''

The kid screwed up his eyes as if he was thinking real
hard. You know, running down a list of all the Swedes in
Oslo. Finally, he shook his head. "No, can't say that I do.
But I wasn't out of Goteberg very much before I was called
up.''

She clucked sympathetically at his provincialism. The baby-
faced blonde of classic anecdote. A real dumb kid. And
yet—there were lots of very clever, high-pressure cuties around
the inner planets these days who had to content themselves
with a one-fifth interest in some abysmal slob who boasted
the barest modicum of maleness. Or a certificate from the
local sperm bank. Blondie here was on her third full husband.

Maybe, I thought, if I were looking for a wife myself, this
is what I'd pick to take the stink of scrambler rays out of my
nose and the yammer-yammer-yammer of Irvingles out of my
ears. Maybe I'd want somebody nice and simple to come
home to from one of those complicated skirmishes with the

Eoti where you spend most of your conscious thoughts trying
to figure out just what battle rhythm the filthy insects are
using this time. Maybe, if I were going to get married, I'd
find a pretty fluffhead like this more generally desirable
than—oh, well. Maybe. Considered as a problem in psychol-
ogy it was interesting.

I noticed she was talking to me. "You've never had a crew
of this type before either, have you, Commander?"

"Zombies, you mean? No, not yet, I'm happy to say."

She made a disapproving pout with her mouth. It was fully
as cute as her approving pouts. "We do not like that word."

"All right, blobs then."

"We don't like bl——that word either. You are talking about
human beings like yourself, Commander. Very much like
yourself."

I began to get sore feet, just the way the kid had out in the
hall. Then I realized she didn't mean anything by it. She
didn't know. What the hell—it wasn't on our orders. I relaxed. "You tell me. What do you call them here?"

The blonde sat up stiffly. "*We* refer to them as soldier
surrogates. The epithet 'zombie' was used to describe the
obsolete Model 21 which went out of production over five
years ago. You will be supplied with individuals based on
Models 705 and 706 which are practically perfect. In fact, in
some respects——"

"No bluish skin? No slow-motion sleepwalking?"

She shook her head violently. Her eyes were lit up. Evidently she'd digested all the promotional literature. Not such
a fluffhead, after all; no great mind, but her husbands had
evidently had someone to talk to in between times. She
rattled on enthusiastically: "The cyanosis was the result of
bad blood oxygenation; blood was our second most difficult
tissue reconstruction problem. The nervous system was the
hardest. Even though the blood cells are usually in the poor-
est shape of all by the time the bodies arrive, we can now
turn out a very serviceable rebuilt heart. But, let there be the
teeniest battle damage to the brain or spine and you have to
start right from scratch. And then the troubles in reconstitu-

tion! My cousin Lorna works in Neural Alignment and she
tells me all you need to make is just one wrong connection—
you know how it is, Commander, at the end of the day your
eyes are tired and you're kind of watching the clock—just
one wrong connection, and the reflexes in the finished individual turn out to be so bad that they just have to send him
down to the third floor and begin all over again. But you
don't have to worry about that. Since Model 663, we've been
using the two-team inspection system in Neural Alignment.
And the 700 series—oh, they've just been *wonderful*."

"That good, eh? Better than the old-fashioned mother's
son type?"

"Well-l-l," she considered. "You'd really be amazed,
Commander, if you could see the very latest performance
charts. Of course, there is always that big deficiency, the one
activity we've never been able to——"

"One thing *I* can't understand," the kid broke in, "why do
they have to use corpses! A body's lived its life, fought its
war—why not leave it alone? I know the Eoti can outbreed us
merely by increasing the number of queens in their flagships;
I know that manpower is the biggest single TAF problem—
but we've been synthesizing protoplasm for a long, long time
now. Why not synthesize the whole damn body, from toe
nails to frontal lobe, and turn out real, honest-to-God androids
that don't wallop you with the stink of death when you meet
them?"

The little blonde got mad. "Our product *does not stink!*
Cosmetics can now guarantee that the new models have even
less of a body odor than you, young man! And we do not
re-activate or revitalize corpses, I'll have you know; what we
do is *reclaim* human protoplasm, we re-use worn-out and
damaged human cellular material in the area where the greatest shortages currently occur, military personnel. You wouldn't
talk about corpses, I assure you, if you saw the condition that
some of those bodies are in when they arrive. Why, sometimes in a whole baling package—a baling package contains
twenty casualties—we don't find enough to make one good,
whole kidney. Then we have to take a little intestinal tissue

here and a bit of spleen there, alter them, unite them carefully, activa——''

''That's what I mean. If you go to all that trouble, why not
start with real raw material?''

''Like what, for example?'' she asked him.

The kid gestured with his black-gloved hands. ''Basic
elements like carbon, hydrogen, oxygen and so on. It would
make the whole process a lot cleaner.''

''Basic elements have to come from somewhere,'' I pointed
out gently. ''You might take your hydrogen and oxygen from
air and water. But where would you get your carbon from?''

''From the same place where the other synthetics manufac-
turers get it—coal, oil, cellulose.''

The receptionist sat back and relaxed. ''Those are organic
substances,'' she reminded him. ''If you're going to use raw
material that was once alive, why not use the kind that comes
as close as possible to the end-product you have in mind? It's
simple industrial economics, Commander, believe me. The
best and cheapest raw material for the manufacture of soldier
surrogates is soldier bodies.''

''Sure,'' the kid said. ''Makes sense. There's no other use
for dead, old, beaten-up soldier bodies. Better'n shoving
them in the ground where they'd be just waste, pure waste.''

Our litte blonde chum started to smile in agreement, then
shot him an intense look and changed her mind. She looked
very uncertain all of a sudden. When the communicator on
her desk buzzed, she bent over it eagerly.

I watched her with approval. Definitely no fluffhead. Just
feminine. I sighed. You see, I figure lots of civilian things
out the wrong way, but only with women is my wrongness an
all-the-time proposition. Proving again that a hell of a lot of
peculiar things turn out to have happened for the best.

''Commander,'' she was saying to the kid. ''Would you go
to Room 1591? Your crew will be there in a moment.'' She
turned to me. ''And Room 1524 for you, Commander, if you
please.''

The kid nodded and walked off, very stiff and erect. I
waited until the door had closed behind him, then I leaned

over the receptionist. "Wish they'd change the Breeding Regulations again," I told her. "You'd make a damn fine rear-echelon orientation officer. Got more of the feel of the Junkyard from you than in ten briefing sessions."

She examined my face anxiously. "I hope you mean that, Commander. You see, we're all very deeply involved in this project. We're extremely proud of the progress the Third District Finishing Plant has made. We talk about the new developments all the time, everywhere—even in the cafeteria. It didn't occur to me until too late that you gentlemen might——" she blushed deep, rich red, the way only a blonde can blush "—might take what I said personally. I'm sorry if I——"

"Nothing to be sorry about," I assured her. "All you did was talk what they call shop. Like when I was in the hospital last month and heard two surgeons discussing how to repair a man's arm and making it sound as if they were going to nail a new arm on an expensive chair. Real interesting, and I learned a lot."

I left her looking grateful, which is absolutely the only way to leave a woman, and barged on to Room 1524.

It was evidently used as a classroom when reconverted human junk wasn't being picked up. A bunch of chairs, a long blackboard, a couple of charts. One of the charts was on the Eoti, the basic information list, that contains all the limited information we have been able to assemble on the bugs in the bloody quarter-century since they came busting in past Pluto to take over the solar system. It hadn't been changed much since the one I had to memorize in high school: the only difference was a slightly longer section on intelligence and motivation. Just theory, of course, but more carefully thought-out theory than the stuff I'd learned. The big brains had now concluded that the reason all attempts at communicating with them had failed was not because they were a conquest-crazy species, but because they suffered from the same extreme xenophobia as their smaller, less intelligent communal insect cousins here on Earth. That is, an ant wanders up to a strange anthill—*zok!* No discussion, he's chopped down at the entrance. And the sentry ants react even faster if it's a creature of another genus. So despite the Eoti science, which in too many respects was more advanced than ours, they were psychologically incapable of the kind of mental projection, or empathy, necessary if one is to realize that a completely alien-looking individual has intelligence, feelings—and rights!—to substantially the same extent as oneself.

Well, it might be so. Meanwhile, we were locked in a murderous stalemate with them on a perimeter of neverending battle that sometimes expanded as far as Saturn and occasionally contracted as close as Jupiter. Barring the invention of a new weapon of such unimaginable power that we could wreck their fleet before they could duplicate the weapon, as they'd been managing to up to now, our only hope was to discover somehow the stellar system from which they came, somehow build ourselves not one starship but a fleet of them—and somehow wreck their home base or throw enough of a scare into it so that they'd pull back their expedition for defensive purposes. A lot of somehows.

But if we wanted to maintain our present position until the *somehows* started to roll, our birth announcements had to take longer to read than the casualty lists. For the last decade, this hadn't been so, despite the more and more stringent Breeding Regulations which were steadily pulverizing every one of our moral codes and sociological advances. Then there was the day that someone in the Conservation Police noticed that almost half our ships of the line had been fabricated from the metallic junk of previous battles. Where was the personnel that had manned those salvage derelicts, he wondered. . . .

And thus what Blondie outside and her co-workers were pleased to call soldier surrogates.

I'd been a computer's mate, second class, on the old *Jenghiz Khan* when the first batch had come aboard as battle replacements. Let me tell you, friends, we had real good reason for calling them zombies! Most of them were as blue as the uniforms they wore, their breathing was so noisy it made you think of asthmatics with built-in public address

systems, their eyes shone with all the intelligence of petro-
leum jelly—*and the way they walked!*

My friend, Johnny Cruro, the first man to get knocked off
in the Great Breakthrough of 2143, used to say that they were
trying to pick their way down a steep hill at the bottom of
which was a large, open, family-size grave. Body held strained
and tense. Legs and arms moving slow, slow, until suddenly
they'd finish with a jerk. Creepy as hell.

They weren't good for anything but the drabbest fatigue
detail. And even then—if you told them to polish a gun
mounting, you had to remember to come back in an hour and
turn them off or they might scrub their way clear through into
empty space. Of course, they weren't all that bad. Johnny
Cruro used to say that he'd met one or two who could achieve
imbecility when they were feeling right.

Combat was what finished them as far as the TAF was
concerned. Not that they broke under battle conditions—just
the reverse. The old ship would be rocking and screaming as
it changed course every few seconds; every Irvingle, scrambler, and nucleonic howitzer along the firing corridor turning
a bright golden yellow from the heat it was generating; a
hoarse yelping voice from the bulkhead loudspeakers pouring
out orders faster than human muscles could move, the shock
troops—their faces ugly with urgency—running crazily from
one emergency station to another; everyone around you working like a blur and cursing and wondering out loud why the
Eoti were taking so long to tag a target as big and as slow as
the Khan . . . and suddenly you'd see a zombie clutching a
broom in his rubbery hands and sweeping the deck in the
slack-jawed, moronic, and horribly earnest way they had. . . .

I remember whole gun crews going amuck and slamming
into the zombies with long crowbars and metal-gloved fists;
once, even an officer, sprinting back to the control room,
stopped, flipped out his side-arm and pumped bolt after bolt
of jagged thunder at a blue-skin who'd been peacefully wip-
ing a porthole while the bow of the ship was being burned
away. And as the zombie sagged uncomprehendingly and
uncomplainingly to the floor plates, the young officer stood

over him and chanted soothingly, the way you do to a boister-
ous dog: "Down, boy, down, *down, down, damn you, down!*"

That was the reason the zombies were eventually pulled
back, not their own efficiency: the incidence of battle psycho
around them just shot up too high. Maybe if it hadn't been for
that, we'd have got used to them eventually—God knows you
get used to everything else in combat. But the zombies
belonged to something beyond mere war.

They were so terribly, terribly unstirred by the prospect of
dying again!

Well, everyone said the new-model zombies were a big
improvement. They'd better be. A sling-shot might be one
thin notch below an outright suicide patrol, but you need peak
performance from every man aboard if it's going to complete
its crazy mission, let alone get back. And it's an awful small
ship and the men have to kind of get along with each other in
very close quarters. . . .

I heard feet, several pairs of them, rapping along the
corridor. They stopped outside the door.

They waited. I waited. My skin began to prickle. And then
I heard that uncertain shuffling sound. They were nervous
about meeting me!

I walked over to the window and stared down at the drill
field where old veterans whose minds and bodies were too
worn out to be repaired taught fatigue-uniformed zombies
how to use their newly conditioned reflexes in close-order
drill. It made me remember a high-school athletic field years
and years ago. The ancient barking commands drifted tinily
up to me: "*Hup*, two, three, four. *Hup*, two, three, four."
Only they weren't using *hup!*, but a newer, different word I
couldn't quite catch.

And then, when the hands I'd clasped behind me had
almost squeezed their blood back into my wrists, I heard the
door open and four pairs of feet clatter into the room. The
door closed and the four pairs of feet clicked to attention.

I turned around.

They were saluting me. Well, what the hell, I told myself,
they were supposed to be saluting me, I was their command-

ing officer. I returned the salute, and four arms whipped down smartly.

I said, "At ease." They snapped their legs apart, arms behind them. I thought about it. I said, "Rest." They relaxed their bodies slightly. I thought about it again. I said, "Hell, men, sit down and let's meet each other."

They sprawled into chairs and I hitched myself up on the instructor's desk. We stared back and forth. Their faces were rigid, watchful: they weren't giving anything away.

I wondered what my face looked like. In spite of all the orientation lectures, in spite of all the preparation, I must admit that my first glimpse of them had hit me hard. They were glowing with health, normality, and hard purpose. But that wasn't it.

That wasn't it at all.

What was making me want to run out of the door, out of the building, was something I'd been schooling myself to expect since that last briefing session in Arizona Base. Four dead men were staring at me. Four very famous dead men.

The big man, lounging all over his chair, was Roger Grey, who had been killed over a year ago when he rammed his tiny scout ship up the forward jets of an Eoti flagship. The flagship had been split neatly in two. Almost every medal imaginable and the Solar Corona. Grey was to be my co-pilot.

The thin, alert man with the tight shock of black hair was Wang Hsi. He had been killed covering the retreat to the asteroids after the Great Breakthrough of 2143. According to the fantastic story the observers told, his ship had still been firing after it had been scrambled fully three times. Almost every medal imaginable and the Solar Corona. Wang was to be my engineer.

The darkish little fellow was Yussuf Lamehd. He'd been killed in a very minor skirmish off Titan, but when he died he was the most decorated man in the entire TAF. A *double* Solar Corona. Lamehd was to be my gunner.

The heavy one was Stanley Weinstein, the only prisoner of war ever to escape from the Eoti. There wasn't much left of him by the time he arrived on Mars, but the ship he came in was the first enemy craft that humanity could study intact. There was no Solar Corona in his day for him to receive even posthumously, but they're still naming military academies after that man. Weinstein was to be my astrogator.

Then I shook myself back to reality. These weren't the original heroes, probably didn't have even a particle of Roger Grey's blood or Wang Hsi's flesh upon their reconstructed bones. They were just excellent and very faithful copies, made to minute physical specifications that had been in the TAF medical files since Wang had been a cadet and Grey a mere recruit.

There were anywhere from a hundred to a thousand Yussuf Lamehds and Stanley Weinsteins, I had to remind myself— and they had all come off an assembly line a few floors down. "Only the brave deserve the future," was the Junkyard's motto, and it was currently trying to assure that future for them by duplicating in quantity any TAF man who went out with especial heroism. As I happened to know, there were one or two other categories who could expect similar honors, but the basic reasons behind the hero-models had little to do with morale.

First, there was that little gimmick of industrial efficiency again. If you're using mass-production methods, and the Junkyard was doing just that, it's plain common sense to turn out a few standardized models, rather than have everyone different—like the stuff an individual creative craftsman might come up with. Well, if you're using standardized models, why not use those that have positive and relatively pleasant associations bound up with their appearance rather than anonymous characters from the designers' drawing boards?

The second reason was almost more important and harder to define. According to the briefing officer, yesterday, there was a peculiar feeling—a superstitious feeling, you might almost say—that if you copied a hero's features, musculature, metabolism, and even his cortex wrinkles carefully enough, well, you might build yourself another hero. Of course, the original personality would never reappear—that had been produced by long years of a specific environment and dozens of other very slippery factors—but it was distinctly possible, the biotechs felt, that a modicum of clever courage resided in the body structure alone. . . .

Well, at least these zombies didn't *look* like zombies!

On an impulse, I plucked the rolled sheaf of papers containing our travel orders out of my pocket, pretended to study it and let it slip suddenly through my fingers. As the outspread sheaf spiraled to the floor in front of me, Roger Grey reached out and caught it. He handed it back to me with the same kind of easy yet snappy grace. I took it, feeling good. It was the way he moved. I like to see a co-pilot move that way.

"Thanks," I said.

He just nodded.

I studied Yussuf Lamehd next. Yes, he had it too. Whatever it is that makes a first-class gunner, he had it. It's almost impossible to describe, but you walk into a bar in some rest area on Eros, say, and out of the five slingshotters hunched over the blow-top table, you know right off which is the gunner. It's a sort of carefully bottled nervousness or a dead calm with a hair-trigger attachment. Whatever it is, it's what you need sitting over a firing button when you've completed the dodge, curve, and twist that's a sling-shot's attacking dash and you're barely within range of the target, already beginning your dodge, curve, and twist back to safety. Lamehd had it so strong that I'd have put money on him against any other gunner in the TAF I'd ever seen in action.

Astrogators and engineers are different. You've just got to see them work under pressure before you can rate them. But, even so, I liked the calm and confident manner with which Wang Hsi and Weinstein sat under my examination. And I liked them.

Right there I felt a hundred pounds slide off my chest. I felt relaxed for the first time in days. I really liked my crew, zombies or no. We'd make it.

I decided to tell them. "Men," I said, "I think we'll really get along. I think we've got the makings of a sweet, smooth sling-shot. You'll find me——"

And I stopped. That cold, slightly mocking look in their eyes. They way they had glanced at each other when I told them I thought we'd get along, glanced at each other and blown slightly through distended nostrils. I realized that none of them had said anything since they'd come in: they'd just been watching me, and their eyes weren't exactly warm.

I stopped and let myself take a long, deep breath. For the first time, it was occurring to me that I'd been worrying about just one end of the problem, and maybe the least important end. I'd been worrying about how I'd react to them and how much I'd be able to accept them as shipmates. They were zombies, after all. It had never occurred to me to wonder how they'd feel about me.

And there was evidently something very wrong in how they felt about me.

"What is it, men?" I asked. They all looked at me inquiringly. "What's on your minds?"

They kept looking at me. Weinstein pursed his lips and tilted his chair back and forth. It creaked. Nobody said anything.

I got off the desk and walked up and down in front of the classroom. They kept following me with their eyes.

"Grey," I said. "You look as if you've got a great big knot inside you. Want to tell me about it?"

"No, Commander," he said deliberately. "I don't want to tell you about it."

I grimaced. "If anyone wants to say anything—anything at all—it'll be off the record and completely off the record. Also for the moment we'll forget about such matters as rank and TAF regulations." I waited. "Wang? Lamehd? How about you, Weinstein?" They stared at me quietly. Weinstein's chair creaked back and forth.

It had me baffled. What kind of gripe could they have against me? They'd never met me before. But I knew one thing: I wasn't going to haul a crew nursing a sub-surface grudge as unanimous as this aboard a sling-shot. I wasn't going to chop space with those eyes at my back. It would be

more efficient for me to shove my head against an Irvingle
lens and push the button.

"Listen," I told them. "I meant what I said about forget-
ting rank and TAF regulations. I want to run a happy ship and
I have to know what's up. We'll be living, the five of us, in
the tightest, most cramped conditions the mind of man has
yet been able to devise; we'll be operating a tiny ship whose
only purpose is to dodge at tremendous speed through the
fire-power and screening devices of the larger enemy craft
and deliver a single, crippling blast from a single oversize
Irvingle. We've got to get along whether we like each other
or not. If we don't get along, if there's any unspoken hostility
getting in our way, the ship won't operate at maximum
efficiency. And that way, we're through before we——"

"Commander," Weinstein said suddenly, his chair coming
down upon the floor with a solid whack, "I'd like to ask you
a question."

"Sure," I said and let out a gust of relief that was the size
of a small hurricane. "Ask me anything."

"When you think about us, Commander, or when you talk
about us, which word do you use?"

I looked at him and shook my head. "Eh?"

"When you talk about us, Commander, or when you think
about us, do you call us zombies? Or do you call us blobs?
That's what I'd like to know, Commander."

He'd spoken in such a polite, even tone that I was a long
time in getting the full significance of it.

"Personally," said Roger Grey in a voice that was just a
little less polite, a little less even, "personally, I think the
Commander is the kind who refers to us as canned meat.
Right, Commander?"

Yussuf Lamehd folded his arms across his chest and seemed
to consider the issue very thoughtfully. "I think you're right,
Rog. He's the canned-meat type. Definitely the canned-meat
type."

"No," said Wang Hsi. "He doesn't use that kind of
language. Zombies, yes; canned meat, no. You can observe
from the way he talks that he wouldn't ever get mad enough

to tell us to get back in the can. And I don't think he'd call us
blobs very often. He's the kind of guy who'd buttonhole
another sling-shot commander and tell him, 'Man, have I got
the sweetest zombie crew you ever saw!' That's the way I
figure him. Zombies.''

And then they were sitting quietly staring at me again. And
it wasn't mockery in their eyes. It was hatred.

I went back to the desk and sat down. The room was very
still. From the yard, fifteen floors down, the marching commands drifted up. Where did they latch on to this zombie-
blob-canned meat stuff? They were none of them more than
six months old; none of them had been outside the precincts
of the Junkyard yet. Their conditioning, while mechanical
and intensive, was supposed to be absolutely foolproof, producing hard, resilient, and entirely human minds, highly
skilled in their various specialties and as far from any kind of
imbalance as the latest psychiatric knowledge could push
them. I knew they wouldn't have got it in their conditioning.
Then *where*——

And then I heard it clearly for a moment. The word. The
word that was being used down in the drill field instead of
Hup! That strange, new word I hadn't been able to make out.
Whoever was calling the cadence downstairs wasn't saying,
"*Hup*, two, three, four."

He was saying, "*Blob*, two, three, four. *Blob*, two, three,
four."

Wasn't that just like the TAF? I asked myself. For that
matter, like any army anywhere anytime? Expending fortunes
and the best minds producing a highly necessary product to
exact specifications, and then, on the very first level of
military use, doing something that might invalidate it completely. I was certain that the same officials who had been
responsible for the attitude of the receptionist outside could
have had nothing to do with the old, superannuated TAF
drill-hacks putting their squads through their paces down
below. I could imagine those narrow, nasty minds, as jeal-
ously proud of their prejudices as of their limited and painfully acquired military knowledge, giving these youngsters

before me their first taste of barracks life, their first glimpse of the "outside." It was so stupid!

But was it? There was another way of looking at it, beyond the fact that only soldiers too old physically and too ossified mentally for any other duty could be spared for this place. And that was the simple pragmatism of army thinking. The fighting perimeters were places of abiding horror and agony, the forward combat zones in which sling-shots operated were even worse. If men or materiel were going to collapse out there, it could be very costly. Let the collapses occur as close to the rear echelons as possible.

Maybe it made sense, I thought. Maybe it was logical to make live men out of dead men's flesh (God knows humanity had reached the point where we had to have reinforcements from *somewhere*!) at enormous expense and with the kind of care usually associated with things like cotton wool and the most delicate watchmakers' tools; and then to turn around and subject them to the coarsest, ugliest environment possible, an environment that perverted their carefully instilled loyalty into hatred and their finely balanced psychological adjustment into neurotic sensitivity.

I didn't know if it was basically smart or dumb, or even if the problem had ever been really weighed as such by the upper, policy-making brass. All I could see was my own problem, and it looked awfully big to me. I thought of my attitude toward these men before getting them, and I felt pretty sick. But the memory gave me an idea.

"Hey, tell me something," I suggested. "What would you call me?"

They looked puzzled.

"You want to know what I call you," I explained. "Tell me first what you call people like me, people who are—who are *born*. You must have your own epithets."

Lamehd grinned so that his teeth showed a bright, mirthless white against his dark skin. "Realos," he said. "We call you people realos. Sometimes, realo trulos."

Then the rest spoke up. There were other names, lots of other names. They wanted me to hear them all. They interrupted each other; they spat the words out as if they were so many missiles; they glared at my face, as they spat them out, to see how much impact they had. Some of the nicknames were funny, some of them were rather nasty. I was particularly charmed by utie and wombat.

"All right," I said after a while. "Feel better?"

They were all breathing hard, but they felt better. I could tell it, and they knew it. The air in the room felt softer now."

"First off," I said, "I want you to notice that you are all big boys and as such, can take care of yourselves. From here on out, if we walk into a bar or a rec camp together and someone of approximately your rank says something that sounds like zombies to your acute ears, you are at liberty to walk up to him and start taking him apart—if you can. If he's of approximately my rank, in all probability, *I'll* do the taking apart, simply because I'm a very sensitive commander and don't like having my men depreciated. And any time you feel that I'm not treating you as human beings, one hundred percent, full solar citizenship and all that I give you permission to come up to me and say, 'Now look *here,* you dirty utie, sir——' "

The four of them grinned. Warm grins. Then the grins faded away, very slowly, and the eyes grew cold again. They were looking at a man who was, after all, an outsider. I cursed.

"It's not as simple as that, Commander," Wang Hsi said, "unfortunately. You can call us hundred-percent human beings, but we're not. And anyone who wants to call us blobs or canned meat has a certain amount of right. Because we're not as good as—as you mother's sons, and we know it. And we'll never be that good. Never."

"I don't know about that," I blustered. "Why, some of your performance charts——"

"Performance charts, Commander," Wang Hsi said softly, "do not a human being make."

On his right, Weinstein gave a nod, thought a bit, and added: "Nor groups of men a race."

I knew where we were going now. And I wanted to smash

my way out of that room, down the elevator, and out of the building before anybody said another word. *This is it,* I told myself: *here we are, boy, here we are.* I found myself squirming from corner to corner of the desk; I gave up, got off it, and began walking again.

Wang Hsi wouldn't let go. I should have known he wouldn't. "Soldier surrogates," he went on, squinting as if he were taking a close look at the phrase for the first time. "Soldier surrogates, but not soldiers. We're not soldiers, because soldiers are men. And we, Commander, are not men."

There was silence for a moment, then a tremendous blast of sound boiled out of my mouth. "And what makes you think that you're *not* men?"

Wang Hsi was looking at me with astonishment, but his reply was still soft and calm. "You know why. You've seen our specifications, Commander. We're not men, real men, because we can't reproduce ourselves."

I forced myself to sit down again and carefully placed my shaking hands over my knees.

"We're as sterile," I heard Yussuf Lamehd say, "as boiling water."

"There have been lots of men," I began, "who have been——"

"This isn't a matter of lots of men," Weinstein broke in. "This is a matter of *all*—all of *us.*"

"Blobs thou art," Wang Hsi murmured. "And to blobs returneth. They might have given at least a few of us a chance. The kids mightn't have turned out so bad."

Roger Grey slammed his huge hand down on the arm of his chair. "That's just the point, Wang," he said savagely. "The kids might have turned out good—too good. Our kids might have turned out to be better than their kids—and where would that leave the proud and cocky, the goddam name-calling, the realo trulo human race?"

I sat staring at them once more, but now I was seeing a different picture. I wasn't seeing conveyor belts moving along slowly covered with human tissues and organs on which earnest biotechs performed their individual tasks. I wasn't seeing a room filled with dozens of adult male bodies suspended in nutrient solution, each body connected to a conditioning machine which day and night clacked out whatever minimum information was necessary for the body to take the place of a man in the bloodiest part of the fighting perimeter.

This time, I saw a barracks filled with heroes, many of them in duplicate and triplicate. And they were sitting around griping, as men will in any barracks on any planet, whether they look like heroes or no. But their gripes concerned humiliations deeper than any soldiers had hitherto known—humiliations as basic as the fabric of human personality.

"You believe, then," and despite the sweat on my face, my voice was gentle, "that the reproductive power was deliberately withheld?"

Weinstein scowled. "Now, Commander. Please. No bedtime stories."

"Doesn't it occur to you at all that the whole problem of our species at the moment is reproduction? Believe me, men, that's all you hear about on the outside. Grammar-school debating teams kick current reproductive issues back and forth in the district medal competitions; every month scholars in archaeology and the botany of fungi come out with books about it from their own special angle. Everyone knows that if we don't lick the reproduction problem, the Eoti are going to lick us. Do you seriously think under such circumstances, the reproductive powers of *anyone* would be intentionally impaired?"

"What do a few male blobs matter, more or less?" Grey demanded. "According to the latest news bulletins, sperm bank deposits are at their highest point in five years. They don't need us."

"Commander," Wang Hsi pointed his triangular chin at me. "Let me ask you a few questions in your turn. Do you honestly expect us to believe that a science capable of reconstructing a living, highly effective human body with a complex digestive system and a most delicate nervous system, all this out of dead and decaying bits of protoplasm, is incapable of reconstructing the germ plasm in one single, solitary case?"

"You have to believe it," I told him. "Because it's so."

Wang sat back, and so did the other three. They stopped looking at me.

"Haven't you ever heard it said," I pleaded with them, "that the germ plasm is more essentially the individual than any other part of him? That some whimsical biologists take the attitude that our human bodies and all bodies are merely vehicles, or hosts, by means of which our germ plasm reproduces itself? It's the most complex bio-technical riddle we have! Believe me, men," I added passionately, "when I say that biology has not yet solved the germ-plasm problem, I'm telling the truth. I know."

That got them.

"Look," I said. "We have one thing in common with the Eoti whom we're fighting. Insects and warm-blooded animals differ prodigiously. But only among the community-building insects and the community-building men are there individuals who, while taking no part personally in the reproductive chain, are of fundamental importance to their species. For example, you might have a female nursery school teacher who is barren but who is of unquestionable value in shaping the personalities and even physiques of children in her care."

"Fourth Orientation Lecture for Soldier Surrogates," Weinstein said in a dry voice. "He got it right out of the book."

"I've been wounded," I said. "I've been seriously wounded fifteen times." I stood before them and began rolling up my right sleeve. It was soaked with my perspiration.

"We can tell you've been wounded, Commander," Lamehd pointed out uncertainly. "We can tell from your medals. You don't have to——"

"And every time I was wounded, they repaired me good as new. Better. Look at that arm." I flexed it for them. "Before it was burned off in a small razzle six years ago, I could never build up a muscle that big. It's a better arm they built on the stump, and, believe me, my reflexes never had it so good."

"What did you mean," Wang Hsi started to ask me, "when you said before——"

"Fifteen times I was wounded," my voice drowned him out, "and fourteen times, the wound was repaired. The fifteenth time—*The fifteenth time*—Well, the fifteenth time it wasn't a wound they could repair. They couldn't help me one little bit the fifteenth time."

Roger Grey opened his mouth.

"Fortunately," I whispered, "it wasn't a wound that showed."

Weinstein started to ask me something, decided against it and sat back. But I told him what he wanted to know.

"A nucleonic howitzer. The way it was figured later, it had been a defective shell. Bad enough to kill half the men on our second-class cruiser. I wasn't killed, but I was in range of the back-blast."

"That back-blast," Lamehd was figuring it out quickly in his mind. "That back-blast will sterilize anybody for two hundred feet. Unless you're wearing——"

"And I wasn't." I had stopped sweating. It was over. My crazy little precious secret was out. I took a deep breath. "So you see—well, anyway, I *know* they haven't solved that problem yet."

Roger Grey stood up and said, "Hey." He held out his hand. I shook it. It felt like any normal guy's hand. Stronger maybe.

"Sling-shot personnel," I went on, "are all volunteers. Except for two categories: the commanders and soldier surrogates."

"Figuring, I guess," Weinstein asked, "that the human race can spare them most easily?"

"Right," I said. "Figuring that the human race can spare them most easily." He nodded.

"Well, I'll be damned," Yussuf Lamehd laughed as he got up and shook my hand, too. "Welcome to our city."

"Thanks," I said. "*Son.*"

He seemed puzzled at the emphasis.

"That's the rest of it," I explained. "Never got married

and was too busy getting drunk and tearing up the pavement on my leaves to visit a sperm bank.''

''Oho,'' Weinstein said, and gestured at the walls with a thick thumb. ''So this is it.''

''That's right: this is it. The Family. The only one I'll ever have. I've got almost enough of these—'' I tapped my medals ''—to rate replacement. As a sling-shot commander, I'm sure of it.''

''All you don't know yet,'' Lamehd pointed out, ''is how high a percentage of replacement will be apportioned to your memory. That depends on how many more of these chest decorations you collect before you become an—ah, should I say *raw material?*''

''Yeah,'' I said, feeling crazily light and easy and relaxed. I'd got it all out and I didn't feel whipped any more by a billion years of reproduction and evolution. And I'd been going to do a morale job on them! ''*Say* raw material, Lamehd.''

''Well, boys,'' he went on, ''it seems to me we want the commander to get a lot more fruit salad. He's a nice guy and there should be more of him in the club.''

They were all standing around me now, Weinstein, Lamehd, Grey, Wang Hsi. They looked real friendly and real capable. I began to feel we were going to have one of the best sling-shots in—— What did I mean *one* of the best? *The* best, mister, *the* best.

''Okay,'' said Grey. ''Wherever and whenever you want to, you start leading us—*Pop.*''

THE HUNTING LODGE

BY RANDALL GARRETT (1927–   )

ASTOUNDING SCIENCE FICTION, JULY

Randall Garrett, under his own name and at least seventeen others, was one of the most prolific writers in the sf field in the years (roughly) 1954–1964. Among his pseudonyms, David Gordon, Darrel T. Langart, and Robert Randall (used for collaborations with Robert Silverberg) are the most familiar, and he was one of those writers who at his best was terrific, and at his average was more than o.k. He seemed to be a favorite of John W. Campbell, and ASTOUNDING was filled with his stories during the above mentioned decade. Among his novels, his most popular is probably TOO MANY MAGICIANS, which features "Lord Darcy," his greatest creation. Also important were his efforts with Laurence M. Janifer, who like Garrett remains an underappreciated talent, under the name "Mark Phillips," a very poor choice, since it increased the confusion readers felt in dealing with Rog Phillips and Peter Phillips, both active writers at that time. The three Garrett-Janifer collaborations, BRAIN TWISTER (1962) and THE IMPOSSIBLES and SUPERMIND (1963), are interesting well-executed novels that certainly deserve to be back in print.

"The Hunting Lodge" shows Garrett at his intricate, fascinating best. (MHG)

* * *

Randall was a real madman, in the pleasant sense of the word. I remember the Thirteenth World Science Fiction Convention, held in Cleveland in 1955. It was the one at which I was Guest of Honor and Randy and I were inseparable for the duration. We two, all by ourselves, accounted for half the noise created by the entire convention. Those were the days when we were young.

He had such talent. He not only wrote excellent science fiction, he wrote absolutely terrific light verse, baked little figurines of characters in the Pogo strip, and knew Gilbert & Sullivan even better than I did.

I last saw him in December 1978, in San Jose, California, where I had traveled by train(!) to give a talk. It was not long after that that he was struck by a bad case of meningitis. He is still alive but he is no longer Randall, alas. (IA)

"We'll help all we can," the Director said, "but if you're caught, that's all there is to it."

I nodded. It was the age-old warning: *If you're caught, we disown you.* I wondered, fleetingly, how many men had heard that warning during the long centuries of human history, and I wondered how many of them had asked themselves the same question I was asking:

Why am *I* risking *my* neck?

And I wondered how many of them had had an answer.

"Ready, then?" the Director asked, glancing at his watch. I nodded and looked at my own. The shadow hands pointed to 2250.

"Here's the gun."

I took it and checked its loading. "Untraceable, I suppose?"

He shook his head. "It can be traced, all right, but it won't lead to us. A gun which couldn't be traced almost certainly would be associated with us. But the best thing to do would be to bring the gun back with you; that way, it's in no danger of being traced."

The way he said it gave me a chill. He wanted me back alive, right enough, but only so there would be no evidence.

"O.K." I said. "Let's go."

I put a nice, big, friendly grin on my face. After all, there was no use making him feel worse than necessary. I knew he didn't like sending men out to be killed. I slipped the sleeve gun into its holder and then faced him.

"Blaze away!"

He looked me over, then touched the hypno controls. A light hit my eyes.

I was walking along the street when I came out of it, heading toward a flitter stand. An empty flitter was sitting there waiting, so I climbed in and sat down.

Senator Rowley's number was ORdway 63-911. I dialed it and leaned back, just as though I had every right to go there.

The flitter lifted perfectly and headed northwest, but I knew perfectly well that the scanners were going full blast, sorting through their information banks to find me.

A mile or so out of the city, the flitter veered to the right, locked its controls, and began to go around in a tight circle.

The viewphone lit up, but the screen stayed blank. A voice said: "Routine check. Identify yourself, please."

Routine! I knew better. But I just looked blank and stuck my right forearm into the checker. There was a short hum while the ultrasonic scanners looked at the tantalum identity plate riveted to the bone.

"Thank you, Mr. Gifford," said the voice. The phone cut off, but the flitter was still going in circles.

Then the phone lit again, and Senator Rowley's face—thin, dark, and bright-eyed—came on the screen.

"Gifford! Did you get it?"

"I got it, sir," I answered quietly.

He nodded, pleased. "Good! I'll be waiting for you."

Again the screen went dark, and this time the flitter straightened out and headed northwest once more.

I tried not to feel too jittery, but I had to admit to myself that I was scared. The senator was dangerous. If he could get a finger into the robot central office of the flitters, there was no way of knowing how far his control went.

He wasn't supposed to be able to tap a flitter any more than he was supposed to be able to tap a phone. But neither one was safe now.

Only a few miles ahead of me was the Lodge, probably the most tightly guarded home in the world.

I knew I might not get in, of course. Senator Anthony Rowley was no fool, by a long shot. He placed his faith in robots. A machine might fail, but it would never be treacherous.

I could see the walls of the Lodge ahead as the flitter began to lose altitude. I could almost feel the watching radar eyes that followed the craft down, and it made me nervous to realize that a set of high-cycle guns were following the instructions of those eyes.

And, all alone in that big mansion—or fortress—sat Senator Rowley like a spider in the middle of an intangible web.

The public flitter, with me in it, lit like a fly on the roof of the mansion. I took a deep breath and stepped out. The multiple eyes of the robot defenses watched me closely as I got into the waiting elevator.

The hard plastic of the little sleeve gun was supposed to be transparent to X rays and sonics, but I kept praying anyway. Suddenly I felt a tingle in my arm. I knew what it was; a checker to see if the molecular structure of the tantalum identity plate was according to government specifications in every respect.

Identity plates were furnished only by the Federal government, but they were also supposed to be the only ones with analyzers. Even the senator shouldn't have had an unregistered job.

To play safe, I rubbed at the arm absently. I didn't know whether Gifford had ever felt that tingle before or not. If he had, he might ignore it, but he wouldn't let it startle him. If he hadn't, he might not be startled, but he wouldn't ignore it. Rubbing seemed the safest course.

The thing that kept running through my mind was—*how much did Rowley trust psychoimpressing*?

He had last seen Gifford four days ago, and at that time, Gifford could no more have betrayed the senator than one of the robots could. Because, psychologically speaking, that's exactly what Gifford had been—a robot. Theoretically, it is impossible to remove a competent psychoimpressing job in less than six weeks of steady therapy. It *could* be done in a little less time, but it didn't leave the patient in an ambient condition. And it couldn't, under any circumstances, be done in four days.

If Senator Rowley was thoroughly convinced I was Gifford, and if he trusted psychoimpression, I was in easy.

I looked at my watch again. 2250. Exactly an hour since I had left. The change in time zones had occurred while I was in the flitter, and the shadow hands had shifted back to accommodate.

It seemed to be taking a long time for the elevator to drop; I could just barely feel the movement. The robots were giving me a very thorough going over.

Finally, the door slid open and I stepped out into the lounge. For the first time in my life, I saw the living face of Senator Anthony Rowley.

The filters built into his phone pickup did a lot for him. They softened the fine wrinkles that made his face look like a piece of old leather. They added color to his grayish skin. They removed the yellowishness from his eyes. In short, the senator's pickup filters took two centuries off his age.

Longevity can't do everything for you, I thought. But I could see what it *could* do, too, if you were smart and had plenty of time. And those who had plenty of time were automatically the smart ones.

The senator extended a hand, "Give me the briefcase, Gifford."

"Yes, sir." As I held out the small blue case, I glanced at my watch. 2255. And, as I watched, the last five became a six.

Four minutes to go.

"Sit down, Gifford." The senator waved me to a chair. I sat and watched him while he leafed through the supposedly secret papers.

Oh, they were real enough, all right, but they didn't contain any information that would be of value to him. He would be too dead for that.

He ignored me as he read. There was no need to watch Gifford. Even if Gifford had tried anything, the robotic brain in the basement of the house would have detected it with at least one of its numerous sensory devices and acted to prevent the senator's death long before any mere human could complete any action.

I knew that, and the senator knew it.

We sat.

2257.

The senator frowned. "This is all, Gifford?"

"I can't be sure, of course, sir. But I will say that any further information on the subject is buried pretty deeply. So well hidden, in fact, that even the government couldn't find it in time to use against you."

"Mmmmmm."

2258.

The senator grinned. "This is it," he said through his tight, thin, old lips. "We'll be in complete control within a year, Gifford."

"That's good, sir. Very good."

It doesn't take much to play the part of a man who's been psychoimpressed as thoroughly as Gifford had been.

2259.

The senator smiled softly and said nothing. I waited tensely, hoping that the darkness would be neither too long nor too short. I made no move toward the sleeve gun, but I was ready to grab it as soon as—

2300!

The lights went out—and came on again.

The senator had time to look both startled and frightened before I shot him through the heart.

I didn't waste any time. The power had been cut off from the Great Northwestern Reactor, which supplied all the juice for the whole area, but the senator had provided wisely for that. He had a reactor of his own built in for emergencies; it had cut in as soon as the Great Northwestern had gone out.

But cutting off the power to a robot brain is the equivalent of hitting a man over the head with a blackjack; it takes time to recover. It was that time lapse which had permitted me to kill Rowley and which would, if I moved fast enough, permit me to escape before its deadly defenses could be rallied against me.

I ran toward a door and almost collided with it before I realized that it wasn't going to open for me. I had to push it aside. I kept on running, heading for an outside entrance. There was no way of knowing how long the robot would remain stunned.

Rowley had figured he was being smart when he built a single centralized computer to take over all the defenses of the house instead of having a series of simple brains, one for each function. And, in a way, I guess he was right; the Lodge could act as a single unit that way.

But Rowley had died because he insisted on that complication; the simpler the brain, the quicker the recovery.

The outside door opened easily enough; the electrolocks were dead, I was still surrounded by walls; the nearest exit was nearly half a mile away. That didn't bother me; I wasn't going to have to use it. There was a high-speed flitter waiting for me above the clouds.

I could hear it humming down toward me. Then I could see it, drifting down in a fast spiral.

Whoom!

I was startled for a timeless instant as I saw the flitter dissolve in a blossom of yellow-orange flame. The flare, marking the end of my escape craft, hung in the air for an endless second and then died slowly.

I realized then that the heavy defenses of the Lodge had come to life.

I didn't even stop to think. The glowing red of the fading explosion was still lighting the ground as I turned and sprinted toward the garage. One thing I knew; the robot would not shoot down one of the senator's own machines unless ordered to do so.

The robot was still not fully awake. It had reacted to the approach of a big, fast-moving object, but it still couldn't see a running man. Its scanners wouldn't track yet.

I shoved the garage doors open and looked inside. The bright lights disclosed ground vehicles and nothing more. The flitters were all on the roof.

I hadn't any choice; I had to get out of there, and fast!

The senator had placed a lot of faith in the machines that guarded the Lodge. The keys were in the lock of one big Ford-Studebaker. I shoved the control from auto to manual, turned the key and started the engines.

As soon as they were humming, I started the car moving. And none too soon, either. The doors of the garage slammed after me like the jaws of a man trap. I gunned the car for the nearest gate, hoping that this one last effort would be successful. If I didn't make it through the outer gate, I might as well give up.

As I approached the heavy outer gates, I could see that they were functioning; I'd never get them open by hand. But the robot was still a little confused. It recognized the car and didn't recognize me. The gates dropped, so I didn't even slow the car. Pure luck again.

And close luck, at that. The gates tried to come back up out of the ground even as the heavy vehicle went over them; there was a loud bump as the rear wheels hit the top of the rising gate. But again the robot was too late.

I took a deep breath and aimed the car toward the city. So far, so good. A clean getaway.

Another of the Immortals was dead. Senator Rowley's political machine would never again force through a vote to give him another longevity treatment, because the senator's political force had been cut off at the head, and the target was gone. Pardon the mixed metaphor.

Longevity treatments are like a drug; the more you have, the more you want. I suppose it had been a good idea a few centuries ago to restrict their use to men who were of such use to the race that they deserved to live longer than the average. But the mistake was made in putting it up to the voting public who should get the treatments.

Of course, they'd had a right to have a voice in it; at the beginning, the cost of a single treatment had been too high for any individual to pay for it. And, in addition, it had been a government monopoly, since the government had paid for the research. So, if the taxpayer's money was to be spent, the taxpayer had a right to say who it was to be spent on.

But if a man's life hangs on his ability to control the public, what other out does he have?

And the longer he lives, the greater his control. A man can become an institution if he lives long enough. And Senator Rowley had lived long enough; he—

Something snickered on the instrument panel. I looked, but I couldn't see anything. Then something moved under my foot. It was the accelerator. The car was slowing.

I didn't waste any time guessing; I knew what was happening. I opened the door just as the car stopped. Fortunately, the doors had only manual controls; simple mechanical locks.

I jumped out of the car's way and watched it as it backed up, turned around, and drove off in the direction of the Lodge. The robot was fully awake now; it had recalled the car. I hadn't realized that the senator had set up the controls in his vehicles so that the master robot could take control away from a human being.

I thanked various and sundry deities that I had not climbed into one of the flitters. It's hard to get out of an aircraft when it's a few thousand feet above the earth.

Well, there was nothing to do but walk. So I walked.

It wasn't more than ten minutes before I heard the buzzing behind me. Something was coming over the road at a good clip, but without headlights. In the darkness, I couldn't see a thing, but I knew it wasn't an ordinary car. Not coming from the Lodge.

I ran for the nearest tree, a big monster at least three feet thick and fifty or sixty feet high. The lowest branch was a heavy one about seven feet from the ground. I grabbed it and swung myself up and kept on climbing until I was a good twenty feet off the ground. Then I waited.

The whine stopped down the road about half a mile, about where I'd left the Ford-Studebaker. Whatever it was prowled around for a minute or two, then started coming on down the road.

When it finally came close enough for me to see it in the moonlight, I recognized it for what it was. A patrol robot. It was looking for me.

Then I heard another whine. But this one was different; it was a siren coming from the main highway.

Overhead, I heard a flitter whistling through the sky.

The police.

The patrol robot buzzed around on its six wheels, turning its search-turret this way and that, trying to spot me.

The siren grew louder, and I saw the headlights in the distance. In less than a minute, the lights struck the patrol robot, outlining every detail of the squat, ugly silhouette. It stopped, swiveling its turret toward the police car. The warning light on the turret came on, glowing a bright red.

The cops slowed down and stopped. One of the men in the car called out, "Senator? Are you on the other end of that thing?"

No answer from the robot.

"I guess he's really dead," said another officer in a low, awed voice.

"It don't seem possible," the first voice said. Then he called again to the patrol robot. "We're police officers. Will you permit us to show our identification?"

The patrol robot clicked a little as the information was relayed back to the Lodge and the answer given. The red warning light turned green, indicating that the guns were not going to fire.

About that time, I decided that my only chance was to move around so that the trunk of the tree was between me and the road. I had to move slowly so they wouldn't hear me, but I finally made it.

I could hear the policeman saying, "According to the information we received, Senator Rowley was shot by his secretary, Edgar Gifford. This patrol job must be hunting him."

"Hey!" said another voice. "Here comes another one! He must be in the area somewhere!"

I could hear the whining of a second patrol robot approaching from the Lodge. It was still about a mile away, judging from the sound.

I couldn't see what happened next, but I could hear the first robot moving, and it must have found me, even though I was out of sight. Directional heat detector, probably.

"In the tree, eh?" said a cop.

Another called: "All right, Gifford! Come on down!"

Well, that was it. I was caught. But I wasn't going to be taken alive. I eased out the sleeve gun and sneaked a peek around the tree. *No use killing a cop,* I thought, *he's just doing his job.*

So I fired at the car, which didn't hurt a thing.

"Look out!"

"Duck!"

"Get that blaster going!"

Good. It was going to be a blaster. It would take off the treetop and me with it. I'd die quickly.

There was a sudden flurry of shots, and then silence.

I took another quick peak and got the shock of my life.

The four police officers were crumpled on the ground, shot down by the patrol robot from the Lodge. One of them—the one holding the blaster—wasn't quite dead yet. He gasped something obscene and fired the weapon just as two more slugs from the robot's turret hit him in the chest.

The turret exploded in a gout of fire.

I didn't get it, but I didn't have time to wonder what was going on. I know a chance when I see one. I swung from the branch I was on and dropped to the ground, rolling over in a bed of old leaves to take up the shock. Then I made a beeline for the police car.

On the way, I grabbed one of the helmets from a uniformed corpse, hoping that my own tunic was close enough to the same shade of scarlet to get me by. I climbed in and got the machine turned around just as the second patrol robot came into sight. It fired a couple of shots after me, but those patrol jobs don't have enough armament to shoot down a police car; they're strictly for hunting unarmed and unprotected pedestrians.

Behind me there were a couple of flares in the sky that reminded me of my own exploding flitter, but I didn't worry about what they could be.

I was still puzzled about the robot's shooting down the police. It didn't make sense.

Oh, well, it had saved my neck, and I wasn't going to pinch a gift melon.

The police car I was in had evidently been the only ground vehicle dispatched toward the Lodge—possibly because it happened to be nearby. It was a traffic-control car; the regular homicide squad was probably using flitters.

I turned off the private road and onto the highway, easing into the traffic-control pattern and letting the car drift along with the other vehicles. But I didn't shove it into automatic. I didn't like robots just then. Besides, if I let the main control panels take over the guiding of the car, someone at headquarters might wonder why car such-and-such wasn't at the Lodge as ordered; they might wonder why it was going down the highway so unconcernedly.

There was only one drawback. I wasn't used to handling a car at a hundred and fifty to two hundred miles an hour. If something should happen to the traffic pattern, I'd have to depend on my own reflexes. And they might not be fast enough.

I decided I'd have to ditch the police car as soon as I could. It was too much trouble and too easy to spot.

I had an idea. I turned off the highway again at the next break, a few miles farther on. There wasn't much side traffic at that time of night, so I had to wait several minutes before the pattern broke again and a private car pulled out and headed down the side road.

I hit the siren and pulled him over to the side.

He was an average-sized character with a belligerent attitude and a fat face.

"What's the matter, officer? There was nothing wrong with that break. I didn't cut out of the pattern on manual, you know. I was—'' He stopped when he realized that my tunic was not that of a policeman. "Why, you're not—''

By then, I'd already cut him down with a stun gun I'd found in the arms compartment of the police car. I hauled him out and changed tunics with him. His was a little loose, but not so much that it would be noticeable. Then I put the helmet on his head and strapped him into the front seat of the police vehicle with the safety belt.

After being hit with a stun gun, he'd be out for a good hour. That would be plenty of time as far as I was concerned.

I transferred as much of the police armory as I thought I'd need into the fat-faced fellow's machine and then I climbed into the police car with him. I pulled the car around and headed back toward the highway.

Just before we reached the control area, I set the instruments for the Coast and headed him west, back the way I had come.

I jumped out and slammed the door behind me as the automatic controls took over and put him in the traffic pattern.

Then I walked back to Fatty's car, got in, and drove back to the highway. I figured I could trust the controls of a private vehicle, so I set them and headed east, toward the city. Once I was there, I'd have to get a flitter, somehow.

I spent the next twenty minutes changing my face. I couldn't do anything about the basic structure; that would have to wait until I got back. Nor could I do anything about the ID plate that was bolted on my left ulna; that, too, would have to wait.

I changed the color of my hair, darkening it from Gifford's gray to a mousy brown, and I took a patch of hair out above my forehead to give me a balding look. The mustache went, and the sides of the beard, giving me a goatee effect. I trimmed down the brows and the hair, and put a couple of tubes in my nostrils to widen my nose.

I couldn't do much about the eyes; my little pocket kit didn't carry them. But, all in all, I looked a great deal less like Gifford than I had before.

Then I proceeded to stow a few weapons on and about my

person. I had taken the sleeve gun out of the scarlet tunic
when I'd put it on the fat-faced man, but his own chartreuse
tunic didn't have a sleeve holster, so I had to put the gun in a
hip pocket. But the tunic was a godsend in another way; it
was loose enough to carry a few guns easily.

The car speaker said: "Attention! You are now approaching Groverton, the last suburb before the city limits. Private
automobiles may not be taken beyond this point. If you wish
to by-pass the city, please indicate. If not, please go to the
free storage lot in Groverton."

I decided I'd do neither. I might as well make the car as
hard to find as possible. I took it to an all-night repair
technician in Groverton.

"Something wrong with the turbos," I told him. "Give
her a complete overhaul."

He was very happy to do so. He'd be mighty unhappy
when the cops took the car away without paying him for it,
but he didn't look as though he'd go broke from the loss.
Besides, I thought it would be a good way to repay Fat-Face
for borrowing his car

I had purposely kept the hood of my tunic up while I was
talking to the auto technician so he wouldn't remember my
new face later, but I dropped the hood as soon as I got to the
main street of Groverton. I didn't want to attract too much
attention.

I looked at my watch. 0111. I'd passed back through the
time-change again, so it had been an hour and ten minutes
since I'd left the Lodge. I decided I needed something to eat.

Groverton was one of those old-fashioned suburbs built
during the latter half of the twentieth century—sponge-glass
streets and sidewalks, aluminum siding on the houses, shiny
chrome-and-lucite business buildings. Real quaint.

I found an automat and went in. There were only a few
people on the streets, but the automat wasn't empty by a long
shot. Most of the crowd seemed to be teen-age kids getting
looped up after a dance. One booth was empty, so I sat down
in it, dialed for coffee and ham and eggs, and dropped in the
indicated change.

Shapeless little blobs of color were bouncing around in the tri-di tank in the wall, giving a surrealistic dance accompaniment to "Anna from Texarkana":

> *You should have seen the way she ate!*
> *Her appetite insatiate*
> *Was quite enough to break your pocketbook!*
> *But with a yeast-digamma steak,*
> *She never made a damn mistake—*
> *What tasty synthefoods that gal could cook!*
> *Oh, my Anna! Her algae Manna*
> *Was tasty as a Manna-cake could be!*
> *Oh, my Anna—from Texarkana!*
> *Oh, Anna, baby, you're the gal for me!*

I sipped coffee while the thing went through the third and fourth verses, trying to figure a way to get into the city without having to show the telltale ID plate in my arm.

"Anna" was cut off in the middle of the fifth verse. The blobs changed color and coalesced into the face of Quinby Lester, news analyst.

"Good morning, free citizens! We are interrupting this program to bring you an announcement of special importance."

He looked very serious, very concerned, and, I thought, just a little bit puzzled. "At approximately midnight last night, there was a disturbance at the Lodge. Four police officers who were summoned to the Lodge were shot and killed by Mr. Edgar Gifford, the creator of the disturbance. This man is now at large in the vicinity. Police are making an extensive search within a five-hundred-mile radius of the Lodge.

"Have you seen this man?"

A tri-di of Gifford appeared in place of Lester's features.

"This man is armed and dangerous. If you see him, report immediately to MONmouth 6-666-666. If your information leads to the capture of Edgar Gifford, you will receive a reward of ten thousand dollars. Look around you! He may be near you now!''

Everybody in the automat looked apprehensively at everybody else. I joined them. I wasn't much worried about being spotted. When everybody wears beards, it's hard to spot a man under a handful of face foliage. I was willing to bet that within the next half hour the police would be deluged with calls from a thousand people who honestly thought they had seen Edgar Gifford.

The cops knew that. They were simply trying to scare me into doing something foolish.

They needn't have done that; I was perfectly capable of doing something foolish without their help.

I thought carefully about my position. I was about fifteen miles from safety. Question: Could I call for help? Answer: No. Because I didn't know the number. I didn't even know who was waiting for me. All that had been erased from my mind when the Director hypnoed me. I couldn't even remember who I was working for or why!

My only chance was to get to Fourteenth and Riverside Drive. They'd pick me up there.

Oh, well, if I didn't make it, I wasn't fit to be an assassin, anyway.

I polished off the breakfast and took another look at my watch. 0147. I might as well get started; I had fifteen miles to walk.

Outside, the streets were fairly quiet. The old-fashioned streets hadn't been built to clean themselves; a robot sweeper was prowling softly along the curb, sucking up the day's debris, pausing at every cross street to funnel the stuff into the disposal drains to be carried to the processing plant.

A few people were walking the streets. Ahead of me, a drunk was sitting on the curb sucking at a bottle that had collapsed long ago, hoping to get one last drop out of it.

I decided the best way to get to my destination was to take Bradley to Macmillan, follow Macmillan to Fourteenth, then stay on Fourteenth until I got to Riverside Drive.

But no free citizen would walk that far. I'd better not look like one. I walked up to the swiller.

"Hey, Joe, how'd you like to make five?"

He looked up at me, trying to focus. "Sure, Sid, sure. Whatta gotta do?"

"Sell me your tunic."

He blinked. "Zissa gag? Ya get 'em free."

"No gag. I want your tunic."

"Sure. Fine. Gimme that five."

He peeled off the charity brown tunic and I handed him the five note. If I had him doped out right, he'd be too drunk to remember what had happened to his tunic. He'd be even drunker when he started on that five note.

I pulled the brown on over the chartreuse tunic. I might want to get into a first-class installation, and I couldn't do it wearing charity brown.

"LOOK OUT!"

CLIK LIK LIK LIK LIK LIK!

I felt something grab my ankle and I turned fast. It was the street cleaner! It had reached out a retractable picker and was trying to lift me into its hopper!

The drunk, who had done the yelling, tried to back away, but he stumbled and banged his head on the soft sidewalk. He stayed down—not out, but scared.

Another claw came out of the cleaner and grabbed my shoulder. The two of them together lifted me off the ground and pulled me toward the open hopper. I managed to get my gun out. These cleaners weren't armored; if I could only get in a good shot—

I fired three times, blowing the pickup antenna off the control dome. When the claws opened, I dropped to the sidewalk and ran. Behind me, the robot, no longer under the direction of the central office, began to flick its claws in and out and run around in circles. The drunk didn't manage to get out from under the treads in time.

A lot of people had stopped to watch the brief tussle, a few of them pretty scared. It was unheard of for a street cleaner to go berserk like that.

I dodged into an alleyway and headed for the second level. I was galloping up the escalator full tilt when the cop saw me. He was on the other escalator, going down, but he didn't stay there long.

"Halt!" he yelled, as he vaulted over the waist-high partition and landed on the UP escalator. By that time, I was already on the second level and running like mad.

"Halt or I fire!" he yelled.

I ducked into a doorway and pulled out the stun gun. I turned just in time to see one of the most amazing sights I have ever been privileged to witness. The cop was running toward me, his gun out, when he passed in front of a bottled goods vendor. At that instant, the vendor opened up, delivering a veritable avalanche of bottles into the corridor. The policeman's foot hit one of the rubbery, bouncing cylinders and slipped just as he pulled the trigger.

His shot went wild, and I fired with the stun gun before the cop could hit the floor. He lay still, bottles rolling all around him.

I turned and ran again. I hadn't gone far before another cop showed up, running toward me. I made a quick turn toward the escalators and went down again toward street level.

The cop wasn't prepared for what happened to him when he stepped on the escalator. He was about halfway down, running, when the belt suddenly stopped and reversed itself. The policeman pitched forward on his face and tumbled down the stair.

I didn't wait to see what happened next. I turned the corner, slowed down, and walked into a bar. I tried to walk slowly enough so that I wouldn't attract attention and headed for the rest room.

I went in, locked the door behind me, and looked around. As far as I could tell, there were no sensory devices in the place, so I pulled the last of my make-up kit out and went to work. This time, I went whole hog. Most of the hair went from the top of my head, and what was left became pure white. I didn't take off the goatee; a beardless man would stand out. But the goatee went white, too.

Then a fine layer of plastic sprayed on my face and hands gave me an elderly network of wrinkles.

All the time I was doing this, I was wondering what was going on with the robots. It was obvious to me that the Lodge was connected illegally with every robot service in the city—possibly in the whole sector.

The street sweeper had recognized me and tried to get me; that was clear enough. But what about the vending machine and the escalator? Was the Lodge's master computer still foggy from the power cutoff? It shouldn't be; not after two hours. Then why had the responses been so slow? Why had they tripped the cops instead of me? It didn't make sense.

That's when it hit me. *Was Rowley really dead?*

I couldn't be absolutely sure, could I? And the police hadn't said anything about a murder. Just a "disturbance." No, wait. The first cops, the ones whose car I'd taken. What had they said the robot reported? I couldn't remember the exact words.

It still didn't settle the question.

For a moment, I found myself wishing we had a government like the United States had had back in the third quarter of the Twentieth Century, back in the days of strong central government, before everybody started screaming about Citizen's Rights and the preservation of the status quo. There wouldn't be any of this kind of trouble now—maybe.

But they had other kinds just as bad.

This wasn't the best of all possible worlds, but I was living in it. Of course, I didn't know how long that happy situation would exist just then.

Somebody rapped on the door.

I didn't know who it was, but I wasn't taking any chances. Maybe it was a cop. I climbed out the back window and headed down the alley toward Bradley Avenue.

If only I could get rid of that plate in my arm! The average citizen doesn't know it, but it isn't really necessary to put your arm in an ID slot to be identified. A sonobeam can pick up a reflected recording from your plate at twenty feet if there's a scanner nearby to direct it.

I walked slowly after running the length of the alley, staying in the shadows as much as possible, trying to keep out of the way of anyone and everyone.

For six blocks or so, I didn't see a soul. Then, just as I turned onto West Bradley, I came face to face with a police car. I froze.

I was ready to pull and shoot; I wanted the cop to kill me before he picked me up.

He slowed up, looked at me sharply, looked at his instrument panel, then drove on. I just stood there, flabbergasted. I knew as well as I knew anything that he'd beamed that plate in my arm!

As the car turned at the next corner, I backed into a nearby doorway, trying to figure out what I should do next. Frankly, I was jumpy and scared; I didn't know what they were up to.

I got even more jumpy when the door behind me gave. I turned fast and made a grab for my gun. But I didn't take it out.

The smoothly dressed girl said: "What's the matter, Grandfather?"

It wasn't until then that I realized how rattled I was. I looked like a very old man, but I wasn't acting like one. I paused to force my mind to adjust.

The girl was in green. The one-piece shortsuit, the sandals, the toenails, fingernails, lips, eyes, and hair. All green. The rest of her was a smooth, even shade of pink.

She said: "You needn't be afraid that anyone will see you. We arrange—Oh!"

I knew what she was oh'ing about. The charity brown of my tunic.

"I'm sorry," she said, frowning. "We can't—"

I cut her off this time. "I have money, my dear," I smiled. "And I'm wearing my own tunic." I flashed the chartreuse on her by opening the collar.

"I see, Grandfather. Won't you come in?"

* * *

I followed the green girl in to the desk of the Program Planner, a girl who was a deep blue in the same way that the first girl was green. I outlined what I wanted in a reedy, anticipating voice and was taken to a private room.

I locked the door behind me. A plaque on the door was dated and sealed with the City stamp.

GUARANTEE OF PRIVACY

> This room has been inspected and sealed against scanners, microphones, and other devices permitting the observation or recording of actions within it, in accordance with the provisions of the Privacy Act.

That was all very fine, but I wouldn't put enough faith in it to trust my life to it. I relaxed in a soft, heavy lounge facing the one-way wall. The show was already going on. I wasn't particularly interested in the fertility rites of the worshipers of Mahrud—not because they weren't intrinsically interesting, but because I had to do some thinking to save my own skin.

Senator Rowley, in order to keep his section under control, had coupled in his own robot's sensory organs with those of the city's Public Services Department and those of various business concerns, most of which were either owned outright or subsidized by the senator.

But something had happened to that computer; for some reason, its actions had become illogical and inefficient. When the patrol car had spotted me on the street, for instance, the sonobeam, which had penetrated the flesh of my arm and bounced off the tantalum plate back to the pickup, had relayed the modified vibrations back to the Central Files for identification. And the Files had obviously given back the wrong information.

What had gone wrong? Was the senator still alive, keeping his mouth shut and his eyes open? If so, what sort of orders was he giving to the robot? I didn't get many answers, and the ones I did get were mutually contradictory.

I was supposed to be back before dawn, but I could see now that I'd never make it. Here in Groverton, there weren't many connections with Public Services; the robot couldn't keep me under observation all the time. But the deeper into the city I penetrated, the more scanners there would be. I couldn't take a private car in, and I didn't dare take a flitter or a ground taxi. I'd be spotted in the subways as soon as I walked in. I was in a fix, and I'd have to think my way out.

I don't know whether it was the music or the soft lights or my lack of sleep or the simple fact that intense concentration is often autohypnotic. At any rate, I dozed off, and the next thing I remember is the girl bringing in the papers.

This gal was silver. I don't know how the cosmeticians had done it, but looking into her eyes was like looking into a mirror; the irises were a glittering silver halo surrounding the dark pupil. Her hair was the same way; not white, but silver.

"Good morning, Grandfather," she said softly. "Here are the newspapers you asked for."

I was thankful for that "Grandfather"; it reminded me that I was an old man before I had a chance to say anything.

"Thank you, my dear, thank you. Just put them here."

"Your coffee will be in in a moment." She moved out as quietly as she had come in.

Something was gnawing at the back of my brain; something like a dream you know you've had but forgotten completely. I concentrated on it a moment, trying to bring it out into the open, but it wouldn't come, so I gave it up and turned to the paper, still warm from the reproducer.

It was splattered all over the front page.

MYSTERIOUS TROUBLE AT THE LODGE

Police Unable to Enter

The Police Department announced this morning that they have been unable, thus far, to pass the defenses of

the Lodge after receiving a call last night that Senator
Rowley had been shot by his secretary, Mr. Edgar Gifford.

Repeated attempts to contact the senator have resulted
in failure, says a Department spokesman.

Thus far, three police flitters under robot control have
been shot down in attempting to land at the Lodge, and
one ground car has been blown up. Another ground car,
the first to respond to the automatic call for help, was
stolen by the fleeing Gifford after killing the four officers
in the car. The stolen vehicle was recovered early this
morning several hundred miles from here, having been
reported by a Mr.——

It went on with the usual statement that the police expected
to apprehend the murderous Mr. Gifford at any moment.

Another small item in the lower left-hand corner registered
the fact that two men had been accidentally caught by a street
cleaner and had proceeded to damage it. One of the men was
killed by the damaged machine, but the other managed to
escape. The dead man was a charity case, named Brodwick,
and his associates were being checked.

So much for that. But the piece that really interested me
was the one that said:

SENATOR LUTHER GRENDON OFFERS AID

"Federal Government Should Keep Hands Off," says
Grendon.

Eastern Sector Senator Grendon said early this morning that he would do all in his power to aid Northwestern
Sector in "apprehending the murderer of my colleague
and bring to justice the organization behind him."

"There is," he said, "no need to call in the Federal
Government at this time. The citizens of an independent
sector are quite capable of dealing with crime within their
own boundaries."

Interviewed later, Senator Quintell of Southwestern
Sector agreed that there was no need to call in the FBI or
"any other Federal Agency."

The other senators were coming in for the kill, even before it was definitely established that the senator was dead.

Well, that was that. I decided I'd better get going. It would be better to travel during the daytime: it's hard for a beam to be focused on an individual citizen in a crowd.

While the other Immortals were foreclosing on Senator Rowley's private property, there might be time for me to get back safely.

The silver girl was waiting for me as I stepped out the door to the private room.

"This way, Grandfather," she said, the ever-present smile on her glittering lips. She started down the corridor.

"This isn't the way out," I said, frowning.

She paused, still smiling. "No, sir, it isn't the way you came in, but, you see, our number has come up. The Medical Board has sent down a checker."

That almost floored me. Somehow, the Lodge had known where I was and had instituted a check against this particular house. That meant that every door was sealed except the one where the robot Medical checker was waiting.

The perfect trap. The checker was armed and armored, naturally; there were often people who did not want to be detained at the hospital—and at their own expense, if they were free citizens.

I walked slowly, as an old man should, stalling for time. The only armament a checker had was a stun gun; that was a point in my favor. But I needed more information.

"My goodness," I said, "you should have called me earlier, my dear, as soon as the checker came."

"It's only been here fifteen minutes, Grandfather," the silver girl answered.

Then there were still plenty of customers in the building!

The girl was just ahead of me in the corridor. I beamed her down with the stun gun and caught her before she hit the floor. I carried her back into the private room I had just left and laid her on the couch.

Then I started pulling down draperies. They were all heavy

synthetic stuff that wouldn't burn unless they were really hot.
I got a good armful, went back into the corridor, and headed
for the opposite end of the building. Nobody bothered me on
the way; everybody was still occupied.

At the end of the hall, I piled the stuff on the floor beneath
some other hangings. Then I took two of the power cartridges
from the stun gun and pried them open. The powder inside
ought to burn nicely. It wouldn't explode unless it was sealed
inside the gun, where the explosion was channeled through
the supersonic whistle in the barrel to form the beam.

I took out my lighter and applied the flame to a sheet of the
newspaper I had brought along, then I laid the paper on top of
the opened cartridges. I got well back and waited.

I didn't take more than a second or two to ignite the
powder. It hissed and went up in a wave of white heat. The
plastic curtains started to smolder. Within less than a minute,
the hallway was full of thick, acrid smoke.

I knew the building wouldn't burn, but I was hoping none
of the other customers was as positive as I.

I yelled "Fire!" at the top of my lungs, then headed for the
stairway and ran to the bottom. I waited just inside the street
door for action.

Outside, I could hear the soft humming of a guard robot,
stationed there by the checker to make sure no one left
through that door.

The smoldering of the curtains put out plenty of smoke
before they got hot enough to turn in the fire alarm and bring
out the fire-fighter robots stationed in the walls. The little
terrier-sized mechanisms scurried all over the place, looking
for heat sources to squirt at. Upstairs, a heavy CO_2 blanket
began to drift down.

I wasn't worried about the fire robots; they didn't have the
sensory apparatus to spot me. All they could find was fire.
They would find it and smother it, but the place was already full
of smoke, which was all I wanted.

It was the smoke that did the job, really. People don't like
to stay in buildings that appear to be burning down, no matter
how safe they think they are. Customers came pouring down

the stairway and out the door like angry wasps out of a disturbed hive. I went with them.

I knew that a fire signal would change the checker's orders. It couldn't keep people inside a burning building. Unfortunately, I hadn't realized to what extent the Lodge would go to get me, or to what extent it was capable of countermanding normal orders.

The guard robot at the door started beaming down everybody as they came out, firing as fast as it could scan and direct. It couldn't distinguish me from the others, of course; not in that mob. But it was hitting everything that moved with its stun beam. Luckily, it couldn't scan and direct fast enough to get everybody; there were too many. I watched and waited for a second or two until the turret was facing away from the corner, then I ran like the very devil, dodging as I ran.

A stun beam hit the fingers of my left hand, and my arm went dead to the elbow. The guard robot had spotted me! I made it around the corner and ducked into a crowd of people who were idly watching the smoke billowing from the upper windows.

I kept moving through the crowd, trying to put as much distance between myself and the checker's guards as possible. The guard evidently hadn't recognized me, personally, as Gifford, because it realized the futility of trying to cut down everyone in Groverton to find me and gave up on the crowd outside. But it kept hitting the ones who came out the door.

I got away fast. The thing really had me worried. I had no desire whatever to get myself mixed up with a nutty robot, but, seemingly, there was no way to avoid it.

I circled around and went down to Corliss Avenue, parallel to Bradley, for about seven blocks before I finally walked back over to Bradley again. Two or three times, police cars came by, but either they didn't test me with their beams or the answers they got weren't incriminating.

I was less than a block from the city limits when something hard and hot and tingling burned through my nerves like acid and I blacked out.

Maybe you've never been hit by a stun beam, but if you've ever had your leg go to sleep, you know what it feels like. And you know what it feels like when you wake up; that painful tingling all over that hurts even worse if you try to move.

I knew better than to try to move. I just lay still, waiting for the terrible tingling to subside. I had been out, I knew, a little less than an hour. I knew, because I'd been hit by stunners before, and I know how long it takes my body to throw off the paralysis.

Somebody's voice said, "He'll be coming out of it anytime now. Shake him and see."

A hand shook me, and I gasped. I couldn't help it; with my nerves still raw from the stunner, it hurt to be shaken that way.

"Sorry, Gifford," said another voice, different from the first. "Just wanted to see. Wanted to see if you were with us."

"Leave him alone a few minutes," the first voice said. "That hurts. It'll wear off quickly."

It was wearing off already. I opened my eyes and tried to see what was going on. At first, the visual pattern was a blithering swirl of meaningless shapes and crackling colors, but it finally settled down to a normal ceiling with a normal light panel in it. I managed to turn my head, in spite of the nerve-shocks, and saw two men sitting in chairs beside the bed.

One of them was short, round, and blond, with a full set of mutton chops, a heavy mustache, and a clean-shaven, firm chin. The other man was taller, muscular, with a full Imperial and smooth cheeks.

The one with the Imperial said, "Sorry we had to shoot you down that way, Gifford. But we didn't want to attract too much attention that close to the city limits."

They weren't cops, then. Of that much I could be certain. At least they weren't the police of this sector. So they were working for one of the other Immortals.

"Whose little boys are you?" I asked, trying to grin.

Evidently I did grin, because they grinned back. "Funny," said the one with the mutton chops, "but that's exactly what we were going to ask you."

I turned my head back again and stared at the ceiling. "I'm an orphan," I said.

The guy with the mutton chops chuckled. "Well," he grinned at the other man, "what do you think of that, Colonel?"

The colonel (*Of what?* I wondered) frowned, pulling heavy brows deep over his gray eyes. His voice came from deep in his chest and seemed to be muffled by the heavy beard.

"We'll level with you, Gifford. Mainly because we aren't sure. Mainly because of that. We aren't sure even you know the truth. So we'll level."

"Your blast," I said.

"O.K., here's how it looks from our side of the fence. It looks like this. You killed Rowley. After fifteen years of faithful service, you killed him. Now we know—even if you don't—that Rowley had you psychoimpressed every six months for fifteen years. Or at least he thought he did."

"He *thought* he did?" I asked, just to show I was interested.

"Well, yes. He couldn't have, really, you see. He couldn't have. Or at least not lately. A psychoimpressed person can't do things like that. Also, we know that nobody broke it, because it takes six weeks of steady, hard therapy to pull a man out of it. And a man's no good after that for a couple more weeks. You weren't out of Rowley's sight for more than four days." He shrugged. "You see?"

"I see," I said. The guy was a little irritating in his manner. I didn't like the choppy way he talked.

"For a while," he said, "we thought it might be an impersonation. But we checked your plate"—he gestured at my arm—"and it's O.K. The genuine article. So it's Gifford's plate, all right. And we know it couldn't have been taken out of Gifford's arm and transferred to another arm in four days.

"If there were any way to check fingerprints and eye patterns, we might be able to be absolutely sure, but the

Privacy Act forbids that, so we have to go on what evidence we have in our possession now.

"Anyway, we're convinced that you are Gifford. So that means somebody has been tampering with your mind. We want to know who it is. Do you know?"

"No," I said, quite honestly.

"You didn't do it yourself, did you?"

"No."

"Somebody's behind you?"

"Yes."

"Do you know who?"

"No. And hold those questions a minute. You said you'd level with me. Who are *you* working for?"

The two of them looked at each other for a second, then the colonel said: "Senator Quintell."

I propped myself up on one elbow and held out the other hand, fingers extended. "All right, figure for yourself. Rowley's out of the picture; that eliminates him." I pulled my thumb in. "You work for Quintell; that eliminates him." I dropped my little finger and held it with my thumb. "That leaves three Immortals. Grendon, Lasser, and Waterford. Lasser has the Western Sector; Waterford, the Southern. Neither borders on Northwestern, so that eliminates them. Not definitely, but probably. They wouldn't be tempted to get rid of Rowley as much as they would Quintell.

"So that leaves Grendon. And if you read the papers, you'll know that he's pushing in already."

They looked at each other again. I knew they weren't necessarily working for Quintell; I was pretty sure it was Grendon. On the other hand, they might have told the truth so that I'd be sure to think it *was* Grendon. I didn't know how deep their subtlety went, and I didn't care. It didn't matter to me who they were working for.

"That sounds logical," said the colonel. "Very logical."

"But we have to know," added Mutton Chops. "We were fairly sure you'd head back toward the city; that's why we set up guards at the various street entrances. Since that part of our prediction worked out, we want to see if the rest of it will.''

"The rest of it?''

"Yeah. You're expendable. We know that. The organization that sent you doesn't care what happens to you now, otherwise they wouldn't have let you loose like that. They don't care what happens to Eddie Gifford.

"So they must have known you'd get caught. Therefore, they've got you hypnoed to a fare-thee-well. And we probably won't find anything under the hypno, either. But we've got to look; there may be some little thing you'll remember. Some little thing that will give us the key to the whole organization.''

I nodded. That was logical, very logical, as the colonel had said. They were going to break me. They could have done it gently, removed every bit of blocking and covering that the hypnoes had put in without hurting me a bit. But that would take time; I knew better than to think they were going to be gentle. They were going to peel my mind like a banana and then slice it up and look at it.

And if they were working for any of the Immortals, I had no doubt that they could do what they were planning. It took equipment, and it took an expert psychometrician, and a couple of good therapists—but that was no job at all if you had money.

The only trouble was that I had a few little hidden tricks that they'd never get around. If they started fiddling too much with my mind, a nice little psychosomatic heart condition would suddenly manifest itself. I'd be dead before they could do anything about it. Oh, I was expendable, all right.

"Do you want to say anything before we start?'' the colonel asked.

"No.'' I didn't see any reason for giving them information they didn't earn.

"O.K.'' He stood up, and so did the mutton-chopper. "I'm sorry we have to do this, Gifford. It'll be hard on you, but you'll be in good condition inside of six or eight months. So long.''

They walked out and carefully locked the door behind them.

I sat up for the first time and looked around. I didn't know where I was; in an hour, I could have been taken a long ways away from the city.

I hadn't been, though. The engraving on the bed said:

DELLFIELD SANATORIUM

I was on Riverside Drive, less than eight blocks from the rendezvous spot.

I walked over to the window and looked out. I could see the roof of the tenth level about eight floors beneath me. The window itself was a heavy sheet of transite welded into the wall. There was a polarizer control to the left to shut out the light, but there was no way to open the window. The door was sealed, too. When a patient got violent, they could pump gas in through the ventilators without getting it into the corridor.

They'd taken all my armament away, and, incidentally, washed off the thin plastic film on my hands and face. I didn't look so old any more. I walked over to the mirror in the wall, another sheet of transite with a reflecting back, and looked at myself. I was a sad-looking sight. The white hair was all scraggly, the whiskers were ditto, and my face looked worried. Small wonder.

I sat back down on the bed and started to think.

It must have been a good two hours later when the therapist came in. She entered by herself, but I noticed that the colonel was standing outside the door.

She was in her mid-thirties, a calm-faced, determined-looking woman. She started off with the usual questions.

"You have been told you are under some form of hypnotic compulsion. Do you consciously believe this?"

I told her I did. There was no sense in resisting.

"Do you have any conscious memory of the process?"

"No."

"Do you have any conscious knowledge of the identity of the therapist?"

I didn't and told her so. She asked a dozen other questions, all standard build-up. When she was through, I tried to ask her a couple of questions, but she cut me off and walked out of the room before I could more than open my yap.

The whole sanatorium was, and probably had been for a long time, in the pay of Quintell or Grendon—or, possibly, one of the other Immortals. It had been here for years, a neat little spy setup nestled deep in the heart of Rowley's territory.

Leaving the hospital without outside help was strictly out. I'd seen the inside of these places before, and I had a healthy respect for their impregnability. An unarmed man was in to stay.

Still, I decided that since something *had* to be done, something *would* be done.

My major worry was the question of whether or not the room was monitored. There was a single scanner pickup in the ceiling with a fairly narrow angle lens in it. That was interesting. It was enclosed in an unbreakable transite hemisphere and was geared to look around the room for the patient. But it was *not* robot controlled. There was evidently a nurse or therapist at the other end who checked on the patients every so often.

But how often?

From the window I could see the big, old-fashioned twelve-hour clock on the Barton Building. I used that to time the monitoring. The scanner was aimed at the bed. That meant it had looked at me last when I was on the bed. I walked over to the other side of the room and watched the scanner without looking at it directly.

It was nearly three quarters of an hour later that the little eye swiveled around the room and came to a halt on me. I ignored it for about thirty seconds, then walked deliberately across the room. The eye didn't follow.

Fine. This was an old-fashioned hospital; I had known that much. Evidently there hadn't been any new equipment installed in thirty years. Whoever operated the scanner simply looked around to see what the patient was doing and then went on to the next one. Hi ho.

I watched the scanner for the rest of the afternoon, timing it. Every hour at about four minutes after the hour. It was nice to know.

They brought me my dinner at 1830. I watched the scanner, but there was no special activity before they opened the door.

They simply swung the door outward; one man stood with a stun gun, ready for any funny business, while another brought in the food.

At 2130, the lights went out, except for a small lamp over the bed. That was fine; it meant that the scanner probably wasn't equipped for infrared. If I stayed in bed like a good boy, that one small light was all they'd need. If not, they turned on the main lights again.

I didn't assume that the watching would be regular, every hour, as it had been during the day. Plots are usually hatched at night, so it's best to keep a closer watch then. Their only mistake was that they were going to watch *me*. And that was perfectly O.K. as far as I was concerned.

I lay in bed until 2204. Sure enough, the scanner turned around and looked at me. I waited a couple of minutes and then got up as though to get a drink at the wash basin. The scanner didn't follow, so I went to work.

I pulled a light blanket off my bed and stuffed a corner of it into the basin's drain, letting the rest of it trail to the floor. Then I turned the water on and went back to bed.

It didn't take long for the basin to fill and overflow. It climbed over the edge and ran silently down the blanket to the floor.

Filling the room would take hours, but I didn't dare go to sleep. I'd have to wake up before dawn, and I wasn't sure I could do that. It was even harder to lay quietly and pretend I was asleep, but I fought it by counting fifty and then turning over violently to wake myself again. If anyone was watching, they would simply think I was restless.

I needn't have bothered. I dropped off—sound asleep. The next thing I knew, I was gagging. I almost drowned; the water had come up to bed level and had flowed into my mouth. I shot up in bed, coughing and spitting.

Fully awake, I moved fast. I pulled off the other blanket and tied it around the pickup in the ceiling. Then I got off the bed and waded in waist-deep water to the door. I grabbed a good hold on the metal dresser and waited.

It must have been all of half an hour before the lights came on. A voice came from the speaker: "Have you tampered with the TV pickup?"

"Huh? Wuzzat?" I said, trying to sound sleepy. "No. I haven't done anything."

"We are coming in. Stand back from the door or you will be shot."

I had no intention of being that close to the door.

When the attendant opened the door, it slammed him in the face as a good many tons of water cascaded onto him. There were two armed men with him, but they both went down in the flood, coughing and gurgling.

Judging very carefully, I let go the dresser and let the swirling water carry me into the hall. I had been prepared and I knew what I was doing; the guards didn't. By turning a little, I managed to hit one of them who was trying to get up and get his stunner into action. He went over, and I got the stunner.

It only lasted a few seconds. The water had been deep in the confines of the little room, but when allowed to expand into the hall, it merely made the floor wet.

I dispatched the guards with the stunner and ran for the nurse's desk, which, I knew, was just around the corner, near the elevators. I aimed quickly and let the nurse have it; he fell over, and I was at the desk before he had finished collapsing.

I grabbed the phone. There wouldn't be much time now.

I dialed. I said: "This is Gifford. I'm in Dellfield Sanatorium, Room 1808."

That was all I needed. I tossed the stunner into the water

that trickled slowly toward the elevators and walked back
toward my room with my hands up.

I'll say this for the staff at Dellfield; they don't get sore
when a patient tries to escape. When five more guards came
down the hall, they saw my raised hands and simply herded
me into the room. Then they watched me until the colonel
came.

"Well," he said, looking things over.

"Well. Neat. Very neat. Have to remember that one.
Didn't do much good, though. Did it? Got out of the room,
couldn't get downstairs. Elevators don't come up."

I shrugged. "Can't blame me for trying."

The colonel grinned for the first time. "I don't. Hate a
man who'd give up—at any time." He lit a cigarette, his gun
still not wavering. "Call didn't do you any good, either. This
is a hospital. Patients have reached phones before. Robot
identifies patient, refuses to relay call. Tough."

I didn't say anything or look anything; no use letting him
think he had touched me.

The colonel shrugged. "All right. Strap him."

The attendants were efficient about it. They changed the
wet bedclothes and strapped me in. I couldn't move my head
far enough to see my hands.

The colonel looked me over and nodded. "You may get
out of this. O.K. by me if you try. Next time, though, we'll
give you a spinal freeze."

He left and the door clicked shut.

Well, I'd had my fun; it was out of my hands now. I
decided I might as well get some sleep.

I didn't hear any commotion, of course; the room was
soundproof. The next thing I knew, there was a Decon robot
standing in the open door. It rolled over to the bed.

"Can you get up?"

These Decontamination robots aren't stupid, by any means.

"No," I said. "Cut these straps."

A big pair of nippers came out and began scissoring through
the plastic webbing with ease. When the job was through, the
Decon opened up the safety chamber in its body.

"Get in."

I didn't argue; the Decon had a stun gun pointed at me.

That was the last I saw of Dellfield Sanatorium, but I had a pretty good idea of what had happened. The Decontamination Squad is called in when something goes wrong with an atomic generator. The Lodge had simply turned in a phony report that there was generator trouble at Dellfield. Nothing to it.

I had seen Decons go to work before; they're smart, efficient, and quick. Each one has a small chamber inside it, radiation shielded to carry humans out of contaminated areas. They're small and crowded, but I didn't mind. It was better than conking out from a psychosomatic heart ailment when the therapists started to fiddle with me.

I smelled something sweetish then, and I realized I was getting a dose of gas. I went by-by.

When I woke up again, I was sick. I'd been hit with a stun beam yesterday and gassed today. I felt as though I was wasting all my life sleeping. I could still smell the gas.

No. It wasn't gas. The odor was definitely different. I turned my head and looked around. I was in the lounge of Senator Anthony Rowley's Lodge. On the floor. And next to me was Senator Anthony Rowley.

I crawled away from him, and then I was *really* sick.

I managed to get to the bathroom. It was a good twenty minutes before I worked up nerve enough to come out again. Rowley had moved, all right. He had pulled himself all of six feet from the spot where I had shot him.

My hunch had been right.

The senator's dead hand was still holding down the programming button on the control panel he had dragged himself to. The robot had gone on protecting the senator because it thought—as it was supposed to—that the senator was still alive as long as he was holding the ORDERS circuit open.

I leaned over and spoke into the microphone. "I will take a flitter from the roof. I want guidance and protection from here to the city. There, I will take over manual control. When I do, you will immediately pull all dampers on your generator.

"Recheck."

The robot dutifully repeated the orders.

After that, everything was simple. I took the flitter to the rendezvous spot, was picked up, and, twenty minutes after I left the Lodge, I was in the Director's office.

He kicked in the hypnoes, and when I came out of it, my arm was strapped down while a surgeon took out the Gifford ID plate.

The Director of the FBI looked at me, grinning. "You took your time, son."

"What's the news?"

His grin widened. "You played hob with everything. The Lodge held off all investigation forces for thirty-odd hours after reporting Rowley's death. The Sector Police couldn't come anywhere near it.

"Meanwhile, funny things have happened. Robot in Groverton kills a man. Medic guard shoots down eighteen men coming out of a burning house. Decon Squad invades Dellfield when there's nothing wrong with the generator.

"Now all hell has busted loose. The Lodge went up in a flare of radiation an hour ago, and since then all robot services in the city have gone phooey. It looks to the citizens as though the senator had an illegal hand in too many pies. They're suspicious.

"Good work, boy."

"Thanks," I said, trying to keep from looking at my arm, where the doctor was peeling back flesh.

The Director lifted a white eyebrow. "Something?"

I looked at the wall. "I'm just burned up, that's all. Not at you; at the whole mess. How did a nasty slug like Rowley get elected in the first place? And what right did he have to stay in such an important job?"

"I know," the Director said somberly. "And that's our job. Immortality is something the human race isn't ready for yet. The masses can't handle it, and the individual can't handle it. And, since we can't get rid of them legally, we have to do it this way. Assassination. But it can't be done overnight.''

"*You've* handled immortality," I pointed out.

"Have I?" he asked softly. "No. No, son. I haven't; I'm using it the same way they are. For power. The Federal government doesn't have any power any more. I have it.

"I'm using it in a different way, granted. Once there were over a hundred Immortals. Last week there were six. Today there are five. One by one, over the years, we have picked them off, and they are never replaced. The rest simply gobble up the territory and the power and split it between them rather than let a newcomer get into their tight little circle.

"But I'm just as dictatorial in my way as they are in theirs. And when the status quo is broken, and civilization begins to go ahead again, I'll have to die with the rest of them.

"But never mind that. What about you? I got most of the story from you under the hypno. That was a beautiful piece of deduction."

I took the cigarette he offered me and took a deep lungful of smoke. "How else could it be? The robot was trying to capture me. But also it was trying to keep anyone else from killing me. As a matter of fact, it passed up several chances to get me in order to keep others from killing me.

"It had to be the senator's last order. The old boy had lived so long that he still wasn't convinced he was dying. So he gave one last order to the robot:

" '*Get Gifford back here—ALIVE!*'

"And then there was the queer fact that the robot never reported that the senator was dead, but kept right on defending the Lodge as though he were alive. That could only mean that the ORDERS circuits were still open. As long as they were, the robot thought the senator was still alive.

"So the only way I could get out of the mess was to let the Lodge take me. I knew the phone at Dellfield would connect me with the Lodge—at least indirectly. I called it and waited.

"Then, when I started giving orders, the Lodge accepted me as the senator. That was all there was to it."

The Director nodded. "A good job, son. A good job."

THE LYSENKO MAZE

BY DAVID GRINNELL
(DONALD A. WOLLHEIM 1914–   )

THE MAGAZINE OF FANTASY AND SCIENCE FICTION,
JULY

"David Grinnell" was the primary pseudonym employed by our own Donald A. Wollheim over a considerable period of years centering on the 1950's. I'll never forget his "The Rag Thing" from an issue of F & SF in 1951, which is surely one of the most frightening stories ever written.

Whenever you reprint your publisher you worry about being perceived as self-serving—with that in mind I'll just say that this Grinnell fellow was a hell of a writer, and may still be, for all I know. (MHG)

You've got to believe this—I didn't know David Grinnell's real identity till Marty told me, and it came about this way.

I had received a group of stories from Marty Greenberg that he recommended for inclusion in this book, and I read each one of them carefully, making notes, then called him up so that we might discuss them.

In the course of the discussion, I said, "But my favorite story in the group was Grinnell's 'Lysenko Maze.' " And Marty said, "Do you know that Grinnell is a pseudonym of Don Wollheim?" And that's how I found out.

Don had a bad year in 1985, but he made a spectacular recovery against what seemed all the odds, and on March 25,

1986, there he was, at a function I was attending, a little too thin, but quite clearly full of life. I was delighted. (IA)

> *By mastering these means, man can create forms that*
> *did not and could not appear*
> *in nature even in millions of years.*
>
> TROFIM DENISOVICH LYSENKO

Professor Borisov had succeeded in shocking his audience. He had had their sympathy for a long time—several months, in fact. Months in which he had slipped across the frontier in Finland, in the dead of winter, months in which he had hidden aboard a Finnish fishing vessel and made his way to Sweden. Months in which he had lived from hand to mouth, a refugee from a political tyranny he despised, without means, until his scientific friends in America had been able to obtain the necessary papers and this most valued post at this cornbelt university's experimental laboratories.

And now this!

The professor waved his hands wildly, a little upset at disturbing his new-found friends. "But of course I am not a Communist—do I have to tell you this again? Do I have to show you what I have gone through? Am I not the same man I was an hour ago, yesterday, last month? A good biologist, a good believer in democracy, in freedom of speech and conscience? *Da!* I am all that—and yet I tell you again, Lysenko is right!"

Melvin Raine shook his head. It had been his responsibility, this invitation to the refugee Russian. It would be on his head if it was now shown that they were harboring a hypocrite. Yet—what Borisov had said was so. There was little doubt of the man's honesty, of his innate personal refusal to compromise with anything he believed false. So what were they now to make of this Lysenko business? Why, how could any self-respecting scientist place credence in that charlatan—in a man of "science" who had to be bolstered up by the dictates of a Politburo of police-state bureaucrats?

Raine voiced his thoughts. "And still you persist in this

strange thing. You betray our intelligence with this belief in
Lysenko's outmoded notions. It is sheer Lamarckism—the
inheritance of acquired characteristics, disproved for a hundred years in a thousand laboratories.''

"Ah, no, no.'' The little Russian was very upset, but very
positive. "It is you who do not understand. I do not approve
of Lysenko's politics: he is a Communist, a Stalinist fanatic. I
am a freeman, a democrat. And yet, I tell you, on this one
thing he could be right and still wrong on a thousand others.
And I tell you also that this one thing I have seen proved in
Russia . . . proved to me, to my satisfaction.''

The men gathered in Raine's rooms were silent. They were
members of the faculty, biologists, teachers of animal hus-
bandry, botanists, men of integrity and learning. It was clear
that Borisov did not have the sympathy of a man there.

"Let me ask you,'' spoke one finally. "Do you think it
was right, let us say, for science, for such a man as Galileo to
be harassed for his opinions by the inquisitorial court?''

"Ah, yes,'' shouted Borisov, "it was wrong of the court—
for in that one thing Galileo was right. But I am glad you
mentioned him. Very glad. For let me ask you this: Galileo
was right in believing his astronomical discoveries and for
saying that the earth did move. But how many other things
that Galileo personally believed were wrong? Did he not
share the ignorance and bias of his time in everything else?
Did he not believe in the divine right of kings, in slavery, in
the permanent servility of serfs and women, in a hundred, a
thousand other such out-moded evils, falsehoods? Would he
not be, by our standards, a hopeless bigot, a reactionary?

"So . . . but in that one thing Galileo was right. So . . . in
this one thing Lysenko is right. He shares the foolishness of
the state around him, but unlike the case of Galileo the fickle
state chooses to uphold this one discovery and suppress his
opponents. Perhaps someday Trofim Denisovich may lose his
political skill, and it will be his opponents who dictate the
Marxist 'truth' concerning genetics. All this is a mere accident of politics. What has it to do with whether his discovery
be true or false?''

Raine leaned forward. He looked at the man, studied him. Borisov's blue eyes were plainly distressed, his face was lined and working. His prematurely gray hair was awry. Yes, the American decided, this man was on the level. Borisov meant what he said, and because he was implicitly honest, he had said it.

"If," and Raine weighed his words carefully, "you have seen proof that Lysenko's theories of evolution and the heredity of acquired characteristics do work, would you be willing to conduct an experiment *here*—under *our* conditions—to prove it again?"

Borisov frowned, ran a hand through his hair. "Yes."

"Then suppose we meet tomorrow and work out the details of this experiment to our mutual satisfaction?"

"Why wait until tomorrow? Let us decide right here upon this experiment. After all, in dealing with generations we may have to need several years for this. . . . Have you any suggestions?"

One of the biology men spoke up, a sly smile on his lips. "What would you say to repeating Weismann's experiment with mice? Shall we breed a race of tailless mice?"

Borisov turned, shook a finger. "Now that is exactly what I mean when I say you do not know what Lysenko is doing. Weismann tried to disprove Lamarck by cutting off the tails of twenty-two generations of mice. And the last generation was born with just the same long tails as the first! Aha, you all say, this proves that you cannot inherit acquired changes! And then you all will get busy saying that Chinese women bound their feet for thousands of years and still were born with normal feet! Aha, you then add, this double proves it! And all that it proves is nothing! Nothing at all, except that nature sneers at foolishness."

He stopped, gathered his breath. "Let me explain and please listen. The mice did not lose their tails because there was no practical reason for them to lose their tails, there was no need for taillessness, there was no environmental necessity for it, it was pointless, senseless, useless. So the mouse breed simply ignored Weismann's scalpel. The Chinese women

were helpless with their feet bound. Their organism rejected
that foolishness. Even if an artificial society wanted it, the
body knew better.

"Now please understand this. A body, a plant, an animal
will pass on an acquired characteristic only when that new
characteristic has been acquired by the individual in answer to
an *urgent need* of the system to maintain itself. A seed that
falls in a strange climate either adapts itself to that climate or
it dies. If it adapts itself, it passes on its adaptation to its
descendants, or they die. Burbank knew this. Plant growers
know this. Only foolish college biologists do not know this."

"How about mutations?" said Raine. "You know that the
means for the creation of new species has been shown to be
by the mutation of the germ cell, by alteration of the chromosomes. In the course of survival, only those mutant individuals who have a beneficial quality from this genetic accident
will live."

"This is not so. Consider the cavern fish," said Borisov.
"This is a thing you Americans discovered. But you ignore it
in your fine theories. These fish, found in lightless caverns,
have no eyes. But you take them out and breed them in
lighted waters, and, presto, in a few generations the eyes are
back. Why? Obviously these fish originally became trapped
in these caverns. In lightlessness, their eyes were useless—
worse, being sensitive, they were a handicap, a menace to
their life. Hence they retracted, generation by generation,
atrophied, until they were born in that atrophied submerged
condition. But back in the light, the need for eyes reasserted
itself, and the eyes returned in a few generations. This is not
mutation, no."

He paused, held up a hand. "Now in this experiment, you
must forget these tailless mice. If you use mice, you must
create a condition which will make them change to survive;
which will make them force the acquisition of some quality
their young will need to have also. You will see. So I suggest
this: why not intelligence? We will force the mice to use their
brains. We will breed thinking mice, because maybe that will
be the easiest experiment for us."

Raine nodded. "I do not believe it will work. But that will be an acceptable basis."

Raine and Borisov and several others worked out the details of the experiment, and within a month the scene was set.

The men who had met that original night gathered at an old farmhouse several miles from the town. The farm and its dilapidated house had been acquired years ago by the college, which had thus far failed to make use of it. Raine and Borisov showed the men in. The interior of the house had been torn out, until the building was like a huge barn, only a hollow shell. It was hard to describe its present contents, save that it looked like nothing so much as a giant abdomen, tightly packed with crisscrossed and interlaced intestines made of tubes ranging from three to ten inches in diameter, some transparent, some translucent, some black plastic. The interior of the house, save for a few corners, a few observation posts set on platforms here and there, was a closed and vastly complex structure of these tubes. The men stared in amazement.

Borisov explained. "We intend to breed mice to have cunning and quickness of thought. This also is an inherited characteristic. We will breed a race of mice that can make deductions, put two and two together, estimate for tomorrow.

"You see, here is Lysenko's law as he condenses it." He took out a little gray-covered pamphlet, found a place, and translated: " *'The alteration of requirements, that is of the heredity of a living body, always reflects the specific effects of conditions of the external environment, provided that they are assimilated by it.'*

"Now, we have created an external environment for these mice. It is this maze, closed from the outside world in every way, and the mice will live and breed entirely within it. We have created, in accord with Lysenko's theory, conditions within this maze which will force the change in the species of mice for the creation of intelligence. That is this. This maze of pipes, which is their home, is basically not too different from the dark holes and cracks they would inhabit in houses. This maze of pipes is full of tricks. It is movable. It will shift its tubes, change connections, in accord with a mathematical rhythm. Systematically, in increasingly complex cycles, the various entry places for food will shift. Day by day they will change, but they will repeat in cycles which the mouse should be able to determine, at first, without too much delay.

"At first the mice will become confused, for to obtain water they must come to one place, salt another, meat a third, fruit a fourth, and so on. And within the lifetime of each mouse they will see the regular alternation of these places. They will have to learn to determine the next day's alternation in advance, for there will never be enough food for all. As this goes on, as future generations come into existence, the pattern will become more complex, new problems will be added, dangers will be placed into the tubes. These mice will have to force themselves to acquire greater and greater skill at solving problems, or die out."

He paused for breath. The men looked at the bewildering maze of tubes, probably miles of it crowded into the space within the wooden farm walls. "There will be lighting cycles within the tubes. There will be heat and cold spells. Mostly there will not be enough heat, by the third or fourth generation surely. But they will have the raw means for making heat, if they can learn to use them. There are special phases through which their development must operate. Light, heat. We are going to give them more oxygen than in the normal atmosphere; this will assist them to think and move faster. Professor Raine has agreed to it. We are even going to feed them supplies of milk formula at first, which is chemically similar to human milk. Lysenko claims that the sap of a foster-parent plant can influence the heredity of a grafted twig from another species. This is permissible in the experiment."

They looked over the maze. Raine unrolled the plans for it, explained the various subtleties, showed them the machinery for operating it, the schedules of food and heat alternations, for creating "season" within the sealed mouse world.

"Professor Borisov and I have our distinct opinions on how this will end. I say that his twentieth generation of mice will be as ignorant as his first, that they will not pass on any basic cunning to their offspring. I say further that if anything strange should develop, I will prove that it is by mutation and that it will display the evidence of it on its own body.''

Borisov shrugged. "You will see. By the way, gentlemen, we are not using laboratory white mice here. We agree that their albinism and their artificial breeding does not correspond with nature's norm. We are starting this experiment with wild gray house mice, captured in the city itself. And—we begin the experiment now.''

He opened a valve in a large tube, took a box from which excited squeaks were coming, and lifted a shutter at the box's side, which he had pressed against the tube's opening. There was a scurrying of little feet as the mice rushed through. Another box was lifted. "The females, now,'' and another scurrying of feet.

"And now we shall see.''

A half year later, Borisov and Raine stood on the upper observation post near the roof of the old house, watching the movements of the little gray mice through the sides of a transparent wide tube. The entry point for fruit was at that spot that hour, and they had just placed the supply there. No mice were in sight when they had done so, but within three minutes, there was a flash of gray and a mouse was at the food, turning it over, nibbling. Then, in a few seconds, there were several mice, and shortly after, a crowd.

Raine snapped his watch shut. "About the same time as yesterday,'' he said. "Not bad. May have been luck.''

Borisov fingered his chin. "Or it may have been an old and experienced mouse simply on the prowl. But I think that first one had figured out where the entry would be.''

Raine leaned over, watching the stream of mice that was now coming and going. "The trouble is that several generations are alive at once. But it does seem true that the younger mice seem to be edging the older ones out.''

"But,'' said Borisov, "just to argue your point, this could be merely agility.''

He noted the time in a large notebook, one of the many

which had been used in the short time so far. There had been
a period within the first few weeks when the mice had had
very great difficulty in finding the food in time. Many of the
original ones had certainly died in that time, starved, or eaten
by their hungry fellows. But definitely they had overcome
this original handicap. Of that there could be no doubt. But
was this the development of intelligence or was it merely a
system of having sentinels dispersed widely at all possible
points? This angle had not occurred to them before.

However, the next steps were already planned. This was a
system of new barriers. When the next food entry points
came around in the complex schedule, there would be additional problems to be solved. But the question was still
whether this was merely a system of food scouts set up by the
older generations and picked up by example by the new ones.
It was hard to tell. . . .

In the next year, Borisov and Raine became more and more
baffled. The mice seemed to have established a fairly standard time for the discovery of the rhythmically changing food
spots. It took usually about two and a half minutes for
discovery and rarely varied. The total number of mice did not
seem to be increasing, but was apparently stationary. There
was no longer any pratical way of determining how many
mice were in the entire maze, but they knew that only a
certain limit could be supported.

However, what they could see of the mice did not seem to
indicate any noticeable physical changes. They did not remove any of the little animals, for the test demanded that the
mouse maze be sealed and stay that way.

It was about two and a quarter years later, about the time
that a twentieth generation might have been in the tubes, that
Raine first spotted the blue mouse. It had originally made its
appearance at one of the food entries among the first five to
find it. By that time the mathematical shifting of the ports had
assumed a complexity that would have confused humans and
would have required a whole month's records to determine its
next shifts. Yet the mice kept on spotting the shifts in time.

Raine pointed out the blue mouse to the Russian. They were again on the upper observation platform. This mouse was actually slightly larger, possibly longer, and his fur was quite definitely more bluish than gray. The tail appeared to be shorter and in some ways he seemed faster.

"Look at that," whispered Raine. "Look at that! Could that be a result?"

Borisov pursed his lips. He had been getting a bit uneasy about the experiment. Even though they were trying for intelligence and not physical change, he had expected that some physical changes would occur as a corollary to the greater brain ability. Man knew too little of nature to predict all the factors that might accompany a change in the direction of a being's existence. Yet all he had seen had been little gray mice that never seemed any different to the eye. But this . . . well . . .

Raine went on, "That mouse has all the appearance of a mutant. An irrelevant color change, an unusual variation in size and length. If it is also intelligent, would it not prove my point and not yours?"

Borisov was shaken more than he would care to admit. "Still," he said, "there might be a factor within the tubes that we do not understand which called forth these changes. We should avoid conclusions until the experiment is over. Should we check the controls, the heat, the inside atmosphere?"

"Hardly necessary," said Raine. "They are checked automatically. The conditions are as they were set and haven't changed. The experiment is approaching its end soon, anyway. We shall soon see."

They watched for the blue mouse day after day and soon came to find it instantly, for it was always among the very first to reach a new food port. Undoubtedly, they realized, here was the first proof that it was not a simple question of mass scouting; for here was an individual who always knew in advance. This one blue mouse must have been able to figure out the now complex mathematical formula for rotation—a pattern which by now would have caused most humans very considerable trouble. Borisov, though, did point out the possibility that there were really many blue mice, a whole generation of them, as the final product of the experiment. But in that case, why was it they never saw more than one of the creatures?

The mouse apparently saw them. For unlike its gray fellows it did not busy itself about the food, carrying the food away into the dark recesses of the tubes. Instead the blue mouse had taken to looking outward, through the glass walls, at them. That was a sign of intelligence, unquestionably.

Now the two experimenters became excited. They speculated on this strange mouse, on what it was doing. For they both had come to regard it as the key to the whole experiment.

More and more the blue mouse seemed obsessed with watching them. Now they noticed once that it dragged something with it toward the transparent food port of that day. Something of straw and shreds. What it was for they could not surmise. Another time the mouse came with a bit of shiny stuff in its jaw. And once Borisov had seen the mouse watching him from a section of the tubes, where no food was expected, simply watching him because from there Borisov could be seen at his desk in a corner of the frame house where he kept the records.

When the trouble came, Raine and Borisov were standing near that desk checking the day's figures. It was night outside, but the lights within the tubes followed their own orbits and at this moment the sealed world of the Lysenko maze was theoretically at "late spring, midday." Borisov had noticed the blue mouse watching their desk from the section of pipe nearest them when he had first entered the building, but he had come to expect that. He was reading off the day's lists, when the lights suddenly flickered.

The two men looked up. "What is happening?" "Is it the dynamo?" Power for the experiment came from the college lines, but there was an emergency dynamo that was supposed to cut in should this power fail. It had not cut in, nor had the regular power failed, yet the lights had flickered.

There was a sound of scurrying within the tubes. A sound as if all the myriad mice within were assembling in one spot nearest them. They saw at that transparent section that this was so, for hundreds of beady eyes were looking out at them and the blue mouse was there in their midst.

Now the lights flickered again, there was a crackling sound, sparks leaped through the air, and the tube fell apart at the point! The men leaped to their feet as a horde of little beasts poured through. There was a smell of smoke, and as the two men rushed into the outside darkness, they saw that the farmhouse was ablaze.

They stood on a knoll watching the building, its records, and the intricate Lysenko maze burning to ashes. Raine grasped Borisov's arm. "You failed. The Lysenko experiment was a failure. It was that blue mouse, you know. And do you know what that blue mouse was?"

The Russian stared at the fire. "It was certainly intelligent. It certainly had contrived a short circuit, and it managed to get all the mice to unite in breaking out. So it was intelligent, and its intelligence came out of the experiment."

"That mouse," shouted Raine triumphantly, "that mouse was *not* like the others! It was a *mutation*, a supermouse, a mutant freak with no relation to its ancestors or to this foolish experiment!"

"Da, da," said the Russian, shaking his head. "I see your point. It makes sense. Those other mice, I have seen them too often. They hadn't changed, they were just gray mice who spread all over the tube confusing all our clever rotations." He sighed deeply.

"Heredity," said Raine, standing in the darkness watching the house burn, "cannot be changed by acquired characteristics. The only mouse that varied, that was above the norm in any way, was simply a freak of nature, an accident of the chromosomes, a mutant, and one that, thank heavens, was probably sterile, since we saw no other bluish mice turning up."

Borisov nodded his head sadly. And sitting on the branches of a bush, in close proximity and a little behind him, three gray mice nodded their heads in agreement. Their prehensile fingers, curled around little bits of sharpened nutshells, carefully noted on scrolls of dried skin what their thought-wave-sensitive brains had just picked up. It was good to know that their opinion of their eccentric blue brother with the dictator complex was verified by the Outside Thinkers. Now they could dispose of his troublesome body in peace and get to work in the real wide world.

FONDLY FAHRENHEIT

BY ALFRED BESTER (1913–   )

THE MAGAZINE OF FANTASY AND SCIENCE FICTION, AUGUST

Alfred Bester sandwiched this excellent story between his two great novels, THE DEMOLISHED MAN (1953) and TIGER, TIGER (1957). 1954 also saw the publication of his fine "5,271,009" (aka "The Starcomber"), again in THE MAGAZINE OF FANTASY AND SCIENCE FICTION, a story that narrowly missed inclusion in this book. A strong element of mystery and crime runs through much of his work during this period, not just in novels like THE DEMOLISHED MAN, but in shorter works like "Time Is the Traitor" (see Volume 13 of this series) and "Star Light, Star Bright" (1953). A number of science fiction practitioners, especially my esteemed co-editor, have skillfully combined the mystery story with sf, but Bester in this story and in the other ones just mentioned provides a tour of the inside of a criminal's mind that has yet to be equaled in our genre. (MHG)

I often speak of "stylistic experimentation" as characteristic of the "new wave" phenomenon of the 1960's, but when I do so, I always hope that no one will ask me to explain what I mean by the phrase. The trouble is that my own style is so plain and forthright and I am so incapable of changing it that I can't conceive of stylistic experimentation, even when I talk about it.

Well, Alfie Bester experiments easily and he turns out powerful stories as a result. In reading the following story, just try to follow the pronouns and you'll see what I mean by stylistic experimentation, or at least one type of it. (IA)

He doesn't know which of us I am these days, but they know one truth. You must own nothing but yourself. You must make your own life, live your own life and die your own death . . . or else you will die another's.

The rice fields on Paragon III stretch for hundreds of miles like checkerboard tundras, a blue and brown mosaic under a burning sky of orange. In the evening, clouds whip like smoke, and the paddies rustle and murmur.

A long line of men marched across the paddies the evening we escaped from Paragon III. They were silent, armed, intent; a long rank of silhouetted statues looming against the smoking sky. Each man carried a gun. Each man wore a walkie-talkie belt pack, the speaker button in his ear, the mirophone bug clipped to his throat, the glowing view-screen strapped to his wrist like a green-eyed watch. The multitude of screens showed nothing but a multitude of individual paths through the paddies. The annunciators uttered no sound but the rustle and splash of steps. The men spoke infrequently, in heavy grunts, all speaking to all.

"Nothing here."
"Where's here?"
"Jenson's fields."
"You're drifting too far west."
"Close in the line there."
"Anybody covered the Grimson paddy?"
"Yeah. Nothing."
"She couldn't have walked this far."
"Could have been carried."
"Think she's alive?"
"Why should she be dead?"

The slow refrain swept up and down the long line of beaters advancing toward the smoky sunset. The line of beaters wavered like a writhing snake, but never ceased its remorseless advance. One hundred men spaced fifty feet apart. Five thousand feet of ominous search. One mile of angry determination stretching from east to west across a compass of heat. Evening fell. Each man lit his search lamp. The writhing snake was transformed into a necklace of wavering diamonds.

"Clear here. Nothing."

"Nothing here."

"Nothing."

"What about the Allen paddies?"

"Covering them now."

"Think we missed her?"

"Maybe.'

"We'll beat back and check."

"This'll be an all-night job."

"Allen paddies clear."

"God damn! We've got to find her!"

"We'll find her."

"Here she is. Sector seven. Tune in."

The line stopped. The diamonds froze in the heat. There was silence. Each man gazed into the glowing green screen on his wrist, tuning to sector seven. All tuned to one. All showed a small nude figure awash in the muddy water of a paddy. Alongside the figure an owner's stake of bronze read: VANDALEUR The ends of the line converged toward the Vandaleur field. The necklace turned into a cluster of stars. One hundred men gathered around a small nude body, a child dead in a rice paddy. There was no water in her mouth. There were fingermarks on her throat. Her innocent face was battered. Her body was torn. Clotted blood on her skin was crusted and hard.

"Dead three-four hours at least."

"Her mouth is dry."

"She wasn't drowned. Beaten to death."

In the dark evening heat the men swore softly. They picked up the body. One stopped the others and pointed to the child's fingernails. She had fought her murderer. Under the nails were particles of flesh and bright drops of scarlet blood, still liquid, still uncoagulated.

"That blood ought to be clotted too."

"Funny."

"Not so funny. What kind of blood don't clot?"

"Android."

"Looks like she was killed by one."

"Vandaleur owns an android."

"She couldn't be killed by an android."

"That's android blood under her nails."

"The police better check."

"The police'll prove I'm right."

"But androids can't kill."

"That's android blood, ain't it?"

"Androids can't kill. They're made that way."

"Looks like one android was made wrong."

"Jesus!"

And the thermometer that day registered 92.9° gloriously Fahrenheit.

So there we were aboard the *Paragon Queen* enroute for Megaster V, James Vandaleur and his android. James Vandaleur counted his money and wept. In the second-class cabin with him was his android, a magnificent synthetic creature with classic features and wide blue eyes. Raised on its forehead in a cameo of flesh were the letters MA, indicating that this was one of the rare multiple aptitude androids, worth $57,000 on the current exchange. There we were, weeping and counting and calmly watching.

"Twelve, fourteen, sixteen. Sixteen hundred dollars," Vandaleur wept. "That's all. Sixteen hundred dollars. My house was worth ten thousand. The land was worth five. There was furniture, cars, my paintings, etchings, my plane, my——— And nothing to show for everything but sixteen hundred dollars. Christ!"

I leaped up from the table and turned on the android. I pulled a strap from one of the leather bags and beat the android. It didn't move.

"I must remind you," the android said, "that I am worth fifty-seven thousand dollars on the current exchange. I must warn you that you are endangering valuable property."

"You damned crazy machine," Vandaleur shouted.

"I am not a machine," the android answered. "The robot is a machine. The android is a chemical creation of synthetic tissue."

"What got into you?" Vandaleur cried. "Why did you do it? Damn you!" He beat the android savagely.

"I must remind you that I cannot be punished," I said. "The pleasure-pain syndrome is not incorporated in the android synthesis."

"Then why did you kill her?" Vandaleur shouted. "If it wasn't for kicks, why did you——"

"I must remind you," the android said, 'that the second-class cabins in these ships are not soundproofed."

Vandaleur dropped the strap and stood panting, staring at the creature he owned.

"Why did you do it? Why did you kill her?" I asked.

"I don't know," I answered.

"First it was malicious mischief. Small things. Petty destruction. I should have known there was something wrong with you then. Androids can't destroy. They can't harm. They——"

"There is no pleasure-pain syndrome incorporated in the android synthesis."

"Then it got to arson. Then serious destruction. Then assault . . . that engineer on Rigel. Each time worse. Each time we had to get out faster. Now it's murder. Christ! What's the matter with you? What's happened?"

"There are no self-check relays incorporated in the android brain."

"Each time we had to get out it was a step downhill. Look at me. In a second-class cabin. Me. James Paleologue Vandaleur. There was a time when my father was the wealthiest—— Now, sixteen hundred dollars in the world. That's all I've got. And you. Christ damn you!"

Vandaleur raised the strap to beat the android again, then

dropped it and collapsed on a berth, sobbing. At last he pulled himself together.

"Instructions," he said.

The multiple aptitude android responded at once. It arose and awaited orders.

"My name is now Valentine. James Valentine. I stopped off on Paragon III for only one day to transfer to this ship for Megaster V. My occupation: Agent for one privately owned MA android which is for hire. Purpose of visit: To settle on Megaster V. Fix the papers."

The android removed Vandaleur's passport and papers from a bag, got pen and ink and sat down at the table. With an accurate, flawless hand—an accomplished hand that could draw, write, paint, carve, engrave, etch, photograph, design, create and build—it meticulously forged new credentials for Vandaleur. Its owner watched me miserably.

"Create and build," I muttered. "And now destroy. Oh, God! What am I going to do? Christ! If I could only get rid of you. If I didn't have to live off you. God! If only I'd inherited some guts instead of you."

Dallas Brady was Megaster's leading jewelry designer. She was short, stocky, amoral and a nymphomaniac. She hired Vandaleur's multiple aptitude android and put me to work in her shop. She seduced Vandaleur. In her bed one night, she asked abruptly: "Your name's Vandaleur, isn't it?"

"Yes," I murmured. Then: "No! No! It's Valentine. James Valentine."

"What happened on Paragon?" Dallas Brady asked. "I thought androids couldn't kill or destroy property. Prime Directives and Inhibitions set up for them when they're synthesized. Every company guarantees they can't."

"Valentine!" Vandaleur insisted.

"Oh, come off it," Dallas Brady said. "I've known for a week. I haven't hollered copper, have I?"

"The name is Valentine."

"You want to prove it? You want I should call the cops?" Dallas reached out and picked up the phone.

"For God's sake, Dallas!" Vandaleur leaped up and struggled to take the phone from her. She fended him off, laughing at him, until he collapsed and wept in shame and helplessness.

"How did you find out?" he asked at last.

"The papers are full of it. And Valentine was a little too close to Vandaleur. That wasn't smart, was it?"

"I guess not. I'm not very smart."

"Your android's got quite a record, hasn't it? Assault. Arson. Destruction. What happened on Paragon?"

"It kidnapped a child. Took her out into the rice fields and murdered her."

"Raped her?"

"I don't know."

"They're going to catch up with you."

"Don't I know it? Christ! We've been running for two years now. Seven planets in two years. I must have abandoned fifty thousand dollars worth of property in two years."

"You better find out what's wrong with it."

"How can I? Can I walk into a repair clinic and ask for an overhaul? What am I going to say? 'My android's just turned killer. Fix it.' They'd call the police right off." I began to shake. "They'd have that android dismantled inside one day. I'd probably be booked as accessory to murder."

"Why didn't you have it repaired before it got to murder?"

"I couldn't take the chance," Vandaleur explained angrily. "If they started fooling around with lobotomies and body chemistry and endocrine surgery, they might have destroyed its aptitudes. What would I have left to hire out? How would I live?"

"You could work yourself. People do."

"Work at what? You know I'm good for nothing. How could I compete with specialist androids and robots? Who can, unless he's got a terrific talent for a particular job?"

"Yeah. That's true."

"I lived off my old man all my life. Damn him! He had to go bust just before he died. Left me the android and that's all. The only way I can get along is living off what it earns."

"You better sell it before the cops catch up with you. You can live off fifty grand. Invest it."

"At 3 percent? Fifteen hundred a year? When the android returns 15 per cent on its value? Eight thousand a year. That's what it earns. No, Dallas. I've got to go along with it."

"What are you going to do about its violence kick?"

"I can't do anything . . . except watch it and pray. What are you going to do about it?"

"Nothing. It's none of my business. Only one thing . . . I ought to get something for keeping my mouth shut."

"What?"

"The android works for me for free. Let somebody else pay you, but I get it for free."

The multiple aptitude android worked. Vandaleur collected its fees. His expenses were taken care of. His savings began to mount. As the warm spring of Megaster V turned to hot summer, I began investigating farms and properties. It would be possible, within a year or two, for us to settle down permanently, provided Dallas Brady's demands did not become rapacious.

On the first hot day of summer, the android began singing in Dallas Brady's workshop. It hovered over the electric furnace which, along with the weather, was broiling the shop, and sang an ancient tune that had been popular half a century before.

> Oh, it's no feat to beat the heat.
> All reet! All reet!
> So jeet your seat
> Be fleet be fleet
> Cool and discreet
> Honey . . .

It sang in a strange, halting voice, and its accomplished fingers were clasped behind its back, writhing in a strange rumba all their own. Dallas Brady was surprised.

"You happy or something?" she asked.

"I must remind you that the pleasure-pain syndrome is not incorporated in the android synthesis," I answered. "All reet! All reet! Be fleet be fleet, cool and discreet, honey . . ."

Its fingers stopped their writhing and picked up a heavy pair of iron tongs. The android poked them into the glowing heart of the furnace, leaning far forward to peer into the lovely heat.

"Be careful, you damned fool!" Dallas Brady exclaimed. "You want to fall in?"

"I must remind you that I am worth fifty-seven thousand dollars on the current exchange," I said. "It is forbidden to endanger valuable property. All reet! All reet! Honey . . ."

It withdrew a crucible of glowing gold from the electric furnace, turned, capered hideously, sang crazily, and splashed a sluggish gobbet of molten gold over Dallas Brady's head. She screamed and collapsed, her hair and clothes flaming, her skin crackling. The android poured again while it capered and sang.

"Be fleet be fleet, cool and discreet, honey . . ." It sang and slowly poured and poured the molten gold. Then I left the workshop and rejoined James Vandaleur in his hotel suite. The android's charred clothes and squirming fingers warned its owner that something was very much wrong.

Vandaleur rushed to Dallas Brady's workshop, stared once, vomited and fled. I had enough time to pack one bag and raise nine hundred dollars on portable assets. He took a third class cabin on the *Megaster Queen* which left that morning for Lyra Alpha. He took me with him. He wept and counted his money and I beat the android again.

And the thermometer in Dallas Brady's workshop registered 98.1° beautifully Fahrenheit.

On Lyra Alpha we holed up in a small hotel near the university. There, Vandaleur carefully bruised my forehead until the letters MA were obliterated by the swelling and the discoloration. The letters would reappear again, but not for several months, and in the meantime Vandaleur hoped the hue and cry for an MA android would be forgotten. The

android was hired out as a common laborer in the university
power plant. Vandaleur, as James Venice, eked out life on
the android's small earnings.

I wasn't too unhappy. Most of the other residents in the
hotel were university students, equally hard up, but delight-
fully young and enthusiastic. There was one charming girl
with sharp eyes and a quick mind. Her name was Wanda, and
she and her beau, Jed Stark, took a tremendous interest in the
killing android which was being mentioned in every paper in
the galaxy.

"We've been studying the case," she and Jed said at one
of the casual student parties which happened to be held this
night in Vandaleur's room. "We think we know what's
causing it. We're going to do a paper." They were in a high
state of excitement.

"Causing what?" somebody wanted to know.

"The android rampage."

"Obviously out of adjustment, isn't it? Body chemistry
gone haywire. Maybe a kind of synthetic cancer, yes?"

"No." Wanda gave Jed a look of suppressed triumph.

"Well, what is it?"

"Something specific."

"What?"

"That would be telling."

"Oh, come on."

"Nothing doing."

"Won't you tell us?" I asked intently. "I . . . We're very
much interested in what could go wrong with an android."

"No, Mr. Venice," Wanda said. "It's a unique idea and
we've got to protect it. One thesis like this and we'll be set
up for life. We can't take the chance of somebody stealing
it."

"Can't you give us a hint?"

"No. Not a hint. Don't say a word, Jed. But I'll tell you
this much, Mr. Venice. I'd hate to be the man who owns that
android."

"You mean the police?" I asked.

"I mean projection, Mr. Venice. Projection! That's the

danger . . . and I won't say any more. I've said too much as is.''

I heard steps outside, and a hoarse voice singing softly: ''Be fleet be fleet cool and discreet, honey . . .'' My android entered the room, home from its tour of duty at the university power plant. It was not introduced. I motioned to it and I immediately responded to the command and went to the beer keg and took over Vandaleur's job of serving the guests. Its accomplished fingers writhed in a private rumba of their own. Gradually they stopped their squirming, and the strange humming ended.

Androids were not unusual at the university. The wealthier students owned them along with cars and planes. Vandaleur's android provoked no comment, but young Wanda was sharp-eyed and quick-witted. She noted my bruised forehead and she was intent on the history-making thesis she and Jed Stark were going to write. After the party broke up, she consulted with Jed walking upstairs to her room.

''Jed, why'd that android have a bruised forehead?''

''Probably hurt itself, Wanda. It's working in the power plant. They fling a lot of heavy stuff around.''

''That all?''

''What else?''

''It could be a convenient bruise.''

''Convenient for what?''

''Hiding what's stamped on its forehead.''

''No point to that, Wanda. You don't have to see marks on a forehead to recognize an android. You don't have to see a trademark on a car to know it's a car.''

''I don't mean it's trying to pass as a human. I mean it's trying to pass as a lower grade android.''

''Why?''

''Suppose it had MA on its forehead.''

''Multiple aptitude? Then why in hell would Venice waste it stoking furnaces if it would earn more—— Oh. Oh! You mean it's—?''

Wanda nodded.

''Jesus!'' Stark pursed his lips. ''What do we do? Call the police?''

"No. We don't know if it's an MA for a fact. If it turns out to be an MA and the killing android, our paper comes first anyway. This is our big chance, Jed. If it's *that* android we can run a series of controlled tests and——"

"How do we find out for sure?"

"Easy. Infrared film. That'll show what's under the bruise. Borrow a camera. Buy some film. We'll sneak down to the power plant tomorrow afternoon and take some pictures. Then we'll know."

They stole down into the university power plant the following afternoon. It was a vast cellar, deep under the earth. It was dark, shadowy, luminous with burning light from the furnace doors. Above the roar of the fires they could hear a strange voice shouting and chanting in the echoing vault: "All reet! All reet! So jeet your seat. Be fleet be fleet, cool and discreet, honey . . ." And they could see a capering figure dancing a lunatic rumba in time to the music it shouted. The legs twisted. The arms waved. The fingers writhed.

Jed Stark raised the camera and began shooting his spool of infrared film, aiming the camera sights at that bobbing head. Then Wanda shrieked, for I saw them and came charging down on them, brandishing a polished steel shovel. It smashed the camera. It felled the girl and then the boy. Jed fought me for a desperate hissing moment before he was bludgeoned into helplessness. Then the android dragged them to the furnace and fed them to the flames, slowly, hideously. It capered and sang. Then it returned to my hotel.

The thermometer in the power plant registered 100.9° murderously Fahrenheit. All reet! All reet!

We bought steerage on the *Lyra Queen* and Vandaleur and the android did odd jobs for their meals. During the night watches, Vandaleur would sit alone in the steerage head with a cardboard portfolio on his lap, puzzling over its contents. That portfolio was all he had managed to bring with him from Lyra Alpha. He had stolen it from Wanda's room. It was labeled ANDROID. It contained the secret of my sickness.

And it contained nothing but newspapers. Scores of

newspapers from all over the galaxy, printed, microfilmed, engraved, etched, offset, photostated . . . Rigel *Star-Banner* . . . Paragon *Picayune* . . . Megaster *Times-Leader* . . . Lalande *Herald* . . . Lacaille *Journal* . . . Indi *Intelligencer* . . . Eridani *Telegram-News*. All reet! All reet!

Nothing but newspapers. Each paper contained an account of one crime in the android's ghastly career. Each paper also contained news, domestic and foreign, sports, society, weather, shipping news, stock exchange quotations, human interest stories, features, contests, puzzles. Somewhere in that mass of uncollated facts was the secret Wanda and Jed Stark had discovered. Vandaleur pored over the papers helplessly. It was beyond him. So jeet your seat!

"I'll sell you," I told the android. "Damn you. When we land on Terra, I'll sell you. I'll settle for 3 per cent on whatever you're worth."

"I am worth fifty-seven thousand dollars on the current exchange," I told him.

"If I can't sell you, I'll turn you in to the police," I said.

"I am valuable property," I answered. "It is forbidden to endanger valuable property. You won't have me destroyed."

"Christ damn you!" Vandaleur cried. "What? Are you arrogant? Do you know you can trust me to protect you? Is that the secret?"

The multiple aptitude android regarded him with calm accomplished eyes. "Sometimes," it said, "it is a good thing to be property."

It was 3 below zero when the *Lyra Queen* dropped at Croydon Field. A mixture of ice and snow swept across the field, fizzing and exploding into steam under the *Queen*'s tail jets. The passengers trotted numbly across the blackened concrete to customs inspection, and thence to the airport bus that was to take them to London. Vandaleur and the android were broke. They walked.

By midnight they reached Piccadilly Circus. The December ice storm had not slackened and the statue of Eros was encrusted with ice. They turned right, walked down to Trafalgar

Square and then along the Strand toward Soho, shaking with cold and wet. Just above Fleet Street, Vandaleur saw a solitary figure coming from the direction of St. Paul's. He drew the android into an alley.

"We've got to have money," he whispered. He pointed at the approaching figure. "He has money. Take it from him."

"The order cannot be obeyed," the android said.

"Take it from him," Vandaleur repeated. "By force. Do you understand? We're desperate."

"It is contrary to my prime directive," I said. "I cannot endanger life or property. The order cannot be obeyed."

"For God's sake!" Vandaleur burst out. "You've attacked, destroyed, murdered. Don't gibber about prime directives. You haven't any left. Get his money. Kill him if you have to. I tell you, we're desperate!"

"It is contrary to my prime directive," the android repeated. "The order cannot be obeyed."

I thrust the android back and leaped out at the stranger. He was tall, austere, competent. He had an air of hope curdled by cyncism. He carried a cane. I saw he was blind.

"Yes?" he said. "I hear you near me. What is it?"

"Sir . . ." Vandaleur hesitated. "I'm desperate."

"We are all desperate," the stranger replied. "Quietly desperate."

"Sir . . . I've got to have some money."

"Are you begging or stealing?" The sightless eyes passed over Vandaleur and the android.

"I'm prepared for either."

"Ah. So are we all. It is the history of our race." The stranger motioned over his shoulder. "I have been begging at St. Paul's, my friend. What I desire cannot be stolen. What is it you desire that you are lucky enough to be able to steal?"

"Money," Vandaleur said.

"Money for what? Come, my friend, let us exchange confidences. I will tell you why I beg, if you will tell me why you steal. My name is Blenheim."

"My name is . . . Vole."

"I was not begging for sight at St. Paul's, Mr. Vole. I was begging for a number."

"A number?"

"Ah yes. Numbers rational, numbers irrational. Numbers imaginary. Positive integers. Negative integers. Fractions, positive and negative. Eh? You have never heard of Blenheim's immortal treatise on Twenty Zeros, or The Differences in Absence of Quantity?" Blenheim smiled bitterly. "I am the wizard of the Theory of Number, Mr. Vole, and I have exhausted the charm of number for myself. After fifty years of wizardry, senility approaches and the appetite vanishes. I have been praying in St. Paul's for inspiration. Dear God, I prayed, if You exist, send me a number."

Vandaleur slowly lifted the cardboard portfolio and touched Blenheim's hand with it. "In here," he said, "is a number. A hidden number. A secret number. The number of a crime. Shall we exchange, Mr. Blenheim? Shelter for a number?"

"Neither begging nor stealing, eh?" Blenheim said. "But a bargain. So all life reduces itself to the banal." The sightless eyes again passed over Vandaleur and the android. "Perhaps the All-Mighty is not God but a merchant. Come home with me."

On the top floor of Blenheim's house we shared a room— two beds, two closets, two washstands, one bathroom. Vandaleur bruised my forehead again and sent me out to find work, and while the android worked, I consulted with Blenheim and read him the papers from the portfolio, one by one. All reet! All reet!

Vandaleur told him so much and no more. He was a student, I said, attempting a thesis on the murdering android. In these papers which he had collected were the facts that would explain the crimes of which Blenheim had heard nothing. There must be a correlation, a number, a statistic, something which would account for my derangement, I explained, and Blenheim was piqued by the mystery, the detective story, the human interest of number.

We examined the papers. As I read them aloud, he listed them and their contents in his blind, meticulous writing. And then I read his notes to him. He listed the papers by type, by type face, by fact, by fancy, by article, spelling, words, theme, advertising, pictures, subject, politics, prejudices. He analyzed. He studied. He meditated. And we lived together in that top floor, always a little cold, always a little terrified, always a little closer . . . brought together by our fear of it, our hatred between us. Like a wedge driven into a living tree and splitting the trunk, only to be forever incorporated into the scar tissue, we grew together. Vandaleur and the android. Be fleet be fleet!

And one afternoon Blenheim called Vandaleur into his study and displayed his notes. "I think I've found it," he said, "but I can't understand it."

Vandaleur's heart leaped.

"Here are the correlations," Blenheim continued. "In fifty papers there are accounts of the criminal android. What is there, outside the depredations, that is also in fifty papers?"

"I don't know, Mr. Blenheim."

"It was a rhetorical question. Here is the answer. The weather."

"What?"

"The weather." Blenheim nodded. "Each crime was committed on a day when the temperature was above 90 degrees Fahrenheit."

"But that's impossible," Vandaleur exclaimed. "It was cool on Lyra Alpha."

"We have no record of any crime committed on Lyra Alpha. There is no paper."

"No. That's right. I——" Vandaleur was confused. Suddenly he exclaimed. "No. You're right. The furnace room. It was hot there. Hot! Of course. My God, yes! That's the answer. Dallas Brady's electric furnace . . . The rice deltas on Paragon. So jeet your seat. Yes. But why? Why? My God, why?"

I came into the house at that moment, and passing the study, saw Vandaleur and Blenheim. I entered, awaiting commands, my multiple aptitudes devoted to service.

"That's the android, eh?" Blenheim said after a long moment.

"Yes," Vandaleur answered, still confused by the discovery. "And that explains why it refused to attack you that night on the Strand. It wasn't hot enough to break the prime directive. Only in the heat . . . The heat, all reet!" He looked at the android. A lunatic command passed from man to android. I refused. It is forbidden to endanger life. Vandaleur gestured furiously, then seized Blenheim's shoulders and yanked him back out of his desk chair to the floor. Blenheim shouted once. Vandaleur leaped on him like a tiger, pinning him to the floor and sealing his mouth with one hand.

"Find a weapon," he called to the android.

"It is forbidden to endanger life."

"This is a fight for self-preservation. Bring me a weapon!" He held the squirming mathematician with all his weight. I went at once to a cupboard where I knew a revolver was kept. I checked it. It was loaded with five cartridges. I handed it to Vandaleur. I took it, rammed the barrel against Blenheim's head and pulled the trigger. He shuddered once.

We had three hours before the cook returned from her day off. We looted the house. We took Blenheim's money and jewels. We packed a bag with clothes. We took Blenheim's notes, destroyed the newspapers; and we left, carefully locking the door behind us. In Blenheim's study we left a pile of crumpled papers under a half inch of burning candle. And we soaked the rug around it with kerosene. No, I did all that. The android refused. I am forbidden to endanger life or property.

All reet!

They took the tubes to Leicester Square, changed trains and rode to the British Museum. There they got off and went to a small Georgian house just off Russell Square. A shingle in the window read: NAN WEBB, PSYCHOMETRIC CONSULTANT. Vandaleur had made a note of the address some weeks earlier. They went into the house. The android waited in the foyer with the bag. Vandaleur entered Nan Webb's office.

She was a tall woman with gray shingled hair, very fine English complexion and very bad English legs. Her features were blunt, her expression acute. She nodded to Vandaleur, finished a letter, sealed it and looked up.

"My name," I said, "is Vanderbilt. James Vanderbilt."

"Quite."

"I'm an exchange student at London University."

"Quite."

"I've been researching on the killing android, and I think I've discovered something very interesting. I'd like your advice on it. What is your fee?"

"What is your college at the university?"

"Why?"

"There is a discount for students."

"Merton College."

"That will be two pounds, please."

Vandaleur placed two pounds on the desk and added to the fee Blenheim's notes. "There is a correlation," he said, "between the crimes of the android and the weather. You will note that each crime was committed when the temperature rose above 90 degrees Fahrenheit. Is there a psychometric answer for this?"

Nan Webb nodded, studied the notes for a moment, put down the sheets of paper and said: "Synesthesia, obviously."

"What?"

"Synesthesia," she repeated. "When a sensation, Mr. Vanderbilt, is interpreted immediately in terms of a sensation from a different sense organ from the one stimulated, it is called synesthesia. For example: A sound stimulus gives rise to a simultaneous sensation of definite color. Or color gives rise to a sensation of taste. Or a light stimulus gives rise to a sensation of sound. There can be confusion or short circuiting of any sensation of taste, smell, pain, pressure, temperature and so on. D'you understand?"

"I think so."

"Your research has uncovered the fact that the android most probably reacts to temperature stimulus above the 90-degree level synesthetically. Most probably there is an endocrine response. Probably a temperature linkage with the android adrenal surrogate. High temperature brings about a response of fear, anger, excitement and violent physical activity . . . all within the province of the adrenal gland."

"Yes. I see. Then if the android were to be kept in cold climates . . ."

"There would be neither stimulus nor response. There would be no crimes. Quite."

"I see. What is projection?"

"How do you mean?"

"Is there any danger of projection with regard to the owner of the android?"

"Very interesting. Projection is a throwing forward. It is the process of throwing out upon another the ideas or impulses that belong to oneself. The paranoid, for example, projects upon others his conflicts and disturbances in order to externalize them. He accuses, directly or by implication, other men of having the very sicknesses with which he is struggling himself."

"And the danger of projection?"

"It is the danger of believing what is implied. If you live with a psychotic who projects his sickness upon you, there is a danger of falling into his psychotic pattern and becoming virtually psychotic yourself. As, no doubt, is happening to you, Mr. Vandaleur."

Vandaleur leaped to his feet.

"You are an ass," Nan Webb went on crisply. She waved the sheets of notes. "This is no exchange student's writing. It's the unique cursive of the famous Blenheim. Every scholar in England knows this blind writing. There is no Merton College at London University. That was a miserable guess. Merton is one of the Oxford colleges. And you, Mr. Vandaleur, are so obviously infected by association with your deranged android . . . by projection, if you will . . . that I hesitate between calling the Metropolitan Police and the Hospital for the Criminally Insane."

I took the gun and shot her.

Reet!

"Antares II, Alpha Aurigae, Acrux IV, Pollux IX, Rigel Centaurus," Vandaleur said. "They're all cold. Cold as a witch's kiss. Mean temperature of 40 degrees Fahrenheit.

Never get hotter than 70. We're in business again. Watch that curve.''

The multiple aptitude android swung the wheel with its accomplished hands. The car took the curve sweetly and sped on through the northern marshes, the reeds stretching for miles, brown and dry, under the cold English sky. The sun was sinking swiftly. Overhead, a lone flight of bustards flapped clumsily eastward. High above the flight, a lone helicopter drifted toward home and warmth.

"No more warmth for us," I said. "No more heat. We're safe when we're cold. We'll hole up in Scotland, make a little money, get across to Norway, build a bankroll and then ship out. We'll settle on Pollux. We're safe. We've licked it. We can live again."

There was a startling *bleep* from overhead, and then a ragged roar: "ATTENTION JAMES VANDALEUR AND ANDROID. ATTENTION JAMES VANDALEUR AND ANDROID!"

Vandaleur started and looked up. The lone helicopter was floating above them. From its belly came amplified commands: "YOU ARE SURROUNDED. THE ROAD IS BLOCKED. YOU ARE TO STOP YOUR CAR AT ONCE AND SUBMIT TO ARREST. STOP AT ONCE!"

I looked at Vandaleur for orders.

"Keep driving," Vandaleur snapped.

The helicopter dropped lower: "ATTENTION ANDROID. YOU ARE IN CONTROL OF THE VEHICLE. YOU ARE TO STOP AT ONCE. THIS IS A STATE DIRECTIVE SUPERSEDING ALL PRIVATE COMMANDS."

"What the hell are you doing?" I shouted.

"A state directive supersedes all private commands," the android answered. "I must point out to you that——"

"Get the hell away from the wheel," Vandaleur ordered. I clubbed the android, yanked him sideways and squirmed over him to the wheel. The car veered off the road in that moment and went churning through the frozen mud and dry reeds. Vandaleur regained control and continued westward through the marshes toward a parallel highway five miles distant.

"We'll beat their God damned block," he grunted.

The car pounded and surged. The helicopter dropped even lower. A searchlight blazed from the belly of the plane.

"ATTENTION JAMES VANDALEUR AND ANDROID. SUBMIT TO ARREST. THIS IS A STATE DIRECTIVE SUPERSEDING ALL PRIVATE COMMANDS."

"He can't submit," Vandaleur shouted wildly. "There's no one to submit to. He can't and I won't."

"Christ!" I muttered. "We'll beat them yet. We'll beat the block. We'll beat the heat. We'll——"

"I must point out to you," I said, "that I am required by my prime directive to obey state directives which supersede all private commands. I must submit to arrest."

"Who says it's a state directive?" Vandaleur said. "Them? Up in that plane? They've got to show credentials. They've got to prove it's state authority before you submit. How d'you know they're not crooks trying to trick us?"

Holding the wheel with one arm, he reached into his side pocket to make sure the gun was still in place. The car skidded. The tires squealed on frost and reeds. The wheel was wrenched from his grasp and the car yawed up a small hillock and overturned. The motor roared and the wheels screamed. Vandaleur crawled out and dragged the android with him. For the moment we were outside the circle of light boring down from the helicopter. We blundered off into the marsh, into the blackness, into concealment . . . Vandaleur running with a pounding heart, hauling the android along.

The helicopter circled and soared over the wrecked car, searchlight peering, loudspeaker braying. On the highway we had left, lights appeared as the pursuing and blocking parties gathered and followed radio directions from the plane. Vandaleur and the android continued deeper and deeper into the marsh, working their way toward the parallel road and safety. It was night by now. The sky was a black matte. Not a star showed. The temperature was dropping. A southeast night wind knifed us to the bone.

Far behind there was a dull concussion. Vandaleur turned, gasping. The car's fuel had exploded. A geyser of flame shot up like a lurid fountain. It subsided into a low crater of burning reeds. Whipped by the wind, the distant hem of flame fanned up into a wall, ten feet high. The wall began marching down on us, crackling fiercely. Above it, a pall of oily smoke surged forward. Behind it, Vandaleur could make out the figures of men . . . a mass of beaters searching the marsh.

"Christ!" I cried and searched desperately for safety. He ran, dragging me with him, until their feet crunched through the surface ice of a pool. He trampled the ice furiously, then flung himself down in the numbing water, pulling the android with us.

The wall of flame approached. I could hear the crackle and feel the heat. He could see the searchers clearly. Vandaleur reached into his side pocket for the gun. The pocket was torn. The gun was gone. He groaned and shook with cold and terror. The light from the marsh fire was blinding. Overhead, the helicopter floated helplessly to one side, unable to fly through the smoke and flames and aid the searchers who were beating far to the right of us.

"They'll miss us," Vandaleur whispered. "Keep quiet. That's an order. They'll miss us. We'll beat them. We'll beat the fire. We'll——"

Three distinct shots sounded less than a hundred feet from the fugitives. *Blam! Blam! Blam!* They came from the last three cartridges in my gun as the marsh fire reached it where it had dropped, and exploded the shells. The searchers turned toward the sound and began working directly toward us. Vandaleur cursed hysterically and tried to submerge even deeper to escape the intolerable heat of the fire. The android began to twitch.

The wall of flame surged up to them. Vandaleur took a deep breath and prepared to submerge until the flame passed over them. The android shuddered and burst into an ear-splitting scream.

"All reet! All reet!" it shouted. "Be fleet be fleet!"

"Damn you!" I shouted. I tried to drown it.

"Damn you!" I cursed him. I smashed his face.

The android battered Vandaleur, who fought it off until it
exploded out of the mud and staggered upright. Before I
could return to the attack, the live flames captured it hypnoti-
cally. It danced and capered in a lunatic rumba before the
wall of fire. Its legs twisted. Its arms waved. The fingers
writhed in a private rumba of their own. It shrieked and sang
and ran in a crooked waltz before the embrace of the heat, a
muddy monster silhouetted against the brilliant sparkling flare.
The searchers shouted. There were shots. The android spun
around twice and then continued its horrid dance before the
face of the flames. There was a rising gust of wind. The fire
swept around the capering figure and enveloped it for a
roaring moment. Then the fire swept on, leaving behind it a
sobbing mass of synthetic flesh oozing scarlet blood that
would never coagulate.

The thermometer would have registered 1200° wondrously
Fahrenheit.

Vandaleur didn't die. I got away. They missed him while
they watched the android caper and die. But I don't know
which of us he is these days. Projection, Wanda warned me.
Projection, Nan Webb told him. If you live with a crazy man
or a crazy machine long enough, I become crazy too. Reet!

But we know one truth. We know they were wrong. The
new robot and Vandaleur know that because the new robot's
started twitching too. Reet! Here on cold Pollux, the robot is
twitching and singing. No heat, but my fingers writhe. No
heat, but it's taken the little Talley girl off for a solitary walk.
A cheap labor robot. A servo-mechanism . . . all I could
afford . . . but it's twitching and humming and walking alone
with the child somewhere and I can't find them. Christ!
Vandaleur can't find me before it's too late. Cool and discreet, honey, in the dancing frost while the thermometer
registers 10° fondly Fahrenheit.

THE COLD EQUATIONS

BY TOM GODWIN (1915–   )

ASTOUNDING SCIENCE FICTION, AUGUST

"The Cold Equations" has been called a "touchstone"
story in the history of American magazine science fiction
because it so clearly reflects the attitudes, world view, and
"feel" of Golden Age sf. Its success is due in no small part to
its combination of sentimentality and hard-nosedness and to
its depiction of the neutrality of the universe.

Godwin is a perfect example of the "one-story" writer, for
he will forever be associated with this story to the almost
total exclusion of all of his other work, which includes THE
SURVIVORS (1958) and its sequel THE SPACE BARBAR-
IANS (1964), as well as BEYOND ANOTHER SUN (1971). In
addition, he published more than twenty stories in the maga-
zines, the last "Before the Willows Ever Walked" in 1980.
Of these, several are worth seeking out, especially "The
Greater Thing" (1954), "The Last Victory" (1957), "Mother
of Invention" (1953), and the excellent "You Created Us."
(MHG)

There are some stories that I will always think of as "John
Campbell" stories, because they so clearly reflect John's
super-hard-nosed philosophy. This story is one of them. I will
never forget John's glee when he told me of "The Cold
Equations" and outlined the plot to me. Nothing could be

closer to his views, and no story made a bigger splash that year, or perhaps for several years.

And yet, although I appreciated its strength and excellence, I refused to accept the force of the situation. I don't want to give away the plot for those of you who have never read the story, but I told John that spaceflight would develop in such a way that the situation in the story would never be acceptable—or necessary.

I think I was right, although at the time John thought it was just my soft-headed idealism. (IA)

He was not alone.

There was nothing to indicate the fact but the white hand of the tiny gauge on the board before him. The control room was empty but for himself; there was no sound other than the murmur of the drives—but the white hand had moved. It had been on zero when the little ship was launched from the *Stardust*; now, an hour later, it had crept up. There was something in the supplies closet across the room, it was saying, some kind of a body that radiated heat.

It could be but one kind of a body—a living, human body.

He leaned back in the pilot's chair and drew a deep, slow breath, considering what he would have to do. He was an EDS pilot, inured to the sight of death, long since accustomed to it and to viewing the dying of another man with an objective lack of emotion, and he had no choice in what he must do. There could be no alternative—but it required a few moments of conditioning for even an EDS pilot to prepare himself to walk across the room and coldly, deliberately, take the life of a man he had yet to meet.

He would, of course, do it. It was the law, stated very bluntly and definitely in grim Paragraph L, Section 8, of Interstellar Regulations: *Any stowaway discovered in an EDS shall be jettisoned immediately following discovery.*

It was the law, and there could be no appeal.

It was a law not of men's choosing but made imperative by the circumstances of the space frontier. Galactic expansion had followed the development of the hyperspace drive and as men scattered wide across the frontier there had come the problem of contact with the isolated first-colonies and exploration parties. The huge hyperspace cruisers were the product of the combined genius and effort of Earth and were long and expensive in the building. They were not available in such numbers that small colonies could possess them. The cruisers carried the colonists to their new worlds and made periodic visits, running on tight schedules, but they could not stop and turn aside to visit colonies scheduled to be visited at another time; such a delay would destroy their schedule and produce a confusion and uncertainty that would wreck the complex interdependence between old Earth and new worlds of the frontier.

Some method of delivering supplies or assistance when an emergency occurred on a world not scheduled for a visit had been needed and the Emergency Dispatch Ships had been the answer. Small and collapsible, they occupied little room in the hold of the cruiser; made of light metal and plastics, they were driven by a small rocket drive that consumed relatively little fuel. Each cruiser carried four EDS's and when a call for aid was received the nearest cruiser would drop into normal space long enough to launch an EDS with the needed supplies or personnel, then vanish again as it continued on its course.

The cruisers, powered by nuclear converters, did not use the liquid rocket fuel but nuclear converters were far too large and complex to permit their installation in the EDS's. The cruisers were forced by necessity to carry a limited amount of the bulky rocket fuel and the fuel was rationed with care; the cruiser's computers determining the exact amount of fuel each EDS would require for its mission. The computers considered the course coordinates, the mass of the EDS, the mass of pilot and cargo; they were very precise and accurate and omitted nothing from their calculations. They could not, however, foresee, and allow for, the added mass of a stowaway.

The *Stardust* had received the request from one of the exploration parties stationed on Woden; the six men of the party already being stricken with the fever carried by the green *kala* midges and their own supply of serum destroyed by the tornado that had torn through their camp. The *Stardust* had gone through the usual procedure; dropping into normal space to launch the EDS with the fever serum, then vanishing again in hyperspace. Now, an hour later, the gauge was saying there was something more than the small carton of serum in the supplies closet.

He let his eyes rest on the narrow white door of the closet. There, just inside, another man lived and breathed and was beginning to feel assured that discovery of his presence would now be too late for the pilot to alter the situation. It *was* too late—for the man behind the door it was far later than he thought and in a way he would find terrible to believe.

There could be no alternative. Additional fuel would be used during the hours of deceleration to compensate for the added mass of the stowaway; infinitesimal increments of fuel that would not be missed until the ship had almost reached its destination. Then, at some distance above the ground that might be as near as a thousand feet or as far as tens of thousands of feet, depending upon the mass of ship and cargo and the preceding period of deceleration, the unmissed increments of fuel would make their absence known; the EDS would expend its last drops of fuel with a sputter and go into whistling free fall. Ship and pilot and stowaway would merge together upon impact as a wreckage of metal and plastic, flesh and blood, driven deep into the soil. The stowaway had signed his own death warrant when he concealed himself on the ship; he could not be permitted to take seven others with him.

He looked again at the telltale white hand, then rose to his feet. What he must do would be unpleasant for both of them; the sooner it was over, the better. He stepped across the control room, to stand by the white door.

"Come out!" His command was harsh and abrupt above the murmur of the drive.

It seemed he could hear the whisper of a furtive movement inside the closet, then nothing. He visualized the stowaway cowering closer into one corner, suddenly worried by the possible consequences of his act and his self-assurance evaporating.

"I said *out!*"

He heard the stowaway move to obey and he waited with his eyes alert on the door and his hand near the blaster at his side.

The door opened and the stowaway stepped through it smiling. "All right—I give up. Now what?"

It was a girl.

He stared without speaking, his hand dropping away from the blaster and acceptance of what he saw coming like a heavy and unexpected physical blow. The stowaway was not a man—she was a girl in her teens, standing before him in little white gypsy sandals with the top of her brown, curly head hardly higher than his shoulder, with a faint, sweet scent of perfume coming from her and her smiling face tilted up so her eyes could look unknowing and unafraid into his as she waited for his answer.

Now what? Had it been asked in the deep, defiant voice of a man he would have answered it with action, quick and efficient. He would have taken the stowaway's identification disk and ordered him into the air lock. Had the stowaway refused to obey, he would have used the blaster. It would not have taken long; within a minute the body would have been ejected into space—had the stowaway been a man.

He returned to the pilot's chair and motioned her to seat herself on the boxlike bulk of the drive-control units that set against the wall beside him. She obeyed, his silence making the smile fade into the meek and guilty expression of a pup that has been caught in mischief and knows it must be punished.

"You still haven't told me," she said. "I'm guilty, so what happens to me now? Do I pay a fine, or what?"

"What are you doing here?" he asked. "Why did you stow away on this EDS?"

"I wanted to see my brother. He's with the government survey crew on Woden and I haven't seen him for ten years, not since he left Earth to go into government survey work."

"What was your destination on the *Stardust?*"

"Mimir. I have a position waiting for me there. My brother has been sending money home all the time to us—my father and mother and I—and he paid for a special course in linguistics I was taking. I graduated sooner than expected and I was offered this job on Mimir. I knew it would be almost a year before Gerry's job was done on Woden so he could come on to Mimir and that's why I hid in the closet, there. There was plenty of room for me and I was willing to pay the fine. There were only the two of us kids—Gerry and I—and I haven't seen him for so long, and I didn't want to wait another year when I could see him now, even though I knew I would be breaking some kind of a regulation when I did it."

I knew I would be breaking some kind of a regulation— In a way, she could not be blamed for her ignorance of the law; she was of Earth and had not realized that the laws of the space frontier must, of necessity, be as hard and relentless as the environment that gave them birth. Yet, to protect such as her from the results of their own ignorance of the frontier, there had been a sign over the door that led to the section of the *Stardust* that housed EDS's; a sign that was plain for all to see and heed:

UNAUTHORIZED PERSONNEL
KEEP OUT!

"Does your brother know that you took passage on the *Stardust* for Mimir?"

"Oh, yes. I sent him a spacegram telling him about my graduation and about going to Mimir on the *Stardust* a month before I left Earth. I already knew Mimir was where he would be stationed in a little over a year. He gets a promotion then, and he'll be based on Mimir and not have to stay out a year at a time on field trips, like he does now."

There were two different survey groups on Woden, and he asked, "What is his name?"

"Cross—Gerry Cross. He's in Group Two—that was the way his address read. Do you know him?"

Group One had requested the serum; Group Two was eight
thousand miles away, across the Western Sea.

"No, I've never met him," he said, then turned to the
control board and cut the deceleration to a fraction of a
gravity; knowing as he did so that it could not avert the
ultimate end, yet doing the only thing he could do to prolong
that ultimate end. The sensation was like that of the ship
suddenly dropping and the girl's involuntary movement of
surprise half lifted her from the seat.

"We're going faster now, aren't we?" she asked. "Why
are we doing that?"

He told her the truth. "To save fuel for a little while."

"You mean, we don't have very much?"

He delayed the answer he must give her so soon to ask:
"How did you manage to stow away?"

"I just sort of walked in when no one was looking my
way," she said. "I was practicing my Gelanese on the native
girl who does the cleaning in the Ship's Supply office when
someone came in with an order for supplies for the survey
crew on Woden. I slipped into the closet there after the ship
was ready to go and just before you came in. It was an
impulse of the moment to stow away, so I could get to see
Gerry—and from the way you keep looking at me so grim,
I'm not sure it was a very wise impulse.

"But I'll be a model criminal—or do I mean prisoner?"
She smiled at him again. "I intended to pay for my keep on
top of paying the fine. I can cook and I can patch clothes for
everyone and I know how to do all kinds of useful things,
even a little bit about nursing."

There was one more question to ask:

"Did you know what the supplies were that the survey
crew ordered?"

"Why, no. Equipment they needed in their work, I
supposed."

Why couldn't she have been a man with some ulterior
motive? A fugitive from justice, hoping to lose himself on a
raw new world; an opportunist, seeking transportation to the

new colonies where he might find golden fleece for the taking; a crackpot, with a mission—

Perhaps once in his lifetime an EDS pilot would find such a stowaway on his ship; warped men, mean and selfish men, brutal and dangerous men—but never, before, a smiling, blue-eyed girl who was willing to pay her fine and work for her keep that she might see her brother.

He turned to the board and turned the switch that would signal the *Stardust*. The call would be futile but he could not, until he had exhausted that one vain hope, seize her and thrust her into the air lock as he would an animal—or a man. The delay, in the meantime, would not be dangerous with the EDS decelerating at fractional gravity.

A voice spoke from the communicator. "*Stardust*. Identify yourself and proceed."

"Barton, EDS 34G11. Emergency. Give me Commander Delhart."

There was a faint confusion of noises as the request went through the proper channels. The girl was watching him, no longer smiling.

"Are you going to order them to come back after me?" she asked.

The communicator clicked and there was the sound of a distant voice saying, "Commander, the EDS requests—"

"Are they coming back after me?" she asked again. "Won't I get to see my brother, after all?"

"Barton?" The blunt, gruff voice of Commander Delhart came from the communicator. "What's this about an emergency?"

"A stowaway," he answered.

"A stowaway?" There was a slight surprise to the question. "That's rather unusual—but why the 'emergency' call? You discovered him in time so there should be no appreciable danger and I presume you've informed Ship's Records so his nearest relatives can be notified."

"That's why I had to call you, first. The stowaway is still aboard and the circumstances are so different—"

"Different?" the commander interrupted, impatience in his

voice. "How can they be different? You know you have a
limited supply of fuel; you also know the law, as well as I do:
'Any stowaway discovered in an EDS shall be jettisoned
immediately following discovery.' "

There was the sound of a sharply indrawn breath from the
girl. *"What does he mean?"*

"The stowaway is a girl."

"What?"

"She wanted to see her brother. She's only a kid and she
didn't know what she was really doing."

"I see." All the curtness was gone from the commander's
voice. "So you called me in the hope I could do something?"
Without waiting for an answer he went on. "I'm sorry—I can
do nothing. This cruiser must maintain its schedule; the life
of not one person but the lives of many depend on it. I know
how you feel but I'm powerless to help you. You'll have to
go through with it. I'll have you connected with Ship's
Records."

The communicator faded to a faint rustle of sound and he
turned back to the girl. She was leaning forward on the
bench, almost rigid, her eyes fixed wide and frightened.

"What did he mean, to go through with it? To jettison me
. . . to go through with it—what did he mean? Not the way it
sounded . . . he couldn't have. What did he mean . . . what
did he really mean?"

Her time was too short for the comfort of a lie to be more
than a cruelly fleeting delusion.

"He meant it the way it sounded."

"No!" She recoiled from him as though he had struck her,
one hand half upraised as though to fend him off and stark
unwillingness to believe in her eyes.

"It will have to be."

"No! You're joking—you're insane! You can't mean it!"

"I'm sorry." He spoke slowly to her, gently. "I should
have told you before—I should have, but I had to do what I
could first; I had to call the *Stardust*. You heard what the
commander said."

"But you can't—if you make me leave the ship, I'll *die*."

"I know."

She searched his face and the unwillingness to believe left her eyes, giving way slowly to a look of dazed terror.

"You—know?" She spoke the words far apart, numb and wonderingly.

"I know. It has to be like that."

"You mean it—you really mean it." She sagged back against the wall, small and limp like a little rag doll and all the protesting and disbelief gone.

"You're going to do it—you're going to make me die?"

"I'm sorry," he said again. "You'll never know how sorry I am. It has to be that way and no human in the universe can change it."

"You're going to make me die and I didn't do anything to die for—I didn't *do* anything—"

He sighed, deep and weary. "I know you didn't, child. I know you didn't—"

"EDS." The communicator rapped brisk and metallic. "This is Ship's Records. Give us all information on subject's identification disk."

He got out of his chair to stand over her. She clutched the edge of the seat, her upturned face white under the brown hair and the lipstick standing out like a blood-red cupid's bow.

"Now?"

"I want your identification disk," he said.

She released the edge of the seat and fumbled at the chain that suspended the plastic disk from her neck with fingers that were trembling and awkward. He reached down and unfastened the clasp for her, then returned with the disk to his chair.

"Here's your data, Records: Identification Number T837—"

"One moment," Records interrupted. "This is to be filed on the gray card, of course?"

"Yes."

"And the time of the execution?"

"I'll tell you later."

"Later? This is highly irregular; the time of the subject's death is required before—"

He kept the thickness out of his voice with an effort. "Then we'll do it in a highly irregular manner—you'll hear the disk read, first. The subject is a girl and she's listening to everything that's said. Are you capable of understanding that?"

There was a brief, almost shocked, silence, then Records said meekly: "Sorry. Go ahead."

He began to read the disk, reading it slowly to delay the inevitable for as long as possible, trying to help her by giving her what little time he could to recover from her first terror and let it resolve into the calm of acceptance and resignation:

"Number T8374 dash Y54. Name: Marilyn Lee Cross, Sex: Female, Born: July 7, 2160. *She was only eighteen.* Height: 5-3. Weight: 110. *Such a slight weight, yet enough to add fatally to the mass of the shell-thin bubble that was an EDS.* Hair: Brown. Eyes: Blue. Complexion: Light. Blood Type: O. *Irrelevant data.* Destination: Port City, Mimir. *Invalid data—*"

He finished and said, "I'll call you later," then turned once again to the girl. She was huddled back against the wall, watching him with a look of numb and wondering fascination.

"They're waiting for you to kill me, aren't they? They want me dead, don't they? You and everybody on the cruiser wants me dead, don't you?" Then the numbness broke and her voice was that of a frightened and bewildered child. "Everybody wants me dead and I didn't *do* anything. I didn't hurt anyone—I only wanted to see my brother."

"It's not the way you think—it isn't that way, at all," he said. "Nobody wants it this way; nobody would ever let it be this way if it was humanly possible to change it?"

"Then why is it! I don't understand. Why is it?"

"This ship is carrying *kala* fever serum to Group One on Woden. Their own supply was destroyed by a tornado. Group Two—the crew your brother is in—is eight thousand miles away across the Western Sea and their helicopters can't cross it to help Group One. The fever is invariably fatal unless the serum can be had in time, and the six men in Group One will die unless this ship reaches them on schedule. These little ships are always given barely enough fuel to reach their destination and if you stay aboard your added weight will cause it to use up all its fuel before it reaches the ground. It will crash, then, and you and I will die and so will the six men waiting for the fever serum."

It was a full minute before she spoke, and as she considered his words the expression of numbness left her eyes.

"Is that it?" she asked at last. "Just that the ship doesn't have enough fuel?"

"Yes."

"I can go alone or I can take seven others with me—is that the way it is "

"That's the way it is."

"And nobody wants me to have to die?"

"Nobody."

"Then maybe— Are you sure nothing can be done about it? Wouldn't people help me if they could?"

"Everyone would like to help you but there is nothing anyone can do. I did the only thing I could do when I called the *Stardust*."

"And it won't come back—but there might be other cruisers, mightn't there? Isn't there any hope at all that there might be someone, somewhere, who could do something to help me?"

She was leaning forward a little in her eagerness as she waited for his answer.

"No."

The word was like the drop of a cold stone and she again leaned back against the wall, the hope and eagerness leaving her face. "You're sure—you *know* you're sure?"

"I'm sure. There are no other cruisers within forty light-years; there is nothing and no one to change things."

She dropped her gaze to her lap and began twisting a pleat of her skirt between her fingers, saying no more as her mind began to adapt itself to the grim knowledge.

*   *   *

It was better so; with the going of all hope would go the fear; with the going of all hope would come resignation. She needed time and she could have so little of it. How much?

The EDS's were not equipped with hull-cooling units; their speed had to be reduced to a moderate level before entering the atmosphere. They were decelerating at .10 gravity; approaching their destination at a far higher speed than the computers had calculated on. The *Stardust* had been quite near Woden when she launched the EDS; their present velocity was putting them nearer by the second. There would be a critical point, soon to be reached, when he would have to resume deceleration. When he did so the girl's weight would be multiplied by the gravities of deceleration, would become, suddenly, a factor of paramount importance; the factor the computers had been ignorant of when they determined the amount of fuel the EDS should have. She would have to go when deceleration began; it could be no other way. When would that be—how long could he let her stay?

"How long can I stay?"

He winced involuntarily from the words that were so like an echo of his own thoughts. How long? He didn't know; he would have to ask the ship's computers. Each EDS was given a meager surplus of fuel to compensate for unfavorable conditions within the atmosphere and relatively little fuel was being consumed for the time being. The memory banks of the computers would still contain all data pertaining to the course set for the EDS; such data would not be erased until the EDS reached its destination. He had only to give the computers the new data; the girl's weight and the exact time at which he had reduced the deceleration to .10.

"Barton." Commander Delhart's voice came abruptly from the communicator, as he opened his mouth to call the *Stardust*. "A check with Records shows me you haven't completed your report. Did you reduce the deceleration?"

So the commander knew what he was trying to do.

"I'm decelerating at point ten," he answered. "I cut the deceleration at seventeen fifty and the weight is a hundred and ten. I would like to stay at point ten as long as the computers say I can. Will you give them the question?"

It was contrary to regulations for an EDS pilot to make any changes in the course or degree of deceleration the computers had set for him but the commander made no mention of the violation, neither did he ask the reason for it. It was not necessary for him to ask; he had not become commander of an interstellar cruiser without both intelligence and an understanding of human nature. He said only: "I'll have that given the computers."

The communicator fell silent and he and the girl waited, neither of them speaking. They would not have to wait long; the computers would give the answer within moments of the asking. The new factors would be fed into the steel maw of the first bank and the electrical impulses would go through the complex circuits. Here and there a relay might click, a tiny cog turn over, but it would be essentially the electrical impulses that found the answer; formless, mindless, invisible, determining with utter precision how long the pale girl beside him might live. Then five little segments of metal in the second bank would trip in rapid succession against an inked ribbon and a second steel maw would spit out the slip of paper that bore the answer.

The chronometer on the instrument board read 18:10 when the commander spoke again.

"You will resume deceleration at nineteen ten."

She looked toward the chronometer, then quickly away from it. "Is that when . . . when I go?" she asked. He nodded and she dropped her eyes to her lap again.

"I'll have the course corrections given you," the commander said. "Ordinarily I would never permit anything like this but I understand your position. There is nothing I can do, other than what I've just done, and you will not deviate from these new instructions. You will complete your report at nineteen ten. Now—here are the course corrections."

The voice of some unknown technician read them to him and he wrote them down on the pad clipped to the edge of the control board. There would, he saw, be periods of deceleration when he neared the atmosphere when the deceleration would be five gravities—and at five gravities, one hundred ten pounds would become five hundred fifty pounds.

The technician finished and he terminated the contact with a brief acknowledgment. Then, hesitating a moment, he reached out and shut off the communicator. It was 18:13 and he would have nothing to report until 19:10. In the meantime, it somehow seemed indecent to permit others to hear what she might say in her last hour.

He began to check the instrument readings, going over them with unnecessary slowness. She would have to accept the circumstances and there was nothing he could do to help her into acceptance; words of sympathy would only delay it.

It was 18:20 when she stirred from her motionlessness and spoke.

"So that's the way it has to be with me?"

He swung around to face her. "You understand now, don't you? No one would ever let it be like this if it could be changed."

"I understand," she said. Some of the color had returned to her face and the lipstick no longer stood out so vividly red. "There isn't enough fuel for me to stay; when I hid on this ship I got into something I didn't know anything about and now I have to pay for it."

She had violated a man-made law that said KEEP OUT but the penalty was not of men's making or desire and it was a penalty men could not revoke. A physical law had decreed: *h amount of fuel will power an EDS with a mass of m safely to its destination* and a second physical law had decreed: *h amount of fuel will not power an EDS with a mass of m plus x safely to its destination.*

EDS's obeyed only physical laws and no amount of human sympathy for her could alter the second law.

"But I'm afraid. I don't want to die—not now. I want to live and nobody is doing anything to help me; everybody is letting me go ahead and acting just like nothing was going to happen to me. I'm going to die and nobody *cares.*"

"We all do," he said. "I do and the commander does and the clerk in Ship's Records; we all care and each of us did what little he could to help you. It wasn't enough—it was almost nothing—but it was all we could do."

"Not enough fuel—I can understand that," she said, as though she had not heard his own words. "But to have to die for it. *Me*, alone—"

How hard it must be for her to accept the fact. She had never known danger of death; had never known the environments where the lives of men could be as fragile and fleeting as sea foam tossed against a rocky shore. She belonged on gentle Earth, in that secure and peaceful society where she could be young and gay and laughing with the others of her kind; where life was precious and well-guarded and there was always the assurance that tomorrow would come. She belonged in that world of soft winds and warm suns, music and moonlight and gracious manners and not on the hard, bleak frontier.

"How did it happen to me, so terribly quickly? An hour ago I was on the *Stardust*, going to Mimir. Now the *Stardust* is going on without me and I'm going to die and I'll never see Gerry and Mama and Daddy again—I'll never see anything again."

He hesitated, wondering how he could explain it to her so she would really understand and not feel she had, somehow, been the victim of a reasonlessly cruel injustice. She did not know what the frontier was like; she thought in terms of safe-and-secure Earth. Pretty girls were not jettisoned on Earth; there was a law against it. On Earth her plight would have filled the newscasts and a fast black Patrol ship would have been racing to her rescue. Everyone, everywhere, would have known of Marilyn Lee Cross and no effort would have been spared to save her life. But this was not Earth and there were no Patrol ships; only the *Stardust*, leaving them behind at many times the speed of light. There was no one to help her, there would be no Marilyn Lee Cross smiling from the newscasts tomorrow. Marilyn Lee Cross would be but a poignant memory for an EDS pilot and a name on a gray card in Ship's Records.

"It's different here; it's not like back on Earth," he said. "It isn't that no one cares; it's that no one can do anything to help. The frontier is big and here along its rim the colonies and exploration parties are scattered so thin and far between. On Woden, for example, there are only sixteen men—sixteen men on an entire world. The exploration parties, the survey crews, the little first-colonies—they're all fighting alien environments, trying to make a way for those who will follow after. The environments fight back and those who go first usually make mistakes only once. There is no margin of safety along the rim of the frontier; there can't be until the way is made for the others who will come later, until the new worlds are tamed and settled. Until then men will have to pay the penalty for making mistakes with no one to help them because there is no one *to* help them."

"I was going to Mimir," she said. "I didn't know about the frontier; I was only going to Mimir and *it's* safe."

"Mimir is safe but you left the cruiser that was taking you there."

She was silent for a little while. "It was all so wonderful at first; there was plenty of room for me on this ship and I would be seeing Gerry so soon . . . I didn't know about the fuel, didn't know what would happen to me—"

Her words trailed away and he turned his attention to the viewscreen, not wanting to stare at her as she fought her way through the black horror of fear toward the calm gray of acceptance.

Woden was a ball, enshrouded in the blue haze of its atmosphere, swimming in space against the background of star-sprinkled dead blackness. The great mass of Manning's Continent sprawled like a gigantic hourglass in the Eastern Sea with the western half of the Eastern Continent still visible. There was a thin line of shadow along the right-hand edge of the globe and the Eastern Continent was disappearing into it as the planet turned on its axis. An hour before the entire continent had been in view, now a thousand miles of it had gone into the thin edge of shadow and around to the night that lay on the other side of the world. The dark blue spot that was Lotus Lake was approaching the shadow. It was somewhere near the southern edge of the lake that Group Two had their camp. It would be night there, soon, and quick behind the coming of night the rotation of Woden on its axis would put Group Two beyond the reach of the ship's radio.

He would have to tell her before it was too late for her to talk to her brother. In a way, it would be better for both of them should they not do so but it was not for him to decide. To each of them the last words would be something to hold and cherish, something that would cut like the blade of a knife yet would be infinitely precious to remember, she for her own brief moments to live and he for the rest of his life.

He held down the button that would flash the grid lines on the view-screen and used the known diameter of the planet to estimate the distance the southern tip of Lotus Lake had yet to go until it passed beyond radio range. It was approximately five hundred miles. Five hundred miles; thirty minutes—and the chronometer read 18:30. Allowing for error in estimating, it could not be later than 19:05 that the turning of Woden would cut off her brother's voice.

The first border of the Western Continent was already in sight along the left side of the world. Four thousand miles across it lay the shore of the Western Sea and the Camp of Group One. It had been in the Western Sea that the tornado had originated, to strike with such fury at the camp and destroy half their prefabricated buildings, including the one that housed the medical supplies. Two days before the tornado had not existed; it had been no more than great gentle masses of air out over the calm Western Sea. Group One had gone about their routine survey work, unaware of the meeting of the air masses out at sea, unaware of the force the union was spawning. It had struck their camp without warning; a thundering, roaring destruction that sought to annihilate all that lay before it. It had passed on, leaving the wreckage in its wake. It had destroyed the labor of months and had doomed six men to die and then, as though its task was accomplished, it once more began to resolve into gentle masses of air. But for all its deadliness, it had destroyed with neither malice nor intent. It had been a blind and mindless force, obeying the laws of nature, and it would have followed the same course with the same fury had men never existed.

Existence required Order and there was order; the laws of nature, irrevocable and immutable. Men could learn to use them but men could not change them. The circumference of a circle was always pi times the diameter and no science of Man would ever make it otherwise. The combination of chemical A with chemical B under condition C invariably produced reaction D. The law of gravitation was a rigid equation and it made no distinction between the fall of a leaf and the ponderous circling of a binary star system. The nuclear conversion process powered the cruisers that carried men to the stars; the same process in the form of a nova would destroy a world with equal efficiency. The laws *were*, and the universe moved in obedience to them. Along the frontier were arrayed all the forces of nature and sometimes they destroyed those who were fighting their way outward from Earth. The men of the frontier had long ago learned the bitter futility of cursing the forces that would destroy them for the forces were blind and deaf; the futility of looking to the heavens for mercy, for the stars of the galaxy swung in their long, long sweep of two hundred million years, as inexorably controlled as they by the laws that knew neither hatred nor compassion.

The men of the frontier knew—but how was a girl from Earth to fully understand? *H amount of fuel will not power an EDS with a mass of m plus x safely to its destination.* To himself and her brother and parents she was a sweet-faced girl in her teens; to the laws of nature she was *x*, the unwanted factor in a cold equation.

She stirred again on the seat. "Could I write a letter? I want to write to Mama and Daddy and I'd like to talk to Gerry. Could you let me talk to him over your radio there?"

"I'll try to get him," he said.

He switched on the normal-space transmitter and pressed

the signal button. Someone answered the buzzer almost immediately.

"Hello. How's it going with you fellows now—is the EDS on its way?"

"This isn't Group One; this is the EDS," he said. "Is Gerry Cross there?"

"Gerry? He and two others went out in the helicopter this morning and aren't back yet. It's almost sundown, though, and he ought to be back right away—in less than an hour at the most."

"Can you connect me through to the radio in his 'copter?"

"Huh-uh. It's been out of commission for two months— some printed circuits went haywire and we can't get any more until the next cruiser stops by. Is it something important—bad news for him, or something?"

"Yes—it's very important. When he comes in get him to the transmitter as soon as you possibly can."

"I'll do that; I'll have one of the boys waiting at the field with a truck. Is there anything else I can do?"

"No, I guess that's all. Get him there as soon as you can and signal me."

He turned the volume to an inaudible minimum, an act that would not affect the functioning of the signal buzzer, and unclipped the pad of paper from the control board. He tore off the sheet containing his flight instructions and handed the pad to her, together with pencil.

"I'd better write to Gerry, too," she said as she took them. "He might not get back to camp in time."

She began to write, her fingers still clumsy and uncertain in the way they handled the pencil and the top of it trembling a little as she poised it between words. He turned back to the viewscreen, to stare at it without seeing it.

She was a lonely little child, trying to say her last good-by, and she would lay out her heart to them. She would tell them how much she loved them and she would tell them to not feel badly about it, that it was only something that must happen eventually to everyone and she was not afraid. The last would be a lie and it would be there to read between the sprawling,

uneven lines; a valiant little lie that would make the hurt all
the greater for them.

Her brother was of the frontier and he would understand.
He would not hate the EDS pilot for doing nothing to prevent
her going; he would know there had been nothing the pilot
could do. He would understand, though the understanding
would not soften the shock and pain when he learned his
sister was gone. But the others, her father and mother—they
would not understand. They were of Earth and they would
think in the manner of those who had never lived where the
safety margin of life was a thin, thin line—and sometimes not
at all. What would they think of the faceless, unknown pilot
who had sent her to her death?

They would hate him with cold and terrible intensity but it
really didn't matter. He would never see them, never know
them. He would have only the memories to remind him; only
the nights to fear, when a blue-eyed girl in gypsy sandals
would come in his dreams to die again—

He scowled at the viewscreen and tried to force his thoughts
into less emotional channels. There was nothing he could do
to help her. She had unknowingly subjected herself to the
penalty of a law that recognized neither innocence nor youth
nor beauty, that was incapable of sympathy or leniency.
Regret was illogical—and yet, could knowing it to be illogical ever keep it away?

She stopped occasionally, as though trying to find the right
words to tell them what she wanted them to know, then the
pencil would resume its whispering to the paper. It was 18:37
when she folded the letter in a square and wrote a name on it.
She began writing another, twice looking up at the chronometer as though she feared the black hand might reach its
rendezvous before she had finished. It was 18:45 when she
folded it as she had done the first letter and wrote a name and
address on it.

She held the letters out to him. "Will you take care of
these and see that they're enveloped and mailed?"

"Of course." He took them from her hand and placed them in a pocket of his gray uniform shirt.

"These can't be sent off until the next cruiser stops by and the *Stardust* will have long since told them about me, won't it?" she asked. He nodded and she went on, "That makes the letters not important in one way but in another way they're very important—to me, and to them."

"I know. I understand, and I'll take care of them."

She glanced at the chronometer, then back to him. "It seems to move faster all the time, doesn't it?"

He said nothing, unable to think of anything to say, and she asked, "Do you think Gerry will come back to camp in time?"

"I think so. They said he should be in right away."

She began to roll the pencil back and forth between her palms. "I hope he does. I feel sick and scared and I want to hear his voice again and maybe I won't feel so alone. I'm a coward and I can't help it."

"No," he said, "you're not a coward. You're afraid, but you're not a coward."

"Is there a difference?"

He nodded. "A lot of difference."

"I feel so alone. I never did feel like this before; like I was all by myself and there was nobody to care what happened to me. Always, before, there was Mama and Daddy there and my friends around me. I had lots of friends, and they had a going-away party for me the night before I left."

Friends and music and laughter for her to remember—and on the viewscreen Lotus Lake was going into the shadow.

"Is it the same with Gerry?" she asked. "I mean, if he should make a mistake, would he have to die for it, all alone and with no one to help him?"

"It's the same with all along the frontier; it will always be like that so long as there is a frontier."

"Gerry didn't tell us. He said the pay was good and he sent money home all the time because Daddy's little shop just brought in a bare living but he didn't tell us it was like this."

"He didn't tell you his work was dangerous?"

"Well—yes. He mentioned that, but we didn't understand. I always thought danger along the frontier was something that was a lot of fun; an exciting adventure, like in the three-D shows." A wan smile touched her face for a moment. "Only it's not, is it? It's not the same at all, because when it's real you can't go home after the show is over."

"No," he said. "No, you can't."

Her glance flicked from the chronometer to the door of the air lock then down to the pad and pencil she still held. She shifted her position slightly to lay them on the bench beside, moving one foot out a little. For the first time he saw that she was not wearing Vegan gypsy sandals but only cheap imitations; the expensive Vegan leather was some kind of grained plastic, the silver buckle was gilded iron, the jewels were colored glass. *Daddy's little shop just brought in a bare living*— She must have left college in her second year, to take the course in linguistics that would enable her to make her own way and help her brother provide for her parents, earning what she could by part-time work after classes were over. Her personal possessions on the *Stardust* would be taken back to her parents—they would neither be of much value nor occupy much storage space on the return voyage.

"Isn't it—" She stopped, and he looked at her questioningly. "Isn't it cold in here?" she asked, almost apologetically, "Doesn't it seem cold to you?"

"Why, yes," he said. He saw by the main temperature gauge that the room was at precisely normal temperature. "Yes, it's colder than it should be."

"I wish Gerry would get back before it's too late. Do you really think he will, and you didn't just say so to make me feel better?"

"I think he will—they said he would be in pretty soon." On the viewscreen Lotus Lake had gone into the shadow but for the thin blue line of its western edge and it was apparent he had overestimated the time she would have in which to talk to her brother. Reluctantly, he said to her, "His camp will be out of radio range in a few minutes; he's on that part

of Woden that's in the shadow"—he indicated the viewscreen—
"and the turning of Woden will put him beyond contact.
There may not be much time left when he comes in—not
much time to talk to him before he fades out. I wish I could
do something about it—I would call him right now if I
could."

"Not even as much time as I will have to stay?"

"I'm afraid not."

"Then—" She straightened and looked toward the air lock
with pale resolution. "Then I'll go when Gerry passes beyond
range. I won't wait any longer after that—I won't have
anything to wait for."

Again there was nothing he could say.

"Maybe I shouldn't wait at all. Maybe I'm selfish—maybe
it would be better for Gerry if you just told him about it
afterward."

There was an unconscious pleading for denial in the way
she spoke and he said, "He wouldn't want you to do that, to
not wait for him."

"It's already coming dark where he is, isn't it? There will
be all the long night before him, and Mama and Daddy don't
know yet that I won't ever be coming back like I promised
them I would. I've caused everyone I love to be hurt, haven't
I? I didn't want to—I didn't intend to."

"It wasn't your fault," he said. "It wasn't your fault at
all. They'll know that. They'll understand."

"At first I was so afraid to die that I was a coward and
thought only of myself. Now, I see how selfish I was. The
terrible thing about dying like this is not that I'll be gone but
that I'll never see them again; never be able to tell them that I
didn't take them for granted; never be able to tell them I
knew of the sacrifices they made to make my life happier,
that I knew all the things they did for me and that I loved
them so much more than I ever told them. I've never told
them any of those things. You don't tell them such things
when you're young and your life is all before you—you're
afraid of sounding sentimental and silly.

"But it's so different when you have to die—you wish you

had told them while you could and you wish you could tell them you're sorry for all the little mean things you ever did or said to them. You wish you could tell them that you didn't really mean to ever hurt their feelings and for them to only remember that you always loved them far more than you ever let them know.''

"You don't have to tell them that," he said. "They will know—they've always known it.''

"Are you sure?" she asked. "How can you be sure? My people are strangers to you.''

"Wherever you go, human nature and human hearts are the same.''

"And they will know what I want them to know—that I love them?''

"They've always known it, in a way far better than you could ever put in words for them.''

"I keep remembering the things they did for me, and it's the little things they did that seem to be the most important to me, now. Like Gerry—he sent me a bracelet of fire-rubies on my sixteenth birthday. It was beautiful—it must have cost him a month's pay. Yet, I remember him more for what he did the night my kitten got run over in the street. I was only six years old and he held me in his arms and wiped away my tears and told me not to cry, that Flossy was gone for just a little while, for just long enough to get herself a new fur coat and she would be on the foot of my bed the very next morning. I believed him and quit crying and went to sleep dreaming about my kitten coming back. When I woke up the next morning, there was Flossy on the foot of my bed in a brand-new white fur coat, just like he had said she would be.

"It wasn't until a long time later that Mama told me Gerry had got the pet-shop owner out of bed at four in the morning and, when the man got mad about it, Gerry told him he was either going to go down and sell him the white kitten right then or he'd break his neck.''

"It's always the little things you remember people by; all the little things they did because they wanted to do them for you. You've done the same for Gerry and your father and mother; all kinds of things that you've forgotten about but that they will never forget.''

"I hope I have. I would like for them to remember me like that.''

"They will.''

"I wish—'' She swallowed. "The way I'll die—I wish they wouldn't ever think of that. I've read how people look who die in space—their insides all ruptured and exploded and their lungs out between their teeth and then, a few seconds later, they're all dry and shapeless and horribly ugly. I don't want them to ever think of me as something dead and horrible, like that.''

"You're their own, their child and their sister. They could never think of you other than the way you would want them to; the way you looked the last time they saw you.''

"I'm still afraid,'' she said. "I can't help it, but I don't want Gerry to know it. If he gets back in time, I'm going to act like I'm not afraid at all and—''

The signal buzzer interrupted her, quick and imperative.

"Gerry!'' She came to her feet. "It's Gerry, now!''

He spun the volume control knob and asked: "Gerry Cross?''

"Yes,'' her brother answered, an undertone of tenseness to his reply. "The bad news—what is it?''

She answered for him, standing close behind him and leaning down a little toward the communicator, her hand resting small and cold on his shoulder.

"Hello, Gerry.'' There was only a faint quiver to betray the careful casualness of her voice. "I wanted to see you—''

"Marilyn!'' There was sudden and terrible apprehension in the way he spoke her name. "What are you doing on that EDS?''

"I wanted to see you,'' she said again. "I wanted to see you, so I hid on this ship—''

"You *hid* on it?''

"I'm a stowaway . . . I didn't know what it would mean—''

"Marilyn!" It was the cry of a man who calls hopeless and desperate to someone already and forever gone from him. "What have you done?''

"I . . . it's not—" Then her own composure broke and the cold little hand gripped his shoulder convulsively. "Don't, Gerry—I only wanted to see you; I didn't intend to hurt you. Please, Gerry, don't feel like that—"

Something warm and wet splashed on his wrist and he slid out of the chair, to help her into it and swing the microphone down to her own level.

"Don't feel like that— Don't let me go knowing you feel like that—"

The sob she had tried to hold back choked in her throat and her brother spoke to her. "Don't cry, Marilyn." His voice was suddenly deep and infinitely gentle, with all the pain held out of it. "Don't cry, Sis—you mustn't do that. It's all right, Honey—everything is all right."

"I—" Her lower lip quivered and she bit into it. "I didn't want you to feel that way—I just wanted us to say good-by because I have to go in a minute."

"Sure—sure. That's the way it will be, Sis. I didn't mean to sound the way I did." Then his voice changed to a tone of quick and urgent demand. "EDS—have you called the *Stardust?* Did you check with the computers?"

"I called the *Stardust* almost an hour ago. It can't turn back, there are no other cruisers within forty light-years, and there isn't enough fuel."

"Are you sure that the computers had the correct data—sure of everything?"

"Yes—do you think I could ever let it happen if I wasn't sure? I did everything I could do. If there was anything at all I could do now, I would do it."

"He tried to help me, Gerry." Her lower lip was no longer trembling and the short sleeves of her blouse were wet where she had dried her tears. "No one can help me and I'm not going to cry any more and everything will be all right with you and Daddy and Mama, won't it?"

"Sure—sure it will. We'll make out fine."

Her brother's words were beginning to come in more faintly and he turned the volume control to maximum. "He's going out of range," he said to her. "He'll be gone within another minute."

"You're fading out, Gerry," she said. "You're going out of range. I wanted to tell you—but I can't, now. We must say good-by so soon—but maybe I'll see you again. Maybe I'll come to you in your dreams with my hair in braids and crying because the kitten in my arms is dead; maybe I'll be the touch of a breeze that whispers to you as it goes by; maybe I'll be one of those gold-winged larks you told me about, singing my silly head off to you; maybe, at times, I'll be nothing you can see but you will know I'm there beside you. Think of me like that, Gerry; always like that and not—the other way."

Dimmed to a whisper by the turning of Woden, the answer came back:

"Always like that, Marilyn—always like that and never any other way."

"Our time is up, Gerry—I have to go now. Good—" Her voice broke in mid-word and her mouth tried to twist into crying. She pressed her hand hard against it and when she spoke again the words came clear and true:

"Good-by, Gerry."

Faint and ineffably poignant and tender, the last words came from the cold metal of the communicator:

"Good-by, little sister—"

She sat motionless in the hush that followed, as though listening to the shadow-echoes of the words as they died away, then she turned away from the communicator, toward the air lock, and he pulled the black lever beside him. The inner door of the air lock slid swiftly open, to reveal the bare little cell that was waiting for her, and she walked to it.

She walked with her head up and the brown curls brushing her shoulders, with the white sandals stepping as sure and steady as the fractional gravity would permit and the gilded buckles twinkling with little lights of blue and red and crystal. He let her walk alone and made no move to help her, knowing she would not want it that way. She stepped into the

air lock and turned to face him, only the pulse in her throat to
betray the wild beating of her heart.

"I'm ready," she said.

He pushed the lever up and the door slid its quick barrier
between them, inclosing her in black and utter darkness for
her last moments of life. It clicked as it locked in place and
he jerked down the red lever. There was a slight waver to the
ship as the air gushed from the lock, a vibration to the wall as
though something had bumped the outer door in passing, then
there was nothing and the ship was dropping true and steady
again. He shoved the red lever back to close the door on the
empty air lock and turned away, to walk to the pilot's chair
with the slow steps of a man old and weary.

Back in the pilot's chair he pressed the signal button of the
normal-space transmitter. There was no response; he had
expected none. Her brother would have to wait through the
night until the turning of Woden permitted contact through
Group One.

It was not yet time to resume deceleration and he waited
while the ship dropped endlessly downward with him and the
drives purred softly. He saw that the white hand of the
supplies closet temperature gauge was on zero. A cold equation had been balanced and he was alone on the ship. Something shapeless and ugly was hurrying ahead of him, going to
Woden where its brother was waiting through the night, but
the empty ship still lived for a little while with the presence
of the girl who had not known about the forces that killed
with neither hatred nor malice. It seemed, almost, that she
still sat small and bewildered and frightened on the metal box
beside him, her words echoing hauntingly clear in the void
she had left behind her:

I didn't do anything to die for—I didn't do anything—

LETTERS FROM LAURA

BY MILDRED CLINGERMAN (1918–   )

THE MAGAZINE OF FANTASY AND SCIENCE FICTION, OCTOBER

*Mildred Clingerman's first story in the science fiction field
was the memorable "Minister Without Portfolio" in the February 1952 issue of THE MAGAZINE OF FANTASY AND
SCIENCE FICTION, and most of her small output of short
stories (there is very little after 1961) would appear in that
magazine. Unlike dozens of other writers in the rich 1960's,
she did have a collection—A CUPFUL OF SPACE (Ballantine,
1961); but she remains largely unknown today. Her talent
can be appreciated by the fact that she had stories selected in
Volumes 2, 5, 6, and 7 of THE BEST FROM FANTASY AND
SCIENCE FICTION, a strikingly high percentage of the total
of stories she had in the magazine in those years. Particularly
noteworthy are "Birds Can't Count" (1955), "Stair Trick"
(1952), and "The Wild Wood" (1957).*

*"Letters From Laura" is an excellent example of Ms.
Clingerman at her best, and a fine example of the sf story
written in the form of a series of letters, one of my favorite
types. (MHG)*

*I have referred in earlier volumes of this series of authors
who seemed to get along with one editor only and who tended
to fade out with that editor. Mildred Clingerman is one of
them, I think.*

She was a favorite of the late, great Anthony Boucher in the days when he edited THE MAGAZINE OF FANTASY AND SCIENCE FICTION. When he retired as editor, she retired as writer. In fact, I don't recall that she ever wrote a story that appeared anywhere but in F & SF during the Boucher regime. (Did she, Marty?) (Yes, but only a few.)

There's absolutely no reason why this should be so. Mildred could clearly write well enough for any editor, and we've been without her for a quarter of a century. It's a shame. (IA)

Monday

Dear Mom:

Stop *worrying*. There isn't a bit of danger. Nobody ever dies or gets hurt or anything like that while time traveling. The young man at the Agency explained it all to me in detail, but I've forgotten most of it. His eyebrows move in the most fascinating way. So I'm going this weekend. I've already bought my ticket. I haven't the faintest idea where I'm going, but that's part of the fun. Grab Bag Tours, they call them. It costs $60 for one day and night, and the Agency supplies you with food concentrates and water capsules—a whole bag full of stuff they send right along with you. I certainly do *not* want Daddy to go with me. I'll tell him all about it when I get back, and then he can go himself, if he still wants to. The thing Daddy forgets is that all the history he reads is mostly just a pack of lies. Everybody says so nowadays, since time travel. He'd spoil everything arguing with the natives, telling them how they were supposed to act. I have to stop now, because the young man from the Agency is going to take me out to dinner and explain about insurance for the trip.

Love,
Laura

Tuesday

Dear Mom:

I can't *afford* to go first class. The Grab Bag Tours are not the leavings. They're perfectly all right. It's just that you sorta

have to rough it. They've been thoroughly explored. I mean
somebody has been there at least once before. I never heard
of a native attacking a girl traveler. Just because I won't
have a guide you start worrying about that. Believe me,
some of those guides from what I hear wouldn't be very
safe, either. Delbert explained it all to me. He's the boy
from the Agency. Did you know that insurance is a very
interesting subject?

Love,

Laura

Friday

Dear Mom:

Everything is set for tomorrow. I'm so excited. I spent
three hours on the couch at the Agency's office—taking the
hypno-course, you know, so I'll be able to speak the language. Later Delbert broke a rule and told me my destination,
so I rushed over to the public library and read bits here and
there. It's ancient Crete! Dad will be so pleased. I'm going to
visit the Minotaur in the Labyrinth. Delbert says he is really
off the beaten track of the tourists. I like unspoiled things,
don't you? The Agency has a regular little room all fixed up
right inside the cave, but hidden, so as not to disturb the
regular business of the place. The Agency is very particular
that way. Time travelers, Delbert says, have to agree to make
themselves as inconspicuous as possible. Delbert says that
will be very difficult for me to do. Don't you think *subtle*
compliments are the nicest? I've made myself a darling
costume—I sat up late to finish it. I don't know that it's
exactly right, historically, but it doesn't really matter, since
I'm not supposed to leave the cave. I have to stay close to my
point of arrival, you understand. Delbert says I'm well covered now with insurance, so don't worry. I'll write the minute
I get back.

Love,

Laura

Friday
Dear Prue:

Tomorrow I take my first time travel tour. I wish you could
see my costume. Very fetching! It's cut so that my breasts are
displayed in the style of ancient Crete. A friend of mine
doubts the authenticity of the dress but says the charms it
shows off are *really* authentic! Next time I see you I'll lend
you the pattern for the dress. But I honestly think, darling,
you ought to get one of those Liff-Up operations first. I've
been meaning to tell you. Of course, I don't need it myself.
I'll tell you all about it (the trip I mean) when I get back.

Love,
Laura

Monday
Dear Prue:

I had the stinkiest time! I'll never know why I let that
character at the travel agency talk me into it. The accommo-
dations were lousy. If you want to know what I think, it's all
a gyp. These Grab Bag Tours, third-class, are just the *leavings*, that they can't sell any other way. I hate salesmen.
Whoever heard of ancient Crete anyway? And the Minotaur.
You would certainly expect him to be a red-blooded he-man,
wouldn't you? He looked like one. Not cute, you know, but
built like a bull, practically. Prue, you just can't *tell* anymore. But I'm getting ahead of myself.

You've heard about that funny dizziness you feel for the
first few minutes on arrival? That part is true. Everything is
supposed to look black at first, but things kept on looking
black even after the dizziness wore off. Then I remembered it
was a cave I was in, but I did expect it to be lighted. I was
lying on one of those beastly little cots that wiggle everytime
your heart beats, and mine was beating plenty fast. Then I
remembered the bag the Agency packs for you, and I sat up
and felt around till I found it. I got out a perma-light and
attached it to the solid rock wall and looked around. The floor
was just plain old dirty dirt. That Agency had me stuck off in
a little alcove, furnished with that sagging cot and a few coat

hangers. The air in the place was rather stale. Let's be honest—it smelled. To console myself I expanded my wrist mirror and put on some more makeup. I was wearing my costume, but I had forgotten to bring a coat. I was freezing. I draped the blanket from the cot around me and went exploring. What a place! One huge room just outside my cubbyhole and corridors taking off in all directions, winding away into the dark. I had a perma-light with me, and naturally I couldn't get lost with my earrings tuned to point of arrival, but it was *weird* wandering around all by myself. I discovered that the corridor I was in curved downward. Later I found there were dozens of levels in the Labyrinth. Very confusing.

I was just turning to go back when something reached out and grabbed for me, from one of those alcoves. I was *thrilled*. I flicked off the light, dropped my blanket, and ran.

From behind I heard a man's voice. "All right, sis, we'll play games."

Well, Prue, I hadn't played hide-and-seek in years (except once or twice at office parties), but I was still pretty good at it. That part was fun. After a time my eyes adjusted to the dark so that I could see well enough to keep from banging into the walls. Sometimes I'd deliberately make a lot of noise to keep things interesting. But do you know what? That character would blunder right by me, and way down at the end of the corridor he'd make noises like "Oho" or "Aha." Frankly, I got discouraged. Finally I heard him grumbling his way back in my direction. I knew the dope would never catch me, so I just stepped out in front of him and said "Wellll?" You know, in that drawly, sarcastic way I have.

He reached out and grabbed me, and then he staggered back—like you've seen actors do in those old, old movies. He kept pounding his forehead with his fist, and then he yelled, "Cheated! Cheated again!" I almost slapped him. Instead I snapped on my perma-light and let him look me over good.

"Well, Buster," I said very coldly, "what do you mean, cheated?"

He grinned at me and shaded his eyes from the light.

"Darling," he said, "you look luscious, indeed, but what the hell are you doing here?"

"I'm sight-seeing," I said. "are you one of the sights?"

"Listen, baby, I *am* the sight. Meet the Minotaur." He stuck out this huge paw, and I shook it.

"Who did you think I was?" I asked him.

"No *who*, but *what*," he said. "Baby, you ain't no virgin."

Well, Prue, really. How can you argue a thing like that? He was completely *wrong* of course, but I simply refused to discuss it.

"I only gobble virgins," he said.

Then he led me down into his rooms, which were really quite comfortable. I couldn't forgive the Agency for that cot, so when I spied his lovely, soft couch draped in pale blue satin, I said, "I'll borrow that if you don't mind."

"It's all yours, kid," the Minotaur said. He meant it, too. You remember how pale blue is one of my best colors? There I was lolling on the couch, looking like the Queen of the Nile, flapping my eyelashes, and what does this churl want to do?

"I'm simply starved for talk," he says. And about what? Prue, when a working girl spends her hard-earned savings on time travel, she has a right to expect something besides *politics*. I've heard there are men, a few shy ones, who will talk very fast to you about science and all that highbrow stuff, hoping maybe you won't notice some of the things they're doing in the *meantime*. But not the Minotaur. Who cares about the government a room's length apart? Lying there, twiddling my fingers and yawning, I tried to remember if Daddy had ever mentioned anything about the Minotaur's being so persnickety. That's the trouble with books. They leave out all the important details.

For instance, did you know that at midnight every night the Minotaur makes a grand tour of the Labyrinth? He wouldn't let me go along. That's another thing. He just says "no" and grins and means it. Now isn't that a typical male trait? I thought so, and when he locked me in his rooms the evening looked like turning into fun. I waited for him to come back with bated breath. But you can't bate your breath forever, and he was gone hours. When he did come back I'd fallen asleep and he woke me up *belching*.

"Please," I said. "Do you have to do that?"

"Sorry, kid," he said. "It's these gaunt old maids. Awful souring to the stomach." It seems this windy diet was one of the things wrong with the government. He was very bitter about it all. Tender virgins, he said, had always been in short supply and now he was out of favor with the new regime. I rummaged around in my wrist bag and found an anti-acid pill. He was delighted. Can you imagine going into a transport over pills?

"Any cute males ever find their way into this place?" I asked him. I got up and walked around. You can loll on a couch just so long, you know.

"No boys!" The Minotaur jumped up and shook his fist at me. I cowered behind some hangings, but I needn't have bothered. He didn't even jerk me out from behind them. Instead he paced up and down and raved about the lies told on him. He swore he'd never eaten boys—hadn't cared for them at all. That creep, Theseus, was trying to ruin him politically. "I've worn myself thin," he yelled, "in all these years of service—" At that point I walked over and poked him in his big, fat stomach. Then I gathered my things together and walked out.

He puffed along behind me wanting to know what was the matter. "Gee, kid," he kept saying, "don't go home mad." I didn't say goodbye to him at all. A spider fell on him and it threw him into a hissy. The last I saw of him he was cursing the government because they hadn't sent him an exterminator.

Well, Prue, so much for the bogey man. Time travel in the raw!

Love,
Laura

Monday

Dear Mom:

Ancient Crete was nothing but politics, not a bit exciting.

You didn't have a single cause to worry. These people are just as particular about girls as you are.

Love,
Laura

Tuesday

Dear Mr. Delbert Barnes:

Stop calling me or I will complain to your boss. You cad. I see it all now. You and your fine talk about how your Agency "fully protects its clients." That's a very high-sounding name for it. Tell me, how many girls do you talk into going to ancient Crete? And do you provide all of them with the same kind of insurance? Mr. Barnes, I don't want any more insurance from you. But I'm going to send you a client for that trip—the haggiest old maid I know. She has buck teeth and whiskers. Insure *her*.

Laura

P.S. Just in case you're feeling smug about me, put this in your pipe and smoke it. The Minotaur *knew*, I can't imagine how, but *you*, Mr. Barnes, *are no Minotaur*.

TRANSFORMER

BY CHAD OLIVER (1928–   )

THE MAGAZINE OF FANTASY AND SCIENCE FICTION,
NOVEMBER

Chad Oliver holds a Ph.D. in anthropology from UCLA, and has taught the subject at the University of Texas since 1955, attaining the rank of Professor in 1968. He has also served as Chairperson of the Department on several occasions. He is the author of two major books in his field, ECOLOGY AND CULTURAL CONTINUITY AS CONTRIBUTING FACTORS IN THE SOCIAL ORGANIZATION OF THE PLAINS INDIANS (1962) and THE KAMBA OF KENYA (1980), the latter partly based on extensive field research carried out in Africa in the early 1960's. He has also authored a textbook, CULTURAL ANTHROPOLOGY: THE DISCOVERY OF HUMANITY (1980).

His academic interests find clear expression in almost all of his science fiction, which now totals some five novels and several dozen short stories. This is especially true of such books as THE SHORES OF ANOTHER SEA (1971) which draws heavily on his African experience, and of SHADOWS IN THE SUN (1954), his first novel. His two collections ANOTHER KIND (1955) and THE EDGE OF FOREVER (1971) are rich storehouses of anthropological lore. His busy academic schedule has kept his total output down, but Oliver is always entertaining and informative.

"Transformer" is one of his strangest stories, and one that

*may or may not actually be science fiction. It hit me as hard
when I read it this year as it did thirty-two years ago. (MHG)*

   *By and large, Marty and I have tried to keep the stories in
this series within rather narrow bounds of the science fictional area. We can only print a few of the stories (of even
the good stories) published in any one year and there's no
need to step outside the limits to horror or to fantasy or to
sword & sorcery.*
   *Consequently, when I read "Transformer" I made a little
note to tell Marty that I was going to throw it out for the
crime of fantasy. But it was the first story I happened to read
in the pile he had sent me and I found I couldn't get it out of
my head. I kept thinking of it as I read the other stories, and I
kept thinking of it when I crawled between the covers and
should have been thinking of my own novel-in-progress.*
   *And I finally decided, "The heck with it. If it affects me
that strongly, I'm going to call it science fiction." And I did.
I never said a word against it when I discussed the stories
with Marty. (IA)*

Our town is turned off now, all gray and lazy, so this seems
like a good time to begin. Let's not kid ourselves about it,
Clyde—I know what you're thinking, and I don't blame you.
You're thinking there's nothing that's as completely and thoroughly boring as some motherly old dame gushing about the
One Hundred and One fugitives from Paradise which are to
be found in Her Home Town. A real insomnia killer, that's
what you're thinking.
   Suppose we get things straight, right from the start.
   I may *look* like one of those sweet little old ladies who
spend all their time in the kitchen slipping apple preserves to
bleary-eyed children, but I can't help what I look like. I never
set foot in a kitchen in my life, and of course there aren't any
kids in our town—not physically anyway. I don't say I'm the
most interesting gal you ever met, Clyde, but I'll tell you for
sure you never yakked with anyone like me before.
   Now, you take our town. It stinks, but we can't get out.

ELM POINT is the name on the station, so that's what we
have to call it, but it's as crazy as the rest of the place.
There's no point in ELM POINT, and the only trees I've seen
are made of sponge rubber. I get restless when the town's
turned off for a long time. I can't sleep. I'm talking to
myself. I'm bored stiff, and so would you be if you had to
live here for your whole life. But I know you're there, Clyde,
or this wouldn't be getting through to you. Don't worry about
it, though.

This is strictly for kicks.

Okay, so let's have some details. I live in a town that's
part of the background for a model railroad. Maybe you think
that's funny, but did you ever live in a subway? I want to be
absolutely clear about this—you're a little dense sometimes,
Clyde. I don't mean that ELM POINT is a town that's located
on a big railroad that's operated in an exemplary, model
manner. No. I mean I live on a *model* railroad, a half-baked
contraption that's set up in a kid's attic. The kid's name is
Willy Roberts, he's thirteen years old, and we don't think
he's a god that created our world. In fact, if you want my
opinion, Willy is a low-grade moron, and a sadist to boot.

So my world is on a big plywood table in an attic. My
town is background atmosphere for a lousy electric train. I
don't know what I'm supposed to be. A motherly old soul
glimpsed through a house window, I guess. An intimate
detail. It gives me a pain.

If you think it's fun to live in a town on a model railroad,
you've got rocks in your head.

Look at it from our point of view. In the first place, ELM
POINT isn't a town at all—it's a collection of weird buildings
that Willy Roberts and his old man took a fancy to and could
afford. It isn't even sharp for a model railroad town; the
whole thing is disgustingly middle class.

Try to visualize it: there's a well in the middle of the table,
a hole for Willy Roberts to get into when he works the
transformer and the electric switches. The whole southern end
of the table is covered with a sagging mountain made out of
chicken wire and wet paper towels. The western side has got

a bunch of these sponge rubber trees I was telling you about, and just beyond them is an empty area called Texas. There are some real dumb cows there and two objectionable citizens who come to our town every Saturday night and try to shoot up the place. The Ohio River starts in the northwestern corner of the table and flows into the southeast. Our town and a mountain take up the northern end of the table and part of the eastern side. That's where I live, as a matter of fact—on the eastern side, between the Ohio River and the water tower.

Now catch this building inventory, Clyde—it'll kill you. We've got a police station and a firehouse in North Flats, at the edge of the mountain where the tunnel comes out. There's a big tin railroad station with a red roof. There's a quaint old frame hotel, and right behind it there's this diner that was supposed to look like an old street-car. There's one gas station with three pumps, but no cars. There's a big double spotlight on a tin tower right across from my house; I have to wear dark glasses all the time. There's seven lower-class frame houses with dirty white curtains in the windows; Humphery and I live in one of them. Humphery—that's my husband, or would be if Willy Roberts had thought to put a preacher in this hole—works in the tin switchman's house up the tracks. Whenever one of those damned trains comes by he has to goose-step out and wave his stupid red lantern. Clyde, he hates it. Then there's a cattle pen on a siding, with no wind to blow the smell away, if you get what I mean.

That's about it—a real Paradise.

Willy's got two trains on the table now. One is a flashy passenger job stashed full of stuck-up aristocrats—you know, the kind who are always reading the *Times* when they go through your town. The other is a freight train that doesn't carry anything; it just grinds around the track like a demented robot, and its only job, as far as *I* can tell, is to shuttle itself onto a siding and look respectful when the passenger train full of city slickers hisses by. As if all this racket weren't enough, Willy's got him a switch engine too, and he keeps it in our front yard. It's got a bell.

There's more, too, but we'll get to that.

How do you like our town, Clyde? Interesting? I want to tell you something else: our town is planning to commit a murder.

Guess who.

You just stick around awhile.

You know, our town is all gray and lazy when the current isn't on, just like I said. Nobody's got much energy; I must be just about the only one awake in ELM POINT at night. It gets pretty lonesome.

But the door to the attic is opening now and here comes Willy the Kid. Hang on, Clyde—all hell will pop loose in a minute. You'll have to excuse me for a minute; I have to wake Humphery up and get him down to his tin house. It's terrible—you almost have to dent Humphery to wake him up like this. And for what? Every time he wakes up he has to go to that damfool switchman's house and make with the red lantern.

Fine thing. Well, I'll be back later. And say, Clyde, if you ever see this Willy character, tell him not to shake the whole lousy table when he drags his body into the well, will you?

Willy Roberts surveyed his model railroad without pleasure. He could remember the time when it had given him a real boot, but after all he was thirteen years old now. He felt slightly ashamed that he should want to mess with it at all, but it was better than getting kicked around in football by all the big guys in the neighborhood. And Sally had said she was going to the show with Dave Toney, damn her.

Willy clicked on the transformer rheostat and watched the lights come on.

He knocked with his knuckles on the blue tin roof of the switchman's house. "Let's get with it, Humphery boy," he said. He always called the switchman Humphery—always had, ever since he was a kid and had carried on long, friendly conversations with the switchman. Boy, what a creep he had used to be! "Come on, Humph, or I'll tear your arm off. Whadaya want, boy—time and a half for overtime? Union

shop? On the ball—here comes the black Express, full of FBI
agents after the atom spies. . . .''

He pressed the START button and the passenger train
slipped its wheels on the tracks and picked up speed. It
zipped by the switchman's shack, and out came Humphery
with his red lantern, right on schedule. "What a brain you
got, Humph," Willy said. "Boy, you're a genius." He
speeded up the passenger train and sent it careening through
the tunnel into ELM POINT. He blew the whistle. He made
artificial black smoke pour out of the locomotive's smokestack.

Willy waited until the Black Express had got by the siding
and wavered into the end mountain tunnel, and then he sent
his freight chugging out of the cattle pen onto the main line.
He sent *that* rattling through ELM POINT, tweaking old
Humphery's cap when he jerked out with his lantern, and
then stopped it on the bridge over the Ohio River. He clapped
his hands together.

The Black Express charged full speed across Texas, knocking a cow off the track, and ploughed full-tilt into the stalled
freight on the bridge. Both engines jumped the track and
landed in the cellophane of the Ohio River. One little man
fell out of the caboose and got caught under a wheel.

Willy grinned.

"Pretty good, hey Humphery?" he said.

He cut the power for a second, righted the trains, and set
them in reverse to see how fast they would go. Then he ran
the freight back onto a siding and began to send the Black
Express backwards and forwards over the switch, so he could
watch old Humphery dart in and out of his tin shack waving
his lantern like a demon.

"Get with it, Humphery," cried Willy. "You only live
once!"

Humphery didn't say anything, Willy noticed.

Too busy, probably.

Well, now you've met our lord and master, Clyde. A real
All-American Junior. I tell you, ELM POINT is a madhouse

when that kid is in the attic. It's bad enough on the rest of us, but it's killing Humphery.

Things have settled down a little at the moment. The freight is sitting in the siding by the cow pen, and Willy's got the passenger job on automatic. Once every 47 seconds it comes yelling and smoking through my side-yard, and five seconds later poor Humphery has to stagger out and wave his red lantern at the snobs in the club car.

The spotlights are on, too, but Willy hasn't turned off the light in the ceiling yet, so it isn't too bad. Willy's sitting in the well reading a sex magazine, so I guess he won't be wrecking any more trains for while.

Maybe you wonder what will happen to the man who fell out of the caboose in the wreck. More likely, you don't care. But I'll tell you his name: Carl. None of us have any last names. Carl's too busted up to fix, so Willy will throw him in the wastebasket. Tender, isn't it? It chokes you all up with sentiment. We'll sort of have a funeral for Carl after the town gets turned off again, if we can stay awake, and you know what we'll be thinking? We'll be thinking that's the end of the road for all of us here in ELM POINT—the wastebasket.

It's a great life. You'd love our town, Clyde.

Let me tell you about our town, Clyde. It's different when the current's turned on. You'd hardly know the old dump, believe me.

Everybody has to go through the proper motions, you see? Like poor old Humphery with his lantern. There's Patrick, the cop, out in front of the police station. He just stands there blowing his tin whistle. Inside, they've got this one prisoner, name of Lefty. He's never been outside a cell; I don't know what he's supposed to have done. Then there's a joker over at the firehouse. All he's done for the last seven years is slide up and down this silly pole. Maybe you think *he* isn't sore at night.

Everyone that can rushes around like mad when the current's on. It's the only time we're really active and feeling good, do you see? We can't add anything to what's already here in ELM POINT, but we can use what we've got as long

as Willy can't see us. Some of us, like poor Humphery or the
policeman, have to work when the current's on, because
that's their job. But some others, the background characters,
can sneak off and visit once in a while. The favorite place is
inside the hollow mountain. You'd be surprised at what goes
on in there, Clyde.

The only rest room in town is in the gas station, and that's
all the place is used for. It's ridiculous. They only know how
to serve one dish at the diner, because that's all that was on
the counter. Bacon and fried eggs and coffee. You think
about it, Clyde. Two meals a day every day for seven years.
That's a lot of bacon and eggs. You lose your taste for them
after awhile.

The train runs right by the side of the hotel, only two
inches away. It rattles the whole thing until it's ready to fall
apart, and every time it goes by it pours black smoke in
through the upstairs window. There's a tenant up there, name
of Martin. He looks like he's made out of soot.

The whole town is knee-deep in dust. Did you ever see a
kid clean anything that belonged to him? And there's no
water, either. That cellophane in the Ohio River may look
good from where you stand, but it's about as wet as the gold
in Fort Knox. Not only that, but it crinkles all the time where
it flows under the bridges. It's enough to drive you bats.

You're beginning to see how it is, Clyde. This town is ripe
for one of those lantern-jawed, fearless crusading reporters—
you know, the kind that wears the snap-brim hat and the pipe
and is always telling the city editor to stop the presses—but
Willy forgot to give us a newspaper.

It isn't much of a life, to my way of thinking. You do the
best you can, and get up whenever some dumb kid hits a
button, and then you get tossed in the wastebasket. It seems
sort of pointless.

You can't really blame us for deciding to kill him, can you
Clyde? What else can we do? After we get rid of him there's
no telling what will happen to us. But it's like living in the
panther cage, you see—a move in any direction is bound to
be an improvement.

Know what we're going to do, Clyde?
We're going to *electrocute* Willy.
With his own electric train.
We think that's pretty sharp.

I don't want you to get the idea that I'm just a sour old
woman, Clyde—a kind of juvenile delinquent with arthritis.
I'm not, really. You know, a long time ago, when Willy
was younger, even ELM POINT wasn't so bad.

Humphery wasn't working so hard then, and at night,
when our town was all gray and lazy, I used to try and write
poetry. I guess you find that pretty hard to swallow, and I
admit that it wasn't very good poetry. Maybe you wonder
what I found to write about in this dump. Well, one night
they left the attic window open and I heard a *real* train, away
off in the distance. I wrote a poem about that. You probably
don't care about poetry, Clyde. Anyhow, if you're like the
creeps around here, you wouldn't admit if it you did.

I'll tell you, though—it's funny. Sometimes, a long time
ago, I'd go and sit down by that silly cellophane river and I'd
almost get to where I liked it here.

If it just hadn't been for that damned train every 47 seconds whenever the current was on . . .

It's too bad Willy had to change, huh Clyde? He wasn't so
bad before—just kinda dumb and goggle-eyed. He and
Humphery used to get along pretty good, but like I say it was
a long time ago.

I can see I'm boring you, talking about the past and all.
You think it's morbid. I guess you're right; I really shouldn't
have mentioned.

Here comes poor old Humphery, dragging in from the
switchman's house. Look at him—man, he's really beat to
the socks. He can hardly put one foot in front of the other.
He's old before his time, Humphery is.

You'll excuse me for a while, won't you? Humphery and I
have to go down to the diner for a cup of coffee. Maybe we'll
have some bacon and eggs too, if we can stand it again. I
hadn't noticed how late it was getting.

We'll have to go to work on that transformer tonight, if
some of us can stay awake. This stuff has got to go, don't
you agree?

I'll see you later, Clyde.

A lot of water has flowed under the bridge since I last had
a bull session with you, Clyde—or at least it *would* have if
there'd been any water in that lousy Ohio River. All it does is
crinkle. You have no idea how that can get on your nerves.

Our town is turned off again, all gray and lazy. I know I
use that phrase too much, but I'm afraid I've got kind of a
literal mind, if you know what I mean. ELM POINT *is* gray
and lazy when the current's turned off, so that's what I say it
is.

I guess I'm a realist, Clyde.

I'm not the only one awake tonight, though, I'll tell you
that. I swear I've never seen so many people up and around at
night in this burg. Even Smoky—he's the guy who has to
slide up and down that pole over at the firehouse—is sort of
waddling around. He's kind of bowlegged, you know.

To tell you the truth, we're all pretty nervous.

A bunch of the guys have been doing their best on the
transformer over in the kid's well. It wasn't easy to get to it,
but they managed it by using one of the crane cars from the
freight train.

It's awfully quiet here in town tonight, even with all the
people up and around. I don't know when I've heard it so
quiet. You probably think we've turned chicken or something. You probably think we're scared.

You're right.

I wonder how you would feel. Have you ever been *discon-
nected*, Clyde?

We've got a chance, the way we figure it. If we can just
get rid of Willy, maybe they'll let us alone for awhile. We'd
have strength enough to send a crew down to plug in the town
once in a while, when nobody was around. It would be so
wonderful—you have no idea. It isn't asking very much, is
it?

Of course, it can't last long. Maybe we'll all get stuffed back in a box after a while. Maybe they'll melt us down. Maybe, if we're lucky, we'll be given away and go to some other town.

But if we can only live a week like human beings, it'll be worth the effort. I guess I'm getting maudlin. Sorry, Clyde. You know how it is when you get old.

Sure, we're scared. Win or lose, though, what are the odds? I ask you. Anything's better than the wastebasket, that's the way we figure it.

The attic door is opening, Clyde. Light is streaming in from the stairs.

I feel terrible.

Here comes Willy.

Willy Roberts wiggled under the table and came up in the control well. The train wasn't a kick like the pinball machine, no argument there, but at least it was cheaper. He hadn't won a free game in a month.

He knocked with his knuckles on the blue tin roof of the switchman's house. "Let's get with it, Humphery boy," he said. "Oil up the old leg and light the red lamp."

Willy surveyed the table top with a jaundiced eye. Let's see now, what were the possibilities? If he played his cards right, it just might be *possible* to set the switch engine on the siding down by the cow pen, and then start the Black Express from the gas station and the freight from Texas. That way, he could have a three-way wreck.

It wouldn't be easy, though. It would take some doing.

He swatted the tin roof of the switchman's shack again and drummed on it with his fingernails. "Dig this, Humphery," he said.

The situation, he reflected, had definite possibilities.

Willy took the transformer rheostat between his thumb and index finger and clicked it on.

Then he pressed the red START button with the middle finger of his right hand.

There was a small yellow spark and a faint smell of

burning insulation. Willy jerked his tingling finger away and stood up straight, staring at his model railroad accusingly.

"Damn it," he said, "that *hurt*."

He reached out quite deliberately and ripped the transformer from its track connection. He pulled out the wall plug with a jerk on the wire. Then he took careful aim and threw the transformer as hard as he could at the spot where the walls converged in the corner of the attic.

The transformer hit with a thud, chipping the wall plaster. It bounced off the wall, crashed into the top of the mountain, and rebounded off again to land with a squashing smash on the police station. The plastic policeman with his tin whistle was under it when it fell.

Willy socked the tin switchman's house with his fingernail, almost knocking it over. "Think you're pretty cool, don't you Humphery boy?" he asked, rubbing his smarting finger. "After all I've done for you, too."

He studied his model railroad thoughtfully for a long time. Finally, Willy made his decision. He was getting too old for this junk anyhow, he reasoned. What he needed was something else.

Willy smiled at the railroad. "You know what I'm going to do to you?" he asked loudly. "I'm going to convert you to cash. How do you like that?"

He turned out the light and left the attic.

No current at all is coming through and our town is black.

How did you like that, Clyde? All that work on the transformer and what do we get? One stinking spark. Like sticking your finger on a lightning bug. Deadly as a water pistol.

I'm not too surprised, to tell you the truth. Patrick the cop warned us; he was in another town before Willy bought him, and they tried the same thing there. Not enough volts for anything but a little shock. Maybe you've been shocked by a model railroad yourself, Clyde. You think about it a little.

Sure, we knew it wouldn't work. So what? You've got to believe in something, Clyde, even when you know you're kidding yourself. What else is there to do? And maybe we could hope that by some chance, just this once . . .

But it's over now, been over for a week. This is the first I've felt like talking. You know. There wasn't much left of Patrick when the transformer hit him. I guess Lefty got his inside—nobody's had enough energy to dig in and see.

Poor old Humphery is hardly himself anymore; he got shaken up pretty badly when Willy socked the switchman's shack. I guess the worst part is mental, though. It's hard to see how things can get much worse in ELM POINT.

Do you know a good psychiatrist, Clyde?

I guess I sound like one of those old bats who spend their waking hours giving recitals of their aches and pains and their sleeping hours dreaming about men under their beds. I'm getting to be crummy company. But it *is* hard to talk now. It used to be that when the transformer was turned off a little current would seep through anyhow, but not anymore. We don't even have a wire into the wall plug. The joint is like a morgue in a coal mine.

I heard footsteps on the stairs.

The door is opening—the light hurts my eyes.

Here they come, Clyde.

A whole *herd* of them.

Willy Roberts rubbed his hands together expectantly. Just about every kid in the neighborhood had showed up, and some of them were fairly well loaded.

"Take it easy, Mac," he said. "One at a time. Let's not mess up the table, guy—this is a valuable set."

Not bad, he told himself. Pretty good in fact. No doubt about it—he had a genius for business.

"Whatcha want for the gas station, Willy?" asked Bruce Golder from down the street.

"What'll you give me?"

"Fifty cents."

"Fifty *cents?*"

"Fifty cents."

"Sold."

Willy pocketed the money. It felt good.

"How about the switchman, Willy?" said Eddie Upman, the rich kid from up the hill.

Willey hesitated, just for a second. He and Humphery had been together for a long time. But what the devil. He wasn't a kid anymore. Humphery had cost five dollars new, and prices had gone up since then.

"Two bucks four bits," Willy announced, crossing his fingers.

"Make it two bucks even," said Eddie Upman, taking out his billfold.

Willy looked around, but no one topped the bid. "Sold," he said, and Eddie Upman took Humphery and put him in a sack.

"Let's get rid of the houses before we start on the track and stuff," Willy said. "Who wants 'em?"

Nobody said anything.

"They're *good* houses," Willy insisted. "People inside and everything. See?"

Silence.

"Aw come on. A buck for the lot."

No takers.

"Fifty cents. This is the last chance on these, you guys. I'll burn 'em before I'll give 'em away."

Mark Borden slowly fumbled in his pockets and came up with a quarter, four nickels, and five pennies. "I'll take them," he said. "I guess I can use them."

"Sold!" said Willy, pocketing the money. "Now, what am I offered for the good mountain? I'll make it easy on you. Let's see, about a buck ought to be right. . . ."

Willy Roberts felt good. The table was being cleaned quicker than he had hoped, and the table itself ought to bring in some real dough. He smiled broadly when Bruce Golder bought the mountain.

Willy knew that he was a real man now.

I'm back, Clyde.

I guess you saw how they fought over me. Willy almost

had to throw me into the fire. I'm a real queen, I am. I drive men mad.

I wish he'd burned me, Clyde. I really do.

I'm determined not to get all morbid and gloomy, so you won't be hearing from me again. I can't hold out much longer, and if I have to make with the blues I'll do it alone.

Maybe you'll be wondering about me—where I am, what I'm doing. Probably you don't give a damn. You're like all the rest of them, aren't you? But just in case—

Let me tell you about our new town, Clyde. It'll kill you. You see, I'm it. Or just about.

That's right. ELM POINT looks like Utopia from where I'm sitting. Mark Borden, the one that bought me, can't afford a real model railroad set-up, and his house doesn't even *have* an attic. So about once a week he takes us all out of his dirty closet, sets up his lousy circle of track, and starts up his wheezing four-car freight train. It isn't even a scale model. Big deal.

He's got four houses that he spaces alongside the track when he's running the train; he doesn't much like the other three that he got from Willy, so he leaves them in the closet *all* the time. That's all there is, Clyde. Just me and the train. The other houses aren't even occupied, and the engineer on the freight is so embittered by now that he won't even wave.

I just sit in my stinking rocking chair and look out the window. Oh, it's delightful. I can see an old blue rug, a dresser with initials cut in it, a pile of dirty clothes in the corner, and a bed that's never made.

Once in a while Mark, the little angel, gets out his lead men and plays Soldier. The first thing he does, see, is to build him a Lincoln Log fort, about a foot from my house. Then he sticks all these lantern-jawed jokers with broken rifles along the walls, and then he backs off about nine feet and sets up his Coast Defense Gun. You'd love that, Clyde. The Coast Defense Gun is a huge blue job that works on a big spring. Mark puts marbles in the barrel, cocks the spring, and then hollers "Fire!" like a maniac. The whole lousy gun jerks up on two folding stilts and hurls all the marbles at the log fort by my house.

Chaos results, Clyde.

Logs fly all over the place. Marbles swish through the air and roll under the bed like thunder. My house has two big holes in it, and all I can do is sit in this quaint old rocker and pray. I don't know whether to pray for a hit or a miss. Periodically, one of the marbles hits a soldier square in the face and knocks his head off.

Charming.

And there's one other minor detail. Ants. We have ants. I don't think I'll tell you about them, though. You just think about it a while.

That's about all. You see how it is, Clyde. I've enjoyed talking to you, but now there doesn't seem to be much to say. I won't bother you anymore.

There's only one thing, Clyde. I wouldn't even ask, but I *am* getting old and corny. It's about Humphery. The one named Eddie Upman bought him, and he's got a lot of money. I heard Willy say so. That probably means a big table and another town and maybe some trees and rivers.

I wouldn't want you to go to any trouble, Clyde. But if you should ever be in Eddie Upman's house, maybe you could go up to the attic for a minute. Maybe you could see Humphery. You wouldn't have to do anything drooley or sentimental; I know you couldn't stand that. But maybe you could sort of accidentally leave the current on low when you leave, without running the trains.

Old Humphery would like that.

Would you do that, Clyde—for me?

THE MUSIC MASTER OF BABYLON

BY EDGAR PANGBORN (1909–1976)

GALAXY SCIENCE FICTION, NOVEMBER

The late Edgar Pangborn returns to these pages (see his "Angel's Egg" in Vol. 13) with one of his finest stories. The arts in general and music in particular have been the subject of numerous stories and novels in science fiction, and at least two anthologies, both excellent, have been published on the theme—James Blish's NEW DREAMS THIS MORNING (1966) and Thomas F. Monteleone's THE ARTS AND BEYOND (1977). A number of sf writers, including Anne McCaffrey and Lloyd Biggle, Jr. have applied their musical expertise to their science fiction. "The Music Master of Babylon" along with 1962's "The Golden Horn" are Pangborn's two major works featuring music, and both contain all the beauty, emotion, and tone that made his work so memorable.

But Isaac is really the music buff of this editorial team, and much better qualified to discuss this story. (MHG)

That's a terrible thing to do to me, Marty. When did I ever pretend to be a music buff?

I like to listen to nineteenth-century romantic music, and I go for the schmaltz of Tschaikovsky and Verdi, and I yield to no one in my appreciation of Gilbert & Sullivan, and I can carry a tune and, for someone without any training at all, I can sing pretty well, but that's as far as it goes. When I read

*this story and say that it is touching, I've gone as far as I can
go in my discussion of the musical aspects of the story.*

   *Edgar Pangborn, by the way, was one of the few prominent
writers of the forties and fifties I never met. (IA)*

For twenty-five years no one came.

   In the seventy-sixth year of his life Brian Van Anda was
still trying not to remember a happy boyhood. To do so was
irrelevant and dangerous, although every instinct of his old
age tempted him to reject the present and live in the lost
times. He would recall stubbornly that the present year, for
example, was 2096 according to the Christian calendar, that
he had been born in 2020, seven years after the close of the
civil war, fifty years before the last war, twenty-five years
before the departure of the First Interstellar. The First and
Second Interstellar would be still on the move, he supposed.
It had been understood, obvious, long ago, that after radio
contact faded out the world would not hear of them again for
many lifetimes, if ever. They would be on the move, farther
and farther away from a planet no longer capable of understanding such matters.

   Brian sometimes recalled his place of birth, New Boston,
the fine planned city far inland from the old metropolis which
a rising sea had reclaimed after the earthquake of 1994. Such
things, places and dates, were factual props, useful when
Brian wanted to impose an external order on the vagueness of
his immediate existence. He tried to make sure they became
no more than that, to shut away the colors, the poignant
sounds, the parks and the playgrounds of New Boston, the
known faces (many of them loved), and the later years when
he had experienced a curious intoxication called fame.

   It was not necessarily better or wiser to reject these memories, but it was safer, and nowadays Brian was often sufficiently tired, sufficiently conscious of his growing weakness
and lonely unimportance, to crave safety as a meadow mouse
craves a burrow.

   He tied his canoe to the massive window which for many
years had been a port and a doorway. Lounging there with a

suspended sense of time, he hardly knew he was listening. In a way, all the twenty-five years had been a listening. He watched Earth's patient star sink toward the rim of the forest on the Palisades. At this hour it was sometimes possible, if the sun-crimsoned water lay still, to cease grieving at the greater stillness.

There must be scattered human life elsewhere, he knew—probably a great deal of it. After twenty-five years alone, that also often seemed irrelevant. At other times than mild evenings—on hushed noons or in the mornings always so empty of human commotion—Brian might lapse into anger, fight the calm by yelling, resent the swift dying of his own echoes. Such moods were brief. A kind of humor remained in him, not to be ruined by any sorrow.

He remembered how, ten months or possibly ten years ago, he had encountered a box turtle in a forest clearing, and had shouted at it: "They went thataway!" The turtle's rigidly comic face, fixed in a caricature of startled disapproval, had seemed to point up some truth or other. Brian had hunkered down on the moss and laughed uproariously until he observed that some of the laughter was weeping.

Today had been rather good. He had killed a deer on the Palisades, and with bow and arrow, not spending a bullet—irreplaceable toy of civilization.

Not that he needed to practice such economy. He could live, he supposed, another ten years at the outside. His rifles were in good condition, his hoarded ammunition would easily outlast him. So would the stock of canned and dried food stuffed away in his living quarters. But there was satisfaction in primitive effort, and no compulsion to analyze the why of it.

The stored food was more important than the ammunition; a time was coming soon enough when he would no longer have the strength for hunting. He would lose the inclination to depart from his fortress for trips to the mainland. He would yield to such timidity or laziness for days, then weeks. Sometime, after such an interlude, he might find himself too feeble to risk climbing the cliff wall into the forest. He would then have the good sense, he hoped, to destroy the canoe, thus making of his weakness a necessity.

There were books. There was the Hall of Music on the next floor above the water, probably safe from its lessening encroachment. To secure fresh water he need only keep track of the tides, for the Hudson had cleaned itself and now rolled down sweet from the lonely uncorrupted hills. His decline could be comfortable. He had provided for it and planned it.

Yet now, gazing across the sleepy water, seeing a broad-winged hawk circle in freedom above the forest, Brian was aware of the old thought moving in him: *If I could hear voices—just once, if I could hear human voices . . .*

The Museum of Human History, with the Hall of Music on what Brian thought of as the second floor, should also outlast his requirements. In the flooded lower floor and basement the work of slow destruction must be going on: Here and there the unhurried waters could find their way to steel and make rust of it; the waterproofing of the concrete was nearly a hundred years old. But it ought to be good for another century or two.

Nowadays the ocean was mild. There were moderate tides, winds no longer destructive. For the last six years there had been no more of the heavy storms out of the south; in the same period Brian had noted a rise in the water level of a mere nine inches. The windowsill, his port, stood six inches above high-tide mark this year. Perhaps Earth was settling into a new amiable mood. The climate had become delightful, about like what Brian remembered from a visit to southern Virginia in his childhood.

The last earthquake had come in 2082—a large one, Brian guessed, but its center could not have been close to the rock of Manhattan. The Museum had only shivered and shrugged—it had survived much worse than that, half a dozen times since 1994. Long after the tremor, a tall wave had thundered in from the south. Its force, like that of others, had mostly been dissipated against the barrier of tumbled rock and steel at the southern end of the submerged island—an undersea dam, man-made though not man-intended—and when it reached

the Museum it did no more than smash the southern windows
in the Hall of Music, which earlier waves had not been able
to reach; then it passed on up the river enfeebled.

The windows of the lower floor had all been broken long
before that. After the earthquake of '82 Brian had spent a
month in boarding up all the openings on the south side of the
Hall of Music—after all, it was home—with lumber painfully
ferried over from mainland ruins. By that year he was sixty-
two years old and not moving with the ease of youth. He
deliberately left cracks and knotholes. Sunlight sifted through
in narrow beams, like the bars of dusty gold Brian could
remember in a hayloft at his uncle's farm in Vermont.

That hawk above the Palisades soared nearer over the river
and receded. Caught in the evening light, he was himself a
little sun, dying and returning.

The Museum had been finished in 2003. Manhattan, strangely
enough, had never taken a bomb, although in the civil war
two of the type called "small clean fission" had fallen on the
Brooklyn and New Jersey sides—so Brian recalled from the
jolly history books which had informed his adolescence that
war was definitely a thing of the past. By the time of the next
last war, in 2070, the sea, gorged on melting ice caps, had
removed Manhattan Island from current history.

Everything left standing above the waters south of the
Museum had been knocked flat by the tornadoes of 2057 and
2064. A few blobs of empty rock still demonstrated where
Central Park and Mount Morris Park had been: not signifi-
cant. Where Long Island once rose, there was a troubled area
of shoals and small islands, probably a useful barrier of
protection for the receding shore of Connecticut. Men had
yielded their great city inch by inch, then foot by foot; a full
mile in 2047, saying: "The flood years have passed their
peak, and a return to normal is expected. Brian sometimes
felt a twinge of sympathy for the Neanderthal experts who
must have told each other to expect a return to normal at the
very time when the Cro-Magnons were drifting in.

In 2057 the Island of Manhattan had to be yielded. New
York City, half-new, half-ancient, sprawled stubborn and

enormous upstream, on both sides of a river not done with its anger. Yet the Museum stood. Aided by sunken rubble of other buildings of its kind, aided also by men because they still had time to move it, the museum stood, and might for a long time yet—weather permitting.

The hawk floated out of sight above the Palisades into the field of the low sun.

The Museum of Human History covered an acre of ground north of 125th Street, rising a modest fifteen stories, its foundation secure in that layer of rock which mimics eternity. It deserved its name; here men had brought samples of everything man-made, literally everything known in the course of human creation since prehistory. Within human limits it was definitive.

No one had felt anything unnatural in the refusal of the Directors of the Museum to move the collection after the building weathered the storm of 2057. Instead, ordinary people donated money so that a mighty abutment could be built around the ground floor and a new entrance designed on the north side of the second. The abutment survived the greater tornado of 2064 without damage, although during those seven years the sea had risen another eight feet in its old ever-new game of making monkeys out of the wise. (It was left for Brian Van Anda, alone, in 2079, to see the waters slide quietly over the abutment, opening the lower regions for the use of fishes and the more secret water-dwellers who like shelter and privacy. In the '90s, Brian suspected the presence of an octopus or two in the vast vague territory that had once been parking lot, heating plant, storage space, air-raid shelter, etc. He couldn't prove it; it just seemed like a decent, comfortable place for an octopus.) In 2070 plans were under consideration for building a new causeway to the Museum from the still expanding city in the north. In 2070, also, the last war began and ended.

When Brian Van Anda came down the river late in 2071, a refugee from certain unfamiliar types of savagery, the Museum was empty of the living. He spent many days in exhaustive exploration of the building. He did this systematically, toiling at last up to the Directors' meeting room on the top floor. There he observed how they must have been holding a conference at the very time when a new gas was tried out over New York in a final effort to persuade the Western Federation that the end justifies the means. (Too bad, Brian sometimes thought, that he would never know exactly what had become of the Asian Empire. In the little splinter state called the Soviet of North America, from which Brian had fled in '71, the official doctrine was that the Asian Empire had won the war and the saviors of humanity would be flying in any day now. Brian had inadvertently doubted this out loud and then stolen a boat and gotten away safely under cover of night.)

Up in the meeting room, Brian had seen how that up-to-date neurotoxin had been no respecter of persons. An easy death, however, by the look of it. He observed also how some things endure. The Museum, for instance: virtually unharmed.

Brian often recalled those moments in the meeting room as a sort of island in time. They were like the first day of falling in love, the first hour of discovering that he could play Beethoven. And a little like the curiously cherished, more than life-size half-hour back there in Newburg, in that ghastly year 2071, when he had briefly met and spoken with an incredibly old man, Abraham Brown. Brown had been President of the Western Federation at the time of the civil war. Later, retired from the uproar of public affairs, he had devoted himself to philosophy, unofficial teaching. In 2071, with the world he had loved in almost total ruin around him, Brown had spoken pleasantly to Brian Van Anda of small things—of chrysanthemums that would soon be blooming in the front yard of the house where he lived with friends, of a piano recital by Van Anda back in 2067 which the old man still remembered with warm enthusiasm.

Only a month later more hell was loose and Brian himself in flight.

Yes, the Museum Directors had died easily. Brooding in

the evening sunlight, Brian reflected that now, all these years later, the innocent bodies would be perfectly decent. No vermin in the Museum. The doorways and the floors were tight, the upper windows unbroken.

One of the white-haired men had had a Ming vase on his desk. He had not dropped out of his chair, but looked as if he had fallen asleep in front of the vase with his head on his arms. Brian had left the vase untouched, but had taken one other thing, moved by some stirring of his own never-certain philosophy and knowing that he would not return to this room, ever.

One of the Directors had been opening a wall cabinet when he fell; the key lay near his fingers. Their discussion had not been concerned only with war, perhaps not at all with war. After all, there were other topics. The Ming vase must have had a part in it. Brian wished he could know what the old man had meant to take from the cabinet. Sometimes he dreamed of conversations with that man, in which the Director told him the truth of this and other matters, but what was certainty in sleep was in the morning gone like childhood.

For himself Brian had taken a little image of rock-hard clay, blackened, two-faced, male and female. Prehistoric, or at any rate wholly savage, unsophisticated, meaningful like the blameless motion of an animal in sunlight. Brian had said: "With your permission, gentlemen." He had closed the cabinet and then, softly, the outer door.

"I'm old, too," Brian said to the red evening. He searched for the hawk and could no longer find it in the deepening sky. "Old, a little foolish—talk aloud to myself. I'll have some Mozart before supper."

He transferred the fresh venison from the canoe to a small raft hitched inside the window. He had selected only choice pieces, as much as he could cook and eat in the few days before it spoiled, leaving the rest for the wolves or any other forest scavengers which might need it. There was a rope strung from the window to the marble steps leading to the next floor of the Museum, which was home.

It had not been possible to save much from the submerged area, for its treasure was mostly heavy statuary. Through the still water, as he pulled the raft along the rope, the Moses of Michelangelo gazed up at him in tranquillity. Other faces watched him; most of them watched infinity. There were white hands that occasionally borrowed motion from ripples made by the raft. "I got a deer, Moses," said Brian Van Anda, smiling down in companionship, losing track of time. . . . "Good night, Moses." He carried his juicy burden up the stairway.

Brian's living quarters had once been a cloakroom for Museum attendants. Four close walls gave it a feel of security. A ventilating shaft now served as a chimney for the wood stove Brian had salvaged from a mainland farmhouse. The door could be tightly locked. There were no windows. You do not want windows in a cave.

Outside was the Hall of Music, a full acre, an entire floor of the Museum, containing an example of every musical instrument that was known or could be reconstructed in the twenty-first century. The library of scores and recordings lacked nothing—except electricity to make the recordings speak. A few might still be made to sound on a hand-cranked phonograph, but Brian had not bothered with that toy for years; the springs were probably rusted.

Brian sometimes took out orchestra and chamber music scores to read at random. Once, reading them, his mind had been able to furnish ensembles, orchestras, choirs of a sort, but lately the ability had weakened. He remembered a day, possibly a year ago, when his memory refused to give him the sound of oboe and clarinet in unison. He had wandered, peevish, distressed, unreasonably alarmed, among the racks and cases of woodwinds and brasses and violins. He tried to sound a clarinet; the reed was still good in the dust proof case, but he had no lip. He had never mastered any instrument except the pianoforte.

He recalled—it might have been that same day—opening a chest of double basses. There was a three-stringer in the group, old, probably from the early nineteenth century, a

trifle fatter than its more modern companions. Brian touched
its middle string in an idle caress, not intending to make it
sound, but it had done so. When in use, it would have been
tuned to D; time had slackened the heavy murmur to A or
something near it. That had throbbed in the silent room with
finality, a sound such as a programmatic composer, say
Tchaikovsky, might have used as a tonal symbol for the
breaking of a heart. It stayed in the air as other instruments
whispered a dim response. "All right, gentlemen," Brian
said, "that was your A. . . ."

Out in the main part of the hall, a place of honor was given
to what may have been the oldest of the instruments, a
seven-note marimba of phonolitic schist discovered in Indo-
China in the twentieth century and thought to be at least
5,000 years of age. The xylophone-type rack was modern.
Brian for twenty-five years had obeyed a compulsion to keep
it free of cobwebs. Sometimes he touched the singing stones,
not for amusement but because there was comfort in it. They
answered to the light tap of a fingernail. Beside them on a
little table of its own he had placed the Stone Age god of two
faces.

On the west side of the Hall of Music, a rather long walk
from Brian's cave, was a small auditorium. Lectures, recitals,
chamber music concerts had been given there in the old days.
The pleasant room held a twelve-foot concert grand, made in
2043, probably the finest of the many pianos in the Hall of
Music, a summit of technical achievement. Brian had done
his best to preserve this beautiful artifact, prayerfully tuning it
three times a year, robbing other pianos in the Museum to
provide a reserve supply of strings, oiled and sealed against
rust. When not in use his great piano was covered by stitched-
together sheets. To remove the cover was a somber ritual.
Before touching the keys, Brian washed his hands with needless fanatical care.

Some years ago he had developed the habit of locking the
auditorium doors before he played. Yet even then he preferred not to glance toward the vista of empty seats, not much
caring whether this inhibition derived from a Stone Age fear

of finding someone there or from a flat civilized understanding that no one could be. It never occurred to him to lock the
one door he used, when he was absent from the auditorium.
The key remained on the inside; if he went in merely to tune
the piano or to inspect the place, he never turned it.

The habit of locking it when he played might have started
(he could not remember) back in the year 2076, when so
many bodies had floated down from the north on the ebb
tides. Full horror had somehow been lacking in the sight of
all that floating death. Perhaps it was because Brian had
earlier had his fill of horrors, or perhaps in 2076 he already
felt so divorced from his own kind that what happened to
them was like the photograph of a war in a distant country.
Some had bobbed and floated quite near the Museum. Most
of them had the gaping obvious wounds of primitive warfare,
but some were oddly discolored—a new pestilence? So there
was (or had been) more trouble up there in what was (or had
been) the short-lived Soviet of North America, a self-styled
"nation" that took in east central New York and most of
New England. So . . . Yes, that was probably the year when
he had started locking the doors between his private concerts
and an empty world.

He dumped the venison in his cave. He scrubbed his
hands, showing high blue veins now, but still tough, still
knowing. Mozart, he thought, and walked, not with much
pleasure of anticipation but more like one externally driven,
through the enormous hall that was so full and yet so empty
and growing dim with evening, with dust, with age, with
loneliness. Music should not be silent.

When the piano was uncovered, Brian delayed. He exer-
cised his hands unnecessarily. He fussed with the candela-
brum on the wall, lighting three candles, then blowing out
two for economy. He admitted presently that he did not want
the emotional clarity of Mozart at all, not now. The darkness
of 2070 was too close, closer than he had felt it for a long
time. It would never have occurred to Mozart, Brian thought,
that a world could die. Beethoven could have entertained the

idea soberly enough, and Chopin probably; even Brahms.
Mozart, Haydn, Bach would surely have dismissed it as
somebody's bad dream, in poor taste. Andrew Carr, who
lived and died in the latter half of the twentieth century, had
endured the idea deep in his bloodstream from the beginning
of his childhood.

The date of Hiroshima was 1945; Carr was born in 1951.
The wealth of his music was written between 1969, when he
was eighteen, and 1984, when he died among the smells of
an Egyptian jail from injuries received in a street brawl.

"If not Mozart," said Brian Van Anda to his idle hands,
"there is always the Project."

To play Carr's last sonata as it should be played—as Carr
was supposed to have said he couldn't play it himself: Brian
had been thinking of that as the Project for many years. It had
begun teasing his mind long before the war, at the time of his
triumphs in a civilized world which had been warmly appreciative of the polished interpretive artist (once he got the
breaks) although no more awake than in any other age to the
creative sort. Back there in the undestroyed society, Brian
had proposed to program that sonata in the company of works
that were older but no greater, and to play it—well, beyond
his best, so that even music critics would begin to see its
importance in history.

He had never done it, had never felt the necessary assurance that he had entered into the sonata and learned the depth
of it. Now, when there was none to hear or care, unless the
harmless brown spiders in the corners of the auditorium had a
taste for music, there was still the Project. *I* hear, Brian
thought. *I* care, and with myself for audience I wish to hear it
once as it ought to be, a final statement for a world that was
(I think) too good to die.

Technically, of course, he had it. The athletic demands
Carr made on the performer were tremendous, but, given
technique, there was nothing impossible about them. Anyone
capable of concert work could at least play the notes at the
required tempi. And any reasonably shrewd pianist could
keep track of the dynamics, saving strength for the shattering

finale. Brian had heard the sonata played by others two or three times in the old days—competently. Competency was not enough.

For example, what about the third movement, the mad scherzo, and the five tiny interludes of quiet scattered through its plunging fury? They were not alike. Related, but each one demanded a new climate of heart and mind—tenderness, regret, simple relaxation. Flowers on a flood—no. Window lights in a storm—no. The innocence of a child in a bombed city—no, not really. Something of all those. Much more, too, defying words.

What of the second movement, the largo, where in a way the pattern was reversed, the midnight introspection interrupted by moments of anger, or longing, or despair like the despair of an angel beating his wings against a prison of glass?

It was a work in which something of Carr's life, Carr's temperament, had to come into you, whether you dared welcome it or not; otherwise your playing was no more than reproduction of notes on a page. Carr's life was not for the contemplation of the timid.

The details were superficially well-known; the biographies were like musical notation, meaningless without interpretation and insight. Carr was a drunken roarer, a young devil-god with such a consuming hunger for life that he choked to death on it. His friends hated him for the way he drained their lives, loving them to distraction and the next moment having no time for them because he loved his work more. His enemies must have had times of helplessly admiring him if only because of a translucent honesty that made him more and less than human. A rugged Australian, not tall but built like a hero, a face all forehead and jaw and glowing hyperthyroid eyes. He wept only when he was angry, the biographic storytellers said. In one minute of talk he might shift from gutter obscenity to some extreme of altruistic tenderness, and from that perhaps to a philosophic comment of cold intelligence. He passed his childhood on a sheep farm, ran away on a freighter at thirteen, was flung out of two respectable conservatories for drunkenness and "public lewdness," then studied like a slave in London with single-minded desperation, as if he knew the time was short. He was married twice and twice divorced. He killed a man in a silly brawl on the New Orleans docks, and wrote his First Symphony while he was in jail for that. He died of stab wounds from a broken bottle in a Cairo jail, and was recognized by the critics. It all had relevancy; relevant or not, if the sonata was in your mind, so was the life.

You had to remember also that Andrew Carr was the last of civilization's great composers. No one in the twenty-first century approached him—they ignored his explorations and carved cherrystones. He belonged to no school, unless you wanted to imagine a school of music beginning with Bach, taking in perhaps a dozen along the way, and ending with Carr himself. His work was a summary as well as an advance along the mainstream into the unknown; in the light of the year 2070, it was also a completion.

Brian was certain he could play the first movement of the sonata as he wished to. Technically it was not revolutionary, and remained rather close to the ancient sonata form. Carr had even written in a double bar for a repeat of the entire opening statement, something that had made his cerebral contemporaries sneer with great satisfaction; it never occurred to them that Carr was inviting the performer to use his head.

The bright-sorrowful second movement, unfashionably long, with its strange pauses, unforeseen recapitulations, outbursts of savage change—that was where Brian's troubles began. ("Reminiscent of Franck," said the hunters for comparisons whom we have always with us.) It did not help Brian to be old, remembering the inner storms of forty years ago and more.

His single candle fluttered. For once Brian had forgotten to lock the door into the Hall of Music. This troubled him, but he did not rise from the piano chair. He chided himself instead for the foolish neuroses of aloneness—what could it matter? Let it go. He shut his eyes. The sonata had long ago been memorized; printed copies were safe in the library. He played the opening of the first movement as far as the double bar, opened his eyes to the friendly black-and-white of clean keys, and played the repetition with new lights, new emphasis. Better than usual, he thought—

Yes. Good. . . . Now that naïve-appearing modulation into A major, which only Carr would have wanted just there in that sudden obvious way, like the opening of a door on shining fields. On toward the climax—*I am playing it, I think*—through the intricate revelations of development and recapitulation. And the conclusion, lingering, half-humorous, not unlike a Beethoven *I'm-not-gone-yet* ending, but with a questioning that was all Andrew Carr. After that—

"No more tonight," said Brian aloud. "Some night, though . . . Not competent right now, my friend." He replaced the cover of the piano and blew out the candle. He had brought no torch, long use having taught his feet every inch of the small journey. It was quite dark. The never-opened western windows of the auditorium were dirty, most of the dirt on the outside, crusted windblown salt.

In this partial darkness something was wrong.

At first Brian found no source for the faint light, dim orange with a hint of motion. He peered into the gloom of the auditorium, fixing his eyes on the oblong of blacker shadow that was the doorway into the Hall of Music. The windows, of course!—he had almost forgotten there were any. The light, hardly deserving the name of light, was coming through them. But sunset was surely past. He had been here a long time, delaying and brooding before he played. Sunset should not flicker.

So there was some kind of fire on the mainland. There had been no thunderstorm. How should fire start, over there where no one ever came?

He stumbled a few times, swearing petulantly, locating the doorway again and groping through it into the Hall of Music. The windows out here were just as dirty; no use trying to see through them. There must have been a time when he had looked through them, enjoyed looking through them. He stood shivering in the marble silence, trying to remember.

Time was a gradual, continual dying. Time was the growth of dirt and ocean salt, sealing in, covering over. He stumbled for his cloakroom cave, hurrying now, and lit two candles. He left one by the cold stove and used the other to light his way down the stairs to his raft; once down there, he blew it out, afraid. The room a candle makes in the darkness is a vulnerable room. Having no walls, it closes in a blindness. He pulled the raft by the guide-rope, gently, for fear of noise.

He found his canoe tied as he had left it. He poked his white head slowly beyond the sill, staring west.

Merely a bonfire gleaming, reddening the blackness of the cliff.

Brian knew the spot, a ledge almost at water level, at one end of it the troublesome path he usually followed in climbing to the forest at the top of the Palisades. Usable driftwood was often there, the supply renewed by the high tides.

"No," Brian said. "Oh, no! . . ."

Unable to accept or believe, or not believe, he drew his head in, resting his forehead on the coldness of the sill, waiting for dizziness to pass, reason to return.

It might have been a long time, a kind of blackout. Now he was again in command of his actions and even rather calm, once more leaning out over the sill. The fire still shone and was therefore not a disordered dream of old age. It was dying to a dull rose of embers.

He wondered about the time. Clocks and watches had stopped long ago; Brian had ceased to want them. A sliver of moon was hanging over the water to the east. He ought to be able to remember the phases, deduce the approximate time from that. But his mind was too tired or distraught to give him the data. Maybe it was somewhere around midnight.

He climbed on the sill and lifted the canoe over it to the motionless water inside. Useless, he decided, as soon as the grunting effort was finished. That fire had been lit before daylight passed; whoever lit it would have seen the canoe, might even have been watching Brian himself come home from his hunting. The canoe's disappearance in the night would only rouse further curiosity. But Brian was too exhausted to lift it back.

And why assume that the maker of the bonfire was necessarily hostile? Might be good company. . . . He pulled his raft through the darkness, secured it at the stairway, and groped back to his cave.

He locked the door. The venison was waiting; the sight made him ravenous. He lit a small fire in the stove, one that he hoped would not still be sending smoke from the ventilator shaft when morning came. He cooked the meat crudely and wolfed it down, all enjoyment gone at the first mouthful. He was shocked to discover the dirtiness of his white beard. He hadn't given himself a real bath in—weeks, was it? He searched for scissors and spent an absentminded while in trimming the beard back to shortness. He ought to take some soap—valuable stuff—down to Moses' room, and wash.

Clothes, too. People probably still wore clothes. He had worn none for years, except for sandals. He used a carrying satchel for trips to the mainland. He had enjoyed the freedom at first, and especially the discovery that in his rugged fifties he did not need clothes even for the soft winters, except perhaps a light covering when he slept. Later, total nakedness had become so natural it required no thought at all. But the owner of that bonfire could have inherited or retained the pruderies of the lost culture.

He checked his rifles. The .22 automatic, an Army model from the 2040's, was the best—any amount of death in that. The tiny bullets carried a paralytic poison: graze a man's finger and he was almost painlessly dead in three minutes. Effective range, with telescopic sights, three kilometers; weight, a scant five pounds. Brian sat a long time cuddling that triumph of military science, listening for sounds that never came. Would it be two o'clock? He wished he could have seen the Time Satellite, renamed in his mind the Midnight Star, but when he was down there at his port, he had not once looked up at the night sky. Delicate and beautiful, bearing its everlasting freight of men who must have been dead now for twenty-five years and who would be dead a very long time—

well, it was better than a clock, if you happened to look at the midnight sky at the right time of the month when the man-made star caught the moonlight. But he had missed it tonight. Three o'clock? . . .

At some time during the long dark he put the rifle away on the floor. With studied, self-conscious contempt for his own weakness, he unlocked the door and strode out noisily into the Hall of Music, with a fresh-lit candle. This same bravado, he knew, might dissolve at the first alien noise. While it lasted, it was invigorating.

The windows were still black with night. As if the candle flame had found its own way, Brian was standing by the ancient marimba in the main hall, the gleam slanting care-lessly away from his gaunt hand. And nearby sat the Stone Age god.

It startled him. He remembered clearly how he himself had placed it there, obeying a half-humorous whim. The image and the singing stones were both magnificently older than history, so why shouldn't they live together? Whenever he dusted the marimba, he dusted the image respectfully, and its table. It would not have needed much urging from the im-pulses of a lonely mind to make him place offerings before it—winking first, of course, to indicate that rituals suitable to a pair of aging gentlemen did not have to be sensible in order to be good.

The clay face remembering eternity was not deformed by the episode of civilization. Chipped places were simple hon-orable scars. The two faces stared mildly from the single head, uncommunicative, serene.

A wooden hammer of modern make rested on the ma-rimba. Softly Brian tapped a few of the stones. He struck the shrillest one harder, waking many slow-dying overtones, and laid the hammer down, listening until the last murmur per-ished and a drop of wax hurt his thumb. He returned to his cave and blew out the candle, never thinking of the door, or if he thought, not caring.

Face down, he rolled his head and clenched his fingers into his pallet, seeking in pain, finding at last the relief of stormy childish weeping in the dark.

Then he slept.

They looked timid. The evidence of it was in their tense squatting pose, not in what the feeble light allowed Brian to see of their faces, which were blank as rock. Hunkered down just inside the doorway of the dim cloakroom cave, a morning grayness from the Hall of Music behind them, they were ready for flight, and Brian's intelligence warned his body to stay motionless. Readiness for flight could also be readiness for attack. He studied them through slit eyelids, knowing he was in deep shadow.

They were very young, sixteen or seventeen, firm-muscled, the boy slim but heavy in the shoulders, the girl a fully developed woman. They were dressed alike: loincloths of some coarse dull fabric, and moccasins that were probably deerhide. Their hair grew nearly to the shoulders and was cut off carelessly, but they were evidently in the habit of combing it. They appeared to be clean. Their complexion, so far as Brian could guess it in the meager light, was brown, like a heavy tan. With no immediate awareness of emotion, he decided they were beautiful, and then within his own poised and perilous silence Brian reminded himself that the young are always beautiful.

The woman muttered softly: "He wake."

A twitch of the man's head was probably meant to warn her to be quiet. He clutched the shaft of a javelin with a metal blade which had once belonged to a breadknife. The blade was polished, shining, lashed to a peeled stick. The javelin trailed, ready for use at a flick of the young man's arm. Brian sighed deliberately. "Good morning."

The man, or boy, said: "Good morning, sa."

"Where do you come from?"

"Millstone." The man spoke automatically, but then his facial rigidity dissolved into astonishment and some kind of distress. He glanced at his companion, who giggled uneasily.

"The old man pretends to not know," she said, and smiled, and seemed to be waiting for the young man's permission to go on speaking. He did not give it, but she continued: "Sa,

the old ones of Millstone are dead." She thrust her hand out
and down, flat, a picture of finality, adding with nervous
haste: "As the Old Man knows. He who told us to call him
Jonas, she who told us to call her Abigail, dead. They are
still-without-moving the full six days, then we do the burial
as they told us. As the Old Man knows."

"But I don't know!" said Brian, and sat up on his pallet
too quickly, startling them. But their motion was backward, a
readying for flight. "Millstone? Where is Millstone?"

They looked wholly bewildered and dismayed. They stood
up with animal grace, stepping backward out of the cave, the
girl whispering in the man's ear. Brian caught two words:
"—is angry."

He jumped up. "Don't go! Please don't go!" He followed
them out of the cave, slowly now, aware that he might be an
object of terror in the half-dark, aware of his gaunt, graceless
age, and nakedness, and dirty hacked-off beard. Almost involuntarily he adopted something of the flat stilted quality of
their speech. "I will not hurt you. Do not go."

They halted. The girl smiled dubiously. The man said:
"We need old ones. They die. He who told us to call him
Jonas said, many days in the boat, not with the sun-path, he
said, across the sun-path, he said, keeping land on the left
hand. We need old ones, to speak the—to speak . . . The Old
Man is angry?"

"No. I am not angry. I am never angry." Brian's mind
groped, certain of nothing. No one came, for twenty-five
years.

Millstone?

There was red-gold on the dirty eastern windows of the
Hall of Music, a light becoming softness as it slanted down,
touching the long rows of cases, the warm brown of an
antique spinet, the clean gold of a twentieth century harp, the
gray of singing stones five thousand years old and a two-
faced god much older than that. "Millstone." Brian pointed
in inquiry, southwest.

The girl nodded, pleased and not at all surprised that he
should know, watching him now with a squirrel's stiff curios-

ity. Hadn't there been a Millstone River in or near Princeton, once upon a time? Brian thought he remembered that it emptied into the Raritan Canal. There was some moderately high ground there. Islands now, no doubt. Perhaps they would tell him. "There were old people in Millstone," he said, trying for peaceful dignity, "and they died. So now you need old ones to take their place."

The girl nodded vigorously many times. Her glance at the young man was shy, possessive, maybe amused. "He who told us to call him Jonas said no marriage without the words of Abraham."

"Abr—" Brian checked himself. If this was religion, it would not do to speak the name Abraham with a rising inflection. "I have been for a long time—" He checked himself again: A man old, ugly, and strange enough to be sacred should never stoop to explain anything.

They were standing by the seven-stone marimba. His hand dropped, his thumbnail clicking against the deepest stone and waking a murmur. The children drew back, alarmed. Brian smiled. "Don't be afraid." He tapped the other stones lightly. "It is only music. It will not hurt you." They were patient and respectful, waiting for more light. He said carefully: "He who told you to call him Jonas—he taught you all the things you know?"

"All things," the boy said, and the girl nodded three or four times, so that the soft brownness of her hair tumbled about her face, and she pushed it back in a small human motion as old as the clay image.

"Do you know how old you are?"

They looked blank. Then the girl said: "Oh—summers!" She held up her two hands with spread fingers, then one hand. "Three fives." She chuckled, and sobered quickly. "As the Old Man knows."

"I am very old," said Brian. "I know many things, but sometimes I wish to forget, and sometimes I wish to hear what others know, even though I may know it myself."

They looked uncomprehending and greatly impressed. Brian felt a smile on his face and wondered why it should be there.

They were nice children. Born ten years after the death of a world; twenty, perhaps. *I think I am seventy-six, but what if I dropped a decade somewhere and never noticed the damned thing?* . . . "He who told you to call him Jonas—he taught you all you know of Abraham?"

At the sound of the name, both made swift circular motions, first at the forehead, then at the breast. "He taught us all things," the young man said. "He, and she who told us to call her Abigail. The hours to rise, to pray, to wash, to eat. The laws for hunting, and I know the Abraham-words for that: Sol-Amra, I take this for my need."

Brian felt lost again, and looked down to the clay faces of the image for counsel, and found none. "They who told you to call them Jonas and Abigail, they were the only ones who lived with you?—the only old ones?"

Again that look of bewilderment and disappointment. "The only ones, sa," the young man said. "As the Old Man knows."

I could never persuade them that, being old, I know very nearly nothing. . . .

Brian straightened to his full great height. The young people were not tall. Though stiff and worn with age, Brian knew he was still overpowering. Once, among men, he had gently enjoyed being more than life-size. As a shield for loneliness and fright within, he now adopted a phony sternness. "I wish to examine you for your own good, my children, about Millstone and your knowledge of Abraham. How many others live at Millstone, tell me."

"Two fives, sa," said the boy promptly, "and I the one who may be called Jonason and this girl who may be called Paula. Two fives and two. We are the biggest. The others are only children, but the one who may be called Jimi has killed his deer; he sees after them now while we go across the sun-path."

Under Brian's questioning, more of the story came, haltingly, obscured by the young man's conviction that the Old Man already knew everything. Sometime, probably in the middle 2080's, Jonas and Abigail (whoever they were) had come on a group of twelve wild children who were keeping alive somehow in a ruined town where their elders had all died. Jonas and Abigail had brought them all to an island they called Millstone. Jonas and Abigail came originally from "up across the sun-path"—the boy seemed to mean north—and they were very old, which might mean, Brian guessed, anything between thirty and ninety. In teaching the children primitive means of survival, Jonas and Abigail had brought off a brilliant success: Jonason and Paula were well-fed, shining with health and the strength of wildness, and clean. Their speech, limited and odd though it was, had not been learned from the ignorant. Its pronunciation faintly suggested New England, so far as it had any local accent. "Did they teach you reading and writing?" Brian asked, and made writing motions on the flat of his palm, which the two watched in vague alarm.

The boy asked: "What is that?"

"Never mind." *I could quarrel with some of your theories, Mister-whom-I-may-call-Jonas.* But maybe, he thought, there had been no books, no writing materials, no way to get them. What's the minimum of technology required to keep the human spirit alive? . . . "Well—well, tell me what they taught you of Abraham. I wish to hear how well you remember."

Both made again the circular motion at forehead and breast, and the young man said with the stiffness of recitation: "Abraham was the Son of Heaven who died that we might live." The girl, her obligation discharged with the religious gesture, tapped the marimba shyly, fascinated, and drew her finger back, smiling up at Brian in apology for naughtiness. "He taught the laws, the everlasting truth of all time," the boy gabbled, "and was slain on the wheel at Nuber by the infidels; therefore since he died for us, we look up across the sun-path when we pray to Abraham Brown who will come again." The boy Jonason sighed and relaxed.

Abraham—Brown? But—

But I knew him. I met him. Nuber? Newburg, temporary capital of the Soviet of—oh, damn that . . . Met him, 2071—the

concert of mine he remembered . . . The wheel? The wheel?
"And when did Abraham die, boy?"

"Oh—" Jonason moved fingers helplessly, embarrassed.
Dates would be no part of the doctrine. "Long ago. A—a—"
He glanced up hopefully. "A thousand years? I think—he
who told us to call him Jonas did not teach us that."

"I see. Never mind. You speak well, boy." *Oh, my good
Doctor, ex-President—after all! Artist, statesman, student of
ethics, agnostic philosopher—all that long life you preached
charity and skepticism, courage without the need of faith, the
positive uses of the suspended judgment. All so clear, simple,
obvious—needing only that little bit more of patience and
courage which your human hearers were not ready to give.
You must have known they were not, but did you know this
would happen?*

Jonas and Abigail—some visionary pair, Brian supposed,
full of this theory and that, maybe gone a bit foolish under
the horrors of those years. Unthinking admirers of Brown, or
perhaps not even that, perhaps just brewing their own syncre-
tism because they thought a religion was needed, and using
Brown's name—why? Because it was easy to remember?
They probably felt some pride of creation in the job; possibly
belief even grew in their own minds as they found the children accepting it and building a ritual life around it.

It was impossible, Brian thought, that Jonas and Abigail
could have met the living Abraham Brown. Brown accepted
mysteries because he faced the limitations of human intelligence; he had only contempt for the needless making of
mysteries. He was without arrogance. No one could have
talked five minutes with him without hearing a tranquil: "I
don't know."

The *wheel* at Nuber?—but Brian realized he would never
learn how Brown actually died. *I hope you suffered no more
than most prophets. . . .*

He was pulled from the pit of abstraction by the girl's awed
question: "What is that?"

She was pointing to the clay image in its dusty sunlight.
Brian was almost deaf to his own words until they were past

recovering: "Oh, that—that is very old. Very old and very sacred." She nodded, round-eyed, and stepped back a pace or two. "And that was all they taught you of Abraham Brown?"

Astonished, the boy asked: "Is it not enough?"

There is always the Project. "Why, perhaps—"

"We know all the prayers, Old Man."

"Yes, yes, I'm sure you do."

"The Old Man will come with us." It was not a question.

"Eh?" *There is always the Project. . . .* "Come with you?"

"We look for old ones." There was a new note in the young man's fine firm voice, and it was impatience. "We traveled many days, up across the sun-path. We want you to speak the Abraham-words for marriage. The old ones said we must not mate as the animals do without the words. We want—"

"Marry, of course," Brian grumbled. *Poor old Jonas and Abigail, faithful to your century, such as it was!* Brian felt tired and confused, and rubbed a great long-fingered hand across his face so that the words might have come out blurred and dull. "Naturally, kids. Beget. Replenish the earth. I'm damned tired. I don't know any special hocus-pocus—I mean, any Abraham-words—for marriage. Just go ahead and breed. Try again—"

"But the Old Ones said—"

"Wait!" Brian cried. "Wait! Let me think. . . . Did he—he who told you to call him Jonas—did he teach you anything about the world as it was in the old days, before you were born?"

"Before—the Old Man makes fun of us."

"No, no." Since he now had to fight down a certain physical fear as well as confusion, Brian spoke more harshly than he intended: "Answer my question! What do you know of the old days? I was a young man once, do you understand that?—as young as you. What do you know about the world I lived in?"

* * *

The young man laughed. There was new-born suspicion in him as well as anger, stiffening his shoulders, narrowing his innocent gray eyes. "There was always the world," he said, "ever since God made it a thousand years ago."

"Was there? . . . I was a musician. Do you know what a musician is?"

The young man shook his head lightly, watching Brian, too alertly, watching his hands, aware of him in a new way, no longer humble. Paula sensed the tension and did not like it. She said worriedly, politely: "We forget some of the things they taught us, sa. They were Old Ones. Most of the days they were away from us in places where we were not to go, praying. Old Ones are always praying."

"I will hear this Old Man pray," said Jonason. The butt of the javelin rested against Jonason's foot, the blade swaying from side to side, a waiting snake's head. A misstep, a wrong word—any trifle, Brian knew, could make them decide he was evil and not sacred. Their religion would inevitably require a devil.

He thought also: *It would merely be one of the ways of dying, not the worst.*

"You shall hear me make music," he said sternly, "and you shall be content with that. Come this way!" In fluctuating despair, he was wondering if any good might come of anger. "Come this way! You shall hear a world you never knew." Naked and ugly, he stalked across the Hall of Music, not looking behind him, though he sensed every glint of light from that bread-knife javelin. "This way!" he shouted. "Come in here!" He flung open the door of the auditorium and strode up on the platform. "Sit down!" he roared at them. "Sit down over there and be quiet, be quiet!"

He thought they did—he could not look at them. He knew he was muttering between his noisy outbursts as he twitched the cover off the piano and raised the lid, muttering bits and fragments from the old times and the new: "They went thataway. . . . Oh, Mr. Van Anda, it just simply goes right through me—I can't express it. Madam, such was my intention, or as Brahms is supposed to have said on a slightly different subject, any ass knows that. . . . Brio, Rubato, and Schmalz went to sea in a—Jonason, Paula, this is a piano-forte; it will not hurt you. Sit there, be quiet, and I pray you listen. . . ."

He found calm. *Now, if ever, when there is living proof that human nature, some sort of human nature, is continuing— now if ever, the Project—*

With the sudden authority that was natural to Andrew Carr, Andrew Carr took over. In the stupendous opening chords of the introduction, Brian very nearly forgot his audience. Not quite. The children had sat down out there in the dusty region where none but ghosts had lingered for twenty-five years, but the piano's first sound brought them to their feet. Brian played through the first four bars, piling the chords like mountains, then held the last one with the pedal and waved his right hand at Jonason and Paula in a furious downward motion.

He thought they understood. He thought he saw them sit down again. But he could pay them no more attention, for the sonata was coming alive under his fingers, waking, growing, rejoicing.

He did not forget the children. They were important, too important, terrifying at the fringe of awareness. But he could not look toward them any more, and presently he shut his eyes.

He had never played like this in the flood of his prime, in the old days, before audiences that loved him. Never.

His eyes were still closed, holding him secure in a world that was not all darkness, when he ended the first movement, paused very briefly, and moved on with complete assurance to explore the depth and height of the second. This was true statement. This was Andrew Carr; he lived, even if after this late morning he might never live again.

And now the third, the storm and the wrath, the interludes of calm, the anger, denials, affirmations. . . .

Without hesitation, without awareness of self, of age or pain or danger or loss, Brian was entering on the broad reaches of the last movement when he glanced out into the auditorium and understood the children were gone.

Too big. It had frightened them away. He could visualize them, stealing out with backward looks of panic, and remembering apparently to close the exit door. To them it was incomprehensible thunder. Children—savages—to see or hear or comprehend the beautiful, you must first desire it. He could not think much about them now, when Andrew Carr was still with him. He played on with the same assurance, the same sense of victory. Children and savages, so let them go, with leave and goodwill.

Some external sound troubled him, something that must have begun under cover of these rising, pealing octave passages—storm waves, each higher than the last, until even the superhuman swimmer must be exhausted. It was some indefinable alien noise, a humming. Wind perhaps. Brian shook his head in irritation, not interrupting the work of his hands. It couldn't matter—everything was here, in the labors his hands still had to perform. The waves were growing more quiet, subsiding, and he must play the curious arpeggios he had never quite understood—but for this interpretation he understood them. Rip them out of the piano like showers of sparks, like distant lightning moving farther and farther away across a world that could never be at rest.

The final section at last. Why, it was a variation—and why had he never quite recognized it?—on a theme of Brahms, from the German Requiem. Quite plain, simple—Brahms would have approved. *Blessed are the dead. . . .* Something more remained to be said, and Brian searched for it through the mighty unfolding of the finale. No hurrying, no crashing impatience any more, but a moving through time without fear of time, through radiance and darkness with no fear of either. *That they may rest from their labors, and their works do follow after them.*

Brian stood up, swaying and out of breath. So the music was over, and the children were gone, but a jangling, humming confusion was filling the Hall of Music out there— hardly a wind—distant but entering with some violence even here, now that the piano was silent. He moved stiffly out of the small auditorium, more or less knowing what he would find.

The noise became immense, the unchecked overtones of the marimba fuming and quivering as the smooth, high ceiling of the Hall of Music caught them and flung them about against the answering strings of pianos and harps and violins, the sulky membranes of drums, the nervous brass of cymbals.

The girl was playing it. Brian laughed once, softly, in the shadows, and was not heard. She had hit on a primeval rhythm natural for children or savages and needed nothing else, banging it out on one stone and another, wanting no rest or variation.

The boy was dancing, slapping his feet and pounding his chest, thrusting out his javelin in time to the clamor, edging up to his companion, grimacing, drawing back in order to return. Neither one was laughing, or close to laughter. Their faces were savage-solemn, grim with the excitement and healthy lust. All as spontaneous as the drumming of partridges. It was a long time before they saw Brian in the shadows.

Reaction was swift. The girl dropped the hammer. The boy froze, his javelin raised, then jerked his head at Paula, who snatched at something—only moments later did Brian understand she had taken the clay image before she fled.

Jonason covered her retreat, stepping backward, his face blank and dangerous with fear. So swiftly, so easily, by grace of great civilized music and a few wrong words, had a sacred Old One become a Bad Old One.

They were gone, down the stairway, leaving the echo of Brian's voice crying: "Don't go! Please don't go!"

Brian followed them. Unwillingly. He was slow to reach the bottom of the stairway; there he looked across the shut-in water to his raft, which they had used and left at the windowsill port. Brian had never been a good swimmer, and would not attempt it now, but clutched the rope and hitched himself hand over hand to the windowsill, collapsing awhile until he found strength to scramble into his canoe and grope for the paddle.

The children's canoe was already far off. Heading up the river, the boy paddling with deep powerful strokes. Up the river, of course. They had to find the right kind of Old Ones. Up across the sun-path.

Brian dug his blade in the quiet water. For a time his rugged, ancient muscles were willing. There was sap in them yet. Perhaps he was gaining. He shouted hugely: "Bring back my two-faced god! And what about my music? You? Did you like it? Speak up!"

They must have heard his voice booming at them. At least the girl looked back, once. The boy, intent on his paddling, did not. Brian roared: "Bring back my little god!"

He was not gaining on them. After all they had a mission. They had to find an Old One with the right Abraham-words. Brian thought: *Damn it, hasn't MY world some rights? We'll see about this!*

He lifted his paddle like a spear, and flung it, knowing even as his shoulder winced with the backlash of the thrust that his action was at the outer limit of absurdity. The children were so far away that even an arrow from a bow might not have reached them. The paddle splashed in the water. Not far away. A small infinity.

It swung about, adjusting to the current, the heavy end pointing downstream, obeying the river and the ebb tide. It nuzzled companionably against a gray-faced chunk of driftwood, diverting it, so that presently the chunk floated into Brian's reach. He flung it back toward the paddle, hoping it might fall on the other side and send the paddle near him, but it fell short. In his unexpectedly painless extremity Brian was not surprised, but merely watched the gray face floating and bobbing along beside him out of reach, and his irritation became partly friendliness. The driftwood fragment suggested the face of a music critic he had once met—New Boston, was it? Denver? London?—no matter.

"Why," he said aloud, detachedly observing the passage

of his canoe beyond the broad morning shadow of the Museum, "why, I seem to have killed myself."

"Mr. Van Anda has abundantly demonstrated a mastery of the instrument and of the"—*Oh, go play solfeggio on your linotype!* —"literature of both classic and contemporary repertory. While we cannot endorse the perhaps overemotional quality of his Bach, and there might easily be two views of his handling of the passage in double thirds which—"

"I can't swim it, you know," said Brian. "Not against the ebb, that's for sure."

"—so that on the whole one feels he has earned himself a not discreditable place among—" Gaining on the canoe, passing it, the gray-faced chip moved on benignly twittering toward the open sea, where the canoe must follow. With a final remnant of strength Brian inched forward to the bow and gathered the full force of his lungs to shout up the river to the children: "Go in peace!"

They could not have heard him. They were too far away, and a new morning wind was blowing, fresh and sweet, out of the northwest.

THE END OF SUMMER

BY ALGIS BUDRYS (1931–   )

ASTOUNDING SCIENCE FICTION, NOVEMBER

Born in Konigsberg, Germany and the son of a Lithuanian diplomat, Algis Budrys was raised in New Jersey, discovered science fiction at an early age, and became a leading author and the leading literary critic of the sf field, a true American success story. He began as an assistant at Gnome Press of beloved memory, then moved to THE MAGAZINE OF FANTASY AND SCIENCE FICTION and numerous other publications, including Regency Books and Playboy Press. He published his first science fiction story in 1952, and since then has produced such outstanding novels as WHO? (1958), ROGUE MOON (1960), and the masterful MICHAELMAS (1977). His book review columns, first with GALAXY and currently for THE MAGAZINE OF FANTASY AND SCIENCE FICTION have set standards that have yet to be equaled within the field. "Book reviews" is a term that does not do justice to the always insightful essays he writes around the books in question. His GALAXY essays have been collected as BENCHMARKS (1985).

1954 saw the publication of his first novel, FALSE NIGHT (aka SOME WILL NOT DIE) AND "The End of Summer," perhaps his finest early story. (MHG)

*   *   *

Budrys' middle name is Jonas, and to his friends he is "A.J."

I remember the Fourteenth World Science Fiction Convention in New York, when A. J., Jim Blish, and I were sitting up in a cafeteria till all hours of the night. (Such all-night sessions usually meant that the practitioners remained sunk in swinish slumber through the daylight hours of the following day, but I made it a practice to simply stay awake and proceed with another day's festivities. I was young then.)

On this occasion, though, it was not happy for me. I was having a kidney stone attack that had made the Convention miserable for me and I did not believe in suffering in silence. I complained bitterly and A.J. and Jim commiserated with me and wasted their night trying to make me feel better. And then at about 3 A.M. I vanished into the men's room and passed the stone and re-emerged feeling wonderful, with A.J. and Jim slapping my back and telling me what a great guy I was.

I have had a soft spot in my heart for those two guys ever since. Jim left us, alas, all too young, but A.J. is still with us. He visited me only a few months ago. (IA)

1

Americaport hadn't changed since he'd last seen it, two hundred years before. It was set as far away from any other civilized area as possible, so that no plane, no matter how badly strayed, could possibly miss its landing and crash into a dwelling. Except for the straight-edged swathe of the highway leading south, it was completely isolated if you forgot the almost deserted tube station. Its edge was dotted by hangars and a few officers, but the terminal building itself was small, and severely functional. Massive with bare concrete, aseptic with steel and aluminum, it was a gray, bleak place in the wilderness.

Kester Fay was so glad to see it that he jumped impatiently from the big jet's passenger lift. He knew he was getting curious looks from the ground crew clustered around the stainless-steel ship, but he would have been stared at in any case, and he had seen the sports car parked and waiting for him beside the Administration Building. He hurried across the field at a pace that attracted still more attention, eager to get his clearance and be off.

He swung his memory vault impatiently by the chain from his wristlet while the Landing Clearance officer checked his passport, but the man was obviously too glad to see someone outside the small circle of airlines personnel. He stalled interminably, and while Fay had no doubt that his life out here bored him to tears, it was becoming harder and harder to submit patiently.

"Christopher Jordan Fay," the man read off, searching for a fresh conversational opening. "Well, Mr. Fay, we haven't seen you here since '753. Enjoy your stay?"

"Yes," he answered as shortly as possible. Enjoyed it? Well, yes, he supposed he had, but it was hard to feel that way since he'd played his old American memories at augmented volume all through the flight across the Atlantic. Lord, but he was tired of Europe at this moment; weary of winding grassy lanes that meandered with classic patience among brooks and along creeks, under old stately trees! "It's good to be back where a man can stretch his legs, though."

The official chuckled politely, stamping forms. "I'll bet it is at that. Planning to stay long?"

Forever, if I can help it, Fay thought first. But then he smiled ruefully. His life had already been an overdue demonstration that forever was a long time. "For a while, at any rate," he answered, his impatience growing as he thought of the car again. He shuffled his feet on the case-hardened flooring.

"Shall I arrange for transportation to New York?"

Fay shook his head. "Not for me. But the man who drove my car up might be a customer."

The official's eyebrows rose, and Fay suddenly remembered that America, with its more liberal social attitudes, might tolerate him more than Europe had, but that there were still plenty of conservatives sheltered under the same banner.

As a matter of fact, he should have realized that the official was a Homebody; a Civil Service man, no doubt. Even with a dozen safe places to put it down within easy reach, he still kept his memory vault chained to his wrist. Fay's own eyebrows lifted, and amusement glittered in his eyes.

"Driving down?" The official looked at Fay with a mixture of respect, envy, and disapproval.

"It's only fifteen hundred miles," Fay said with careful nonchalance. Actually, he felt quite sure that he was going to throttle the man if he wasn't let out of here and behind the wheel soon. But it would never do to be anything but bored in front of a Homebody. "I expect to make it in about three days," he added almost yawning.

"Yes, sir," the man said, instantly wrapping himself in a mantle of aloof politeness, but muttering "Dilly!" almost audibly.

He'd hit home with that one, all right! Probably, the man had never set foot in an automobile. Certainly, he considered it a barefaced lie that anyone would undertake to average fifty m.p.h. during a driving day. Safe cushiony pneumocars were his speed—and he an airlines employee!

Fay caught himself hastily. Everybody had a right to live any way he wanted to, he reminded himself.

But he could not restrain an effervescent grin at the man's sudden injured shift to aloofness.

"All right, sir," the official said crisply, returning Fay's passport. "Here you are. No baggage, of course?"

"Of course," Fay said agreeably, and if that had been intended as a slur at people who traveled light and fast, it had fallen exceedingly flat. He waved his hand cheerfully as he turned away, while the official stared at him sourly. "I'll be seeing you again, I imagine."

"I'm afraid not, sir," the man answered with a trace of malevolence. "United States Lines is shutting down passenger service the first of next dekayear."

Momentarily nonplussed, Fay hesitated. "Oh? Too bad. No point to continuing, though, is there?"

"No, sir. I believe you were our first in a hectoyear and a

half." Quite obviously, he considered that as much of a mark
of Cain as necessary.

"Well . . . must be dull out here, eh?"

He cocked a satiric eye at the man and was gone, chuck-
ling at that telling blow while the massive exit door swung
ponderously shut behind him.

The car's driver was obviously a Worker who'd taken on
the job because he needed money for some obscure, Worker-
ish purpose. Fay settled the business in the shortest possible
time, counting out hundred-dollar bills with a rapid shuffle.
He threw in another for good measure, and waved the man
aside, punching the starter vibrantly. He was back, he was
home! He inhaled deeply, breathing the untrammeled air.

Curled around mountains and trailed gently through val-
leys, the road down through New York State was a joy. Fay
drove it with a light, appreciative smile, guiding his car
exuberantly, his muscles locked into communion with the
automobile's grace and power as his body responded to each
banked turn, each surge of acceleration below the downward
crest of a hill. There was nothing like this in Europe—nothing.
Over there, they left no room for his kind among their stately
people.

He had almost forgotten what it was like to sit low behind
the windscreen of a two-seater and listen to the dancing
explosions of the unmuffled engine. It was good to be back,
here on this open, magnificent road, with nothing before or
behind but satin-smooth ferro-concrete, and heaped green
mountains to either side.

He was alone on the road, but thought nothing of it. There
were very few who lived his kind of life. Now that his first
impatience had passed, he was sorry he hadn't been able to
talk to the jet's pilot. But that, of course, had been out of the
question. Even with all the safety interlocks, there was the
chance that one moment's attention lost would allow an
accident to happen.

So, Fay had spent the trip playing his memory on the

plane's excellent equipment, alone in the comfortable but small compartment forward of the ship's big cargo cabin.

He shrugged as he nudged the car around a curve in the valley. It couldn't be helped. It was a lonely life, and that was all there was to it. He wished there were more people who understood that it was the *only* life—the only solution to the problem which had fragmented them into so many social patterns. But there were not. And, he supposed, they were all equally lonely. The Homebodies, the Workers, the Students, and the Teachers. Even, he conceded, the Hoppers. He'd Hopped once himself, as an experiment. It had been a hollow, hysteric experience.

The road straightened, and, some distance ahead, he saw the white surface change to the dark macadam of an urban district. He slowed in response, considering the advisability of switching his safeties in, and decided it was unnecessary as yet. He disliked being no more than a pea in a safetied car's basket, powerless to do anything but sit with his hands and feet off the controls. No; for another moment, he wanted to be free to turn the car nearer the shoulder and drive through the shade of the thick shrubbery and overhanging trees. He breathed deeply of the faint fragrance in the air and once more told himself that *this* was the only way to live, the only way to find some measure of vitality. A Dilly? Only in the jealous vocabularies of the Homebodies, so long tied to their hutches and routines that the scope of mind and emotion had narrowed to fit their microcosm.

Then, without warning, still well on the white surface of open road, the brown shadow darted out of the bushes and flung itself at his wheels, barking shrilly.

He tried to snap the car out of the way, his face suddenly white, but the dog moved unpredictably, its abrupt yell of pain louder than the scream of Fay's brakes. He felt the soft bump, and then his foot jerked away from the clutch and the car stalled convulsively. Even with his engine dead and the car still, he heard no further sound from the dog.

Then he saw the Homebody boy running toward him up the road, and the expression of his face changed from shocked unpleasantness to remorseful regret. He sighed and climbed out of the car clumsily, trying to think of something to say.

The boy came running up and stopped beside the car, looking up the road with his face drawn into tearful anger.

"You *ran* over Brownie!"

Fay stared helplessly down at the boy. "I'm sorry, son," he said as gently as he could. He could think of nothing really meaningful to tell him. It was a hopeless situation. "I . . . I shouldn't have been driving so fast."

The boy ran to the huddled bundle at the shoulder of the road and picked it up in his arms, sobbing. Fay followed him, thinking that ten thousand years of experience were not enough—that a hundred centuries of learning and acquiring superficial maturity were still insufficient to shield the emotions trapped in a young boy's body, at the mercy of his glandular system, under a shock like this.

"Couldn't you see him?" the boy pleaded.

Fay shook his head numbly. "He came out of the shrubs—"

"You shouldn't have been driving so fast. You should have—"

"I know." He looked uselessly back up the road, the trees bright green in the sunshine, the sky blue.

"I'm sorry," he told the boy again. He searched desperately for something, some way, to make recompense. "I wish it hadn't happened." He thought of something, finally. "I . . . I know it wouldn't be the same thing, but I've got a dog of my own—a basset hound. He's coming over from Europe on a cargo ship. When he gets here, would you like to have him?"

"Your *own* dog?" For a moment the boy's eyes cleared, but then he shook his head hopelessly. "It wouldn't work out," he said simply, and then, as though conscious of guilt at even considering that any other dog could replace his, tightened his arms on the lifeless bundle.

No, it hadn't been such a good idea, Fay realized. If he weren't so snarled up in remorse and confusion, he'd have seen that. Ugly had been his dog and couldn't be separated from him, or he from Ugly. He realized even more strongly just precisely what he had done to the boy.

"Something wrong? Oh—" The Homebody man who had come up the road stopped beside them, his face turning grave. Fay looked at him in relief.

"I had my automatics off," he explained to the man. "I wouldn't have, if I'd known there was a house around here, but I didn't see anything. I'm terribly sorry about the . . . about Brownie."

The man looked again at the dog in the boy's arms, and winced. Then he sighed and shrugged helplessly. "Guess it was bound to happen sometime. Should have been on a leash. There's still a law of averages."

Fay's fist clenched behind his back, out of sight. The well-worn words bit deep at the very foundation of his vitality, and his mind bridled, but in another moment the spasm of reflexive fear was gone, and he was glad he'd had this harmless outlet for his emotions. Besides, the man was right, and at this moment Fay was forced to be honest enough with himself to admit it. There was still a law of averages, whether Fay and his Dilly kind liked it or not.

"Go on back to the house, Son," the man said with another sigh. "There's nothing we can do for Brownie. We'll bury him later. Right now you ought to wash up. I'll be along in a minute."

It was the way he said it—the fatalistic acceptance that no matter what the honest folk did, some blundering, heedless dilettante was going to thwart them—that scored Fay's emotions.

The boy nodded wordlessly, still crying, and began to walk away without looking at Fay again.

But Fay couldn't let him go. Like a man who picks at a splinter, he could not let this pass so simply. "Wait!" he said urgently.

The boy stopped and looked at him woodenly.

"I . . . I know there's nothing—I mean," Fay stumbled, "Brownie was your dog, and there can't be another one like

him. But I do a lot of traveling—" He stopped again, flush-
ing at the Homebody man's knowing look, then pushed on
regardless. "I see a lot of people," he went on. "I'll try to
find you a dog that hasn't ever belonged to anybody. When I
do, I'll bring him to you. I promise."

The boy's lips twitched, suddenly revealing what ten thousand years had taught him. "Thanks, mister," he said half-
scornfully, and walked away, cradling his dog.

He hadn't believed him, of course. Fay suddenly realized
that no one ever believed a Dilly, whether he was telling the
truth or not. He realized, too, that he had done the best he
could, and nevertheless failed. He looked regretfully after the
boy.

"You didn't have to do that," the man said softly, and Fay
noted that some of his reserve and half-contemptuous politeness were gone. "I don't know whether to believe you or not,
you didn't have to do that. Anyway, I'll edit the dog out of
his memories tonight. My wife and I'll clean the place up,
and he won't notice anything." He paused, reflecting, his
eyes dark. "Guess Madge and I'll cut it out of our own
minitapes, too."

Fay clenched his teeth in sudden annoyance. Nobody ever
believed a Dilly. "No," he said. "I wish you wouldn't do
that. I meant what I said." He shook his head again. "I don't
like editing. There's always a slip somewhere, and then you
know you've got a hole in your memory, but you can never
remember what it was."

The man looked at him curiously. "Funny thing for one of
you people to say. I always heard you went for editing in a
big way—"

Fay kept his face from showing his thoughts. There it was
again—that basic lack of understanding and a complete unwillingness to check second-hand tales. The very essence of
his kind of life was that no memory, no experience, should
not be lived and preserved. Besides, he'd always heard that it
was the Homebodies who had to edit whole hectoyears to
keep from going mad with boredom.

"No," he contented himself with saying. "You're confusing us with the Hoppers. *They'll* try anything."

The man curled his lip at the mention, and Fay reflected that the introduction of a common outsider seemed helpful in circumstances like this.

"Well . . . maybe you're right," the man said, still not completely trustful, but willing to take the chance. He gave Fay his name, Arnold Riker, and his address. Fay put the slip of paper carefully in his memory vault.

"Anytime I lose that, I'll have lost my memory, too," he commented.

The man grinned wryly. "More likely, you'll remember to forget it tonight," he said, some of his distrust returning at the sight of the spooled tapes.

Fay took that without protest. He supposed Riker had a right to feel that way. "Can I drive you down to your house?"

The man flicked an expressive glance along the car's length and shook his head. "Thanks. I'll walk. There's still a law of averages."

And you can take that phrase and carve it on Humanity's headstone, Fay thought bitterly, but did not reply.

He climbed into the car, flicked on the automatics, and froze, completely immobile from sharply ingrained habit that was the only way to avoid the careless move that just might open the safety switch. He did not even turn his head to look at the man he left behind as the car started itself slowly away, nor did he catch more than a passing glimpse of the house where the boy and his dog had lived together for ten kiloyears.

We guard our immortality so carefully, he thought. *So very, very carefully. But there's still a law of averages.*

2

Perversely, he drove more rapidly than normal for the rest of the trip. Perhaps he was trying to reaffirm his vitality. Perhaps he was running away. Perhaps he was trying to cut down the elapsed time between towns, where his automatics threaded him though the light pedestrian traffic and sent him farther down the road, with each new danger spot safely behind him. At any rate, he arrived at his Manhattan apartment while it was still daylight, stepping off the continuous-impulse elevator with his eyes discontented.

The apartment, of course, was just as he had left it two hectoyears ago. The semi-robots had kept it sealed and germicidal until the arrival of his return message yesterday.

He could imagine the activity that had followed, as books and music tapes were broken out of their helium-flooded vaults, rugs and furnishings were stripped of their cocoons, aerated, and put in place. From somewhere, new plants had come and been set in the old containers, and fresh liquor put in the cabinet. There would be food in the kitchen, clothes in the wardrobes—the latest styles, of course, purchased with credits against the left-behind apparel of two hectoyears before—and there were the same, old, familiar paintings on the walls. Really old, not just By-Product stuff.

He smiled warmly as he looked around him, enjoying the swell of emotion at the apartment's comfortable familiarity. He smiled once more, briefly, at the thought that he must some day devise a means of staying in a sealed apartment—wearing something like a fishing lung, perhaps—and watch the semi-robots at their refurbishing process. It must be a fascinating spectacle.

But his glance had fallen on the memory vault which he had unchained and put on a coffee table. It faced him with the ageless, silent injunction painted on each of its faces: PLAY ME, and underneath this the block of smaller lettering that he, like everybody else, knew by heart:

If your surroundings seem unfamiliar, or you have any other reason to suspect that your environment and situation are not usual, request immediate assistance from any other individual. He is obligated by strict law to direct you to the nearest free public playback booth, where you will find further instructions. Do not be alarmed, and follow these directions without anxiety, even if they seem strange to you. In extreme situations, stand still and do not move. Hold this box in front of you with both hands. This is a universally recognized signal of distress. Do not let anyone take this box away from you, no matter what the excuse offered.

He wondered momentarily—what had made him notice it; he knew it so well that the pattern of type had long ago become no more than a half-seen design with a recognition value so high that it had lost all verbal significance.

Was it some sort of subconscious warning? He checked his memory hastily, but relaxed when he found none of the telltale vagueness of detail that meant it was time to let everything else wait and get a playback as fast as possible. He had refreshed his memory early this morning, before starting the last leg of his trip, and it seemed to be good for several more hours, at least.

What was it, then?

He frowned and went to the liquor cabinet, wondering if some train of thought had been triggered off by the accident and was trying to call attention to itself. And when he dropped into an easy-chair a few minutes later, a drink in his hand and his eyes still brooding over the vault's legend, he realized that his second guess had been the right one. As usual, one level of his mind had been busy digesting while the surface churned in seeming confusion.

He smiled ruefully. Maybe he wasn't quite as much of a Dilly as he looked and would have liked to believe. Still, a man couldn't live ten thousand years and not put a few things together in his head. He took a sip of his drink and stared out over the city in the gathering twilight. Somewhere in the graceful furniture behind him, a photo-electric relay clicked, and his high-fidelity set began to play the Karinius *Missa*. The apartment had not forgotten his moods.

No, he thought, the machines never forget. Only men forgot, and depended on machines to help them remember. He stared at the vault, and a familiar sophistry occurred to him. "Well," he asked the box labeled PLAY ME, "which *is* my brain—you or the gray lump in my head?"

The answer depended on his moods, and on his various audiences. Tonight, alone, in an uncertain mood, he had no answer.

He took another drink and sat back, frowning.

At best, he'd offered the boy a shoddy substitute. Even presuming that the passage of ten kiloyears had somehow still left room for a dog without a master, the animal would have to be re-familiarized with the boy at least once or twice a day.

Why? Why did dogs who had always had the same master remember him without any difficulty, even though they seemed to have to reinvestigate their surroundings periodically? Why would Ugly, for instance, remember him joyfully when his ship came? And why would Ugly have to be re-familiarized with this apartment, in which he'd lived with Fay, off and on, for all this time?

The Kinnard dog, whose master insisted on building each new house in a carbon-copy of the previous, didn't have anywhere near as much trouble. Why?

He'd heard rumors that some people were recording canine memories on minitape, but that sort of story was generally classified along with the jokes about the old virgin who switched vaults with her nubile young niece.

Still and all, there might be something in that. He'd have to ask Monkreeve. Monkreeve was the Grand Old Man of the crowd. He had memories the rest of them hadn't even thought of yet.

Fay emptied his glass and got up to mix another drink. He was thinking harder than he had for a long time—and he could not help feeling that he was making a fool of himself. Nobody else had ever asked questions like this. Not where others could hear them, at any rate.

He sat back down in his chair, fingers laced around the glass while the *Missa* ended and the *Lieutenant Kije* suite caught up the tempo of the city as it quickened beneath showers of neon.

PLAY ME. Like a music tape, the memory vault held his life

tightly knit in the nested spindles of bright, imperishable minitape.

What, he suddenly asked himself, would happen if he didn't play it tonight?

"If your surroundings seem unfamiliar, or you have any other reason to suspect your environment and situation are not usual . . .

"Obligated by strict law to direct you . . .

"Do not be alarmed . . ."

What? What was behind the whispered stories, the jokes:

'What did the girl in the playback booth say to the young man who walked in by mistake?

"Man, this has been the *busiest* Twenty-seventh of July!" (Laughter.)

The thought struck him that there might be all sorts of information concealed in his fund of party conversation.

"If you wish to get to heaven,
Stay away from twenty-seven."

And there it was again. Twenty-seven. July Twenty-seventh, this time conglomerated with a hangover reference to religion. And that was interesting, too. Man had religions, of course—schismatic trace sects that offered no universally appealing reward to make them really popular. But they must have been really big once, judging by the stamp they'd left on oaths and idiomatic expressions. Why? What did they have? Why had two billion people integrated words like "Heaven," "Lord God," and "Christ" into the language so thoroughly that they had enduured ten kiloyears?

July Twenty-seventh when? Year?

What would happen to him if he ignored PLAY ME just this once?

He had the feeling that he knew all this; that he had learned it at the same time that he had learned to comb his hair and cut his fingernails, take showers and brush his teeth. But he did all that more or less automatically now.

Maybe it was time he thought about it.

But nobody else did. Not even Monkreeve.

So what? Who was Monkreeve, really? Didn't the very fact

that he had thought of it make it all right? That *was* the basis
on which they judged everything else, wasn't it?

That boy and his dog had really started something.

He realized several things simultaneously, and set his glass
down with a quick *thump*. He couldn't remember the dog's
name. And he was definitely letting the simple problem of
following his conscience—and his wounded pride—lead him
into far deeper intellectual waters than any boy and his dog
had a right.

His cheeks went cold as he tried to remember the name of
this morning's hotel, and he shivered violently. He looked at
the box labeled PLAY ME.

"Yes," he told it. "Yes, definitely."

3

Fay awoke to a bright, sunny morning. The date on his
calendar-clock was 16 April 11958, and he grinned at it while
he removed the vault's playback contacts from the bare places
on his scalp. He noted that all the memories he had brought
back from Europe had been re-recorded for the apartment's
spare vault, and that the current minitape had advanced the
shining notch necessary to record yesterday.

He looked at that notch and frowned. It looked like an
editing scratch, and was. It was always there, every morning,
but he knew it covered nothing more than the normal Traumatic pause between recording and playback. He'd been told
that it was the one memory nobody wanted to keep, and
certainly he'd never missed editing it—or, of course, remembered doing it. It was a normal part of the hypnotic action
pattern set by the recorder to guide him when he switched
over from record to playback, his mind practically blank by
that time.

He'd never seen a tape, no matter whose, that did not bear
that one scratch to mark each day. He took pride in the fact
that a good many tapes were so hashed out and romanticized
as to be almost pure fiction. He hadn't been lying to the boy's
father—and he noted the presence of that memory with the

utmost satisfaction—he had a driving basic need to see everything, hear everything, sense each day and its events to their
fullest, and to remember them with sharp perfect clarity.

He laughed at the vault as he kicked it shut on his way to
the bathroom. "Not until tonight," he said to PLAY ME, and
then teetered for a breathless moment as he struggled to
regain his balance. He set his foot down with a laugh, his
eyes sparkling.

"Who needs a car to live dangerously?" he asked himself.
But that brought back the memory of the boy, and his lips
straightened. Nevertheless, it was a beautiful day, and the
basic depression of yesterday was gone. He thought of all the
people he knew in the city, one of whom, at least, would be
sure to have a contact somewhere or the other that would
solve his problem for him.

He ate his breakfast heartily, soaking for an hour in the
sensual grip of his bathtub's safety slinging while he spooned
the vitalizing porridge, then shrugged into a violet bathrobe
and began calling people on the telephone.

He hadn't realized how long he'd been gone, he reflected,
after Vera, his welcome to her apartment finished, had left
him with a drink while she changed. It was, of course, only
natural that some of the old crowd had changed their habits or
themselves gone traveling in his absence. Nevertheless, he
still felt a little taken aback at the old phone numbers that
were no longer valid, or the really astonishing amount of
people who seemed to have edited him out of their memories.
Kinnard, of all people! And Lorraine.

Somehow, he'd never thought Lorraine would go editor.

"Ready, Kes?"

Vera was wearing a really amazing dress. Apparently,
America had gone back toward conservatism, as he might
have guessed from his own wardrobe.

Vera, too, had changed somehow—too subtly for him to
detect, here in surroundings where he had never seen her
before. Hadn't she always been resistant to the fad of completely doing apartments over every seventy years? He seemed
to remember it that way, but even with minitapes, the evi-

dence of the eye always took precedence over the nudge of memory. Still, she at least knew where Monkreeve was, which was something he hadn't been able to find out for himself.

"Uh-huh. Where're we going?"

She smiled and kissed the tip of his nose. "Relax, Kes. Let it happen."

"Um."

"Grasshoppers as distinct from ants, people given to dancing and similar gay pursuits, or devotees to stimulants," Monkreeve babbled, gesturing extravagantly. "Take your pick of derivations." He washed down a pill of some sort and braced himself theatrically. "I've given up on the etymology. What'd you say your name was?"

Fay grimaced. He disliked Hoppers and Hopper parties—particularly in this instance. He wished heartily that Vera had told him what had happened to Monkreeve before she brought him here.

He caught a glimpse of her in the center of a hysterical knot of people, dancing with her seven petticoats held high.

"Who*ee!*" Monkreeve burst out, detecting the effects of the pill among the other explosions in his system. Fay gave him a searching look, and decided, from the size of his pupils, that he could probably convince himself into an identical state on bread pills, and more than likely was.

"Got a problem, hey, Lad?" Monkreeve asked wildly. "Got a dog problem." He put his finger in his mouth and burlesqued Thought. "Got a dog, got a problem, got a problem, got a dog," he chanted. "Hell!" he exploded, "go see old Williamson. Old Williamson knows everything. Ask him anything. Sure," he snickered, "ask him anything."

"Thanks, Monk," Fay said. "Glad to've met you," he added in the accepted polite form with editors, and moved toward Vera.

"Sure, sure, Kid. Ditto and check. Whatcha say your name was?"

Fay pretended to be out of earshot, brushed by a couple

who were dancing in a tight circle to no music at all, and delved into the crowd around Vera.

"Hi, Kes!" Vera exclaimed, looking up and laughing. "Did Monk give you any leads?"

"Monk has a monkey on his back, he thinks," Fay said shortly, a queasy feeling in his throat.

"Well, why not try that on the kid? He might like a change." Vera broke into fresh laughter. Suddenly an inspiration came to her, and she began to sing.

"Oh where, oh where, has my little dog gone? Oh where, oh where can he be?"

The rest of the crowd picked it up. Vera must have told them about his search, for they sang it with uproarious gusto.

Fay turned on his heel and walked out.

The halls of the University library were dim gray, padded with plastic sponge, curving gently with no sharp corners. Doorways slid into walls, the sponge muffled sound, and he wore issued clothes into which he had been allowed to transfer only those personal items which could not possibly cut or pry. Even his vault had been encased in a ball of cellular sponge plastic, and his guide stayed carefully away from him, in case he should fall or stumble. The guide carried a first-aid kit, and like all the library staff, was a certified Doctor of Theoretical Medicine.

"This is Dr Williamson's interview chamber," the guide told him softly, and pressed a button concealed under the sponge. The door slid back, and Fay stepped into the padded interior of the chamber, divided down the middle by a sheet of clear, thick plastic. There was no furniture to bump into, of course. The guide made sure he was safely in, out of the door's track, and closed it carefully after he had stepped out.

Fay sat down on the soft floor and waited. He started wondering what had happened to the old crowd, but he had barely found time to begin when the door on the other side of the partition opened and Dr Williamson came in. Oddly enough, his physiological age was less than Fay's, but he

carried himself like an old man, and his entire manner radiated the same feeling.

He looked at Fay distastefully. "Hopper, isn't it? What're
you doing here?"

Fay got to his feet. "No, sir. Dilly, if you will, but not a
Hopper." Coming so soon after the party, Wiliamson's remark bit deep.

"Six of one, half a dozen of the other, in time," Williamson said curtly. "Sit down." He lowered himself slowly,
testing each new adjustment of his muscles and bones before
he made the next. He winced faintly when Fay dropped to the
floor with defiant overcarelessness. "Well—go on. You
wouldn't be here if the front desk didn't think your research
was at least interesting."

Fay surveyed him carefully before he answered. Then he
sighed, shrugged mentally, and began. "I want to find a dog
for a little boy," he said, feeling more than foolish.

Williamson snorted: "What leads you to believe this is the
ASPCA?"

"ASPCA, sir?"

Williamson threw his hands carefully up to heaven and
snorted again. Apparently, everything Fay said served to
confirm some judgment of mankind on his part.

He did not explain, and Fay finally decided he was waiting. There was a minute's pause, and then Fay said awkwardly: "I assume that's some kind of animal shelter. But
that wouldn't serve my purpose. I need a dog that . . . that
remembers."

Williamson put the tips of his fingers together and pursed
his lips. "So. A dog that remembers, eh?" He looked at Fay
with considerably more interest, the look in his eyes sharpening.

"You look like any other brainless jackanapes," he mused,
"but apparently there's some gray matter left in your artfully
coiffed skull after all." Williamson was partially bald.

"What would you say," Williamson continued, "if I offered to let you enroll here as an Apprentice Liberor?"

"Would I find out how to get that kind of dog?"

A flicker of impatience crossed Williamson's face. "In time, in time. But that's beside the point."

"I . . . I haven't got much time, sir," Fay said haltingly. Obviously, Williamson had the answer to his question. But would he part with it, and if he was going to, why this rigmarole?

Williamson gestured with careful impatience. "Time is unimportant. And especially here, where we avoid the law of averages almost entirely. But there are various uses for time, and I have better ones than this. Will you enroll? Quick, man!"

"I—Dr Williamson, I'm grateful for your offer, but right now all I'd like to know is how to get a dog." Fay was conscious of a mounting impatience of his own.

Williamson got carefully to his feet and looked at Fay with barely suppressed anger.

"Young man, you're living proof that our basic policy is right. I wouldn't trust an ignoramus like you with with the information required to cut his throat.

"Do you realize where you are?" He gestured at the walls. "In this building is the world's greatest repository of knowledge. For ten thousand years we have been accumulating opinion and further theoretical data on every known scientific and artistic theory extant in 1973. We have data that will enable Man to go to the stars, travel ocean bottoms, and explore Jupiter. We have here the raw material of symphonies and sonatas that make your current addictions sound like a tin-cup beggar's fiddle. We have the seed of paintings that would make you spatter whitewash over the daubs you treasure, and verse that would drive you mad. And you want me to find you a dog!"

Fay had gotten to his own feet. Williamson's anger washed over him in battering waves, but one thing remained clear, and he kept to it stubbornly.

"Then you won't tell me."

"No, I will *not* tell you! I thought for a moment that you had actually managed to perceive something of your environment, but you have demonstrated my error. You are dismissed." Williamson turned and stamped carefully out of his half of the interview chamber, and the door slid open behind Fay.

Still and all, he had learned something. He had learned that there was something important about dogs not remembering, and he had a date: 1973.

He sat in his apartment, his eyes once more fixed on PLAY ME, and tried a thought on for size: 27 July 1973.

It made more sense that way than it did when the two parts were separated—which could mean nothing, of course. Dates were like the jigsaw puzzles that were manufactured for physiological four-year-olds: they fit together no matter how the pieces were matched.

When had the human race stopped having children?

The thought smashed him bolt upright in his chair, spilling his drink.

He had never thought of that. Never once had he questioned the fact that everyone was frozen at some apparently arbitrary physiological age. He had learned that such-and-such combined anatomical and psychological configuration was indicative of one physiological age, that a different configuration indicated another. Or had he? Couldn't he tell instinctively—or, rather, couldn't he tell as though the word "age" were applicable to humans as well as inanimate objects?

A lesser thought followed close on the heels of the first: exactly the same thing could be said of dogs, or canaries or parakeets, as well as the occasional cat that hadn't gone wild.

"Gone" wild? Hadn't most cats always been wild?

Just exactly what memories were buried in his mind, in hiding—or rather, since he was basically honest with himself, what memories had he taught himself to ignore? And why?

His skin crawled. Suddenly, his careful, flower-to-flower world was tinged with frost around him, and brown, bare, and sharply ragged stumps were left standing. The boy and his dog had been deep water indeed—for his tentative toe had baited a monster of continuous and expanding questions to fang him with rows of dangerous answers.

He shook himself and took another drink. He looked at PLAY ME, and knew where the worst answers must be.

4

He awoke, and there were things stuck to his temples. He pulled them loose and sat up, staring at the furnishings and the machine that sat beside his bed, trailing wires.

The lights were on, but the illumination was so thoroughly diffused that he could not find its source. The furniture was just short of the radical in design, and he had certainly never worn pajamas to bed. He looked down at them and grunted.

He looked at the machine again, and felt his temples where the contacts had rested. His fingers came away sticky, and he frowned. Was it some sort of encephalograph? Why?

He looked around again. There was a faint possibility that he was recovering from psychiatric treatment, but this was certainly no sanatorium room.

There was a white placard across the room, with some sort of printing on it. Since it offered the only possible source of information, he got off the bed cautiously and, when he encountered no dizziness or weakness, crossed over to it. He stood looking at it, lips pursed and brow furrowed, while he picked his way through the rather simplified orthography.

Christopher Jordan Fay:

If your surroundings seem unfamiliar, or you have any other reason to suspect that your environment and situation are unusual, do not be alarmed, and follow these directions without anxiety, even if they seem strange to you. If you find yourself unable to do so, for any reason whatsoever, please return to the bed and read the instructions printed on the machine beside it. In this case, the nearest "free public playback booth" is the supplementary cabinet you see built into the head of the bed. Open the doors and read the supplementary instructions printed inside. In any case, do not be alarmed, and if you are unable or unwilling to perform any of the actions requested above simply dial "0" on the telephone you see across the room.

Fay looked around once more, identified the various objects, and read on.

The operator, like all citizens, is required by strict law to furnish you with assistance.

If, on the other hand, you feel sufficiently calm or are commensurately curious, please follow these directions:

Return to the bed and restore the contacts to the places where they were attached. Switch the dial marked "Record-Playback-Auxiliary Record" to the "Auxiliary Record" position. You will then have three minutes to place your right forearm on the grooved portion atop the machine. Make certain your arm fits snugly—the groove is custom-molded to accept your arm perfectly in one position only.

Finally, lie back and relax. All other actions are automatic.

For your information, you have suffered from loss of memory, and this device will restore it to you.

Should you be willing to follow the above directions, please accept our thanks.

Fay's tongue bulged his left cheek, and he restrained a grin. Apparently, his generator had been an unqualified success. He looked at the printing again, just to be certain, and confirmed the suspicion that it had been done by his own hand. Then, as a conclusive check, he prowled the apartment in search of a calendar. He finally located the calendar-clock, inexpertly concealed in a bureau drawer, and looked at the date.

That was his only true surprise. He whistled shrilly at the date, but finally shrugged and put the clock back. He sat down in a convenient chair, and pondered.

The generator was working just as he'd expected, the signal bouncing off the heavyside layer without perceptible loss of strength, covering the Earth. As to what would happen when it exhausted its radioactive fuel in another five thousand years, he had no idea, but he suspected that he would simply refuel it. Apparently, he still had plenty of money, or whatever medium of exchange existed in the future—or, rather existed now. Well, he'd provided for it.

Interesting, how his mind kept insisting it was 27 July 1973. This tendency to think of the actual date as "the future" could be confusing if he didn't allow for it.

Actually, he was some ten-thousand-and-thirty-eight years old, rather than the thirty-seven his mind insisted on. But his memories carried him only to 1973, while, he strongly suspected, the Kester Fay who had written the naïve message had memories that *began* shortly thereafter.

The generator broadcast a signal which enabled body cells to repair themselves with one hundred percent perfection, rather than the usual less-than-perfect of living organisms. The result was that none of the higher organisms aged, in any respect. Just the higher ones, fortunately, or there wouldn't even be yeast derivatives to eat.

But, of course, that included brain cells, too. Memory was a process of damaging brain cells much as a phonograph recording head damaged a blank record disk. In order to re-live the memory, the organism had only to play it back, as a record is played. Except that, so long as the generator continued to put out the signal, brain cells, too, repaired themselves completely. Not immediately, of course, for the body took a little time to act. But no one could possibly sleep through a night and remember anything about the day before. Amnesia was the price of immortality.

He stood up, went to the liquor cabinet he'd located in his search, and mixed himself a drink, noticing again how little, actually, the world had progressed in ten thousand years. Cultural paralysis, more than likely, under the impact of two and a half billion individuals each trying to make his compromise with the essential boredom of eternal life.

The drink was very good, the whisky better than any he was used to. He envied himself.

They'd finally beaten amnesia, as he suspected the human race would. Probably by writing notes to themselves at first, while panic and hysteria cloaked the world and 27 July marched down through the seasons and astronomers went mad.

The stimulated cells, of course, did not repair the damage done to them before the generator went into operation. They took what they already had as a model, and clung to it fiercely.

He grimaced. Their improved encephalograph probably rammed in so much information so fast that their artificial memories blanketed the comparatively small amount of information which they had acquired up to the 27th. Or, somewhat more likely, the period of panic had been so bad that they refused to probe beyond it. If that was a tape-recording encephalograph, editing should be easily possible.

"I suspect," he said aloud, "that what I am remembering now is part of a large suppressed area in my own memory." He chuckled at the thought that his entire life had been a blank to himself, and finished the drink.

And what he was experiencing now was an attempt on his own part to get that blank period on tape, circumventing the censors that kept him from doing it when he had his entire memory.

And that took courage. He mixed another drink and toasted himself. "Here's to you, Kester Fay +. I'm glad to learn I've got guts."

The whiskey was extremely good.

And the fact that Kester Fay had survived the traumatic hiatus between the Twenty-seventh and the time when he had his artificial memory was proof that They hadn't gotten to him before the smash-up.

Paranoid, was he?

He'd stopped the accelerating race toward Tee-Total War, hadn't he?

They hadn't been able to stop him, that was certain. He'd preserved the race of Man, hadn't he?

Psychotic? He finished the drink and chuckled. Intellectually, he had to admit that anyone who imposed immortality on all his fellow beings without asking their permission was begging for the label.

But, of course, he knew he wasn't psychotic. If he were, he wouldn't be so insistent on the English "Kester" for a nickname rather than the American "Chris."

He put the glass down regretfully. Ah, well—time to give himself *all* his memories back. Why was his right arm so strong?

He lay down on the bed, replaced the contacts, and felt the needle slip out of its recess in the forearm trough and slide into a vein.

Scopolamine derivative of some sort, he decided. Machinery hummed and clicked in the cabinets at the head of the bed, and a blank tape spindle popped into position in the vault, which rested on a specially-built stand beside the bed.

Complicated, he thought dimly as he felt the drug pumping into his system. I could probably streamline it down considerably.

He found time to think once more of his basic courage. Kester Fay must still be a rampant individual, even in his stagnant, conservative, ten-thousand-year-weighty civilization.

Apparently, nothing could change his fundamental character.

He sank into a coma with a faint smile.

The vault's volume control in the playback cycle was set to "Emergency Overload." Memories hammered at him ruthlessly, ravaging brain tissue, carving new channels through the packed silt of repair, foaming, bubbling, hissing with voracious energy and shattering impetus.

His face ran through agonized changes in his sleep. He pawed uncertainly and feebly at the contacts on his scalp, but the vital conditioning held. He never reached them, though he tried, and, failing, tried, and tried through the long night, while sweat poured down his face and soaked into his pillow, and he moaned, while the minitapes clicked and spun, one after the other, and gave him back the past.

It was 27 July 1973, and he shivered with cold, uncompre-

hendingly staring at the frost on the windows, with the note
dated 27/7/73 in his hand.

It was 27 July 1973, and he was faint with hunger as he
tried to get the lights to work. Apparently, the power was off.
He struck a match and stared down at the series of notes,
some of them smudged with much unremembered handling,
all dated 27 July 1973.

It was 27 July 1973, and the men who tried to tell him it
was really Fall in 1989, clustered around his bed in the
crowded hospital ward, were lying. But they told him his
basic patents on controlled artificial radioactivity had made it
possible to power the complicated machinery they were teaching him to use. And though, for some reason, money as an
interest-gathering medium was no longer valid, they told him
that in his special case, in gratitude, they'd arranged things so
there'd be a series of royalties and licensing fees, which
would be paid into his accounts automatically. He wouldn't
even have to check on them, or know specifically where they
came from. But the important part came when they assured
him that the machinery—the "vault," and the "minitapes,"
whatever they were, would cure his trouble.

He was grateful for that, because he'd been afraid for a
long time that he was going insane. Now he could forget his
troubles.

Kester Fay pulled the vault contacts off his forehead and
sat up to see if there was an editing scratch on the tape.

But, of course, there wasn't. He knew it before he'd raised
his head an inch, and he almost collapsed, sitting on the edge
of the bed with his head in his hands.

He was his own monster. He had no idea of what most of
the words he'd used in those memories had meant, but even
as he sat there, he could feel his mind hesitatingly making the
linkages and assigning tags to the jumbled concepts and
frightening rationalizations he'd already remembered.

He got up gingerly, and wandered about the apartment,
straightening out the drawers he'd upset during his amnesiac

period. He came to the empty glass, frowned at it, shrugged, and mixed a drink.

He felt better afterward, the glow of 100 Proof working itself into his system. The effects wouldn't last, of course—intoxication was a result of damage to the brain cells—but the first kick was real enough. Moreover, it was all he'd gotten accustomed to, during the past ten kiloyears, just as the Hoppers could drug themselves eternally.

Moreover, ten thousand years of having a new personality seemed to have cured the psychosis he'd had with his old one. He felt absolutely no desire to change the world single-handed.

Had it, now? Had it? Wasn't being a dilettante the result of an inner conviction that you were too good for routine living?

And didn't he want to turn the generator off, now that he knew what it did and where it was?

He finished the drink and bounced the glass in his palm. There was nothing that said he had to reach a decision right this minute. He'd had ten kiloyears. It could wait a little longer.

He bathed to the accompaniment of thoughts he'd always ignored before—thoughts about things that weren't his problem, then. Like incubators full of babies ten kiloyears old, and pregnant women, and paralytics.

He balanced that against hydrogen bombs, and still the scales did not tip.

Then he added something he had never known before, but that he had now, and understood why no one ever ventured to cross Twenty-seven, or to remember it if he had. For one instant, he, too, stopped still at his bath and considered ripping the memory out of his minitapes.

He added Death.

But he knew he was lost, now. For better or worse, the water had closed over his head, and if he edited the memory now, he would seek it out again some day. For a moment, he wondered if that was precisely what he had done, countless times before.

He gave it up. It could wait—if he stayed sane. At any rate, he knew how to get the little boy his dog, now.

He built a signal generator to cancel out the effect of the big one, purring implacably in its mountain shaft, sending out its eternal, unshieldable signal. He blanketed one room of his apartment with the canceling wave, and added six months to his age by staying in it for hours during the eighteen months it took to mate Ugly and raise the best pup, for the stimulating wave was the answer to sterility, too. Fetuses could not develop.

He cut himself from the Dilly crowd, what was left of it, and raised the pup. And it was more than six months he added to his age, for all that time he debated and weighed, and remembered.

And by the time he was ready, he still did not know what he was going to do about the greater problem. Still and all, he had a new dog for the boy.

He packed the canceling generator and the dog in his car, and drove back up the road he had come.

Finally, he knocked on Riker's door, the dog under one arm, the generator under the other.

Riker answered his knock and looked at him curiously.

"I'm . . . I'm Kester Fay, Mr Riker," he said hesitatingly. "I've brought your boy that dog I promised."

Riker looked at the dog and the bulky generator under his arm, and Fay shifted his load awkwardly, the dangling vault interfering with his movements. Light as it was, the vault was a bulky thing. "Don't you remember me?"

Riker blinked thoughtfully, his forehead knotting. Then he shook his head. "No . . . no, I guess not, Mr Fay." He looked suspiciously at Fay's clothes, which hadn't been changed in three days. Then he nodded.

"Uh . . . I'm sorry, mister, but I guess I must have edited it." He smiled in embarrassment. "Come to think of it, I've wondered if we didn't have a dog sometime. I hope it wasn't too important to you."

Fay looked at him. He found it impossible to think of anything to say. Finally, he shrugged.

"Well," he said, "your boy doesn't have a dog now, does he?"

Riker shook his head. "Nope. You know—it's a funny thing, what with the editing and everything, but he knows a kid with a dog, and sometimes he pesters the life out of me to get him one." Riker shrugged. "You know how kids are."

"Will you take this one?" He held out the squirming animal.

"Sure. Mighty grateful. But I guess we both know this won't work out too well." He reached out and took the dog.

"This one sure will," Fay said. He gave Riker the generator. "Just turn this on for a while in the same room with your son and the dog. It won't hurt anything, but the dog'll remember."

Riker looked at him skeptically.

"Try it," Fay said, but Riker's eyes were narrowing, and he gave Fay both the dog and the generator back.

"No, thanks," he said. "I'm not trying anything like that from a guy that comes out of nowhere in the middle of the night."

"Please, Mr Riker. I promise—"

"Buddy, you're trespassing. I won't draw more than half a hectoyear if I slug you."

Fay's shoulders slumped. "All right," he sighed, and turned around. He heard Riker slam the heavy door behind him.

But as he trudged down the walk, his shoulders lifted, and his lips set in a line.

There has to be an end somewhere, he thought. Each thing has to end, or there will never be any room for beginnings. He turned around to be sure no one in the house was watching, and released the dog. He'd be found in the morning, and things might be different by then.

He climbed into the car and drove quickly away, leaving the dog behind. Somewhere outside of town, he threw the canceling generator outside, onto the concrete highway, and heard it smash. He unchained his memory vault, and threw it out, too.

There had to be an end. Even an end to the starlit nights and the sound of a powerful motor. An end to the memory of sunset in the Piazza San Marco, and the sight of snow on Chamonix. An end to good whisky. For him, there had to be an end—so that others could come after. He pointed the car toward the generator's location, and reflected that he had twenty or thirty years left, anyway.

He flexed his curiously light arm.

THE FATHER-THING

BY PHILIP K. DICK (1928–1982)

THE MAGAZINE OF FANTASY AND SCIENCE FICTION, DECEMBER

Philip K. Dick returns (see his wonderful "Imposter" in Volume 15 of this series) with one of his most frightening stories and one of his most typical. "Typical" for Phil Dick means that things or people are not what they seem to be, that reality itself is uncertain. We have now reached a point in this series where there is more good material than we have room for, a situation that will get worse as we go through the years. This is especially true of long stories and novellas, and we regret that we are unable to include Phil Dick's excellent "The Golden Man," surely one of 1954's finest works.

Isaac, you chose this story for your anthology TOMORROW'S CHILDREN (1966), further evidence of your good taste. (MHG)

Yes, Marty, but TOMORROW'S CHILDREN was published twenty years ago and I haven't read the story since. Then, when the pile of possible candidates for this volume arrived, I read it again (not relying on memory) and felt the same horror I felt in 1966.

Let me say something about horror. There is a narrow overlap between science fiction and fantasy and usually there is no difficulty in telling them apart. "Transformer," earlier in the volume, is much more fantasy than science fiction.

Horror, however, is a feeling you get. It can be based on crime or on madness as in some of the stories of Edgar Allan Poe and then it is "straight-horror." Or it can be based on tales of the supernatural or mystic as in some of the stories of M. R. James and of H. P. Lovecraft. And the feeling can arise out of science fictional situations.

In the case of "The Father-Thing", there is no question but that it is a science fiction story. However, it elicits horror very efficiently and many people might think of it as a horror story first. (IA)

"Dinner's ready," commanded Mrs. Walton. "Go get your father and tell him to wash his hands. The same applies to you, young man." She carried a steaming casserole to the neatly set table. "You'll find him out in the garage."

Charles hesitated. He was only eight years old, and the problem bothering him would have confounded Hillel. "I—" he began uncertainly.

"What's wrong?" June Walton caught the uneasy tone in her son's voice and her matronly bosom fluttered with sudden alarm. "Isn't Ted out in the garage? For heaven's sake, he was sharpening the hedge shears a minute ago. He didn't go over to the Andersons', did he? I told him dinner was practically on the table."

"He's in the garage," Charles said. "But he's—talking to himself."

"Talking to himself!" Mrs. Walton removed her bright plastic apron and hung it over the doorknob. "Ted? Why, he never talks to himself. Go tell him to come in here." She poured boiling black coffee in the little blue-and-white china cups and began ladling out creamed corn. "What's wrong with you? Go tell him!"

"I don't know which of them to tell," Charles blurted out desperately. "They both look alike."

June Walton's fingers lost their hold on the aluminum pan; for a moment the creamed corn slushed dangerously. "Young man—" she began angrily, but at that moment Ted Walton came striding into the kitchen, inhaling and sniffing and rubbing his hands together.

"Ah," he cried happily. "Lamb stew."

"Beef stew," June murmured. "Ted, what were you doing out there?"

Ted threw himself down at his place and unfolded his napkin. "I got the shears sharpened like a razor. Oiled and sharpened. Better not touch them—they'll cut your hand off." He was a good-looking man in his early thirties: thick blond hair, strong arms, competent hands, square face and flashing brown eyes. "Man, this stew looks good. Hard day at the office—Friday, you know. Stuff piles up and we have to get all the accounts out by five. Al McKinley claims the department could handle twenty percent more stuff if we organized our lunch hours; staggered them so somebody was there all the time." He beckoned Charles over. "Sit down and let's go."

Mrs. Walton served the frozen peas. "Ted," she said, as she slowly took her seat, "is there anything on your mind?"

"On my mind?" He blinked. "No, nothing unusual. Just the regular stuff. Why?"

Uneasily, June Walton glanced over at her son. Charles was sitting bolt-upright at his place, face expressionless, white as chalk. He hadn't moved, hadn't unfolded his napkin or even touched his milk. A tension was in the air; she could feel it. Charles had pulled his chair away from his father's; he was huddled in a tense little bundle as far from his father as possible. His lips were moving, but she couldn't catch what he was saying.

"What is it?" she demanded, leaning toward him.

"*The other one,*" Charles was muttering under his breath. "The other one came in."

"What do you mean, dear?" June Walton asked out loud. "What other one?"

Ted jerked. A strange expression flitted across his face. It vanished at once; but in the brief instant Ted Walton's face lost all familiarity. Something alien and cold gleamed out, a twisting, wriggling mass. The eyes blurred and receded, as an archaic sheen filmed over them. The ordinary look of a tired, middle-aged husband was gone.

And then it was back—or nearly back. Ted grinned and began to wolf down his stew and frozen peas and creamed corn. He laughed, stirred his coffee, kidded and ate. But something was terribly wrong.

"The other one," Charles muttered, face white, hands beginning to tremble. Suddenly he leaped up and backed away from the table. "Get away!" he shouted. "Get out of here!"

"Hey," Ted rumbled ominously. "What's got into you?" He pointed sternly at the boy's chair. "You sit down there and eat your dinner, young man. Your mother didn't fix it for nothing."

Charles turned and ran out of the kitchen, upstairs to his room. June Walton gasped and fluttered in dismay. "What in the world—"

Ted went on eating. His face was grim; his eyes were hard and dark. "That kid," he grated, "is going to have to learn a few things. Maybe he and I need to have a little private conference together."

Charles crouched and listened.

The father-thing was coming up the stairs, nearer and nearer. "Charles!" it shouted angrily. "Are you up there?"

He didn't answer. Soundlessly, he moved back into his room and pulled the door shut. His heart was pounding heavily. The father-thing had reached the landing; in a moment it would come into his room.

He hurried to the window. He was terrified; it was already fumbling in the dark hall for the knob. He lifted the window and climbed out on the roof. With a grunt he dropped into the flower garden that ran by the front door, staggered and gasped, then leaped to his feet and ran from the light that streamed out the window, a patch of yellow in the evening darkness.

He found the garage; it loomed up ahead, a black square against the skyline. Breathing quickly, he fumbled in his pocket for his flashlight, then cautiously slid the door up and entered.

The garage was empty. The car was parked out front. To the left was his father's workbench. Hammers and saws on the wooden walls. In the back were the lawnmower, rake, shovel, hoe. A drum of kerosene. License plates nailed up everywhere. Floor was concrete and dirt; a great oil slick stained the center, tufts of weeds greasy and black in the flickering beam of the flashlight.

Just inside the door was a big trash barrel. On top of the barrel were stacks of soggy newspapers and magazines, moldy and damp. A thick stench of decay issued from them as Charles began to move them around. Spiders dropped to the cement and scampered off; he crushed them with his foot and went on looking.

The sight made him shriek. He dropped the flashlight and leaped wildly back. The garage was plunged into instant gloom. He forced himself to kneel down, and for an ageless moment, he groped in the darkness for the light, among the spiders and greasy weeds. Finally he had it again. He managed to turn the beam down into the barrel, down the well he had made by pushing back the piles of magazines.

The father-thing had stuffed it down in the very bottom of the barrel. Among the old leaves and torn-up cardboard, the rotting remains of magazines and curtains, rubbish from the attic his mother had lugged down here with the idea of burning someday. It still looked a little like his father, enough for him to recognize. He had found it—and the sight made him sick to his stomach. He hung on to the barrel and shut his eyes until finally he was able to look again. In the barrel were the remains of his father, his real father. Bits the father-thing had no use for. Bits it had discarded.

He got the rake and pushed it down to stir the remains. They were dry. They cracked and broke at the touch of the rake. They were like discarded snakeskin, flaky and crumbling, rustling at the touch. *An empty skin.* The insides were gone. The important part. This was all that remained, just the brittle, cracking skin, wadded down at the bottom of the trash barrel in a little heap. This was all the father-thing had left; it had eaten the rest. Taken the insides—and his father's place.

A sound.

He dropped the rake and hurried to the door. The father-thing was coming down the path, toward the garage. Its shoes crushed the gravel; it felt its way along uncertainly. "Charles!" it called angrily. "Are you in there? Wait'll I get my hands on you, young man!"

His mother's ample, nervous shape was outlined in the bright doorway of the house. "Ted, please don't hurt him. He's all upset about something."

"I'm not going to hurt him," the father-thing rasped; it halted to strike a match. "I'm just going to have a little talk with him. He needs to learn better manners. Leaving the table like that and running out at night, climbing down the roof—"

Charles slipped from the garage; the glare of the match caught his moving shape, and with a bellow the father-thing lunged forward.

"Come here!"

Charles ran. He knew the ground better than the father-thing; it knew a lot, had taken a lot when it got his father's insides, but nobody knew the way like *he* did. He reached the fence, climbed it, leaped into the Andersons' yard, raced past their clothesline, down the path around the side of their house, and out on Maple Street.

He listened, crouched down and not breathing. The father-thing hadn't come after him. It had gone back. Or it was coming around the sidewalk.

He took a deep, shuddering breath. He had to keep moving. Sooner or later it would find him. He glanced right and left, made sure it wasn't watching, and then started off at a rapid dog-trot.

"What do you want?" Tony Peretti demanded belligerently. Tony was fourteen. He was sitting at the table in the oak-paneled Peretti dining room, books and pencils scattered around him, half a ham-and-peanut-butter sandwich and a Coke beside him. "You're Walton, aren't you?"

Tony Peretti had a job uncrating stoves and refrigerators after school at Johnson's Appliance Shop, downtown. He was big and blunt-faced. Black hair, olive skin, white teeth. A couple of times he had beaten up Charles; he had beaten up every kid in the neighborhood.

Charles twisted. "Say, Peretti. Do me a favor?"

"What do you want?" Peretti was annoyed. "You looking for a bruise?"

Gazing unhappily down, his fists clenched, Charles explained what had happened in short, mumbled words.

When he had finished, Peretti let out a low whistle. "No kidding."

"It's true." He nodded quickly. "I'll show you. Come on and I'll show you."

Peretti got slowly to his feet. "Yeah, show me. I want to see."

He got his b.b. gun from his room, and the two of them walked silently up the dark street, toward Charles' house. Neither of them said much. Peretti was deep in thought, serious and solemn-faced. Charles was still dazed; his mind was completely blank.

They turned down the Anderson driveway, cut through the back yard, climbed the fence, and lowered themselves cautiously into Charles's back yard. There was no movement. The yard was silent. The front door of the house was closed.

They peered through the living-room window. The shades were down, but a narrow crack of yellow streamed out. Sitting on the couch was Mrs. Walton, sewing a cotton T-shirt. There was a sad, troubled look on her large face. She worked listlessly, without interest. Opposite her was the father-thing. Leaning back in his father's easy chair, its shoes off, reading the evening newspaper. The TV was on, playing to itself in the corner. A can of beer rested on the arm of the easy chair. The father-thing sat exactly as his own father had sat; it had learned a lot.

"Looks just like him," Peretti whispered suspiciously. "You sure you're not bulling me?"

Charles led him to the garage and showed him the trash

barrel. Peretti reached his long tanned arms down and carefully pulled up the dry, flaking remains. They spread out,
unfolded, until the whole figure of his father was outlined.
Peretti laid the remains on the floor and pieced broken parts
back into place. The remains were colorless. Almost transparent. An amber yellow, thin as paper. Dry and utterly lifeless.

"That's all," Charles said. Tears welled up in his eyes.
"That's all that's left of him. The thing has the insides."

Peretti had turned pale. Shakily, he crammed the remains
back in the trash barrel. "This is really something," he
muttered. "You say you saw the two of them together?"

"Talking. They both looked exactly alike. I ran inside."
Charles wiped the tears away and sniveled; he couldn't hold it
back any longer. "It ate him while I was inside. Then it came
in the house. It pretended it was him. But it isn't. It killed
him and ate his insides."

For a moment Peretti was silent. "I'll tell you something,"
he said suddenly. "I've heard about this sort of thing. It's a
bad business. You have to use your head and not get scared.
You're not scared, are you?"

"No," Charles managed to mutter.

"The first thing we have to do is figure out how to kill it."
He rattled his b.b. gun. "I don't know if this'll work. It must
be plenty tough to get hold of your father. He was a big
man." Peretti considered. "Let's get out of here. It might
come back. They say that's what a murderer does."

They left the garage. Peretti crouched down and peeked
through the window again. Mrs. Walton had got to her feet.
She was talking anxiously. Vague sounds filtered out. The
father-thing threw down its newspaper. They were arguing.

"For God's sake!" the father-thing shouted. "Don't do
anything stupid like that."

"Something's wrong," Mrs. Walton moaned. "Something
terrible. Just let me call the hospital and see."

"Don't call anybody. He's all right. Probably up the street
playing."

"He's never out this late. He never disobeys. He was
terribly upset—afraid of you! I don't blame him." Her voice

broke with misery. "What's wrong with you? You're so strange." She moved out of the room, into the hall. "I'm going to call some of the neighbors."

The father-thing glared after her until she had disappeared. Then a terrifying thing happened. Charles gasped; even Peretti grunted under his breath.

"Look," Charles muttered. "What—"

"Golly," Peretti said, black eyes wide.

As soon as Mrs. Walton was gone from the room, the father-thing sagged in its chair. It became limp. Its mouth fell open. Its eyes peered vacantly. Its head fell forward, like a discarded rag doll.

Peretti moved away from the window. "That's it," he whispered. "That's the whole thing."

"What is it?" Charles demanded. He was shocked and bewildered. "It looked like somebody turned off its power."

"Exactly." Peretti nodded slowly, grim and shaken. "It's controlled from outside."

Horror settled over Charles. "You mean, something outside our world?"

Peretti shook his head with disgust. "Outside the house! In the yard. You know how to find?"

"Not very well." Charles pulled his mind together. "But I know somebody who's good at finding." He forced his mind to summon the name. "Bobby Daniels."

"That little black kid? Is he good at finding?"

"The best."

"All right," Peretti said. "Let's go get him. We have to find the thing that's outside. That made *it* in there, and keeps it going . . ."

"It's near the garage," Peretti said to the small, thin-faced black boy who crouched beside them in the darkness. "When it got him, he was in the garage. So look there."

"In the garage?" Daniels asked.

"*Around* the garage. Walton's already gone over the garage, inside. Look around outside. Nearby."

There was a small bed of flowers growing by the garage,

and a great tangle of bamboo and discarded debris between the garage and the back of the house. The moon had come out; a cold, misty light filtered down over everything. "If we don't find it pretty soon," Daniels said, "I got to go back home. I can't stay up much later." He wasn't any older than Charles. Perhaps nine.

"All right," Peretti agreed. "Then get looking."

The three of them spread out and began to go over the ground with care. Daniels worked with incredible speed; his thin little body moved in a blur of motion as he crawled among the flowers, turned over rocks, peered under the house, separated stalks of plants, ran his expert hands over leaves and stems, in tangles of compost and weeds. No inch was missed.

Peretti halted after a short time. "I'll guard. It might be dangerous. The father-thing might come and try to stop us." He posted himself on the back step with his b.b. gun while Charles and Bobby Daniels searched. Charles worked slowly. He was tired, and his body was cold and numb. It seemed impossible, the father-thing and what had happened to his own father, his real father. But terror spurred him on; what if it happened to his mother, or to him? Or to everyone? Maybe the whole world.

"I found it!" Daniels called in a thin, high voice. "You all come around here quick!"

Peretti raised his gun and got up cautiously. Charles hurried over; he turned the flickering yellow beam of his flashlight where Daniels stood.

The boy had raised a concrete stone. In the moist, rotting soil the light gleamed on a metallic body. A thin, jointed thing with endless crooked legs was digging frantically. Plated, like an ant; a red-brown bug that rapidly disappeared before their eyes. Its rows of legs scabbled and clutched. The ground gave rapidly under it. Its wicked-looking tail twisted furiously as it struggled down the tunnel it had made.

Peretti ran into the garage and grabbed up the rake. He pinned down the tail of the bug with it. "Quick! Shoot it with the b.b. gun!"

Daniels snatched the gun and took aim. The first shot tore the tail of the bug loose. It writhed and twisted frantically; its tail dragged uselessly and some of its legs broke off. It was a foot long, like a great millipede. It struggled desperately to escape down its hole.

"Shoot again," Peretti ordered.

Daniels fumbled with the gun. The bug slithered and hissed. Its head jerked back and forth; it twisted and bit at the rake holding it down. Its wicked specks of eyes gleamed with hatred. For a moment it struck futilely at the rake; then abruptly, without warning, it thrashed in a frantic convulsion that made them all draw away in fear.

Something buzzed through Charles's brain. A loud humming, metallic and harsh, a billion metal wires dancing and vibrating at once. He was tossed about violently by the force; the banging crash of metal made him deaf and confused. He stumbled to his feet and backed off; the others were doing the same, white-faced and shaken.

"If we can't kill it with the gun," Peretti gasped, "we can drown it. Or burn it. Or stick a pin through its brain." He fought to hold onto the rake, to keep the bug pinned down.

"I have a jar of formaldehyde," Daniels muttered. His fingers fumbled nervously with the b.b. gun. "How do this thing work? I can't seem to—"

Charles grabbed the gun from him. "I'll kill it." He squatted down, one eye to the sight, and gripped the trigger. The bug lashed and struggled. Its force-field hammered in his ears, but he hung on to the gun. His finger tightened . . .

"All right, Charles," the father-thing said. Powerful fingers gripped him, a paralyzing pressure around his wrists. The gun fell to the ground as he struggled futilely. The father-thing shoved against Peretti. The boy leaped away and the bug, free of the rake, slithered triumphantly down its tunnel.

"You have a spanking coming, Charles," the father-thing droned on. "What got into you? Your poor mother's out of her mind with worry."

It had been there, hiding in the shadows. Crouched in the

darkness watching them. Its calm, emotionless voice, a dreadful parody of his father's, rumbled close to his ear as it pulled him relentlessly toward the garage. Its cold breath blew in his voice, an icy-sweet odor, like decaying soil. Its strength was immense; there was nothing he could do.

"Don't fight me," it said calmly. "Come along, into the garage. This is for your own good. I know best, Charles."

"Did you find him?" his mother called anxiously, opening the back door.

"Yes, I found him."

"What are you going to do?"

"A little spanking." The father-thing pushed up the garage door. "In the garage." In the half light a faint smile, humorless and utterly without emotion, touched its lips. "You go back in the living room, June. I'll take care of this. It's more in my line. You never did like punishing him."

The back door reluctantly closed. As the light cut off, Peretti bent down and groped for the b.b. gun. The father-thing instantly froze.

"Go on home, boys," it rasped.

Peretti stood undecided, gripping the b.b. gun.

"Get going," the father-thing repeated. "Put down that toy and get out of here." It moved slowly toward Peretti, gripping Charles with one hand, reaching toward Peretti with the other. "No b.b. guns allowed in town, sonny. Your father know you have that? There's a city ordinance. I think you better give me that before—"

Peretti shot it in the eye.

The father-thing grunted and pawed at its ruined eye. Abruptly it slashed out at Peretti. Peretti moved down the driveway, trying to cock the gun. The father-thing lunged. Its powerful fingers snatched the gun from Peretti's hands. Silently, the father-thing mashed the gun against the wall of the house.

Charles broke away and ran numbly off. Where could he hide? It was between him and the house. Already, it was coming back toward him, a black shape creeping carefully, peering into the darkness, trying to make him out. Charles retreated. If there were only some place he could hide . . .

The bamboo.

He crept quickly into the bamboo. The stalks were huge and old. They closed after him with a faint rustle. The father-thing was fumbling in its pocket; it lit a match, then the whole pack flared up. "Charles," it said. "I know you're here, some place. There's no use hiding. You're only making it more difficult."

His heart hammering, Charles crouched among the bamboo. Here, debris and filth rotted. Weeds, garbage, papers, boxes, old clothing, boards, tin cans, bottles. Spiders and salamanders squirmed around him. The bamboo swayed with the night wind. Insects and filth.

And something else.

A shape, a silent, unmoving shape that grew up from the mound of filth like some nocturnal mushroom. A white column, a pulpy mass that glistened moistly in the moonlight. Webs covered it, a moldy cocoon. It had vague arms and legs. An indistinct half-shaped head. As yet, the features hadn't formed. But he could tell what it was.

A mother-thing. Growing here in the filth and dampness, between the garage and the house. Behind the towering bamboo.

It was almost ready. Another few days and it would reach maturity. It was still a larva, white and soft and pulpy. But the sun would dry and warm it. Harden its shell. Turn it dark and strong. It would emerge from its cocoon, and one day when his mother came by the garage . . .

Behind the mother-thing were other pulpy white larvae, recently laid by the bug. Small. Just coming into existence. He could see where the father-thing had broken off; the place where it had grown. It had matured here. And in the garage, his father had met it.

Charles began to move numbly away, past the rotting boards, the filth and debris, the pulpy mushroom larvae. Weakly, he reached out to take hold of the fence—and scrambled back.

Another one. Another larva. He hadn't seen this one at

first. It wasn't white. It had already turned dark. The web, the pulpy softness, the moistness, were gone. It was ready. It stirred a little, moved its arm feebly.

The Charles-thing.

The bamboo separated, and the father-thing's hand clamped firmly around the boy's wrist. "You stay right here," it said. "This is exactly the place for you. Don't move." With its other hand it tore at the remains of the cocoon binding the Charles-thing. "I'll help it out—it's still a little weak."

The last shred of moist gray was stripped back, and the Charles-thing tottered out. It floundered uncertainly, as the father-thing cleared a path for it toward Charles.

"This way," the father-thing grunted. "I'll hold him for you. When you've fed you'll be stronger."

The Charles-thing's mouth opened and closed. It reached greedily toward Charles. The boy struggled wildly, but the father-thing's immense hand held him down.

"Stop that, young man," the father-thing commanded. "It'll be a lot easier for you if you—"

It screamed and convulsed. It let go of Charles and staggered back. Its body twitched violently. It crashed against the garage, limbs jerking. For a time it rolled and flopped in a dance of agony. It whimpered, moaned, tried to crawl away. Gradually it became quiet. The Charles-thing settled down in a silent heap. It lay stupidly among the bamboo and rotting debris, body slack, face empty and blank.

At last the father-thing ceased to stir. There was only the faint rustle of the bamboo in the night wind.

Charles got up awkwardly. He stepped down onto the cement driveway. Peretti and Daniels approached, wide-eyed and cautious. "Don't go near it," Daniels ordered sharply. "It ain't dead yet. Takes a little while."

"What did you do?" Charles muttered.

Daniels set down the drum of kerosene with a gasp of relief. "Found this in the garage. We Danielses always used kerosene on our mosquitoes, back in Virginia."

"Daniels poured kerosene down the bug's tunnel," Peretti explained, still awed. "It was his idea."

Daniels kicked cautiously at the contorted body of the father-thing. "It's dead, now. Died as soon as the bug died."

"I guess the others'll die, too," Peretti said. He pushed aside the bamboo to examine the larvae growing here and there among the debris. The Charles-thing didn't move at all, as Peretti jabbed the end of a stick into its chest. "This one's dead."

"We better make sure," Daniels said grimly. He picked up the heavy drum of kerosene and lugged it to the edge of the bamboo. "It dropped some matches in the driveway. You get them, Peretti."

They looked at each other.

"Sure," Peretti said softly.

"We better turn on the hose," Charles said. "To make sure it doesn't spread."

"Let's get going," Peretti said impatiently. He was already moving off. Charles quickly followed him, and they began searching for the matches in the moonlit darkness.

THE DEEP RANGE

BY ARTHUR C. CLARKE (1917–   )

STAR SCIENCE FICTION 4

Science fiction writers have been speculating about life under water since at least 1870, when the publication of Jules Verne's TWENTY THOUSAND LEAGUES UNDER THE SEA caused a sensation in Europe. Since then, numerous writers have imagined previously unknown life-forms, great cities, and future wars under water, both on our own Earth and on other planets. A representative list would include Stanton A. Coblentz's THE SUNKEN WORLD (1928), Isaac Asimov's LUCKY STARR AND THE OCEANS OF VENUS (1957), and Frank Herbert's THE DRAGON IN THE SEA (1956).

In particular, dolphins and whales have been very popular in science fiction, sometimes as protagonists, frequently as victims of human exploitation. Two excellent novels of this type are THE DAY OF THE DOLPHIN (1969) by Robert Merle and THE JONAH KIT (1975) by Ian Watson. Arthur C. Clarke is, among many other things, an expert skin diver with long experience under the sea. This excellent story reflects his interest and his expertise, and was later expanded into a successful novel in 1957. (MHG)

I have a certain grouping which I call "respectable science fiction." I don't talk about it much, but it's the kind of science fiction story that deals with a future so sensible that people outside the science fiction field refer to it very earnestly and seriously in their own discussions of the future.

Obviously, as the human population rises, we're going to have to find food for it if we are to avoid catastrophe. The sea is one source but not if we simply plunder it. We've got to progress from the simple food-gathering stage to "aquaculture" in which we encourage the growth of edible sea-creatures and cull them for our food.

The analogy with agriculture and with herding is obvious and Arthur carries the analogy to a logical extreme. "The Deep Range" is frequently referred to by futurists. I know that I have referred to it many times in my own futurist essays, much as I hate to give Arthur the satisfaction. (IA)

There was a killer loose on the range. A 'copter patrol, five hundred miles off Greenland, had seen the great corpse staining the sea crimson as it wallowed in the waves. Within seconds, the intricate warning system had been alerted: men were plotting circles and moving counters on the North Atlantic chart—and Don Burley was still rubbing the sleep from his eyes as he dropped silently down to the twenty-fathom line.

The pattern of green lights on the tell-tale was a glowing symbol of security. As long as that pattern was unchanged, as long as none of those emerald stars winked to red, all was well with Don and his tiny craft. Air—fuel—power—this was the triumvirate which ruled his life. If any of them failed, he would be sinking in a steel coffin down toward the pelagic ooze, as Johnnie Tyndall had done the season before last. But there was no reason why they should fail; the accidents one foresaw, Don told himself reassuringly, were never the ones that happened.

He leaned across the tiny control board and spoke into the mike. Sub 5 was still close enough to the mother ship for radio to work, but before long he'd have to switch to the sonics.

"Setting course 255, speed 50 knots, depth 20 fathoms, full sonar converage. . . . Estimated time to target area, 70 minutes. . . . Will report at 10-minute intervals. That is all. . . . Out.''

The acknowledgment, already weakening with range, came back at once from the *Herman Melville*.

"Message received and understood. Good hunting. What about the hounds?"

Don chewed his lower lip thoughtfully. This might be a job he'd have to handle alone. He had no idea, to within fifty miles either way, where Benj and Susan were at the moment. They'd certainly follow if he signaled for them, but they couldn't maintain his speed and would soon have to drop behind. Besides, he might be heading for a pack of killers, and the last thing he wanted to do was to lead his carefully trained porpoises into trouble. That was common sense and good business. He was also very fond of Susan and Benj.

"It's too far, and I don't know what I'm running into," he replied. "If they're in the interception area when I get there, I may whistle them up."

The acknowledgment from the mother ship was barely audible, and Don switched off the set. It was time to look around.

He dimmed the cabin lights so that he could see the scanner screen more clearly, pulled the polaroid glasses down over his eyes, and peered into the depths. This was the moment when Don felt like a god, able to hold within his hands a circle of the Atlantic twenty miles across, and to see clear down to the still-unexplored deeps, three thousand fathoms below. The slowly rotating beam of inaudible sound was searching the world in which he floated, seeking out friend and foe in the eternal darkness where light could never penetrate. The pattern of soundless shrieks, too shrill even for the hearing of the bats who had invented sonar a million years before man, pulsed out into the watery night: the faint echoes came tingling back as floating, blue-green flecks on the screen.

Through long practice, Don could read their message with effortless ease. A thousand feet below, stretching out to his submerged horizon, was the scattering layer—the blanket of life that covered half the world. The sunken meadow of the sea, it rose and fell with the passage of the sun, hovering always at the edge of darkness. But the ultimate depths were no concern of his. The flocks he guarded, and the enemies who ravaged them, belonged to the upper levels of the sea.

Don flicked the switch of the depth-selector, and his sonar beam concentrated itself into the horizonal plane. The glimmering echoes from the abyss vanished, but he could see more clearly what lay around him here in the ocean's stratospheric heights. That glowing cloud two miles ahead was a school of fish; he wondered if Base knew about it, and made an entry in his log. There were some larger, isolated blips at the edge of the school—the carnivores pursuing the cattle, insuring that the endlessly turning wheel of life and death would never lose momentum. But this conflict was no affair of Don's; he was after bigger game.

Sub 5 drove on toward the west, a steel needle swifter and more deadly than any other creature that roamed the seas. The tiny cabin, lit only by the flicker of lights from the instrument board, pulsed with power as the spinning turbines thrust the water aside. Don glanced at the chart and wondered how the enemy had broken through this time. There were still many weak points, for fencing the oceans of the world had been a gigantic task. The tenuous electric fields, fanning out between generators may miles apart, could not always hold at bay the starving monsters of the deep. They were learning, too. When the fences were opened, they would sometimes slip through with the whales and wreak havoc before they were discovered.

The long-range receiver bleeped plaintively, and Don switched over to TRANSCRIBE. It wasn't practical to send speech any distance over an ultrasonic beam, and code had come back into its own. Don had never learned to read it by ear, but the ribbon of paper emerging from the slot saved him the trouble.

COPTER REPORTS SCHOOL 50-100 WHALES HEADING 95 DEGREES GRID REF X186475 Y438034 STOP. MOVING AT SPEED. STOP. MELVILLE. OUT.

Don started to set the coordinates on the plotting grid, then saw that it was no longer necessary. At the extreme edge of his screen, a flotilla of faint stars had appeared. He altered course slightly, and drove head-on toward the approaching herd.

The copter was right: they were moving fast. Don felt a mounting excitement, for this could mean that they were on the run and luring the killers toward him. At the rate at which they were traveling he would be among them in five minutes. He cut the motors and felt the backward tug of water bringing him swiftly to rest.

Don Burley, a knight in armor, sat in his tiny dim-lit room fifty feet below the bright Atlantic waves, testing his weapons for the conflict that lay ahead. In these moments of poised suspense, before action began, his racing brain often explored such fantasies. He felt a kinship with all shepherds who had guarded their flocks back to the dawn of time. He was David, among ancient Palestinian hills, alert for the mountain lions that would prey upon his father's sheep. But far nearer in time, and far closer in spirit, were the men who had marshaled the great herds of cattle on the American plains, only a few lifetimes ago. They would have understood his work, though his implements would have been magic to them. The pattern was the same; only the scale had altered. It made no fundamental difference that the beasts Don herded weighed almost a hundred tons, and browsed on the endless savannahs of the sea.

The school was now less than two miles away, and Don checked his scanner's continuous circling to concentrate on the sector ahead. The picture on the screen altered to a fan-shaped wedge as the sonar beam started to flick from side to side; now he could count every whale in the school, and even make a good estimate of its size. With a practiced eye, he began to look for stragglers.

Don could never have explained what drew him at once toward those four echoes at the southern fringe of the school. It was true that they were a little apart from the rest, but others had fallen as far behind. There is some sixth sense that a man acquires when he has stared long enough into a sonar screen—some hunch which enables him to extract more from the moving flecks than he has any right to do. Without conscious thought, Don reached for the control which would start the turbines whirling into life. Sub 5 was just getting under way when three leaden thuds reverberated through the hull, as if someone was knocking on the front door and wanted to come in.

"Well I'm damned," said Don. "How did *you* get here?" He did not bother to switch on the TV; he'd know Benj's signal anywhere. The porpoises must have been in the neighborhood and had spotted him before he'd even switched on the hunting call. For the thousandth time, he marveled at their intelligence and loyalty. It was strange that Nature had played the same trick twice—on land with the dog, in the ocean with the porpoise. Why were these graceful sea-beasts so fond of man, to whom they owed so little? It made one feel that the human race was worth something after all, if it could inspire such unselfish devotion.

It had been known for centuries that the porpoise was at least as intelligent as the dog, and could obey quite complex verbal commands. The experiment was still in progress, but if it succeeded then the ancient partnership between shepherd and sheep-dog would have a new lease on life.

Don switched on the speakers recessed into the sub's hull and began to talk to his escorts. Most of the sounds he uttered would have been meaningless to other human ears; they were the product of long research by the animal psychologists of the World Food Administration. He gave his orders twice to make sure that they were understood, then checked with the sonar screen to see that Benj and Susan were following astern as he had told them to.

The four echoes that had attracted his attention were clearer and closer now, and the main body of the whale pack had swept past him to the east. He had no fear of a collision; the great animals, even in their panic, could sense his presence as easily as he could detect theirs, and by similar means. Don wondered if he should switch on his beacon. They might recognize its sound pattern, and it would reassure them. But the still unknown enemy might recognize it, too.

He closed for an interception, and hunched low over the screen as if to drag from it by sheer will power every scrap of information the scanner could give. There were two large echoes, some distance apart, and one was accompanied by a pair of smaller satellites. Don wondered if he was already too late. In his mind's eye, he could picture the death struggle taking place in the water less than a mile ahead. Those two fainter blips would be the enemy—either shark or grampus—worrying a whale while one of its companions stood by in helpless terror, with no weapons of defense except its mighty flukes.

Now he was almost close enough for vision. The TV camera in Sub 5's prow strained through the gloom, but at first could show nothing but the fog of plankton. Then a vast shadowy shape began to form in the center of the screen, with two smaller companions below it. Don was seeing, with the greater precision but hopelessly limited range of ordinary light, what the sonar scanners had already told him.

Almost at once he saw his mistake. The two satellites were calves, not sharks. It was the first time he had ever met a whale with twins; although multiple births were not unknown, a cow could suckle only two young at once and usually only the stronger would survive. He choked down his disappointment; this error had cost him many minutes and he must begin the search again.

Then came the frantic tattoo on the hull that meant danger. It wasn't easy to scare Benj, and Don shouted his reassurance as he swung Sub 5 round so that the camera could search the turgid waters. Automatically, he had turned toward the fourth blip on the sonar screen—the echo he had assumed, from its size, to be another adult whale. And he saw that, after all, he had come to the right place.

"Jesus!" he said softly. "I didn't know they came that big." He'd seen larger sharks before, but they had all been harmless vegetarians. This, he could tell at a glance, was a Greenland shark, the killer of the northern seas. It was supposed to grow up to thirty feet long, but this specimen was bigger than Sub 5. It was every inch of forty feet from snout to tail, and when he spotted it, it was already turning in toward the kill. Like the coward it was, it had launched its attack at one of the calves.

Don yelled to Benji and Susan, and saw them racing ahead into his field of vision. He wondered fleetingly why porpoises had such an overwhelming hatred of sharks; then he loosed his hands from the controls as the autopilot locked on to the target. Twisting and turning as agilely as any other sea-creature of its size, Sub 5 began to close in upon the shark, leaving Don free to concentrate on his armament.

The killer had been so intent upon his prey that Benj caught him completely unawares, ramming him just behind the left eye. It must have been a painful blow: an iron-hard snout, backed by a quarter-ton of muscle moving at fifty miles an hour is something not to be laughed at even by the largest fish. The shark jerked round in an impossibly tight curve, and Don was almost jolted out of his seat as the sub snapped on to a new course. If this kept up, he'd find it hard to use his Sting. But at least the killer was too busy now to bother about his intended victims.

Benj and Susan were worrying the giant like dogs snapping at the heels of an angry bear. They were too agile to be caught in those ferocious jaws, and Don marveled at the coordination with which they worked. When either had to surface for air, the other would hold off for a minute until the attack could be resumed in strength.

There was no evidence that the shark realized that a far more dangerous adversary was closing in upon it, and that the porpoises were merely a distraction. That suited Don very nicely; the next operation was going to be difficult unless he could hold a steady course for at least fifteen seconds. At a pinch he could use the tiny rocket torps to make a kill. If he'd been alone, and faced with a pack of sharks he would certainly have done so. But it was messy, and there was a better way. He preferred the technique of the rapier to that of the hand-grenade.

Now he was only fifty feet away, and closing rapidly. There might never be a better chance. He punched the launching stud.

From beneath the belly of the sub, something that looked like a sting-ray hurtled forward. Don had checked the speed of his own craft; there was no need to come any closer now. The tiny, arrow-shaped hydrofoil, only a couple of feet across, could move far faster than his vessel and would close the gap in seconds. As it raced forward, it spun out the thin line of the control wire, like some underwater spider laying its thread. Along that wire passed the energy that powered the Sting, and the signals that steered it to its goal. Don had completely ignored his own larger craft in the effort of guiding this underwater missile. It responded to his touch so swiftly that he felt he was controlling some sensitive high-spirited steed.

The shark saw the danger less than a second before impact. The resemblance of the Sting to an ordinary ray confused it, as the designers had intended. Before the tiny brain could realize that no ray behaved like this, the missile had struck. The steel hypodermic, rammed forward by an exploding cartridge, drove through the shark's horny skin, and the great fish erupted in a frenzy of terror. Don backed rapidly away, for a blow from that tail would rattle him around like a pea in a can and might even cause damage to the sub. There was nothing more for him to do, except to speak into the microphone and call off his hounds.

The doomed killer was trying to arch its body so that it could snap at the poisoned dart. Don had now reeled the Sting back into its hiding place, pleased that he had been able to retrieve the missile undamaged. He watched without pity as the great fish succumbed to its paralysis.

Its struggles were weakening. It was swimming aimlessly back and forth, and once Don had to sidestep smartly to avoid a collision. As it lost control of buoyancy, the dying shark drifted up to the surface. Don did not bother to follow; that could wait until he had attended to more important business.

He found the cow and her two calves less than a mile away, and inspected them carefully. They were uninjured, so there was no need to call the vet in his highly specialized two-man sub which could handle any cetological crisis from a stomach-ache to a Caesarian. Don made a note of the mother's number, stenciled just behind the flippers. The calves, as was obvious from their size, were this season's and had not yet been branded.

Don watched for a little while. They were no longer in the least alarmed, and a check on the sonar had shown that the whole school had ceased its panicky flight. He wondered how they knew what had happened; much had been learned about communication among whales, but much was still a mystery.

"I hope you appreciate what I've done for you, old lady," he muttered. Then, reflecting that fifty tons of mother love was a slightly awe-inspiring sight, he blew his tanks and surfaced.

It was calm, so he cracked the airlock and popped his head out of the tiny conning tower. The water was only inches below his chin, and from time to time a wave made a determined effort to swamp him. There was little danger of this happening, for he fitted the hatch so closely that he was quite an effective plug.

Fifty feet away, a long slate-colored mound, like an over-turned boat, was rolling on the surface. Don looked at it thoughtfully and did some mental calculations. A brute this size should be valuable; with any luck there was a chance of a double bonus. In a few minutes he'd radio his report, but for the moment it was pleasant to drink the fresh Atlantic air and to feel the open sky above his head.

A gray thunderbolt shot up out of the depths and smashed back onto the surface of the water, smothering Don with spray. It was just Benj's modest way of drawing attention to himself; a moment later the porpoise had swum up to the conning tower, so that Don could reach down and tickle its head. The great, intelligent eyes stared back into his; was it pure imagination, or did an almost human sense of fun also lurk in their depths?

Susan, as usual, circled shyly at a distance until jealousy overpowered her and she butted Benj out of the way. Don distributed caresses impartially and apologized because he had nothing to give them. He undertook to make up for the omission as soon as he returned to the *Herman Melville*.

"I'll go for another swim with you, too," he promised, "as long as you behave yourselves next time." He rubbed thoughtfully at a large bruise caused by Benj's playfulness, and wondered if he was not getting a little too old for rough games like this.

"Time to go home," Don said firmly, sliding down into the cabin and slamming the hatch. He suddenly realized that he was very hungry, and had better do something about the breakfast he had missed. There were not many men on earth who had earned a better right to eat their morning meal. He had saved for humanity more tons of meat, oil and milk than could easily be estimated.

Don Burley was the happy warrior, coming home from one battle that man would always have to fight. He was holding at bay the specter of famine which had confronted all earlier ages, but which would never threaten the world again while the great plankton farms harvested their millions of tons of protein, and the whale herds obeyed their new masters. Man had come back to the sea after aeons of exile; until the oceans froze, he would never be hungry again. . . .

Don glanced at the scanner as he set his course. He smiled as he saw the two echoes keeping pace with the central splash of light that marked his vessel. "Hang around," he said. "We mammals must stick together." Then, as the autopilot took over, he lay back in his chair.

And presently Benj and Susan heard a most peculiar noise, rising and falling against the drone of the turbines. It had filtered faintly through the thick walls of Sub 5, and only the sensitive ears of the porpoises could have detected it. But intelligent beasts though they were, they could hardly be expected to understand why Don Burley was announcing, in a highly unmusical voice, that he was Heading for the Last Round-up. . . .

BALAAM

BY ANTHONY BOUCHER (1911-1968)

9 TALES OF SPACE AND TIME

1954 was the year that the late J. Francis McComas left the co-editorship of THE MAGAZINE OF FANTASY AND SCIENCE FICTION, leaving the publication in the good hands of Tony Boucher (William Anthony Parker White), and this is another opportunity to pay tribute to two men who did much for both genres. Boucher is the one that is always mentioned when one speaks of F & SF, but their partnership was a real collaboration, and McComas would continue as advisory editor for several more years. 1954 was also the midpoint of Boucher's tenure with the magazine, since he stepped down as editor in 1958.

Tony Boucher (it rhymes with voucher) was an excellent writer as well as an editor, but his total output was relatively small in science fiction. "Balaam" appeared in the original anthology 9 TALES OF SPACE AND TIME, a sort of follow up to 1951's NEW TALES OF SPACE AND TIME, both of which were edited by Raymond J. Healy, who was McComas' co-editor of the landmark anthology ADVENTURES IN TIME AND SPACE (1946), a wonderful book that is thankfully still in print. Here, Boucher again turns his attention to religion, a subject that he explored in several other stories including "The Quest for Saint Aquin" (see Volume 13 of this series). (MHG)

*   *   *

*I always considered Tony Boucher as the G. K. Chesterton
of science fiction. Like Chesterton, Boucher wrote both detective stories and fantasies and often threatened to blur the
boundary between the two. What's more Boucher, like Chesterton, was a Catholic. Boucher, however, was one from
birth so that he didn't have the sometime abrasive assertive-
ness of the convert who feels he must forever defend his
conversion.*

*Then, too, Tony differed from Chesterton in that the former
wrote science fiction as well, and very good science fiction.*

*Incidentally, I want to say something about Balaam. De-
spite the fact that he did not curse Israel but blessed it, he is
treated as a villain by the Biblical writers. I consider this a
case of sectarian malice. (IA)*

"What is a '*man?*' " Rabbi Chaim Acosta demanded, turning
his back on the window and its view of pink sand and infinite
pink boredom. "You and I, Mule, in our respective ways,
work for the salvation of *man*—as you put it, for the brotherhood of *men* under the fatherhood of God. Very well, let us
define our terms: Whom, or more precisely *what*, are we
interested in saving?"

Father Aloysius Malloy shifted uncomfortably and reluctantly closed the *American Football Yearbook* which had
been smuggled in on the last rocket, against all weight regulations, by one of his communicants. I honestly like Chaim, he
thought, not merely (or is that the right word?) with brotherly
love, nor even out of the deep gratitude I owe him, but with
special individual liking; and I respect him. He's a brilliant
man—too brilliant to take a dull post like this in his stride.
But he *will* get off into discussions which are much too much
like what one of my Jesuit professors called "disputations."

"What did you say, Chaim?" he asked.

The Rabbi's black Sephardic eyes sparkled. "You know
very well what I said, Mule; and you're stalling for time.
Please indulge me. Our religious duties here are not so ardu-
ous as we might wish; and since you won't play chess . . ."

". . . and you," said Father Malloy unexpectedly, "refuse to take any interest in diagraming football plays . . ."

"*Touché*. Or am I? Is it my fault that as an Israeli I fail to share the peculiar American delusion that football means something other than rugby and soccer? Whereas chess—" He looked at the priest reproachfully. "Mule," he said, "you have led me into a digression."

"It was a try. Like the time the whole Southern California line thought I had the ball for once and Leliwa walked over for the winning TD."

"What," Acosta repeated, "is *man?* Is it by definition a member of the genus *H. sapiens* inhabiting the planet Sol III and its colonies?"

"The next time we tried the play," said Malloy resignedly, "Leliwa was smeared for a ten-yard loss."

The two *men* met on the sands of Mars. It was an unexpected meeting, a meeting in itself uneventful, and yet one of the turning points in the history of *men* and their universe.

The *man* from the colony base was on a routine patrol—a patrol imposed by the captain for reasons of discipline and activity-for-activity's-sake rather than from any need for protection in this uninhabited waste. He had seen, over beyond the next rise, what he would have sworn was the braking blaze of a landing rocket—if he hadn't known that the next rocket wasn't due for another week. Six and a half days, to be exact, or even more exactly, six days, eleven hours, and twenty-three minutes, Greenwich Interplanetary. He knew the time so exactly because he, along with half the garrison, Father Malloy, and those screwball Israelis, was due for rotation then. So no matter how much it looked like a rocket, it couldn't be one; but it was something happening on his patrol, for the first time since he'd come to this god-forsaken hole, and he might as well look into it and get his name on a report.

The *man* from the spaceship also knew the boredom of the empty planet. Alone of his crew, he had been there before, on the first voyage when they took the samples and set up the

observation autoposts. But did that make the captain even
listen to him? Hell, no; the captain knew all about the planet
from the sample analyses and had no time to listen to a guy
who'd really been there. So all he got out of it was the
privilege of making the first reconnaissance. Big deal! One
fast look around reconnoitering a few googols of sand grains
and then back to the ship. But there was some kind of glow
over that rise there. It couldn't be lights; theirs was the scout
ship, none of the others had landed yet. Some kind of phos-
phorescent life they'd missed the first time round. . . ? Maybe
now the captain would believe that the sample analyses didn't
tell him everything.

The two *men* met at the top of the rise.

One *man* saw the horror of seemingly numberless limbs, of
a headless torso, of a creature so alien that it walked in its
glittering bare flesh in this freezing cold and needed no
apparatus to supplement the all but nonexistent air.

One *man* saw the horror of an unbelievably meager four
limbs, of a torso topped with an ugly lump like some unnatural growth, of a creature so alien that it smothered itself with
heavy clothing in this warm climate and cut itself off from
this invigorating air.

And both *men* screamed and ran.

"There is an interesting doctrine," said Rabbi Acosta,
"advanced by one of your writers, C. S. Lewis . . ."

"He was an Episcopalian," said Father Malloy sharply.

"I apologize." Acosta refrained from pointing out that
Anglo-Catholic would have been a more accurate term. "But
I believe that many in your church have found his writings,
from your point of view, doctrinally sound? He advances the
doctrine of what he calls *hnaus*—intelligent beings with souls
who are the children of God, whatever their physical shape or
planet of origin."

"Look, Chaim," said Malloy with an effort toward patience. "Doctrine or no doctrine, there just plain aren't any
such beings. Not in this solar system anyway. And if you're

going to go interstellar on me, I'd just as soon read the men's
microcomics.''

"Interplanetary travel existed only in such literature once.
But of course if you'd rather play chess . . .''

"My specialty," said the man once known to sports writers as Mule Malloy, "was running interference. Against you
I need somebody to run interference *for*."

"Let us take the sixteenth psalm of David, which you call
the fifteenth, having decided, for reasons known only to your
God and mine, that psalms nine and ten are one. There is a
phrase in there which, if you'll forgive me, I'll quote in
Latin; your Saint Jerome is often more satisfactory than any
English translator. *Benedicam Dominum, qui tribuit mihi
intellectum.*''

"*Blessed be the Lord, who schools me,*" murmured Malloy,
in the standard Knox translation.

"But according to Saint Jerome: *I shall bless the Lord,
who bestows on me*—just how should one render *intellectum?*
—not merely *intellect*, but *perception, comprehension* . . .
what Hamlet means when he says of *man*: *In apprehension
how like a god!*''

Words change their meanings.

Apprehensively, one *man* reported to his captain. The captain first swore, then scoffed, then listened to the story again.
Finally he said, "I'm sending a full squad back with you to
the place where—maybe—you saw this thing. If it's for real,
these mother-dighting bug-eyed monsters are going to curse
the day they ever set a God-damned tentacle on Mars." The
man decided it was no use trying to explain that the worst of
it was it *wasn't* bug-eyed; any kind of eyes in any kind of
head would have been something. And they weren't even
quite tentacles either. . . .

Apprehensively, too, the other *man* made his report. The
captain scoffed first and then swore, including some select
remarks on underhatched characters who knew all about a
planet because they'd been there once. Finally he said, "We'll
see if a squad of real observers can find any trace of your

egg-eating limbless monsters; and if we find them, they're going to be God-damned sorry they were ever hatched.'' It was no use, the *man* decided, trying to explain that it wouldn't have been so bad if it *had* been limbless, like in the picture tapes; but just *four* limbs. . . .

"What is a *man?*" Rabbi Acosta repeated, and Mule Malloy wondered why his subconscious synapses had not earlier produced the obvious appropriate answer.

"Man," he recited, *"is a creature composed of body and soul, and made to the image and likeness of God."*

"From that echo of childish singsong, Mule, I judge that is a correct catechism response. Surely the catechism must follow it up with some question about that likeness? Can it be a likeness in"—his hand swept up and down over his own body with a graceful gesture of contempt—*"this* body?"

"This likeness to God is chiefly in the soul."

"Aha!" The Sephardic sparkle was brighter than ever.

The words went on, the centers of speech following the synaptic patterns engraved in parochial school as the needle followed the grooves of an antique record. *"All creatures bear some resemblance to God inasmuch as they exist. Plants and animals resemble Him insofar as they have life . . ."*

"I can hardly deny so profound a statement."

". . . but none of these creatures is made to the image and likeness of God. Plants and animals do not have a rational soul, such as man has, by which they might know and love God."

"As do all good *hnaus.* Go on; I am not sure that our own scholars have stated it so well. Mule, you are invaluable!"

Malloy found himself catching a little of Acosta's excitement. He had known these words all his life; he had recited them the Lord knows how many times. But he was not sure that he had ever listened to them before. And he wondered for a moment how often even his Jesuit professors, in their profound consideration of the x^n's of theology, had never paused to reconsider these childhood ABC's.

"How is the soul like God?" He asked himself the next

catechistic question, and answered, *"The soul is like God because it is a spirit having understanding and free will and is destined . . ."*

"Reverend gentlemen!" The reverence was in the words only. The interrupting voice of Captain Dietrich Fassbänder differed little in tone from his normal address to a buck private of the Martian Legion.

Mule Malloy said, "Hi, Captain." He felt half relieved, half disappointed, as if he had been interrupted while unwrapping a present whose outlines he was just beginning to glimpse. Rabbi Acosta smiled wryly and said nothing.

"So this is how you spend your time? No Martian natives, so you practice by trying to convert each other, is that it?"

Acosta made a light gesture which might have been polite acknowledgment of what the captain evidently considered a joke. "The Martian day is so tedious we have been driven to talking shop. Your interruption is welcome. Since you so rarely seek out our company, I take it you bring some news. Is it, God grant, that the rotation rocket is arriving a week early?"

"No, damn it," Fassbänder grunted. (He seemed to take a certain pride, Malloy had observed, in carefully not tempering his language for the ears of clergymen.) "Then I'd have a German detachment instead of your Israelis, and I'd know where I stood. I suppose it's all very advisable politically for every state in the UW to contribute a detachment in rotation; but I'd sooner either have my regular legion garrison doubled, or two German detachments regularly rotating. That time I had the pride of Pakistan here . . . Damn it, you new states haven't had time to develop a military tradition!"

"Father Malloy," the Rabbi asked gently, "are you acquainted with the sixth book of what you term the Old Testament?"

"Thought you fellows were tired of talking shop," Fassbänder objected.

"Rabbi Acosta refers to the Book of Joshua, Captain. And I'm afraid, God help us, that there isn't a state or a tribe that hasn't a tradition of war. Even your Prussian ancestors might

have learned a trick or two from the campaigns of Joshua—or
for that matter, from the Cattle Raid on Cooley, when the
Hound of Cullen beat off the armies of Queen Maeve. And
I've often thought, too, that it'd do your strategists no harm
to spend a season or two at quarterback, if they had the wind.
Did you know that Eisenhower played football, and against
Jim Thorpe once at that? And . . ."

"But I don't imagine," Acosta interposed, "that you came
here to talk shop either, Captain?"

"Yes," said Captain Fassbänder, sharply and unexpectedly. "My shop and, damn it, yours. Never thought I'd see
the day when I . . ." He broke off and tried another approach. "I mean, of course, a chaplain is part of an army.
You're both army officers, technically speaking, one of the
Martian Legion, one in the Israeli forces; but it's highly
unusual to ask a man of the cloth to . . ."

"To praise the Lord and pass the ammunition, as the folk
legend has it? There are precedents among my people, and
among Father Malloy's as well, though rather different ideas
are attributed to the founder of his church. What is it, Captain? Or wait, I know: We are besieged by alien invaders and
Mars needs every able-bodied man to defend her sacred
sands. Is that it?"

"Well . . . God damn it . . ." Captain Fassbänder's cheeks
grew purple. ". . . YES!" he exploded.

The situation was so hackneyed in 3V and microcomics
that it was less a matter of explaining it than of making it
seem real. Dietrich Fassbänder's powers of exposition were
not great, but his sincerity was evident and in itself convincing.

"Didn't believe it myself at first," he admitted. "But he
was right. Our patrol ran into a patrol of . . . of *them*. There
was a skirmish; we lost two men but killed one of the things.
Their small arms use explosive propulsion of metal much like
ours; God knows what they might have in that ship to counter
our A-warheads. But we've got to put up a fight for Mars;
and that's where you come in."

The two priests looked at him wordlessly, Acosta with a

faint air of puzzled withdrawal, Malloy almost as if he expected the captain to start diagraming the play on a blackboard.

"You especially, Rabbi. I'm not worried about your boys,
Father. We've got a Catholic chaplain on this rotation because this bunch of legionnaires is largely Poles and Irish-
Americans. They'll fight all right, and we'll expect you to
say a field Mass beforehand, and that's about all. Oh, and
that fool gunner Olszewski has some idea he'd like his
A-cannon sprinkled with holy water; I guess you can handle
that without any trouble.

"But your Israelis are a different problem, Acosta. They
don't know the meaning of discipline—not what we call
discipline in the legion; and Mars doesn't mean to them what
it does to a legionnaire. And besides a lot of them have got a
. . . hell, guess I shouldn't call it superstition, but a kind of
. . . well, reverence—awe, you might say—about you, Rabbi.
They say you're a miracle-worker.''

"He is,'' said Mule Malloy simply. "He saved my life.''

He could still feel that extraordinary invisible power (a
"force-field,'' one of the technicians later called it, as he
cursed the shots that had destroyed the machine past all
analysis) which had bound him helpless there in that narrow
pass, too far from the dome for rescue by any patrol. It was
his first week on Mars, and he had hiked too long, enjoying
the easy strides of low gravity and alternately meditating on
the versatility of the Creator of planets and on that Year Day
long ago when he had blocked out the most famous of
All-American line-backers to bring about the most impressive
of Rose Bowl upsets. Sibiryakov's touchdown made the head-
lines; but he and Sibiryakov knew why that touchdown happened, and he felt his own inner warmth . . . and was that
sinful pride or just self-recognition? And then he was held as
no line had ever held him and the hours passed and no one on
Mars could know where he was and when the patrol arrived
they said, "The Israeli chaplain sent us.'' And later Chaim
Acosta, laconic for the first and only time, said simply, "I
knew where you were. It happens to me sometimes.''

Now Acosta shrugged and his graceful hands waved deprecation. "Scientifically speaking, Captain, I believe that I have, on occasion, a certain amount of extrasensory perception and conceivably a touch of some of the other *psi* faculties. The Rhinists at Tel Aviv are quite interested in me; but my faculties too often refuse to perform on laboratory command. But 'miracle-working' is a strong word. Remind me to tell you some time the story of the guaranteed genuine miracle-working rabbi from Lwow."

"Call it miracles, call it ESP, you've got something, Acosta . . ."

"I shouldn't have mentioned Joshua," the rabbi smiled. "Surely you aren't suggesting that I try a miracle to win your battle for you?"

"Hell with that," snorted Fassbänder. "It's your men. They've got it fixed in their minds that you're a . . . a saint. No, you Jews don't have saints, do you?"

"A nice question in semantics," Chaim Acosta observed quietly.

"Well, a prophet. Whatever you people call it. And we've got to make men out of your boys. Stiffen their backbones, send 'em in there knowing they're going to win."

"Are they?" Acosta asked flatly.

"God knows. But they sure as hell won't if they don't think so. So it's up to you.'

"What is?"

"They may pull a sneak attack on us, but I don't think so. Way I see it, they're as surprised and puzzled as we are; and they need time to think the situation over. We'll attack before dawn tomorrow; and to make sure your Israelis go in there with fighting spirit, you're going to curse them."

"Curse my men?"

"Potztausend Sapperment noch einmal!" Captain Fassbänder's English was flawless, but not adequate to such a situation as this. "Curse *them!* The . . . the *things,* the aliens, the invaders, whatever the *urverdammt* bloody hell you want to call them!"

He could have used far stronger language without offending either chaplain. Both had suddenly realized that he was perfectly serious.

"A formal curse, Captain?" Chaim Acosta asked. "Anathema maranatha? Perhaps Father Malloy would lend me bell, book, and candle?"

Mule Malloy looked uncomfortable. "You read about such things, Captain," he admitted. "They were done, a long time ago. . . ."

"There's nothing in your religion against it, is there, Acosta?"

"There is . . . precedent," the Rabbi confessed softly.

"Then it's an order, from your superior officer. I'll leave the mechanics up to you. You know how it's done. If you need anything . . . what kind of bell?"

"I'm afraid that was meant as a joke, Captain."

"Well, these *things* are no joke. And you'll curse them tomorrow morning before all your men."

"I shall pray," said Rabbi Chaim Acosta, "for guidance . . ." But the captain was already gone. He turned to his fellow priest. "Mule, you'll pray for me too?" The normally agile hands hung limp at his side.

Mule Malloy nodded. He groped for his rosary as Acosta silently left the room.

Now entertain conjecture of a time when two infinitesimal forces of *men*—one half-forgotten outpost garrison, one small scouting fleet—spend the night in readying themselves against the unknown, in preparing to meet on the morrow to determine, perhaps, the course of centuries for a galaxy.

Two *men* are feeding sample range-finding problems into the computer.

"That God-damned Fassbänder," says one. "I heard him talking to our commander. 'You and your men who have never understood the meaning of discipline. . . !' "

"Prussians," the other grunts. He has an Irish face and an American accent. "Think they own the earth. When we get through here, let's dump all the Prussians into Texas and let 'em fight it out. Then we can call the state Kilkenny."

"What did you get on that last? . . . Check. Fassbänder's 'discipline' is for peace—spit-and-polish to look pretty here in our sandy pink nowhere. What's the pay-off? Fassbänder's great-grandfathers were losing two world wars while mine were creating a new nation out of nothing. Ask the Arabs if we have no discipline. Ask the British . . ."

"Ah, the British. Now *my* great-grandfather was in the IRA . . ."

Two *men* are integrating the electrodes of the wave-hurler.

"It isn't bad enough we get drafted for this expedition to nowhere; we have to have an egg-eating Nangurian in command."

"And a Tryldian scout to bring the first report. What's your reading there? . . . Check."

" 'A Tryldian to tell a lie and a Nangurian to force it into truth,' " the first quotes.

"Now, brothers," says the *man* adjusting the microvernier on the telelens, "the Goodman assures us these monsters are true. We must unite in love for each other, even Tryldians and Nangurians, and wipe them out. The Goodman has promised us his blessing before battle . . ."

"The Goodman," says the first, "can eat the egg he was hatched from."

"The Rabbi," says a *man* checking the oxyhelms, "can take his blessing and shove it up Fassbänder. I'm no Jew in his sense. I'm a sensible, rational atheist who happens to be an Israeli."

"And I," says his companion, "am a Romanian who believes in the God of my fathers and therefore gives allegiance to His state of Israel. What is a Jew who denies the God of Moses? To call him still a Jew is to think like Fassbänder."

"They've got an edge on us," says the first. "*They* can breathe here. These oxyhelms run out in three hours. What do we do then? Rely on the Rabbi's blessing?"

"I said the God of my fathers, and yet my great-grandfather thought as you do and still fought to make Israel live anew. It

was his son who, like so many others, learned that he must
return to Jerusalem in spirit as well as body."

"Sure, we have the Great Revival of orthodox religion. So
what did it get us? Troops that need a Rabbi's blessing before
a commander's orders."

"Many men have died from orders. How many from
blessings?"

"I fear that few die well who die in battle . . ." the *man*
reads in Valkram's great epic of the siege of Tolnishri.

". . . for how [the *man* is reading of the eve of Agincourt
in his micro-Shakespeare] *can they charitably dispose of
anything when blood is their argument?"*

". . . and if these do not die well [so Valkram wrote] *how
grievously must their bad deaths be charged against the
Goodman who blesses them into battle . . ."*

"And why not?" Chaim Acosta flicked the question away
with a wave of his long fingers.

The bleep (even Acosta was not so linguistically formal as
to call it a bubble jeep) bounced along over the sand toward
the rise which overlooked the invaders' ship. Mule Malloy
handled the wheel with solid efficiency and said nothing.

"I *did* pray for guidance last night," the rabbi asserted,
almost as if in self-defense. "I . . . I had some strange
thoughts for a while; but they make very little sense this
morning. After all, I am an officer in the army. I do have a
certain obligation to my superior officer and to my men. And
when I became a rabbi, a teacher, I was specifically ordained
to decide questions of law and ritual. Surely this case falls
within that authority of mine."

Abruptly the bleep stopped.

"What's the matter, Mule?"

"Nothing . . . Wanted to rest my eyes a minute . . . Why
did you become ordained, Chaim?"

"Why did you? Which of us understands all the infinite

factors of heredity and environment which lead us to such a choice? Or even, if you will, to such a being chosen? Twenty years ago it seemed the only road I could possibly take; now . . . We'd better get going, Mule.''

The bleep started up again.

''A curse sounds so melodramatic and medieval; but is it in essence any different from a prayer for victory, which chaplains offer up regularly? As I imagine you did in your field Mass. Certainly all of your communicants are praying for victory to the Lord of Hosts—and as Captain Fassbäander would point out, it makes them better fighting men. I will confess that even as a teacher of the law, I have no marked doctrinal confidence in the efficacy of a curse. I do not expect the spaceship of the invaders to be blasted by the forked lightning of Yahveh. But my men have an exaggerated sort of faith in me, and I owe it to them to do anything possible to strengthen their morale. Which is all the legion or any other army expects of chaplains anyway; we are no longer priests of the Lord, but boosters of morale—a type of sublimated YMCA secretary. Well, in my case, say YMHA.''

The bleep stopped again.

''I never knew your eyes to be so sensitive before,'' Acosta observed tartly.

''I thought you might want a little time to think it over,'' Malloy ventured.

''I've thought it over. What else have I been telling you? Now please, Mule. Everything's all set. Fassbäander will explode completely if I don't speak of my curse into this mike in two minutes.''

Silently Mule Malloy started up the bleep.

''Why did I become ordained?'' Acosta backtracked. ''That's no question really. The question is why have I remained in a profession to which I am so little suited. I will confess to you, Mule, and to you only, that I have not the spiritual humility and patience that I might desire. I itch for something beyond the humdrum problems of a congregation or an army detachment. Sometimes I have felt that I should drop every-
 ~g else and concentrate on my *psi* faculties, that they might

lead me to this goal I seek without understanding. But they
are too erratic. I know the law, I love the ritual, but I am not
good as a rabbi, a teacher, because . . .''

For the third time the bleep stopped, and Mule Malloy
said, ''Because you are a saint.''

And before Chaim Acosta could protest, he went on, ''Or a
prophet, if you want Fassbänder's distinction. There are all
kinds of saints and prophets. There are the gentle, humble,
patient ones like Francis of Assisi and Job and Ruth—or do
you count women? And there are God's firebrands, the ones
of fierce intellect and dreadful determination, who shake the
history of God's elect, the saints who have reached through
sin to salvation with a confident power that is the reverse of
the pride of the Lucifer, cast from the same ringing metal.''

''Mule. . . !'' Acosta protested. ''This isn't you. These
aren't your words. And you didn't learn these in parochial
school . . .''

Malloy seemed not to hear him. ''Paul, Thomas More,
Catherine of Siena, Augustine,'' he recited in rich cadence.
''Elijah, Ezekiel, Judas Maccabeus, Moses, David . . . You
are a prophet, Chaim. Forget the rationalizing double talk of
the Rhinists and recognize whence your powers come, how
you were guided to save me, what the 'strange thoughts' were
that you had during last night's vigil of prayer. You are a
prophet—and you are not going to curse *men*, the children of
God.''

Abruptly Malloy slumped forward over the wheel. There
was silence in the bleep. Chaim Acosta stared at his hands as
if he knew no gesture for this situation.

''Gentlemen!'' Captain Fassbänder's voice was even more
rasping than usual over the telecom. ''Will you please get the
blessed lead out and get up that rise? It's two minutes, twenty
seconds, past zero!''

Automatically Acosta depressed the switch and said, ''Right
away, Captain.''

Mule Malloy stirred and opened his eyes. ''Was that
Fassbänder?''

"Yes . . . But there's no hurry, Mule. I can't understand it. What made your. . . ?"

"I don't understand it, either. Never passed out like that before. Doctor used to say that head injury in the Wisconsin game might—but after thirty years . . ."

Chaim Acosta sighed. "You sound like my Mule again. But before . . ."

"Why? Did I say something? Seems to me like there was something important I wanted to say to you."

"I wonder what they'd say at Tel Aviv. Telepathic communication of subconscious minds? Externalization of thoughts that I was afraid to acknowledge consciously? Yes, you said something, Mule; and I was as astonished as Balaam when his ass spoke to him on his journey to . . . Mule!"

Acosta's eyes were blackly alight as never before, and his hands flickered eagerly. "Mule, do you remember the story of Balaam? It's in the fourth book of Moses . . ."

"Numbers? All I remember is he had a talking ass. I suppose there's a pun on *Mule?*"

"Balaam, son of Beor," said the Rabbi with quiet intensity, "was a prophet in Moab. The Israelites were invading Moab, and King Balak ordered Balaam to curse them. His ass not only spoke to him; more important, it halted and refused to budge on the journey until Balaam had listened to a message from the Lord . . .

"You were right, Mule. Whether you remember what you said or not, whether your description of me was God's truth or the telepathic projection of my own ego, you were right in one thing: These invaders are *men*, by all the standards that we debated yesterday. Moreover they are *men* suited to Mars; our patrol reported them as naked and unprotected in this cold and this atmosphere. I wonder if they have scouted this planet before and selected it as suitable; that could have been some observation device left by them that trapped you in the pass, since we've never found traces of an earlier Martian civilization.

"Mars is not for us. We cannot live here normally; our scientific researches have proved fruitless; and we maintain an inert, bored garrison only because our planetary ego can-

not face facts and surrender the symbol of our 'conquest of
space.' These other *men* can live here, perhaps fruitfully,to
the glory of God and eventually to the good of our own world
as well, as two suitably populated planets come to know each
other. You were right; I cannot curse *men*."

"GENTLEMEN!"

Deftly Acosta reached down and switched off the telecom.
"You agree, Mule?"

"I . . . I . . . I guess I drive back now, Chaim?"

"Of course not. Do you think I want to face Fassbänder
now? You drive on. At once. Up to the top of the rise. Or
haven't you yet remembered the rest of the story of Balaam?
He didn't stop at refusing to curse his fellow children of God.
Not Balaam."

"He blessed them."

Mule Malloy had remembered that. He had remembered
more, too. The phonograph needle had coursed through the
grooves of Bible study on up to the thirty-first chapter of
Numbers with its brief epilog to the story of Balaam:

*So Moses ordered a muster of men sufficient to wreak the
Lord's vengeance on the Midianites. . . . All the menfolk
they killed, the chiefs of the tribe . . . Balaam, too, the son of
Beor, they put to the sword.*

He looked at the tense face of Chaim Acosta, where exulta-
tion and resignation blended as they must in a man who
knows at last the pattern of his life, and realized that Chaim's
memory, too, went as far as the thirty-first chapter.

And there isn't a word in the Bible as to what became of
the ass, thought Mule Malloy, and started the bleep up the
rise.

MAN OF PARTS

BY H. L. GOLD (1914–   )

9 TALES OF SPACE AND TIME

One of the ways that science fiction is unique is the fact that most of its great magazine and original anthology editors have also been excellent writers themselves; I have not checked this carefully, but this seems less the case with mystery and Western editors, although there are obviously a number of people like Ellery Queen who excelled in both areas. One of the patterns among sf editor/writers is for the editing to take place at the expense of the writing—good examples include Anthony Boucher, John W. Campbell, Jr., Damon Knight (while he was busy with the ORBIT series), and of course, Horace L. Gold, the great editor of GALAXY SCIENCE FICTION from its founding in 1950 until his retirement in 1961. Although he has published a small number of stories from about 1967, the great bulk of his science fiction and fantasy is pre-1955, and the best of it can be found in his wonderful and long-out-of-print collection THE OLD DIE RICH AND OTHER SCIENCE FICTION STORIES (1955). His editorial genius has completely overshadowed his excellence as a writer, but the author of stories like "Trouble With Water," "The Biography Project," and "Love in the Dark" deserves to be remembered.

He was able to squeeze out a few stories during his editor years, of which "Man of Parts" is one of the best. (MHG)

* * *

*Horace was one of the triad of great editors of the 1950's;
the other two being John Campbell and Tony Boucher. It was
Horace's tragedy that whereas John managed to blind everyone with his verbal pyrotechnics, and Tony managed to hold
everyone with his sheer lovability—Horace masked his editorial genius under a kind of abrasiveness that alienated his
writers.*

*The result was that after his retirement, he seemed to fall
into a kind of obscurity, as though other science fiction
personalities preferred not to talk about him. (I talk about
him, of course, but perhaps not always reverently.)*

*I have not seen Horace in many years, since he moved to
the west coast, but I understand that his life has been a sad
one as he has felt underappreciated by the field to which he
gave so much and for which he did so much. And in this, he
is right! He did as much for the 1950's as John Campbell did
for the 1940's, and why isn't this acknowledged more than it
is? (IA)*

There wasn't a trace of amnesia or confusion when Major
Hugh Savold, of the Fourth Earth Expedition against Vega,
opened his eyes in the hospital. He knew exactly who he was,
where he was, and how he had gotten there.

His name was Gam Nex Biad.

He was a native of the planet named Dorfel.

He had been killed in a mining accident far underground.

The answers were preposterous and they terrified Major
Savold. Had he gone insane? He must have, for his arms
were pinned tight in a restraining sheet. And his mouth was
full of bits of rock.

Savold screamed and wrenched around on the flat, comfortable boulder on which he had been nibbling. He spat out
the rock fragments that tasted—*nutritious.*

Shaking, Savold recoiled from something even more fright-
ful than the wrong name, wrong birthplace, wrong accident,
and shockingly wrong food.

A living awl was watching him solicitously. It was as tall

as himself, had a pointed spiral drill for a head, three knee-action arms ending in horn spades, two below them with numerous sensitive cilia, a row of socketed bulbs down its front, and it stood on a nervously bouncing bedspring of a leg.

Savold was revolted and tense with panic. He had never in his life seen a creature like this.

It was Surgeon Trink, whom he had known since infancy.

"Do not be distressed," glowed the surgeon's kindly lights. "You are everything you think you are."

"But that's impossible! I'm an Earthman and my name is Major Hugh Savold!"

"Of course."

"Then I can't be Gam Nex Biad, a native of Dorfel!"

"But you are."

"I'm not!" shouted Savold. 'I was in a one-man space scout. I sneaked past the Vegan cordon and dropped the spore-bomb, the only one that ever got through. The Vegans burned my fuel and engine sections full of holes. I escaped, but I couldn't make it back to Earth. I found a planet that was pockmarked worse than our moon. I was afraid it had no atmosphere, but it did. I crash-landed." He shuddered. "It was more of a crash than a landing."

Surgeon Trink brightened joyfully. "Excellent! There seems to be no impairment of memory at all."

"No?" Savold yelled in terror. "Then how is it I remember being killed in a mining accident? I was drilling through good hard mineral ore, spinning at a fine rate, my head soothingly warm as it gouged into the tasty rock, my spades pushing back the crushed ore, and I crashed right out into a fault . . ."

"Soft shale," the surgeon explained, dimming with sympathy. "You were spinning too fast to sense the difference in density ahead of you. It was an unfortunate accident. We were all very sad."

"And I was killed," said Savold, horrified. *"Twice!"*

"Oh, no. Only once. You were badly damaged when your

machine crashed, but you were not killed. We were able to repair you."

Savold felt fear swarm through him, driving his ghastly thoughts into a quaking corner. He looked down at his body, knowing he couldn't see it, that it was wrapped tightly in a long sheet. He had never seen material like this.

He recognized it instantly as asbestos cloth.

There was a row of holes down the front. Savold screamed in horror. The socketed bulbs lit up in a deafening glare.

"Please don't be afraid!" The surgeon bounced over concernedly, broke open a large mica capsule, and splashed its contents on Savold's head and face. "I know it's a shock, but there's no cause for alarm. You're not in danger, I assure you."

Savold found himself quieting down, his panic diminishing. No, it wasn't the surgeon's gentle, reassuring glow that was responsible. It was the liquid he was covered with. A sedative of some sort, it eased the constriction of his brain, relaxed his facial muscles, dribbled comfortingly into his mouth. Half of him recognized the heavy odor and the other half identified the taste.

It was lubricating oil.

As a lubricant, it soothed him. But it was also a coolant, for it cooled off his fright and disgust and let him think again.

"Better?" asked Surgeon Trink hopefully.

"Yes, I'm calmer now," Savold said, and noted first that his voice sounded quieter, and second that it wasn't his voice—he was communicating by glows and blinks of his row of bulbs, which, as he talked, gave off a cold light like that of fireflies. "I think I can figure it out. I'm Major Hugh Savold. I crashed and was injured. You gave me the body of a . . ." he thought about the name and realized that he didn't know it, yet he found it immediately ". . . a Dorfellow, didn't you?"

"Not the whole body," the surgeon replied, glimmering with confidence again as his bedside manner returned. "Just the parts that were in need of replacement."

Savold was revolted, but the sedative effect of the lubricating oil kept his feelings under control. He tried to nod in understanding. He couldn't. Either he had an unbelievably stiff neck . . . or no neck whatever.

"Something like our bone, limb, and organ banks," he said. "How much of me is Gam Nex Biad?"

"Quite a lot, I'm afraid." The surgeon listed the parts, which came through to Savold as if he were listening to a simultaneous translation: from Surgeon Trink to Gam Nex Biad to him. They were all equivalents, of course, but they amounted to a large portion of his brain, skull, chest, internal and reproductive organs, midsection, and legs.

"Then what's left of me?" Savold cried in dismay.

"Why, part of your brain—a very considerable part, I'm proud to say. Oh, and your arms. Some things weren't badly injured, but it seemed better to make substitutions. The digestive and circulatory system, for instance. Yours were adapted to foods and fluids that aren't available on Dorfel. Now you can get your sustenance directly from the minerals and metals of the planet, just as we do. If I hadn't, your life would have been saved, but you would have starved to death."

"Let me up," said Savold in alarm. "I want to see what I look like."

The surgeon looked worried again. He used another capsule of oil on Savold before removing the sheet.

Savold stared down at himself and felt revulsion trying to rise. But there was nowhere for it to go and it couldn't have gotten past the oil if there had been. He swayed sickly on his bedspring leg, petrified at the sight of himself.

He looked quite handsome, he had to admit—Gam Nex Biad had always been considered one of the most crashing bores on Dorfel, capable of taking an enormous leap on his magnificently wiry leg, landing exactly on the point of his head with a swift spin that would bury him out of sight within instants in even the hardest rock. His knee-action arms were splendidly flinty; he knew they had been repaired with some other miner's remains, and they could whirl him through a self-drilled tunnel with wonderful speed, while the spade hands could shovel back ore as fast as he could dig it out. He

was as good as new . . . except for the disgustingly soft,
purposeless arms.

The knowledge of function and custom was there, and the
reaction to the human arms, and they made explanation unnecessary, just as understanding of the firefly language had
been there without his awareness. But the emotions were
Savold's and they drove him to say fiercely, "You didn't
have to change me altogether. You could have just saved my
life so I could fix my ship and get back . . ." He paused
abruptly and would have gasped if he had been able to.
"Good Lord! Earth Command doesn't even know I got the
bomb through! If they act fast, they can land without a bit of
opposition!" He spread all his arms—the two human ones,
the three with knee-action and spades, the two with the
sensitive cilia—and stared at them bleakly. "And I have a
girl back on Earth . . ."

Surgeon Trink glowed sympathetically and flashed with
pride. "Your mission seems important somehow, though its
meaning escapes me. However, we have repaired your machine . . ."

"You *have*?" Savold interrupted eagerly.

"Indeed, yes. It should work better than before." The
surgeon flickered modestly. "We do have some engineering
skill, you know."

The Gam Nex Biad of Savold did know. There were the
underground ore smelters and the oil refineries and the giant
metal awls that drilled out rock food for the manufacturing
centers, where miners alone could not keep up with the
demand, and the communicators that sent their signals clear
around the planet through the substrata of rock, and more,
much more. This, insisted Gam Nex Biad proudly, was a
civilization, and Major Hugh Savold, sharing his knowledge,
had to admit that it certainly was.

"I can take right off, then?" Savold flared excitedly.

"There is a problem first," glowed the surgeon in some
doubt. "You mention a 'girl' on this place you call 'Earth.' I
gather it is a person of the opposite sex."

"As opposite as anybody can get. Or was," Savold added

moodily. "But we have limb and organ banks back on Earth.
The doctors there can do a repair job. It's a damned big one,
I know, but they can handle it. I'm not so sure I like carrying
Gam Nex Biad around with me for life, though. Maybe they
can take him out and . . ."

"Please," Surgeon Trink cut in with anxious blinkings.
"There is a matter to be settled. When you refer to the 'girl,'
you do not specify that she is your mate. You have not been
selected for each other yet?"

"Selected?" repeated Savold blankly, but Gam Nex Biad
supplied the answer—the equivalent of marriage, the mates
chosen by experts on genetics, the choice being determined
by desired transmittable aptitudes. "No, we were just going
together. We were not mates, but we intended to be as soon
as I got back. That's the other reason I have to return in a
hurry. I appreciate all you've done, but I really must . . ."

"Wait," the surgeon ordered.

He drew an asbestos curtain that covered part of a wall.
Savold saw an opening in the rock of the hospital, a hole-
door through which bounced half a dozen little Dorfellows
and one big one . . . straight at him. He felt what would have
been his heart leap into what would have been his chest if he
had had either. But he couldn't even get angry or shocked or
nauseated; the lubricating oil cooled off all his emotions.

The little creatures were all afire with childish joy. The big
one sparkled happily.

"Father!" blinked the children blindingly.

"Mate!" added Prad Fim Biad in a delighted exclamation
point.

"You see," said the surgeon to Savold, who was shrinking
back, "you already have a mate and a family."

It was only natural that a board of surgeons should have
tried to cope with Savold's violent reaction. He had fought
furiously against being saddled with an alien family. Even
constant saturation with lubricating oil couldn't keep that
rebellion from boiling over.

On Earth, of course, he would have been given immediate

psychotherapy, but there wasn't anything of the sort here. Dorfellows were too granitic physically and psychologically to need medical or psychiatric doctors. A job well done and a family well raised—that was the extent of their emotionalism. Savold's feelings, rage and resentment and a violent desire to escape, were completely beyond their understanding. He discovered that as he angrily watched the glittering debate.

The board quickly determined that Surgeon Trink had been correct in adapting Savold to the Dorfel way of life. Savold objected that the adaptation need not have been so thorough, but he had to admit that, since they couldn't have kept him fed any other way, Surgeon Trink had done his best in an emergency.

The surgeon was willing to accept blame for having introduced Savold so bluntly to his family, but the board absolved him—none of them had had any experience in dealing with an Earth mentality. A Dorfellow would have accepted the fact, as others with amnesia caused by accidents had done. Surgeon Trink had had no reason to think Savold would not have done the same. Savold cleared the surgeon entirely of admitting that the memory was there, but, like all the other memories of Gam Nex Biad's, had been activated only when the situation came up. The board had no trouble getting Savold to agree that the memory would have returned sooner or later, no matter how Surgeon Trink handled the introduction, and that the reaction would have been just as violent.

"And now," gleamed the oldest surgeon on the board, "the problem is how to help our new—and restored—brother adjust to life on this world."

"That isn't the problem at all!" Savold flared savagely. "I have to get back to Earth and tell them I dropped the bomb and they can land safely. And there's the girl I mentioned. I want to marry her—become her mate, I mean."

"*You* want to become her mate?" the oldest surgeon blinked in bewilderment. "It is *your* decision?"

"Well, hers, too."

"You mean you did the selecting yourselves? Nobody chose for you?"

Savold attempted to explain, but puzzled glimmers and Gam Nex Biad's confusion made him state resignedly, "Our customs are different. We choose our own mates." He thought of adding that marriages were arranged in some parts of the world, but that would only have increased their baffled lack of understanding.

"And how many mates can an individual have?" asked a surgeon.

"Where I come from, one."

"The individual's responsibility, then, is to the family he has. Correct?"

"Of course."

"Well," said the oldest surgeon, "the situation is perfectly clear. You have a family—Prad Fim Biad and the children."

"They're not my family," Savold objected. "They're Gam Nex Biad's and he's dead."

"We respect your customs. It is only fair that you respect ours. If you had had a family where you come from, there would have been a question of legality, in view of the fact that you could not care for them simultaneously. But you have none and there is no such question."

"Customs? Legality?" asked Savold, feeling as lost as they had in trying to comprehend an alien society.

"A rebuilt Dorfellow," the oldest surgeon said, "is required to assume the obligations of whatever major parts went into his reconstruction. You are almost entirely made up of the remains of Gam Nex Biad, so it is only right that his mate and children should be yours."

"I won't do it!" Savold protested. "I demand the right to appeal!"

"On what grounds?" asked another surgeon politely.

"That I'm not a Dorfellow!"

"Ninety-four point seven per cent of you is, according to Surgeon Trink's requisition of limbs and organs. How much more of a citizen can any individual be?"

Gam Nex Biad confirmed the ruling and Savold subsided. While the board of surgeons discussed the point it had begun with—how to adapt Savold to life on Dorfel—he thought the situation through. He had no legal or moral recourse. If he was to get out of his predicament, it would have to be through shrewd resourcefulness and he would never have become a major in the space fleet if he hadn't had plenty of that.

Yeah, shrewd resourcefulness, thought Savold bitterly, jouncing unsteadily on his single bedspring leg on a patch of unappealing topsoil a little distance from the settlement. He had counted on something that didn't exist here—the kind of complex approach that Earth doctors and authorities would have used on his sort of problem, from the mitigation of laws to psychological conditioning, all of it complicated and every stage allowing a chance to work his way free.

But the board of surgeons had agreed on a disastrously simple course of treatment for him. He was not to be fed by anybody and he could not sleep in any of the underground rock apartments, including the dormitory for unmated males.

"When he's hungry enough, he'll go back to mining," the oldest surgeon had told the equivalent of a judge, a local teacher who did part-time work passing on legal questions that did not have to be ruled on by the higher courts. "And if he has no place to stay exept with Gam Nex Biad's family, which is his own, naturally, he'll go there when he's tired of living out in the open all by himself."

The judge thought highly of the decision and gave it official approval.

Savold did not mind being out in the open, but he was far from being all by himself. Gam Nex Biad was a constant nuisance, nagging at him to get in a good day's drilling and then go home to the wife, kiddies, and their cozy, hollowed-out quarters, with company over to celebrate his return with a lavish supply of capsuled lubricating oil. Savold obstinately refused, though he found himself salivating or something very much like it.

The devil of the situation was that he *was* hungry and there was not a single bit of rock around to munch on. That was the purpose of this fenced-in plot of ground—it was like hard labor in the prisons back on Earth, where the inmates ate only if they broke their quota of rock, except that here the inmates would eat the rock they broke. The only way Savold could get out of the enclosure was by drilling under the high fence. He had already tried to bounce over it and discovered he couldn't.

"Come on," Gam Nex Biad argued in his mind. "Why fight it? We're a miner and there's no life like the life of a miner. The excitement of boring your way through a lode, making a meal out of the rich ore! Miners get the choicest tidbits, you know—that's our compensation for working so hard and taking risks."

"Some compensation," sneered Savold, looking wistfully up at the stars and enviously wishing he were streaking between them in his scout.

"A meal of iron ore would go pretty well right now, wouldn't it?" Gam Nex Biad tempted. "And I know where there are some veins of tin and sulphur. You don't find *them* lying around on the surface, eh? Nonminers get just traces of the rare metals to keep them healthy, but we can stuff ourself all we want . . ."

"Shut up!"

"And some pools of mercury. Not big ones, I admit, but all we'd want is a refreshing gulp to wash down those ores I was telling you about."

Resisting the thought of the ores was hard enough, for Savold was rattlingly empty, but the temptation of the smooth, cool mercury would have roused the glutton in anyone.

"All right," he growled, "but get this straight—we're not going back to your family. They're your problem, not mine."

"But how could I go back to them if you won't go?"

"That's right. I'm glad you see it my way. Now where are those ores and the pools of mercury?"

"Dive," said Gam Nex Biad. "I'll give you the directions."

Savold took a few bounces to work up speed and spin, then shot into the air and came down on the point of his awl-shaped head, which bit through the soft topsoil as if through—he shuddered—so much water. As a Dorfellow, he had to avoid water; it eroded and corroded and caused deposits of rust in the digestive and circulatory systems. There was a warmth that was wonderfully soothing and he was drilling into rock. He ate some to get his strength back, but left room for the main meal and the dessert.

"Pretty nice, isn't it?" asked Gam Nex Biad as they gouged a comfortable tunnel back toward the settlement. "Nonminers don't know what they're missing."

"Quiet," Savold ordered surlily, but he had to confess to himself that it was pleasant. His three knee-action arms rotated him at a comfortable speed, the horn spades pushing back the loose rock; and he realized why Gam Nex Biad had been upset when Surgeon Trink left Savold's human arms attached. They were in the way and they kept getting scratched. The row of socketed bulbs gave him all the light he needed. That, he decided, had been their original purpose. Using them to communicate with must have been one of the first steps toward civilization.

Savold had been repressing thoughts ever since the meeting of the board of surgeons. Experimentally, he called his inner partner.

"Um?" asked Gam Nex Biad absently.

"Something I wanted to discuss with you," Savold said.

"Later. I sense the feldspar coming up. We head north there."

Savold turned the drilling over to him, then allowed the buried thoughts to emerge. They were thoughts of escape and he had kept them hidden because he was positive that Gam Nex Biad would have betrayed them. He had been trying incessantly, wheedlingly, to sell Savold on mining and returning to the family.

The hell with that, Savold thought grimly now. He was getting back to Earth somehow—Earth Command first, Marge second. No, surgery second, Marge third, he corrected. She wouldn't want him this way . . .

"Manganese," said Gam Nex Biad abruptly, and Savold shut off his thinking. "I always did like a few mouthfuls as an appetizer."

The rock had a pleasantly spicy taste, much like a cocktail before dinner. Then they went on, with the Dorfellow giving full concentration to finding his way from deposit to deposit.

The thing to do, Savold reasoned, was to learn where the scout ship was being kept. He had tried to sound out Gam Nex Biad subtly, but it must have been too subtle—the Dorfellow had guessed uninterestedly that the ship would be at one of the metal fabricating centers, and Savold had not dared ask which one. Gam Nex Biad couldn't induce him to become a miner and Dorfellow family man, but that didn't mean he could escape over Gam Nex Biad's opposition.

Savold did not intend to find out. Shrewd resourcefulness, that was the answer. It hadn't done him much good yet, but the day he could not outfox these rock-eaters, he'd turn in his commission. All he had to do was find the ship . . .

Bloated and tired, Savold found himself in a main tunnel thoroughfare back to the settlement. The various ores, he disgustedly confessed to himself, were as delicious as the best human foods, and there was nothing at all like the flavor and texture of pure liquid mercury. He discovered some in his cupped cilia hands.

"To keep around for a snack?" he asked Gam Nex Biad.

"I thought you wouldn't mind letting Prad Fim and the children have some;" the Dorfellow said hopefully. "You ought to see them light up whenever I bring it home!"

"Not a chance! We're not going there, so I might as well drop it."

Savold had to get some sleep. He was ready to topple with exhaustion. But the tunnels were unsafe—a Dorfellow traveling through one on an emergency night errand would crash into him hard enough to leave nothing but flinty splinters. And the night air felt chill and hostile, so it was impossible to sleep above ground.

"Please make up your mind," Gam Nex Biad begged. "I can't stay awake much longer and you'll just go blundering around and get into trouble."

"But they've got to put us up somewhere," argued Savold. "How about the hospital? We're still a patient, aren't we?"

"We were discharged as cured. And nobody else is allowed to let us stay in any apartment . . . except one."

"I know, I know," Savold replied with weary impatience. "Forget it. We're not going there."

"But it's so comfortable there . . ."

"Forget it I told you!"

"Oh, all right," Gam Nex Biad said resignedly. "But we're not going to find anything as pleasant and restful as my old sleeping boulder. It's soft limestone, you know, and grooved to fit our body. I'd like to see anybody *not* fall asleep instantly on that good old flat boulder . . ."

Savold tried to resist, but he was worn out from the operation, hunger, digging, and the search for a place to spend the night.

"Just take a *look* at it, that's all," Gam Nex Biad coaxed. "If you don't like it, we'll sleep anywhere you say. Fair enough?"

"I suppose so," admitted Savold.

The hewn-rock apartment was quiet, at least; everybody was asleep. He'd lie down for a while, just long enough to get some rest, and clear out before the household awoke . . .

But Prad Fim and the children were clustered around the boulder when he opened his eyes. Each of them had five arms to fight off. And there were Surgeon Trink, the elder of the board of surgeons, and the local teacher-judge all waiting to talk to him when the homecoming was over with.

"The treatment worked!" cried the judge. "He came back!"

"I never doubted it," the elder said complacently.

"You know what this means?" Surgeon Trink eagerly asked Savold.

"No, what?" Savold inquired warily, afraid of the answer.

"You can show us how to operate your machine," declared the judge. "It isn't that we lack engineering ability, you understand. We simply never had a machine as large and complex before. We could have, of course—I'm sure you are aware of that—but the matter just didn't come up. We could work it out by ourselves, but it would be much easier to have you explain it.''

''By returning, you've shown that you have regained some degree of stability,'' added the elder. ''We couldn't trust you with the machine while you were so disturbed.''

''Did you know this?'' Savold silently challenged Gam Nex Biad.

''Well, certainly,'' came the voiceless answer.

''Then why didn't you tell me? Why did you let me go floundering around instead?''

''Because you bewilder me. This loathing for our body, which I'd always been told was quite attractive, and dislike of mining and living with our own family—wanting to reach this thing you call Earth Command and the creature with the strange name. Marge, isn't it? I could never guess how you would react to anything. It's not easy living with an alien mentality.''

''You don't have to explain. I've got the same problem, remember.''

''That's true,'' Gam Nex Biad silently agreed. ''But I'm afraid you'll have to take it from here. All I know is mining, not machines or metal fabricating centers.''

Savold repressed his elation. The less Gam Nex Biad knew from this point on, the less he could guess—and the smaller chance there was that he could betray Savold.

''We can leave right now,'' the judge was saying. ''The family can follow as soon as you've built a home for them.''

''Why should they follow?'' Savold demanded. ''I thought you said I was going to be allowed to operate the ship.''

''Demonstrate and explain it, really,'' the judge amended. ''We're not absolutely certain that you are stable, you see. As for the family, you're bound to get lonesome . . .''

Savold stared at Prad Fim and the children. Gam Nex Biad was brimming with affection for them, but Savold saw them only as hideous ore-crushing monsters. He tried to keep them from saying good-bye with embraces, but they came at him with such violent leaps that they chipped bits out of his body with their grotesque pointed awl heads. He was glad to get away, especially with Gam Nex Biad making such a damned slobbering nuisance of himself.

"Let's go!" he blinked frantically at the judge, and dived after him into an express tunnel.

While Gam Nex Biad was busily grieving, Savold stealthily worked out his plans. He would glance casually at the ship, glow some mild compliment at the repair job, make a pretense at explaining how the controls worked—and blast off into space at the first opportunity, even if he had to wait for days. He knew he would never get another chance; they'd keep him away from the ship if that attempt failed. And Gam Nex Biad was a factor, too. Savold had to hit the take-off button before his partner suspected or their body would be paralyzed in the conflict between them.

It was a very careful plan and it called for iron discipline, but that was conditioned into every scout pilot. All Savold had to do was maintain his rigid self-control.

He did—until he saw the ship on the hole-pocked plain. Then his control broke and he bounced with enormous, frantic leaps into the airlock and through the corridors to the pilot room.

"Wait! Wait!" glared the judge, and others from the fabricating center sprang toward the ship.

Savold managed to slam the airlock before Gam Nex Biad began to fight him, asking in frightened confusion, "What are you doing?" and locking their muscles so that Savold was unable to move.

"What am I doing?" glinted Savold venomously. "Getting off your lousy planet and back to a world where people live like people instead of like worms and moles!"

"I don't know what you mean," said the Dorfellow anxiously, "but I can't let you do anything until the authorities say it's all right."

"You can't stop me!" Savold exulted. "You can paralyze everything *except my own arms*!"

And that, of course, was the ultimate secret he had been hiding from Gam Nex Biad.

Savold slammed the take-off button. The power plant roared and the ship lifted swiftly toward the sky.

It began to spin.

Then it flipped over and headed with suicidal velocity toward the ground.

"They did something wrong to the ship!" cried Savold.

"Wrong?" Gam Nex Biad repeatedly vacantly. "It seems to be working fine."

"But it's supposed to be heading *up*!"

"Oh, no," said Gam Nex Biad. "Our machines never go that way. There's no rock up there."

ANSWER

BY FREDRIC BROWN (1906–1972)

ANGELS AND SPACESHIPS

This justly famous story first appeared in the author's 1954 collection ANGELS AND SPACESHIPS, from his long-time publisher E. P. Dutton. The book also contained the first publication of several other well known Brown short-short stories, including "Pattern" and "Preposterous."

Isaac, we have discussed Fredric Brown's career in several earlier volumes in this series, and I know that a short-short speaks for itself, but it seems to me that a few words about "good" vs. "evil" machines may be in order here. (MHG)

Well, now, Marty, I'm not sure that what Fred's story should inspire is a discussion as to whether machines are good or evil. What has always struck me about this marvelous vignette since I first read it (and wished with such earnestness and fervor that I had written it myself) is that it raises the question of whether God is good or evil.

The machine struck down the person who tried to interfere with it, but God does that frequently. In David's reign, the ark of the Covenant was brought to Jerusalem and a certain Uzzah reached out to steady the ox-cart when it seemed that it might overturn and tumble the ark into the road. For doing this (which sounds reasonable enough to us mere mortals) God struck him down—see 2 Samuel 6:1-8.

To be sure, everyone says that God is good, and loving, and kind, and merciful. That's what they say. If, however, one glances over the historical record, and supposes it all to be under God's strict control, then it seems to me it might be possible to argue that God is evil. (IA)

Dwar Ev ceremoniously soldered the final connection with gold. The eyes of a dozen television cameras watched him and the sub-ether bore throughout the universe a dozen pictures of what he was doing.

He straightened and nodded to Dwar Reyn, then moved to a position beside the switch that would complete the contact when he threw it. The switch that would connect, all at once, all of the monster computing machines of all the populated planets in the universe—ninety-six billion planets—into the supercircuit that would connect them all into one supercalculator, one cybernetics machine that would combine all the knowledge of all the galaxies.

Dwar Reyn spoke briefly to the watching and listening trillions. Then after a moment's silence he said, "Now, Dwar Ev."

Dwar Ev threw the switch. There was a mighty hum, the surge of power from ninety-six billion planets. Lights flashed and quieted along the miles-long panel.

Dwar Ev stepped back and drew a deep breath. "The honor of asking the first question is yours, Dwar Reyn."

"Thank you," said Dwar Reyn. "It shall be a question which no single cybernetics machine has been able to answer."

He turned to face the machine. "Is there a God?"

The mighty voice answered without hesitation, without the clicking of a single relay.

"Yes, *now* there is a God."

Sudden fear flashed on the face of Dwar Ev. He leaped to grab the switch.

A bolt of lightning from the cloudless sky struck him down and fused the switch shut.